STARS
MAGE

MAGE
PROVOCATEUR

BOOK TWO
OF THE RED FALCON TRILOGY

Mage-Provocateur © 2018 Glynn Stewart

This edition published in 2018 by:
Faolan's Pen Publishing Inc.
22 King St. S, Suite 300
Waterloo, Ontario
N2J 1N8 Canada

ISBN-13: 978-1-988035-36-9 (print)
A record of this book is available from Library and Archives Canada.
Printed in the United States of America
1 2 3 4 5 6 7 8 9 10

First edition
First printing: March 2018

Illustration © 2018 Jeff Brown Graphics
Read more books from Glynn Stewart at faolanspen.com

STARSHIP'S
MAGE

MAGE

PROVOCATEUR

BOOK TWO
OF THE RED FALCON TRILOGY

GLYNN STEWART

**FAOLAN'S PEN
PUBLISHING**

faolanspen.com

CHAPTER 1

THE YOUNG WOMAN across the table from Captain David Rice seemed utterly unperturbed by the panel interview. She just barely qualified for the Senior Ship's Mage position she'd applied for aboard the jump freighter *Peregrine*, but there was no sign of that in the slim red-headed Mage's poised form.

"All right, Miss McLaughlin," the stockily built Captain of the freighter *Red Falcon*—and owner of the soon-to-be-commissioned *Peregrine*—said. "Everyone in this room knows that we're going to have at least half a dozen more-qualified candidates for *Peregrine*'s Senior Ship's Mage.

"So, I suggest you tell us why Captain Campbell should hire *you*."

Jenna Campbell sat to his right, the stoutly built blonde woman his strong right hand. After ten years as his XO, however, there was no question who would be the Captain when he'd purchased a second ship.

Grace McLaughlin smiled.

"I can think of a few reasons," she told them. "Firstly, I served as Ship's Mage aboard *Gentle Rains of Summer* for over two years, rising from the most junior Mage to second-most senior through my skills.

"Captain Michaels and Ship's Mage Caomhánach have both provided glowing references that I have supplied you," she continued. "The only reason I'm looking to leave *Gentle Rains* is that Mage Caomhánach has no intention of retiring anytime soon, so I've advanced as far as I can under Captain Michaels."

And David was quite certain she knew he and Michaels were old friends. That was part of how McLaughlin's friend had ended up as Ship's Mage aboard David's old ship, *Blue Jay*.

"I've read Mage Caomhánach's reference," the third person on the hiring side of the table noted. Ship's Mage Maria Isabella Soprano had rapidly become David's strong left hand, even if her presence had dragged him into working with the Protectorate's Martian Interstellar Security Service.

"It's glowing and adorable," Soprano continued in her calm, lightly accented voice. "But sufficiently short on details to easily be the kind of letter you write a politically connected subordinate as a favor."

McLaughlin's smile didn't even waver.

"I would be glad to demonstrate my skills to you, Mage Soprano," she said firmly. "I'm no Navy Mage and I doubt I am as powerful as you, ma'am, but I am more than capable of fulfilling both the jumping and the defensive portions of the Ship's Mage job.

"I understand you've had some difficulties with the crime syndicates?" she concluded.

David chuckled.

"You know Damien Montgomery," he noted. Everything in David's life right now still seemed to come back to hiring that one Mage. Now they *both* served the Protectorate, though David understood that Montgomery was somewhere in the Sol System, training to be some kind of uber-Mage.

Even that was probably more than he *should* know.

McLaughlin coughed and flushed slightly.

"I know Damien, yes," she confirmed. "Part of my reason for applying with your crew was that I know he works for you."

"Damien worked for me, yes," David told her. "He left us for the service of the Mage-King eighteen months ago or so now. He was a capable subordinate and a dear friend."

"That he was," she agreed, her eyes flickering aside. David figured he'd just lost a quarter or so of her interest now she knew she wouldn't be working with Montgomery again.

That was...fascinating, and he smiled at her.

"I hope that doesn't render this interview pointless?" he asked.

She laughed.

"No," she told him. "I'll admit that working with Damien again would be a large bonus, but your new shipping line is intriguing to me—and getting in at the beginning looks like a good idea to me!"

After the young Mage had gone on her way, David refilled his officers' coffees and looked at the two women questioningly.

"Well?"

"If we could bring her in on the secret, I'd take her as a junior on *Red Falcon* instantly," Soprano replied. "I'm not so sure at making her senior on a ship—especially with a first-time Captain; no offense, Jenna."

Campbell snorted.

"None taken. I'll note that if she was on *Falcon*, she'd inevitably be working with Xi Wu, at least, if not LaMonte herself. How many of Damien's ex-girlfriends do you really *want* on a ship?"

David laughed.

"Given Miss LaMonte's demonstrated lethality to anyone who threatens her friends, that's a trick question," he pointed out. "It's irrelevant in any case; the Agency has already made up the Mage complement for *Red Falcon*."

Maria Soprano had, apparently, been an agent for MISS since she'd come aboard. His own membership in the organization was more recent—and was why they now owned *Peregrine*.

He and Soprano had been tasked to go poke several of the galaxy's more dangerous underground organizations with a stick. He wasn't taking anyone on that mission who didn't know what they were getting into, so he was shuffling a large chunk of his crew over to *Peregrine* and replacing them with a mix of MISS personnel and people the Agency had cleared.

An even larger portion of his crew was ex-Navy now than *Red Falcon* had carried before—and since *Falcon* was a former armed Navy auxiliary, the big ship had always had a solid cohort of Navy crew and Marines.

"Almost as important, though," Campbell noted, "is that rumor has it that Sherwood is calling home any of their Ship's Mages they can find for a new security force. Anyone want to bet that the Governor *hasn't* already sent a letter to his granddaughter?

"Or that Miss McLaughlin won't disappear back home to answer the call?"

"I'm not taking that bet," David agreed. "So, she's off the list, then. You're going to want an experienced senior Ship's Mage in any case, XO. I'm not prepared to send you off into the black without the best I can give you."

Campbell chuckled.

"I know, boss," she replied. "What about you? I know the Navy gave you a new tactical officer, but who gets my job?"

He shook his head.

"I was waiting until LaMonte finished her Mate certification to make the decision," he admitted. "I was *planning* on making LaMonte our new Fourth Mate and Chief Engineer, bumping Kellers to the XO slot."

Soprano chuckled.

"I'm going to guess our friend Kellers shut *that* down fast?"

"Before I'd even finished the offer," David agreed. "However, since *I'm* not a first-time Captain, and I have First and Fourth Mates I can rely on..."

A merchant freighter usually had three Mate-certified officers, people who were qualified to take over command if something happened to the Captain. First Officer was the Ship's Mage, Second Officer was the executive officer, and the Third Officer was the Chief Engineer.

Armed ships like *Red Falcon*—and like *Peregrine* once her refit was complete—moved the Chief Engineer to Fourth Officer and inserted a tactical officer as Third Mate.

"You're making LaMonte XO?" Soprano asked carefully. "She's a little...young."

"She is," David confirmed. "And she's dating both our second-most senior pilot and our second-most senior Mage," he continued, shaking his head at the complexity of the relationship mess going on with his mid-twenties officers. "A complication I expect *you*, Ship's Mage, to keep an eye on.

"That said, she's one of the best programmers I've ever met, good with people, and a solid engineer," he continued. "I'll teach her to fly the ship, and the other three Mates can keep her feet on solid ground. She'll be fine."

"Sink or swim with that Mate certification, huh?" Campbell noted.

"She'll swim," David replied confidently. "If I didn't think so, I wouldn't be tossing her in the deep end."

The Tau Ceti System was the heart of the Royal Martian Navy's presence outside the Sol System, and the entirety of David Rice's little shipping line was docked at one of the civilian stations orbiting the massive military shipyard complex.

Red Falcon had only recently left the military yard, the RMN technicians far more capable of dealing with the armed megafreighter's idiosyncrasies than most yards. She was a big mushroom-shaped vessel, with a rotating hab-ring tucked underneath a heavy armored dome containing her main water tanks and most of her arsenal.

Next to the twenty-megaton ship, *Peregrine* looked tiny. That was deceptive at best. The *Maui*-class heavy freighter was rated for twelve million tons of cargo, four times David's old *Blue Jay*, if still far less than *Falcon*.

Of course, the *Maui* class normally only carried a half-dozen of the Rapid-Fire Laser Anti-Missile turrets for self-defense, with no heavier armament. *Peregrine* was nearing the end of a two-month refit in the capable hands of one of Tau Ceti's more reliable contractors.

When it was done, she'd still be a fusion-drive ship with rotating ribs for gravity—but she'd be a civilian ship with four battle lasers, a complete suite of gravity runes for her Mages to keep charged, and sixteen missile launchers.

David had made far too many enemies over the years to send people out under his banner without making sure they could protect themselves.

The transfer pod he and his senior officers were aboard slowed to a halt in the zero-gravity section of the station docks. Two bays next to each other were now labeled with the simple text of his expanded company: RICE SHIPPING INTERSTELLAR.

"If I'm reading my mail right, our new tactical officer should be reporting aboard this evening," David told his companions. "I'll stay aboard until then. You two?"

"I'm going to go take a walk around my ship," Campbell replied. She was still sleeping aboard *Falcon*, but *Peregrine* was intact enough that her captain-to-be could walk her decks now.

"I'm going to get a drink," Soprano said. "The ship is getting stuffy."

He chuckled. Fast as she was, any lengthy voyage would involve them spending weeks or even months locked aboard *Red Falcon*. *Stuffy* wasn't something the environmental plant would permit.

"Don't stay out too late, and *behave*," he ordered his Ship's Mage. "Tau Ceti may be safe, but..."

"I still have friends here," she replied. "I'll be fine."

CHAPTER 2

KELLY LAMONTE entered her Captain's office with a certain degree of hesitation. It had seemed so clear to her when she'd started the Mate certification program: she'd get the certificate and then her career would take off.

That had been when she'd been aboard a ship she'd been afraid would fall apart around her. It had been post-Damien Montgomery but before Xi Wu and Mike Kelzin. Before *Red Falcon* and their conflict with Azure Legacy and the Legatans.

Before her ship had helped end a pirate fleet and become an unofficial covert operations ship for the Protectorate.

Now...she wasn't quite sure *what* to do with the certificate that said she could be one of the senior non-Mage officers of a starship. The MISS courses in hacking and programming she'd taken hadn't helped either. They'd expanded her skills to a level she couldn't help wanting to try out...and no ordinary ship was going to give her that chance.

"Have a seat, Kelly," Rice told her, gesturing to the chair across his desk. "Coffee?"

"Please," she agreed, nervously tugging on her hair—currently a natural-looking red—for a moment before folding her hands in her lap. She couldn't be certain, but she'd thought she'd seen her Captain conceal a smile at the nervous gesture.

Rice returned to the desk with two mugs of coffee and slid one over to her.

"I saw the posting from the Shippers' Academy," he said. "Congratulations."

"Thank you, Captain," Kelly replied. "They don't tell us much other than 'You passed.' You can kind of guess how you did on the different sections, but they don't tell you."

She knew, for example, that there was no way she'd excelled on the normal-space flight portion of the test. Campbell had helped teach her, but she knew she lacked the instinct that Campbell or Kelly's own boyfriend had for maneuvers.

"Officially, they don't tell anybody," Rice agreed. "Unofficially, your Captain can usually get at least a rundown from your tester."

She sat up straight, leveling a curious gaze on her boss.

"Can you tell me?" she asked frankly.

He laughed.

"You sure you want to know?"

"I need to know where I still need to improve," she said instantly.

"You're a freshly minted ship's mate, Kelly," Rice said gently. "You need improvement *everywhere*; that's the nature of the world. That said..." He held up a finger.

"To no one's surprise, you nearly maxed out the programming and engineering portions of the test. You did almost as well on the personnel interactions and counseling portions, which I'll admit I didn't expect. You were fine on the rest but, bluntly, got a pity pass on normal-space flight."

She winced.

"I didn't think pity passes were a thing," she admitted. Somehow, that was more important than the nearly max grade on almost half the components of the testing.

"They're what happens when your history and the rest of your testing say you'll make an exemplary officer," Rice told her gently, "but you fail one or two components by a slim margin.

"If you stay with us, we'll make sure you get more practice and training at the stick," he continued. "You're fine on the software side, the navigation, but given the kind of scrapes we get into, we need a live hand on the controls more often than most."

"'If I stay'?" she repeated.

"You now have your Mate's certificate, a mechanical engineering degree, eight years' experience, and a stack of glowing recommendations as long as your arm," her Captain pointed out. "This is Tau Ceti, Kelly. You could walk off *Red Falcon* and have six interviews scheduled by the end of the day and be in a Chief Engineer slot *somewhere* by the end of the week.

"I don't want you to feel obligated to stay," he concluded. "We'd love to keep you, but we don't have a perfect slot to drop you into. There are ships out there that could be a better fit for your skills and experience, much as I hate to say it."

"And how many of them have stopped a war?" she asked quietly.

Rice coughed.

"I'll note that I don't think *we've* stopped any wars," he replied. "Though I'll admit that we've probably helped delay a civil war by short-circuiting some of Legatus's plans.

"But, yes, *Red Falcon* is probably the only covert Agency ship available," he admitted. "With your qualifications, though, you could probably talk your way into the Navy with a near-guaranteed rapid promotion scale."

"Probably," she agreed with a smile. "But I'm guessing you *do* have some openings for me?"

Rice chuckled.

"I do," he confirmed. "None are what I hoped, but, as I doubt surprises you, Kellers refuses to leave *Red Falcon*'s engineering section."

Kelly wasn't surprised at all, sadly. The perfect job for her would have been to take over for Kellers in the engineering section she knew inside and out, with the people she already knew.

"The first option is probably the most obvious," Rice continued. "While we've interviewed several solid candidates, *Peregrine* doesn't have a Chief Engineer yet.

"You'd be building a department up from scratch, which is a solid opportunity but very much the deep end for your first department," he noted. "Kellers would backstop your hiring and we'll be sending some key personnel over from *Red Falcon*, but you'd be an inexperienced officer with a new department on a new ship.

"I have confidence that you and Captain Campbell could make it work, but I'll warn you ahead of time that it'll be an uphill struggle."

"It would be a challenge," Kelly admitted slowly, "but I think I could do it."

The challenge was tempting all on its own. It wasn't often you were offered the opportunity to stretch your skills that far. Leaving her partners behind on *Red Falcon* would be...suboptimal, but her understanding was that the two ships should be meeting up relatively regularly.

"So do I, or I wouldn't be offering it to you," Rice told her. "But if you want to stay on *Red Falcon*, I do have another option."

Kelly nodded, leaning back in her chair to let him speak. The only way she could see to stay on *Falcon* would be to remain as a secondary engineering officer, maybe with a bump in authority to make her Kellers's second-in-command.

She could do that, and it would be good experience, but she wasn't sure it would be worth it. She knew she could make more of a difference aboard *Red Falcon* than aboard *Peregrine*, but she couldn't hamper her own career, either.

"James Kellers, obviously, is staying on as Chief Engineer, and Maria isn't going anywhere," Rice reminded her. "Connor Daniels, our new Third Officer will be arriving later today, freshly retired from the Navy and connected to us by the Agency.

"That does leave one open position for a Mate-certified officer," he concluded.

Kelly stared at him in silence for several long seconds. He couldn't be saying what she thought he was saying.

"*Red Falcon*'s crew is one of the better ones I've worked with," Rice noted. "Our ridiculous proportion of ex-Navy probably has something to do with that, but with three experienced ship's officers and a solid crew, we can probably handle bringing a green executive officer up to speed."

His words were still barely processing. That was a massive offer—an *insane* offer.

"It's the deep end," he continued. "Nothing deeper, in fact, but Maria has been executive officer aboard a warship, and I still remember most of the drill myself. You'll have to hit the ground running, but we can at least point the way for you.

"If you want the job."

"You." She paused, considering. "You want to make me XO. Second Officer."

"Yes," Rice confirmed. "We'll back you all the way. Both Maria and I know what you need to do, and we'll make sure you keep your head above water." He grinned. "I can't promise that James will go easy on you, but we'll make sure Connor knows you're his boss.

"Two options, Kelly," he continued. "I won't tell you which is better. Both would be challenges. The *Peregrine* role is probably closer to what you *should* be doing at this point in your career.

"But I think you can do the XO role here. I'd rather have someone whose skills I know and that I know I can trust at my right hand, Kelly.

"What do you say?"

She exhaled sharply, shaking her head as she looked up to meet her Captain's gaze.

Executive officer. Second Officer of an armed megafreighter, a covert ops ship that was going to go looking for trouble. If she wanted to make a difference, she couldn't see anywhere better to be.

"Hell, yes," she told him. "I'm not leaving this ship if I've a choice, Captain, so if you want to stick me on your bridge, I guess I'm learning to fly this barge."

"Hey!" her Captain objected. "Call my *Falcon* a barge again and I might change my mind!"

Kelly wasn't sure if Rice had told people in advance of his plan or if *Red Falcon*'s Chief of Security had been advised afterward.

Or, potentially, had worked it out on his own. "Chief" Ivan Skavar was also *Lieutenant* Ivan Skavar, Royal Martian Marine Corps Forward Combat Intelligence—and he saluted briskly as he met her in the corridor.

"XO, the new tactical officer just reported aboard," he informed her brightly. "I figured you and the Captain would need to sort out your plan before meeting with him, so one of my girls is showing him to his quarters."

Right. Quarters. She was going to have to move—had Campbell even moved out yet?

It was the executive officer's job to know that. She'd hit the ground, but she wasn't running fast enough yet.

"I'll consult with Rice," she confirmed. "XO? Does everyone know already?"

Skavar laughed.

"I don't know about everyone, but I did the math two days ago—and you just spent an hour closeted with the Skipper. Two plus two equals new executive officer, I think. Am I wrong?"

She chuckled. Skavar was ten years older than her, but there was something infectious in the Marine officer's sense of the world.

"You're not wrong," she confirmed. "I'll ping the Skipper and see what he thinks, but right off the bat..."

Kelly checked her wrist-comp. The smooth plastic tablet strapped to her arm was linked in to *Falcon*'s far more powerful computers, and since it now had the executive officer's codes, it could access the Captain's and Ship's Mage's schedule.

"Let me confirm with Rice"—she had, after all, been executive officer for under an hour—"but it looks like Maria is due back aboard in forty minutes and we're all free in ninety."

"Sounds like a plan, ma'am," Skavar replied. "I'll make sure Mr. Connor Daniels is where he needs to be."

CHAPTER 3

SOMEHOW, MARIA SOPRANO wasn't surprised to find her evening interrupted by one of MISS's seemingly ubiquitous polite older men. It took her a moment to recognize Brent Alois, the silver-haired gentleman who'd originally recruited her.

"Brent," she greeted him, trading a nod with her old friend behind the bar. "Xu, drinks for us both?"

"I see you two are getting along better now," Alexis Xu rumbled, the big shaven-headed Asian man smiling at her. "Things worked out, did they?"

She shook her head, a shadow passing over her thoughts as she remembered people who were no longer around to say that things had "worked out."

"In some ways," she admitted. "Not in others."

"I know how that goes," the bartender agreed, sliding two beers across the bar. "You know which booths have privacy fields," he continued.

Shaking her head, Maria led Alois to the farthest back booth. The agent followed her unspoken suggestion and carried the beers behind her, taking a seat across from her and smiling sadly.

"I've heard the details of your trip," he noted. "The Hand was impressed. I hear we even drafted your new boss."

"Among others," she agreed. "What's this about, Brent?"

"About forty percent checking in on my recruit," he told her calmly. "Sixty percent passing on data. Nature of the job, Maria, is that you'll get bits of the mission from various sources."

She sighed.

"I suppose I should have expected the cloak-and-dagger bullshit when I agreed to be a spy, huh?" she asked.

"Yep," he agreed. "My understanding is that you'll be getting the data on what you're supposed to be doing via your new gunnery officer. The piece I've got is how you get there."

"I'm listening," Maria replied.

"Cobalt Interstellar Elements is shipping a massive cargo of refining gear to the Desdemona System," Alois told her. "Their original shipper has fallen through and it's a fifteen-megaton cargo—most of the core pieces of a new orbital platform destined for Desdemona IV. They'll realize *Red Falcon* is perfect pretty quickly."

"And I'm sure MISS had nothing to do with the falling-through or how quickly they'll realize that," Maria said dryly, earning herself a chuckle from the man.

"Not that I can admit to, no," he confirmed. "In Desdemona, you'll want to look for a shipper named Jan Lomond. I'm not sure what we've got on them, but they're sending a cargo *Red Falcon's* size over to the UnArcana world of Snap."

Alois shrugged.

"I have not been briefed on why we want you in Snap or what's going on there," he admitted. "My job was to pass on how you're getting there without drawing attention.

"I've also got a heads-up for you: Stealey's heading this way, she'll want to meet with you and Rice as she passes through. I suspect that will be the third and final part of your briefing," Alois concluded, "but it's not my place to make guesses like that."

Maria laughed.

"Sure it isn't, *Major* Alois," she replied. "Sure it isn't."

"Whatever it takes to do the job," he replied, offering his hand across the table. "From what I've heard, you've done a better job of digging your way up than I dared even hope when we first met, Mage Soprano.

"I'm pleased to have been of service," he concluded. "And it sounds like we're all the better off for it."

She smiled.

"It hasn't been easy," she admitted, "but it's been good—and we've done good. I plan on keeping that up."

Most of their meeting ended up being quiet catch-up, the senior MISS agent curious about how Maria was adapting to life aboard a civilian starship. When they were done, Alois insisted on picking up the tab.

On his way out, he paused and leaned back on the table to bring himself back into the field of the white-noise generator.

"I know I'm the one who dragged you into all of this," he said quietly, "but listen to me for a moment: be careful. Watch your back."

He shook his head.

"The Agency is traditionally better-intentioned than many organizations like it in history, but remember that at our best, we're interstellar covert ops—but at our worst, we're interstellar secret police.

"It's far too easy for someone sitting in a ship or an office a hundred light-years from anywhere to decide a risk is worth the benefit. They aren't the ones who do the bleeding and dying if the risk goes wrong."

Maria smiled thinly.

"I've seen what happens when the back office decides not everyone needs to know what's going on," she said quietly. "I have no intention of watching *Falcon*'s crew suffer the same fate."

"We're out there for a reason," Alois told her. "But take care of yourself, Maria."

"Why, Major Alois, whatever would your wife think?" she told him with a wicked grin.

"She'd think I was being the overprotective team dad she married still," he replied with his own grin. "You know what I mean."

"I do," she agreed. "We'll be fine, Major Alois. I promise."

"I'll hold you to that!"

As she was returning to *Red Falcon* via the zero-gravity docks, Maria's wrist-comp pinged with a note from the Captain informing her that the new Third Officer was aboard and asking if she was available to meet with him.

She checked and fired a note back saying she was, before accelerating her course. It only took her a few minutes to make it to *Falcon*, though the ship's own impressive length delayed her making it to the Captain's office.

Maria was still there before the new officer, arriving to find Captain Rice in his usual space behind his desk—and Kelly LaMonte ensconced in the seat to the Captain's right that had been Jenna Campbell's usual spot.

"I see the promotion went through on schedule," she said with a chuckle. "Welcome to the hot seat, Second Officer."

"Oh, don't worry," LaMonte replied with her own smile. "I plan on hiding from any real heat behind you for at least, oh, two days."

"Take at *least* a week," Maria told the younger woman. "Trust me, I'm pretty fire-retardant."

"Maybe," LaMonte agreed easily, "but I'll be a shitty XO if someone else is taking my heat, won't I?"

Maria bowed her head in acknowledgement. The new XO at least had a handle on where she needed to be. That was a good sign.

"Ivan is bringing Mr. Daniels down as we speak," Rice told his two senior officers. "He comes highly recommended and this is mostly a meet-and-greet, but Kelly, I suggest you let Maria and me take the lead.

"That said, you *are* the XO, so don't hesitate to speak up if you see something that needs saying."

"All right," LaMonte said, her voice calm but steady. She seemed to be handling the deep end relatively well, from what Maria could see.

A sharp rap on the door interrupted any further preparation, and Ivan Skavar escorted the new Third Officer in.

Connor Daniels was a rippling hunk of a man, almost distractingly attractive to Maria's eyes. He was tall and broad-shouldered, with perfectly tousled brown hair and eminently kissable lips.

Ivan Skavar was equally tall and broad-shouldered, but his dark hair and sharp features made him pale into near-insignificance next to the specimen he was escorting.

The man's attractiveness, however, was not enough for Maria to miss that the Chief of Security had escorted Daniels all the way into the office. That shouldn't have been required, and the Chief's body language was wrong for it to be as simple as two alpha males posturing at each other.

Something about the new officer had the Marine concerned, but Skavar didn't say a word. He just escorted Daniels into the room, showed the ex-Navy man to his seat, and left with a silent salute.

He didn't say a word...but his presence alone spoke volumes, and Maria studied Daniels with a far more critical eye than she might otherwise have. She was used to men being distracted by her chest, but most got over it in short order.

The new tactical officer's gaze lingered on her figure for a good second longer than appropriate—and lingered on LaMonte's much less voluptuous form for almost as long before leveling on the Captain...without meeting either woman's gaze.

"Captain Rice," he introduced himself, and his voice was a baritone purr that ran right down Maria's spine.

"Pleasure to meet you. Connor Daniels, formerly of His Majesty's Starship *Measures of Safety*," he continued, offering his hand.

Rice shook the younger man's hand, then gestured to the two women with his chin.

"Likewise, Officer Daniels," he said slowly. "This is Mage Maria Soprano, Senior Ship's Mage and First Officer, and Officer Kelly LaMonte, Executive and Second Officer. You'll be working closely with both of them as you get situated."

Daniels turned his gaze on LaMonte, managing to physically look down on the smaller woman despite being seated.

"That sounds like fun," he murmured. "Miss LaMonte is the executive officer, though? She seems...young."

"Miss LaMonte has saved this ship and her crew from all kinds of problems," Rice replied. Something in his careful tone told Maria he'd also picked up on Skavar's silent warning. "I hope you won't have a problem working under her?"

"I'll have no problem at all working *under* her," Daniels replied cheekily, and for one long, glorious, moment of temptation, Maria considered teleporting him into the vacuum outside the ship.

That was probably overkill.

"I'd suggest refraining from comments like that," Rice told the new officer, his voice very low. "This isn't a small ship, Officer Daniels, but her crew is smaller than you may be used to. We're a family here, and we look after each other."

"Of course, of course," he agreed. "Outside the Navy, of course, there's fewer fraternization rules, eh, XO?"

The idiot had the gall to wink at LaMonte, who straightened and leveled him with a death glare she must have been practicing for months.

"There are still, however, standards of consent, discretion, and common decency, Officer Daniels," LaMonte said icily. "Do you expect to continue having difficulties meeting those?"

The young woman flashed Rice and Maria a quick glance. Maria managed to not openly send her a thumbs-up—and Rice made a very clear "go ahead" gesture.

"Just talking crap, miss," Daniels replied easily. "Don't mean anything by it. You'll learn to tell the difference with more experience."

"That, Officer Daniels, should be *ma'am*, not *miss*," LaMonte said coldly. "It seems my question didn't quite register. Are you prepared to follow orders and do your job? Or is my being younger and female going to be a problem?"

"Miss, you being female is the *opposite* of a problem," he said with a grin. He finally actually met LaMonte's gaze as he spoke, however, and the smile faded.

LaMonte looked at her seniors again, and Maria caught David's single, cold nod.

"Speak to Chief Skavar about having your things delivered on your way out," LaMonte told the ex-Navy man gently. "I don't think you're going to fit in with *Red Falcon*'s crew, and it's better for us to get that sorted out right now."

Daniels looked shocked.

"Hey, now, this is a covert ops ship, ain't it?" he demanded. "I was *assigned* here. That's—"

"That's not how this works," Rice cut him off. "This is *my* ship, Mr. Daniels. The Agency assists in making sure we have qualified crew, but they appear to have made a mistake in this case.

"I would suggest you learn to keep your mouth shut better in future," the Captain concluded. "MISS is hardly fond of people who blabber classified information at the drop of a hat.

"Chief Skavar will escort you off *Red Falcon*," Rice continued, backing up LaMonte completely. "I apologize for the waste of everyone's time this appears to have been, Mr. Daniels."

CHAPTER 4

"CONNOR DANIELS is currently very, very grumpy at you, Captain," Hand Alaura Stealey told David as she poured herself a generous splash of scotch into a glass.

It had been five days since they'd kicked their intended Third Officer off of *Red Falcon*, and David had joined the Hand of the Mage-King of Mars in her hotel suite on his own. Based off his own experience with in-suite hotel bars, he'd have hesitated to be quite so free with the alcohol, but the Hand didn't seem perturbed by any amount of liquor, in his experience.

And, well, it wasn't like one of the dozen or so personal representatives of humanity's ruler really needed to worry about the budget.

"Mr. Daniels strikes me in desperate need of some remedial growing-up," David noted as he poured himself a glass of water. "I am somehow unsurprised that the Navy was happy to see the back of him."

"I saw your comments," Stealey agreed. She was an average-looking woman of average height with iron-gray hair and a perpetually sour expression. "I passed on some of my own to the case officer with MISS."

She shook her head.

"To be fair to the man, it wasn't like Daniels being a sexist pig made it into his jacket," she concluded. "Though it bloody well *should* have. A few ears at the Navy will be bent before this is over."

"And Daniels?" David asked.

"Daniels and his demonstrated big mouth have found themselves a comfortable posting to a survey ship heading to somewhere beyond the back of nowhere," Stealey said grimly. "I feel a bit guilty for the survey ship's crew, but the Captain seemed to understand what we were handing her.

"And this way, he's a long way away from anyone he can leak information to."

She shook her head.

"Lacking a gunnery officer is going to be a headache, though," she said. "The wheels are in motion to get you to Snap—Alois passed on the details, I hope?"

"He did," David confirmed. "I put out some feelers of my own, and I have found a man who could do the job. If you're willing to wave the golden hand and make certain problems go away."

Stealey sighed, tapping the closed-fist icon of her office that hung on her chest.

"What kind of problems, Captain Rice?"

"Alexander Jeeves is an old friend from my own Navy days," he told her. "He's...an irrevocable idiot and walked himself into a lot of trouble with the wrong people, but he already owes me one and was a half-decent tactical officer in the day."

Stealey leveled a hard gray glare on him.

"What kind of problems, Captain Rice?" she repeated.

He sighed.

"Jeeves is in a Protectorate penitentiary for arms smuggling," David admitted. "He got tied up in some kind of deal with the Mafia and, so far as I can tell, got left holding the bag when much smarter people got out of Dodge.

"I visited him after I found out where he was. He's doing about as well as anyone can in prison, but I suspect he'd be more useful to *everyone* on my bridge."

"You want me to see an arms smuggler released into your custody to serve as your tactical officer, Captain Rice?"

"It would certainly give us some bona fides for the kind of trouble you want me to get into," he pointed out.

Stealey laughed.

"That's fair," she allowed. "I'll talk to some people and pull the full re-cord of just what he got locked up for. I make no promises, Rice, but if he looks trustworthy, you're right in that he'd open up some doors we can use."

"Speaking of which," Rice noted. "Snap, huh?"

Stealey nodded in answer to his question, stepping over to the screen that covered one wall of the suite's living room. Currently, it was showing the view from the protective fortification protecting Tau Ceti *f* from the system's eternal bombardment of rocks.

As David looked at it past her, one of the station's lasers flared to life, a line of bright light that turned a rock too small and too far away to be seen into a glowing streak of light, an artificial shooting star.

"Snap," she agreed. "We couldn't have you go there directly from Tau Ceti. For one thing, it would be too obvious. For another, Snap is pretty insular, so there *aren't* any shipments going there from here."

"I know the name and that's it's an UnArcana World," David admit-ted. "That's it."

"That's all most people know," Stealey said. "Even for an UnArcana World, Snap is...xenophobic. It's not just that they don't like Mages; they don't like *anybody*."

She shook her head.

"It's not religious or anything," she explained. "They're just very in-sular. Since there are things they can't make themselves, however, they have interstellar trade that's filtered through some very specific channels.

"Basically, nobody from outside the Snap System is even permitted in orbit of Flytrap, the habitable planet," she told him. "The fifth planet, the next one out from Flytrap, is Junkrat. Junkrat has several orbital sta-tions that are *technically* run by Snap's government."

"That sounds more complicated than it should be," David said.

"It is," she agreed. "Snap doesn't bother to actually police Junkrat Orbital. The main station is safe enough, but that's because Legatus runs it. The rest..."

She shook her head.

"It's a criminal organization's dream," she said. "Massive transship-ment facilities with minimal to no oversight. Even *Amber* keeps better track of what moves through their space than Snap does of what moves through Junkrat.

"It's an entirely different story if you move over to Flytrap," she continued. "You wouldn't make it there, for one. Snap may not build starships, but they've got some *very* effective long-range missiles based out of orbital platforms.

"Build them big enough and you, too, can have a fusion-drive missile that rivals the performance of everyone else's antimatter birds."

David winced. Given the difference in performance between his handful of Navy-built antimatter missiles and his police-grade fusion missiles, those had to be *huge* missiles.

"Even Snap has limits on what they're prepared to tolerate—or so the crime families assume, at least—which has led to Junkrat being something of a neutral ground for criminals," she continued.

"There's no official enforcement like there was on Darkport, but everyone is there to do business, and nobody wants trouble. If you cause trouble, no one will do business with you," she summarized.

"Sounds like a wonderful place to visit and a horrible place to live," David replied. "Why are you sending me there?"

"MISS intelligence suggests that the Azure Legacy is attempting to broker a peace between the various remnant factions of the Blue Star Syndicate," Stealey said flatly.

Azure Legacy was an organization created by Mikhail Azure's will after that crime lord had died trying to hunt Rice and his ship down. It had two purposes, as he understood it: to kill the people who'd killed Mikhail Azure, and to make sure the Syndicate didn't fall apart.

Since the Syndicate had done a solid job of falling apart and they hadn't managed to kill David yet, he figured they had to be pretty frustrated.

"Not everyone is in, but the estimates I'm seeing suggest that if Legacy pulls this meeting off, they'll re-concentrate about seventy percent of the Syndicate's resources under one banner. They wouldn't be the largest crime organization again...but they'd be close."

"Damn. I see why we need to stop it. Do you have a plan for me beyond 'show up and look intimidating'?"

She chuckled humorlessly.

"More 'show up and look like a target,'" she admitted. "Our hope is that your presence will distract the Legacy and cause them to come after you, hopefully undermining their authority with the fragment syndicates *and* exposing the whole summit for our operatives on the station.

"We want to break up this meeting and prevent any chance of the Blue Star Syndicate re-forming," Stealey told him. "But this *also* gives us the opportunity to tag a number of the leaders of the successor organizations we haven't IDed yet. If we can make them and follow them home, we have the chance to dismantle that same seventy percent of the Syndicate's leftovers."

"That seems worth the try, at least, my lady," David admitted. "I have a meeting with the shipper to get us to Desdemona in the morning. We'll get the wheels moving. Do we have more detailed information?"

She slid a data chip out of her pocket and dropped it on the table.

"Everything we know about the Legacy's summit and the power players in Junkrat," she told him. "I'll take a look at your friend, too, see if I think he's safe enough to hand over."

"If I'm walking into this kind of den of vipers, I could use a solid hand on *Falcon's* guns."

"I know," she agreed. "But there's a limit to the level of scum I'm willing to trust you with, Rice!"

CHAPTER 5

"CAPTAIN RICE, a pleasure to speak to you," the man on the screen greeted David. "I am Roger Yukimura, Vice President of Special Projects for Cobalt Interstellar Elements."

Yukimura was a slim man with bleached-white hair that reached down to his shoulders, and long delicate fingers that were in full view as he held a cup of tea in front of himself.

He didn't seem to be drinking the tea so much as using it as a prop, but David had dealt with stranger.

"A pleasure indeed," David replied cheerfully. "Your agent told me that you had a large cargo that needed to be delivered quickly and safely? *Red Falcon* excels at all three of those things: with our antimatter engines, we clear the gravity well faster than most freighters, and with four Mages aboard, we move between systems faster as well.

"And, well, if anyone decides to tangle with your cargo, *Falcon* retains a portion of the armament from her Navy days," he concluded. "Whatever you need delivered, Mr. Yukimura, we can get it there."

In truth, *Red Falcon* retained the entirety of her Navy armament, though in naval service her magazines had been entirely filled with antimatter-drive missiles. The launchers could still handle fusion-drive missiles, however, and the battle lasers were still very intact.

"So I'm told," Yukimura allowed. "You understand, Captain, that Cobalt rarely relies on small-scale shippers, however capable their vessel.

"This cargo for the Desdemona System was originally booked with Chevalier, and I remain surprised by their failure to fulfill their contract."

David managed not to visibly whistle silently. Chevalier Arcane Transshipment had been the very first interstellar shipping line and remained one of the largest and richest, even though their immense megafreighters almost never left the Core Worlds.

"Desdemona is a MidWorld, I suppose," he said carefully. "I didn't think Chevalier left the Core anymore."

Yukimura took one hand off his teacup for long enough to make a languid dismissive gesture.

"I suppose not. Negotiations between Cobalt and Chevalier around contract penalties continue, but that is irrelevant to our current discussion," he admitted. "We are almost two weeks late in moving this cargo now.

"Without it, the new refinery facility in Desdemona cannot be completed. The system government gave us quite generous terms to operate in their space, which means there are also significant penalties if the plant does not come online and begin providing employment as promised."

"We can get your cargo to Desdemona in under four days from it being loaded," David told the executive. Desdemona was forty light-years from Tau Ceti, three full days plus a few extra jumps for his Mages, and it would take them about ten hours to get out to and in from jump distance.

"Four days?" Yukimura noted. "Chevalier wasn't prepared to promise less than a week."

"Chevalier doesn't have antimatter drives and only carries three Mages per ship as standard," David noted. "I may only have two-thirds the cargo capacity of one of their big ships, but I'd bet against them in any race."

"Which fate, it seems, now requires me to do as well," Yukimura concluded. "Standard carriage terms for a fifty-light-year transit, with a twenty-five-percent bonus for delivery inside five days." He shrugged slowly, delicately. "The same terms we agreed to with Chevalier."

"If you can have the cargo aboard inside twenty-four hours, that's entirely acceptable," David replied. "If your people fail to have the cargo loaded in time, that five-day timeline will need to be extended."

The executive's eyes flashed, the first sign of real energy from the man in the entire conversation.

"Our people have access to the best gear in the system," he declared.

"Then you'll have no problem allowing for loading delays in the bonus timeline," David said brightly.

"Captain, there are some…gentlemen here at the main boarding tube with a package for you," Skavar's dry tones echoed over David's wrist-comp shortly after his meeting with Yukimura.

"I'll be right down," David promised.

He could guess just what kind of "package" would be showing up on his doorstep today, a bit over a day since meeting with Hand Stealey and her promising to look into Alexander Jeeves's case.

So, when he arrived at the docking tube to find a wiry, dirty-looking little man in prison fatigues and shackles half-suspended between two burly officers in Tau Ceti System Police uniforms, he wasn't entirely surprised.

"You ordered a felon, sir?" Skavar whispered to David as he approached. "He doesn't look like much."

"Neither would you after two years in a Protectorate medium-security facility," David murmured back. "Give the man a chance."

He stepped past his guards and nodded crisply to the two TCSPD men.

"You were looking for me?" he asked.

"You Rice?" the bigger of them asked.

"I'm Captain David Rice, owner of the *Falcon* shipping line and Captain of this ship, yes," David replied levelly.

"I'm Sergeant Stanka Chilikov," the officer introduced himself. "I have orders to transfer one Alexander Jeeves into your custody."

Jeeves managed to stand somewhat straighter. His permanent slouch slipped away enough to reveal that he was actually of average height, despite his wiry appearance.

"I'm being released?" he asked.

"No," Chilikov said bluntly. "You're not being released; you're not being pardoned. Your sentence has been commuted to a work term under Captain Rice per authority higher than I can argue with."

"Huh." Jeeves studied David. "You're looking good, Chief. I guess Captain now?"

"You know; you don't guess," David said dryly. They'd met before. "Want a job?"

"I'm not under the impression I get a *choice*," the dirty little man noted.

"Oh, you have a choice," Sergeant Chilikov said sweetly. "If you don't want to work for the Captain, you and I get back on the shuttle we arrived on and you go back to breaking rocks for the greater good."

Jeeves paused dramatically, then his face turned thoughtful.

"What's the job?" he asked bluntly. "There are things I'd rather break rocks than do."

"Gunnery officer aboard a civilianized Armed Auxiliary Fast Heavy Freighter," David told him. "Don't piss off the XO or the Ship's Mage. Some other complications, but those are confidential company data." He eyed the cops. He trusted them as much as he trusted anyone, but they didn't need to know that *Falcon* was a covert ops ship.

"I don't need *more* time on my sentence, David," Jeeves said quietly. "I get myself in enough trouble on my own."

David laughed.

"Believe me, Alexander Jeeves, I don't promise not to get you in trouble," he told his old comrade. "I *do* promise that none of that trouble is going to add to your jail time. Deal?"

Jeeves looked at Chilikov and his companion and shrugged.

"The Sergeant isn't nearly the sourpuss he's pretending to be," he noted, "but medium-security facilities are *boring*.

"If you can lend me a shower and some clean clothes in, oh, the next five minutes, we have a deal."

"We can do that," David promised.

"Then deal."

David had known exactly how much stuff Jeeves would be arriving with, so he'd made sure the Third Officer's quarters were stocked with basic toiletries and clothes in the man's size.

Shaved, showered, and dressed in an unmarked ship's uniform, Alexander Jeeves could almost pass for the soldier he'd once been. He'd kept the shoulder-length hair, though, and there was a twitchiness to the man he hadn't had when he'd been in the Navy.

"There's still a catch to all of this," David warned as Jeeves took a careful seat on the couch in what would hopefully be his new suite. "Stuff that your escorting Sergeant wasn't cleared for."

"*Cleared for*," Jeeves echoed, then glanced around the room. "This is a civvy ship now, I'm told. *You're* definitely a civilian now. Not Navy. So, who the hell is clearing whom for what?"

"I'd say that it was just company-confidential information, but you need to know what you're getting into before it's too late to get out," David told him. "You can still get out if you choose, so we're clear."

"That much fun, huh?" his old friend asked. "All right, Chief, lay it on me."

"Firstly, don't call me Chief," David replied. "'Chief' on this boat is either James Kellers, Chief Engineer and Fourth Officer; or Ivan Skavar, Chief of Security. Clear?"

"Habit," Jeeves admitted. "Sorry, Skipper."

"Better. Now, you're right, we're not Navy," David confirmed. "Until relatively recently, I was a private shipper with odd connections. Now... now we're MISS."

"Covert ops. Fuck." There was no heat to Jeeves's words.

"You know Mikhail Azure is dead and the Blue Star Syndicate is falling apart," David said. "I imagine that made it into prison."

"Yeah. Not many people talking up just how, though."

"We killed him," David Rice said flatly. "He chased us across half the damn Protectorate, caught up to us, and my Ship's Mage vaporized him and his ship."

Jeeves was silent.

"You're serious."

"Perfectly. In exchange, my Mage got drafted to the Mage-King's service and I got this ship," David concluded. "And, of course, an entire organization of assassins and bounty hunters looking to avenge Azure.

"So, we ended up working with the Agency. And now I work *for* the Agency, as does every senior officer on this ship."

"Which now includes me."

"You can still back out," David noted.

Jeeves laughed.

"You poked an epic knee in the Syndicate's eye and need someone to watch your back while they sharpen the knife?" he replied. "No, Skipper, I'm in. I'm guessing we're heading out to poke them in the eye again?"

"Lure them into a trap, hopefully," David said. "See if we can catch some Legatan spies while we're at it. Make the galaxy a safer place in general."

"I'm no good at that on my own," his old friend said seriously. "I tried and ended up getting conned into running guns *for* the Syndicate. I've got your back, Skipper."

"Good. Now all you need to do is *not* piss off the XO and Ship's Mage."

"Have you ever known me to do anything except make friends?" Jeeves replied, pressing a hand to his heart.

"Yeah. That's what I'm afraid of."

CHAPTER 6

"WE ARE CLEAR of the gravity well and ready to jump," LaMonte reported from the navigation station on the bridge. "All cargo is locked in place and hanging on solidly. No issues."

David nodded wordlessly as he double-checked all of the metrics himself. He trusted LaMonte, but this was her first flight out as XO.

Red Falcon was purring along. The hab ring was rotating smoothly underneath the shield dome, the engines were happily turning hydrogen and antihydrogen into thrust, and the cargo suspended along the stem between the two sections of the ship had all been well attached.

Cobalt Interstellar Elements' people had done their job well and quickly. *Falcon* had actually left ten hours before he'd hoped, barely giving Jeeves's delivery of new clothes time to arrive before they'd set off.

He didn't *need* the twenty-five-percent bonus, not when he could turn over standard carriage rate contracts in half the time of most of his competitors, but it didn't hurt, either. Plus, his standing policy was to pay out a good chunk of that kind of bonus to the crew.

Starship captains, especially those who owned multiple ships, were far from poor. Starship crews were often less lucky. There were few jobs aboard a jump-ship that paid poorly, per se, but there were always some crew members who were perpetually in money troubles.

In David's experience, Jeeves was of that category no matter what the man was making. He was also, despite his amazing ability to find trouble, one of the better team leads *Red Falcon*'s Captain had ever met, and he was already settling in to lead the armed freighter's gunnery crews.

So far, he'd drunk all of his new team under the table on the way out of Tau Ceti and was now making them do targeting exercises with blistering hangovers.

"Stand down the exercises, Guns," David ordered. "We don't want to be lighting up space with a laser when we jump."

"Understood," Jeeves replied crisply. "Captain says you folks get a break." He paused. "In fact, you've all done okay. Assuming no one ambushes us after the jump, Bravo and Charlie shifts can stand down for a rest cycle.

"Sorry, Alpha shift, you get the short straw today." He grinned into the mike. "Bravo gets it next time."

David couldn't hear the responding groans, but he was sure they'd been loud, extended, and melodramatic. The gunners knew their new boss's type, and Jeeves seemed to know their numbers in turn.

"Mage Wu," David greeted his now-second-most senior Mage as he activated the screen to the simulacrum chamber. "I show the ship green to jump. How are things looking back there?"

Kelly LaMonte's girlfriend smiled thinly, the petite Chinese woman floating in the middle of the starry chamber at the core of the starship. Her hands rested on the liquid silver simulacrum that magically mirrored the entirety of *Red Falcon* on a smaller scale.

"Our calculations are complete and I read the space around as safe to jump. With your permission, Captain Rice?"

He smiled.

"Carry on, Mage Wu. You are authorized to jump the ship."

He'd barely finished speaking when there was an infinitesimal moment of *change*...and the stars were suddenly slightly different.

"Kelly?" he asked.

"Nav software running," his new XO replied. She waited. "Navigation confirms successful jump. We are bang on target at Jump One along the Tau Ceti–Desdemona route."

"Mage Barrow is up next," Xi Wu reported. "In two hours."

With four Mages aboard, David had no need to push them past the standard one-jump-every-eight-hours routine. *Red Falcon* could still outrun most of her competitors—and since every Mage on his ship *could* do a six-hour jump when needed, she could also outrun her enemies.

David Rice might, officially, be a spy in the employ of the Protectorate of the Mage-King of Mars...but he was, at heart, a merchant-ship captain. The last thing he was expecting when he entered his office and sat down at his computer was for a message to start playing without him doing anything.

Hand Alaura Stealey's image looked up at him from the monitor growing out of his desk, a wry smirk on the old woman's face.

"If you're seeing this, then you've completed your first jump away from Tau Ceti and were probably about to sit down for a relaxing cup of coffee or some such," she told him brightly.

David looked down at the empty mug sitting on the edge of his desk. He hadn't made it that far before the preprogrammed image had interrupted him.

"There's a lot of different strings to our bow here, Captain Rice, and some of them are even more cloak-and-dagger than the rest," she continued after a moment. "I apologize for the secrecy, but there are layers that I cannot risk being leaked at all.

"What we have begun doing is leaking the location where Mikhail Azure died," she told him. "Depending on the rumor, either there's nothing there, or either *Blue Jay* or *Azure Gauntlet* were left there to drift, in various states of disrepair."

He sighed.

Either of those would be tempting prizes to a lot of criminals. It had been an open secret, in the end, that Damien Montgomery had somehow turned *Blue Jay*'s jump matrix—the set of runes any starship had that allowed a Mage to teleport it between the stars—into a true amplifier matrix.

An amplifier matrix could amplify *any* spell, not just the jump spell, which made it a powerful weapon. They were restricted to the Royal Martian Navy...but *Blue Jay* would have been a template for any decently trained Rune Scribe to duplicate what Montgomery had done.

The Navy had destroyed his ship to prevent that.

Damien Montgomery himself had destroyed *Azure Gauntlet*, Mikhail Azure's stolen cruiser flagship, by using *Blue Jay*'s amplifier matrix to detonate the warship's antimatter stockpiles.

There was nothing left of either vessel, but even rumors of their presence would be tempting bait.

"We expect the rumors themselves to lure some more foolish players into our web," Stealey noted. "And that is the reason I gave the agents involved. High in my thinking, however, is that the rumors give *you* a weapon, Captain Rice.

"There is only one person the Syndicate or Legatus would trust to know the location of Azure's death with full accuracy," she said. "You."

Her wry smirk turned evil.

"It turns out that the Navy has four *Minotaur*-class cruisers, the same class as *Gauntlet*. A little bit of paint and some engine tuning, and presto! We now have four ships that can pretend to be *Azure Gauntlet*.

"They will be rotated through that location for the next year or until I feel we've dragged as many flies into our trap as we're going to get."

The smile faded.

"It gives you leverage, Captain, but it also gives you an out," she told him. "Something you can trade for your life—the location of a crippled but repairable ship.

"And if they come looking for it with you as their prisoner, I promise you, David Rice, the Navy will rescue you. We owe you far more than that."

The message ended, and David stared at the blank screen for a few moments. The cloak-and-dagger mess was already getting on his nerves, but he could see why that needed to stay secret.

The rumors were one thing, but the fact that the rumors were a trap needed to stay quiet to let the trap work. The chance to lure his enemies into the Navy's web was tempting, too.

He could see uses for Stealey's trap.

And with all that the Blue Star Syndicate had done, he didn't even feel guilty for it.

A full day and twelve more jumps later, the ship was beginning to settle into routine again. David could always tell the point where the crew began to settle down for a voyage. There'd be breaks and cargo off-loading and on-loading, but it would be a while before *Red Falcon* settled into one place for any extended period again.

Assuming, of course, that nobody shot his ship up this time. He wasn't willing to take that bet.

He did take advantage of the seeming quiet to cook for his senior officers. It was a ritual David saw no need to give up, especially now that they were the inner circle of a covert operations team as well as the officers of his ship!

There were a few extras in the room for supper, of course. He had his four senior officers, but he also had Ivan Skavar, the Chief of Security, and Fulbert Nicolas, his First Pilot.

If it had been a less formal affair, there might have been others—both of Kelly LaMonte's partners, for example, were relatively senior members of the ship's crew—but there was a limit to how much David could cook in his little kitchen and to how many people he could fit in his Captain's dining room.

Red Falcon had more space than *Blue Jay* had had, but its military designers had included an officers' mess for if the Captain wanted to dine with all of his officers—and the thought of the Captain cooking up

---

a massive dish of butter chicken lasagne with his own hands wouldn't have occurred to them.

Many modern cuisines were a result of cultural blending on new worlds. This one, however, he understood dated back to North America—the original cultural blender.

"How are everyone's departments shaping up?" he asked as he scooped out the steaming pasta.

"Security is Security," Skavar said with a shrug. "We're Marines pretending to be civilians; what do you expect?"

David chuckled.

"Trouble, that's what I expect. How much of it have we got?"

"Not much," the Marine told him. "The fact that everyone on the ship now knows what's going on helps avoid our old problem of my people running their mouths off to get laid."

LaMonte coughed pointedly as she took a seat next to Skavar, who had the courtesy to flush—said running of the mouth had occurred when one of Skavar's squad leaders had tried to get her and Wu into bed at the same time.

It hadn't ended well for the Marine in question by any measure.

"I'm still feeling my way around the ship outside of Engineering and my shiny new admin group," LaMonte said, answering the question herself and letting Skavar off the hook for his people's earlier mistakes.

"Bran Wiltshire and I go way back, and the man knows the admin inside and out," she continued. "I have no worries there, just finding my feet so to speak."

"Engineering's fine," Kellers grunted. "You promoted my best helper past me, but we'll make do."

"You didn't want the job," David reminded his engineer, who promptly filled his mouth to avoid answering.

"We've got a *lot* of shuttlecraft," Nicolas noted, the gaunt blond man filling his plate with far more vegetables and pasta than anyone would have expected, looking at him. "But my people know their jobs and we didn't lose many when we 'officially' went covert ops.

"Speaking of which, though"—he glanced at Skavar as he took a seat—"am I supposed to admit I know about the squadron of assault shuttles you tucked in Kelzin's Bravo Bay?"

"I stuck five hundred tons of munitions in your storage lockers, First Pilot," Skavar replied. "I bloody well *hope* you know about the spacecraft they're for!"

Jeeves chuckled, shaking his head as he took his own plate.

"Quite the affair we've got going on here," he noted aloud. "Assault shuttles, Marines...and it's not like the Navy actually took any of *Falcon's* guns out. Who do you have to kill to get this kind of setup, Skipper?"

"Mikhail Azure," at least four people chorused back instantly.

Jeeves laughed in response.

"Fair enough," he conceded. "All of the beams, turrets, and launchers check out green. My crews are solid—better than I was expecting, to be honest. I wouldn't want to fight a cruiser in this ship, but we could probably tangle with a rogue destroyer or two.

"Presuming we stayed out of amplifier range, anyway," he concluded, with a glance at Soprano.

"That's our job," she said grimly. "Wu's taking things a bit rough, but she's one of the best I've ever seen as civilians go. Barrow and Nguyen are ex-Navy, but I think Wu may actually edge them out for sheer power.

"Once I've got them all trained up to what I want, we'll take you wherever you want to go and get you *out* of any trouble you happen to find."

"That's what we're all here for," David concluded. "Our job is to get in trouble and live through it. I'm glad we all understand that!"

CHAPTER 7

ONE POSITIVE POINT in favor of moving massive industrial equipment, Kelly supposed, was that it didn't require much in terms of watching. It didn't even require the usual systems checks that they'd have to do on the standard ten-thousand-ton shipping containers.

There were enough of those in the cargo, but the core pieces for Cobalt Interstellar Elements' new refinery came in massive, half-kilometer-tall, single-piece components. Once strapped into place, the massive chunks of silent machinery didn't really require supervision.

They were also, however, massive chunks of *fascinating* technology, and Kelly LaMonte was an engineer. Primarily a software and electronics engineer, to be sure, but she didn't know any engineer who could spend four days a few minutes' walk away from the galaxy's most advanced version of *anything* without taking a peek.

Which left her poking her way along the computing core of what would shortly be the primary smelter for the Cobalt Desdemona Orbital Refinery. The section was sealed but didn't have atmosphere or gravity of its own, which left her in a vac-suit with magnetic boots and a flashlight.

There wasn't much they could do if something had broken in the pre-built segment, but the contract also required them to make sure everything was transporting safely, so Kelly figured she'd take the chance to take a look.

The gun was *probably* overkill, but she'd spent too long aboard *Red Falcon* to consider anything paranoid. She shone the flashlight around the control center, taking an extra few seconds to appreciate the sheer scale and complexity of the hardware,

The real key to what would make the station tick was the software, but even if she was feeling like violating their contract that badly, the segments didn't have power. There was a Desdemona-built fusion plant waiting for them at their destination.

Turning to run the light over another wall, she caught what she thought was movement. That was impossible—she knew there was no one else outside *Red Falcon's* hull. She was the one who had to sign off on EVAs. There shouldn't be anything moving on the half-kilometer-long chunk of space station she was inspecting.

Saying hello would be pointless in vacuum, but she flashed her light twice, waiting for a response. Nothing. But there *was* a hatch in the middle of the wall where she'd thought she'd seen something.

For a moment, she considered dismissing it as a trick of the light.

Then she drew the gun and turned up the lock on her mag-boots to absorb recoil if needed. If someone was aboard the orbital refinery pieces, *Red Falcon* had a problem.

Kelly took a moment to localize where the stranger must have been coming from—and going *to*—and realized they had a problem.

She tapped her communicator with her chin, cycling through the channels for the one she wanted as she slowly approached the door.

"Skavar, it's LaMonte," she greeted the Security Chief. "We have an issue."

There was a pregnant pause.

"Okay, XO, last I checked you were doing EVA sweeps of our cargo. I don't like the idea of an issue out there."

"Pretty sure I spotted movement, a potential stowaway," she told him. "Except I'm standing right beside probably the single most expensive and fragile piece of equipment in this whole assemblage.

"My quick and dirty mental math puts our client in *serious* trouble if they have any more delays in bringing the platform online," Kelly continued. "Reading the papers the Skipper gave me says the penalties are to the tune of about ten percent of CIE's annual profit...per day."

"You think we've got a saboteur."

"I'm *afraid* we have a saboteur," she agreed. "Can you get some of your people into suits and ready to follow me out? We have real exosuit combat gear, right?"

"Enough," Skavar said grimly. "You need to hold in place until I get backup to you, XO," he continued. "Are you even armed?"

"MARP-15," she told him. The Martian Armaments Rocket-Propelled Fifteen-Millimeter pistol was a low-recoil hand cannon designed for exactly this environment. Its rounds shouldn't penetrate the refinery's walls but would do an ugly number on any vac-suit they hit.

"Okay, better than nothing," the Marine agreed. "Still, wait for the backup."

"Skavar...we've swept the cargo for thermals every twelve hours since we loaded it aboard," she told him. "If there *is* someone out there, they're hiding and hiding well. Which means if I don't follow them and see where they go..."

"*Fuck,*" he hissed. "Fine. Be careful. I'm pretty sure my contract says *ugly* things about losing senior officers!"

"I was born careful," she promised lightly.

"I've met the people you date," the Marine replied. "Stay alive, Ms. LaMonte. We're coming in after you."

Nodding wordlessly—for herself more than Skavar—Kelly stepped up to the hatch. She left the channel open so the security detail could trace her, but her focus was on the here and now.

The hatch should have been sealed, requiring the codes she'd got from Cobalt to open. Instead, it opened at a touch, not even properly closed.

Someone else was *definitely* aboard.

-⟩-

The lack of sound had been irrelevant before. Now it was nerve-wracking, an additional factor to edge on Kelly's fears as she stepped through the door, looking for any sign of the intruder.

Other than the unlocked hatch, nothing was immediately obvious, and she was concerned she'd spent too much time checking in with Skavar—and then her light flicked down the hallway and over an *open* hatchway.

All of the hatches on the station pieces should have been locked and secured against acceleration. *Red Falcon* had been dragging them along at ten gravities for most of the first day, after all, and that was enough to cause serious damage if anything wasn't secured.

Kelly made her way down the hall to the open hatch, peering through to find an empty shaft that would eventually contain an elevator. The shaft ran the entire half-kilometer length of the smelter—it was missing its car primarily so the workers fitting out the chunk of space station could use it as a walkway.

She shone her light down the shaft, trying to see if she could find some evidence of her intruder—and then received a sharp lesson in why carrying a flashlight in a dark space wasn't necessarily the best idea.

Some instinct caused her to jerk her head back out of the elevator shaft a fraction of a moment before the first bullets smacked into where she'd been leaning out. Her engineer's mind cataloged them as frangible rounds—not the rocket-propelled ammunition her weapon was loaded with, but regular bullets designed not to damage the hull.

"Skavar, I'm under fire," she reported swiftly. "What's the ETA on my backup?"

"Six, seven minutes," the Marine replied instantly. "Fall back, wait for support."

She watched the metal of the wall vibrate. Someone was now moving up the empty elevator shaft.

"I'm not sure that's an option," she told him. "Going to see if I can buy some time."

There wasn't much point shouting. With no atmosphere, no one could hear anyone—and if their intruders had introduced themselves by shooting at her, they clearly weren't planning on talking.

Kelly leaned out more carefully this time, with her flashlight turned off, looking in the direction the gunfire had come from.

She couldn't see much. A hint of movement. Maybe a glint of light. It was enough to return the favor, her MARP-15 vibrating sharply as she sent a trio of rounds back at the people who'd fired at her.

The light from the tiny rocket engines was enough for her to pick out someone in an unusually bulky vac-suit—not the armored exosuit used by Marines or hazardous-environment workers, but much thicker than the standard suit she wore—before they raised a weapon of their own and she ducked back out of the line of fire.

"So, Skavar, any idea what a suit halfway between a vac-suit and an exosuit would be?" she asked sweetly. "Any relation to why our friend wouldn't show up on thermal scanners?"

"Cooled stealth suits," the Marine said instantly. "They're used for commando ops—and while not exactly *secret,* aren't really public knowledge, either."

"So, not regular saboteurs, then?"

Skavar chuckled bitterly.

"No, just *expensive* saboteurs," he replied. "We're moving in; get out of their way, XO!"

That turned out to be easier said than done. Kelly had a decent idea of at least where to start looking for their stowaway now, so she began moving back toward the control center and its attached computer core.

She needed to make sure that whoever these people were, they didn't get into that core. Every other component of the station could be worked around or just delay the final product. If the computer core for the smelter was damaged or destroyed, the entire refinery would be disabled until a new one could be manufactured and shipped out.

The silence of vacuum betrayed her, however, and Kelly didn't realize that the person shooting at her had been a distraction until she ran into their partner. She turned a corner and found herself with the barrel of a carbine poking directly into the chest plate of her vac-suit.

The bulky stealth suit the intruder wore concealed their face along with everything else. Kelly could see them clearly through her own transparent faceplate, but either their faceplate was one-way or they were viewing the world through cameras.

Keeping one hand on the trigger of their gun, their other hand pointed at her gun and then away. The message was clear enough and Kelly released the rocket pistol, giving a slight shove so it drifted away.

"XO, we show you stopped," Skavar's voice sounded in her ears. "What's going on?"

If she said anything, her captor would see her speak and know she had an open channel. She could see that ending poorly for her as the stranger gestured for her to keep walking toward the control center.

She obeyed, her captor keeping pace with her as she moved. They wore the same kind of military-grade magnetic boots she did, carefully keeping one foot on the ground as each broke clear.

"Kelly?" Skavar sounded worried now. "Telemetry shows the channel is open but I'm not hearing anything."

"Ambushed," she muttered, keeping her lips as still as she could. The one word didn't seem to catch her captor's attention, but she couldn't risk more.

Skavar was silent for longer than she'd expected.

"Okay, took us a second run-through of the recording to catch that," his voice finally replied. "Listen, a fire team of Marines just boarded. They're headed towards your position now, but if they're wearing commando stealth suits, SmartDarts aren't going to cut it."

SmartDarts were the auto-calibrating taser rounds loaded into a modern stungun. They assessed their victim and delivered a carefully calculated nonlethal shock—but given the bulk of the suits she could see, the darts wouldn't penetrate to the skin.

That meant Skavar's people were coming in with real guns, and if they accidentally shot her, she'd be bleeding out.

In a zero-gee vacuum.

"I'm going to keep talking you through their approach," Skavar told her. "When I give the word, I need you to shut off your mag-boots and kick off, you hear me? It's risky," he admitted frankly, "but less dangerous than you being in the line of fire."

"If you can hear me and understand, tap your chin against the mike."

With a careful look at her escort, Kelly obeyed.

"Good," the Chief of Security said with a sigh of relief. "Our guess is that these guys are corporate mercs, black hats for hire sent in by Cobalt's competitors.

"Their main plan went out the window the moment you saw them, but these guys will have a backup plan and it could very easily involve blowing the entire cargo—and *Red Falcon*!—to hell."

He paused.

"Fire team is on the same deck as you; they're moving in your direction. How many of them are there? Tap the mike with your chin for each one."

She was about to tap once, and then saw her escort glance back. The second intruder, the one who'd shot at her in the elevator shaft, stepped up on her other side a moment later.

She tapped the mike twice. Whoever these people were, she doubted this was going to end well.

"All right, XO, the Marines are just around the corner," Skavar said quietly. "When I say go, go."

Seconds ticked away in seeming eternities as her captors suddenly stopped, trapping her between them as they presumably carried on a conversation via encrypted channels of some kind.

Trapped as she was between the two intruders, Skavar's original plan wasn't going to work. If Kelly just kicked off, one of them would be able to grab her. She needed a new plan and fast.

"Okay," the Marine breathed in her ear. "*Go.*"

She killed her mag-boots, pushing off into the air. The intruders turned to grab her—and she turned her mag-boots back on, locking one foot onto each captor's chest.

It wasn't a long-term plan. Kelly certainly wasn't getting *away* with her boots magnetically locked to the intruders' armor.

But it put said armor—and the intruders it contained—between her and Skavar's Marines as they came around the corner. Their flashlights were invisible to the naked eye but were clearly enough for them to see everything.

And aim.

Gunfire flashed in the corridor, and locked to Kelly as they were, the intruders couldn't twist around to return fire in time. Both jerked as bullets struck home, then went limp.

With a sick feeling, Kelly released her mag-boots and launched off the intruders back toward the floor—carefully ignoring the globules of blood slowly starting to be pumped out into the corridor.

CHAPTER 8

"CORPORAL SPIROS," the senior of the three Marines introduced herself immediately as she linked into Kelly's channel. "Are you okay, XO?"

Kelly didn't know Sylvana Spiros well—she'd really only had the chance to get to know Skavar and the squad leaders—but right now, she was ecstatic to see any of *Red Falcon*'s security detail.

"I'm fine," she said shortly. "Anyone else coming?"

"I just boarded," Skavar told her briskly over the radio. "With the rest of First Squad. Anyone want to place bets on whether there were only two?"

"Not a chance," Kelly replied sharply. "I want this segment swept from top to bottom, Chief Skavar."

"I agree," he said. "I don't think that the XO needs to be here while we do that, though."

"How well do you know the layout of a refinery smelter core?" she asked.

He coughed.

"Not well," he admitted. "You?"

"I studied the specifications and have them loaded in my wrist-comp," she told him. "Which, given where I ran into our commando-out-fitted friends, means I think I know where they were hiding."

"Okay," the Security Chief replied as he came around the corner, the now-visible flashlights from the half-dozen Marines with him lighting up the corridor as bright as daylight, "that's a legit reason to stick around.

"*Behind* the guys and gals in exosuits, you read me?"

"I read you, Ivan," she admitted. Technically, she could give him orders. In reality, Skavar could spare the single exosuited Marine it would take to haul *Red Falcon*'s vac-suited-but-petite executive officer back into their ship.

"Good." The Marine was probably nodding, but there was no way to tell through the ceramic helmet of Skavar's exosuit armor. He crossed to the two dead intruders hanging in the strangely limp way only the dead or unconscious in mag-boots could.

One armored finger poked at the closer one, causing the body to twist and spurt out several more globules of blood. Kelly swallowed her gorge, trying to focus on the armor.

She'd directly or indirectly killed several hundred people who'd been chasing her crew over the last few years, but this was the first time she'd seen someone die right in front of her.

"Not Marine-issue," Skavar said absently. "Same tech, though. Either someone saw them in action and copied the idea, or Corps Logistics needs to have some long talks with their suppliers.

"Wouldn't last forever, though," he continued. "They need to re-charge coolant every twenty-four hours, tops. They couldn't rely on knowing when we'd be sweeping."

"I figured," Kelly pointed out, looking away from the bodies. "The core has a water reserve tank near the bottom. It's *supposed* to be empty, but it's double-walled and could have been partially filled without us noticing the mass."

"That would definitely work," he agreed. "All right, XO, point the way. From *behind* the armor."

The repetition wasn't necessary. Kelly had no desire to get shot at anymore today.

The passage down the elevator shaft went smoothly enough, the Marines sweeping the path ahead of Kelly and Skavar as they moved toward the theoretical "bottom" of the station segment.

"Scans aren't showing anything," Spiros reported. "Are we sure there's anything down here?"

"The scans weren't showing anything before, either," Kelly told her. "Whoever these jackasses are, they've done a good job of hiding from us so far. I'm guessing they weren't planning to be caught at all."

"Which means they probably have an escape ship," the Marine reminded them. "And that would mean..."

The realization that the boarders had to have at least one Mage came about half a second too late, light flickering up and down the corridor as magical lightning flared to life.

"Back, back!" Skavar snapped. "Counter-Mage protocols; locate the target!"

Gunfire added to the chaos now. Kelly couldn't tell how many shooters were backing up the Mage—but she quickly realized that their attackers had badly underestimated *Red Falcon*'s security detachment.

A trained Combat Mage could burn through exosuits and take down even prepared and ready Marines in the heavy battle armor. But that was an entirely different level of training and power than most Mages had access to, and the Jump Mage down the hall was no Combat Mage.

The Marines were shaken and shocked but uninjured—and the enemy gunfire was mostly frangible rounds that shattered on their armor.

"Move up," Skavar ordered, reversing his order of a minute before. "Before they go for bigger guns!"

Kelly was going to suggest they try to take prisoners, but shut herself up before she started giving unnecessary advice. Ivan Skavar knew his job better than she did.

What she knew was starships and space stations, which meant she had the schematics and could find another way around the boarders' position—especially as they rapidly demonstrated that, yes, they did have at least one gun capable of punching through exosuits.

"Akkerman is wounded," Spiros barked, yanking her subordinate back and out of the immediate line of fire. "Suit sealed around it, but they've got at least one man-portable penetrator rifle."

"And they've fallen back into the halls and the Mage knows what they're dealing with now," Skavar agreed grimly. "One way in and I guarantee the buggers have set the penetrator up to cover it."

"One way into that level from this elevator shaft," Kelly interjected. "There's a way around, should let us drop onto that level near the access to the water tanks."

"Not bad, XO," Skavar replied. "Spiros—keep Chau, Reyes and Smith, cover Akkerman and keep the pressure up.

"Everyone else, come with me. We're following the XO."

"All right," Kelly agreed with a sharp sigh. "But what about their ship?"

"What about it?"

"Get our pilots out looking for it," she told him. "It can't be big or we'd have noticed it being attached to the station segments in port, so your assault shuttles should be able to cripple it—and if we know where it's coming from, Jeeves can shoot it down if they try and run."

"And if we know where it is, we can make sure they can't run," Skavar said with satisfaction. "Prisoners would be nice. This headache will be much more worth it if we can hang it around the neck of the pricks who hired this lot."

Levering open the doors to the level three floors up from where the boarders had dug in proved harder than expected. The hatch Kelly had first found had already been opened, and she'd presumed her access codes from Cobalt would work.

They didn't. The elevator, it turned out, wasn't hooked into the reserve battery power that had been put in for the surveys. Fortunately, she had Marines in exosuits who were able to take care of that, but she now understood why the earlier access had been left open.

There was no way to close the hatch behind them.

"All right, people, this is Bravo Flight Leader," Mike Kelzin's voice cut into the channel. "We've got three of these bad girls out in the air, and we are beginning our sweep of the smelter. Any thoughts as to where they may have attached their ship?"

Of *course* Kelly's boyfriend had decided to take one of the assault shuttles out himself. She was suddenly glad that they hadn't asked for Mage support—her girlfriend was about as capable of staying out of trouble as her boyfriend.

Or, well, herself.

"I'm guessing they've set themselves up around the base where they could hide themselves," she told Kelzin. "The ship will be docked close to the water reserve tanks, probably covered with some kind of camo fabric to make it blend in to all but the closest scans."

She considered for a moment.

"Run both infrared and radar scans in parallel," she ordered. "If they've done it well—and I see no reason to think they haven't based off everything *else* they've pulled so far—it'll look perfectly normal to both...but you'll inevitably have some discrepancy between them.

"Not enough to show up normally, but..."

"But enough for us to pick it out since we're looking for it," Kelzin replied instantly. "Especially with three scan sources. Swinging down— and if they try to run for it, we'll stop them.

"I promise."

"Thank you," Kelly replied softly, then turned to point the Marines towards a hatch covering an emergency ladder. That, at least, was hooked up to the reserve power and opened to her codes.

"Three floors, straight down," she told the Marines. "We'll come out just up the corridor from the water tanks. Not sure where our friends will have settled in."

"LaMonte, Skavar, Kelzin," Rice's voice cut in. "We're going to broadcast a surrender demand and try to get prisoners that way, and these guys are almost certainly going to try and cut their losses at some point—these aren't suicide bombers.

"Most likely, they're going to try to run. We want them alive if we can, but don't take any risks."

"Yes, sir," Kelly chirped, following Skavar and his Marines down the ladder. Without gravity, they were walking along the wall of its tube rather than using the rungs themselves.

A moment later, the broadband transmission from *Red Falcon* overwhelmed everyone's radio.

"Unidentified stowaways, this is Captain David Rice of the merchant ship *Red Falcon*. You have illegally boarded my cargo and fired on my crew.

"If you continue to resist, my people will use whatever force is necessary to bring you down and secure our cargo. If you surrender, I will see you peacefully delivered to Protectorate authorities.

"This offer is limited. If you keep shooting, it will expire *damn* quickly.

"Rice out."

Kelly and Skavar's team paused by the exit onto the lowest level for several seconds.

"Hey, Spiros, did anyone stop shooting?" Skavar asked, his voice falsely light.

"No," the Corporal said flatly. "In fact, I think they found a second penetrator rifle. Chau's got a flesh wound, nothing serious after the suit sealed it up, but they're getting closer. I'd love that flanking maneuver *anytime* now."

"Coming right up," he replied, nodding to Kelly.

The engineer plugged in the code and overrode the door, leaving space for the exosuited troopers to charge through before her and take any unexpected fire.

There was none.

"Okay, what now?" Skavar said to her.

"That way"—she pointed—"is the water tanks, where I suspect we'll find an emergency hab-bubble with attached heat sinks suspended in a water level that shouldn't be there at all.

"Their ship is *probably* further in that direction."

"That way"—she gestured in the opposite direction—"is where the buggers are shooting up your people at the elevator shaft."

The Marine considered the situation for all of about three seconds.

"Sergeant Weaver, take your Charlie fire team and stick with the XO," he snapped. "Check out the water tanks.

"Everyone else is with me. We have a counter-ambush to arrange."

Kelly wasn't even sure which of the blank-faced armored form was Sergeant Cho Weaver, but the Marines clearly knew. Moments after Skavar had given his orders, half of the Marines were leaving with the Security Chief and half were gathered around her.

"Where to, ma'am?" Weaver asked.

"Down that hall," Kelly ordered, repeating her gesture.

"All right. Stay behind us," the Sergeant instructed. "I'm not explaining to the Captain how you got hurt."

"I have *no* desire to get hurt," Kelly agreed, letting the four hulking suits of battle armor cut ahead of her. "Mike, do you have their ship yet?"

"We're running the data back to *Falcon*'s computers," the pilot replied. "Give me a moment... Yes.

"Yes, we have their ship," he confirmed. "Gods, that thing is tiny. Are we sure it can jump?"

"They wouldn't have brought it with them if it couldn't," she replied grimly. "Captain Rice? Skipper? I think this is your call."

"Can you disable their escape ship without harming the cargo?" Rice asked.

Kelzin sucked in a breath.

"I can't," he admitted after a moment. "But, as it happens, Sergeant Davis happened to sneak onto my shuttle on the way out, and *she* happens to be fully qualified on this bird's weapons. Sergeant?"

Silent seconds.

"Seventy-thirty," the woman finally said. "No guarantees unless they actually launch. Precision is all fine and dandy, but a thirty-millimeter slug at three thousand kilometers a second doesn't leave any room for error."

"Hold fire," Rice ordered with a sigh. "If they do launch, summon them to surrender once.

"Then blow them to hell."

The open emergency access hatch for the water reserve tank was almost a relief to Kelly. She'd have been thoroughly upset with herself if she'd led the Marines here and there *hadn't* been anything hidden in the water tank.

"Stand back," Weaver told her. "Okafor, sweep ahead."

The indicated Marine moved up to the hatch, checking through it with the tip of his weapon first.

"Tank looks about a quarter-full," he reported. "Some kind of transparent tube attached to the other side of the hatch, running down into the water. Think I see an airlock at the other end." He paused. "Cheap plastic airlock."

"Like I said, hab bubble," Kelly agreed. "Submersed in water with added heat sinks, it wouldn't show up at all on our thermal scanners. Clever bastards."

"Pretty fragile, though," Weaver concluded. "Depending on where we shoot it, they could drown, asphyxiate, freeze...or all three. Not much resistance they could put up."

"No. I suggest we ask for surrenders?"

She couldn't see Weaver's nod, but the exosuit gestured for Okafor to continue. The Marine turned off his mag-boots and launched himself down the tube to slam into the airlock. A speaker attachment connected to the airlock and Okafor barked orders through it.

They waited.

"No response, Sergeant," the Marine told them after a minute. "From this range, I think I've got a clean thermal reading...it's showing the bubble as empty."

"If they're moving out, that makes sense," Weaver noted. "Damn."

The Sergeant's faceless helmet turned to Kelly for a moment.

"Punch through," she ordered briskly. "If the bubble's clear, we need to know, and if they're playing games...fuck 'em."

Exosuits had originally been built as protective hard shells for hazardous-environment workers. Their weight had required additional muscle augmentation, which had only been added to when the design had been coopted as powered combat armor.

The hab bubble's flimsy airlock didn't survive Okafor's first attempt to open it up, the trooper's two-meter-tall ceramic war suit ripping through the exterior shell like paper.

"Yeah," he said flatly a moment later. "Empty. Not super-comfortable, even, but at least we have some intel out of this."

"There are eight bedrolls, that gives us a likely minimum if not a max."

"That's more than we knew a moment ago," Weaver agreed. "Pull back out, I think we need to head to the ship."

"Agreed," Kelly said, running through the map on her comp. "Based off Kelzin's locator, the best way is that way." She pointed.

"All right, folks, our would-be ambushers have surrendered," Skavar cut in. "We've got two more dead and two prisoners. No Mage. I don't suppose you got them?"

"There's nobody here," Kelly told him. "They abandoned the bubble. There was only beds for eight, though."

"And if they were staying in the bubble and keeping exertions minimal, they weren't hot-bunking," Skavar agreed. "So, we're missing two, including the Mage."

"They've got to be headed for the ship," Kelly replied. "*Cut and run* is their best option at this point."

"Can you get there first?"

She looked at Weaver and then at her map.

"Depends on when they started moving," she admitted. "But we can get there quickly."

"Good enough. Keep following the XO, Weaver."

The boarder's Mage had to have started running for the escape ship as soon as she'd realized there were exosuits in the security team. Kelly and her team were barely halfway to where she guessed it was docked when Kelzin cut into the channel again.

"Uh-oh. I've got fusion plant ignition on the ship." She could almost hear him shake his head. "No other heat signatures, it's got to be *freezing* in there, but she's booting up fast."

"How fast?" Rice demanded.

Kelly ran the numbers in her head. From a cold start, their regular shuttles could be live in ten minutes, but the assault shuttles...

"Ninety seconds, tops," she told them. "She's supposed to be a fast-escape ship; she'll use the same rapid-boost tech as the assault shuttles. She'll have power and engines in under ninety seconds. Life support and guns will be later, but she'll move and she can jump as soon as the Mage is at the simulacrum."

"A ship that small...she's already *at* the simulacrum," Rice said grimly. "Maria—can she jump still attached to the cargo?"

"No," the Ship's Mage replied instantly. "The spell would try and jump everything attached to the ship. It won't work without the runes being specifically designed to encompass a cargo space."

"She'll need to get...fifty, maybe a hundred meters clear."

That wasn't a lot of time. Kelly wasn't the only one thinking that.

"Transmitting a warning now," Kelzin said grimly. "The moment they bounce clear, we're going to shoot them down."

"Do it," Rice ordered grimly.

Kelly slowed, carefully locking her mag-boots to the ground. Whatever happened now, there was no point in her team rushing through the station segment.

"Looks like a sixty-second boot time," the pilot continued. "That's *better* than our assault shuttles... No response to our warning.

"She's moving. Take the shot, Davis!"

There was no sound audible from inside the station. Nothing to mark the moment when an assault shuttle fired railgun rounds at one percent of the speed of light. Just...silence.

"Clean hits," Kelzin reported after a moment. "She's breaking up."

"Move in and sweep for survivors," Rice ordered. "Skavar, sweep the station segment for any other stowaways and police up debris and corpses.

"XO?"

"Yes, sir?" Kelly replied carefully.

"Well done. Now get the *hell* back aboard *Red Falcon*."

CHAPTER 9

"I'M SORRY, *what* happened en route?" the woman on the screen demanded.

"It appears, Ms. Lauren, that one of Cobalt's competitors hired mercenaries to attempt to render the smelter components nonfunctional in transit," David told her calmly.

From the way Avril Lauren, Cobalt Interstellar Element's System Executive Officer for Desdemona, whitened at his description, he might well have underestimated the impact on Cobalt if the station implementation was delayed.

Lauren was pale-skinned to begin with, the sallow tones of someone who spent most of their life under artificial light aboard space stations and starships, and her black hair had glittering streaks of silver in it. There was no give in her ice-blue eyes, however, and fear promptly turned to determination.

"I presume you do not know who?"

"We do not," David admitted. "We did, however, take two prisoners. We don't have jurisdiction to interrogate them, but Desdemona Security..."

"Most definitely does," Lauren finished for him in a satisfied tone. "Please forward DesSec and my own staff everything you have on the incident, Captain. Was there any damage to the cargo?"

"So far as my Chief Engineer and XO can tell, all components are intact. Obviously, we can't confirm or guarantee functionality, but we haven't located any damage."

"Thank deity," she breathed. "I will be frank, Captain Rice: this shipment has been a nightmare from the beginning, and I'm already dreading our activation delays. My copy of the contract says you were owed a bonus for rapid delivery, which you have made despite the interferences."

She smiled.

"We'll have to wait for the final dockyard approval that everything is on hand, but I'm happy to confirm that the delivery bonus has been secured. When can we expect you in Puck orbit?"

Puck had been the Desdemona System's fourth planet, a shattered world that some unimaginable disaster had split in six pieces that still shared roughly the same orbit. The exposed planetary core was why Cobalt was there at all.

The wreck was actually in the Goldilocks zone, and Puck might have been inhabitable before it had split apart. The fifth planet, Beatrice, was a cold planet in the middle of an ice age, but its equatorial regions were surprisingly warm and welcoming to the folks who'd settled there.

"About seven hours," he told her. "I'll contact DesSec and make sure they have a contingent ready to collect our prisoners upon arrival."

"I appreciate it, Captain. You've done Cobalt some massive favors that weren't in your contract, and I promise you, you will be compensated for them," she assured him.

"I'm not going to argue," David replied with a smile. "But believe me, Ms. Lauren, *nobody* likes armed stowaways shooting at their crew."

She was about to disconnect but paused at that.

"Were any of your crew injured?" she asked. "Can we provide assistance?"

"A few injuries, nothing severe," he replied, surprised and heartened at her concern. "Our ship's doctor has everything under control."

"Good, good. If your doctor requires any assistance or resources, do not hesitate to ask," she told him. "Cobalt is in your debt, and not all liabilities can be settled with cash."

Maneuvering through the debris fields around Puck was not an exercise for the faint of heart. It couldn't be left entirely to the computers—the administration tracked the vast majority of the objects floating around the wrecked planet, but there were always items that wouldn't be picked up until the last moment.

An even tougher exercise, in David Rice's opinion, was watching your brand-new XO, who you *knew* was a mediocre pilot at best, maneuver through those debris fields. LaMonte was utterly focused on her controls and the proximity radar, guiding the massive freighter in toward the main transshipment platform.

David *could* take control back, but only if he wanted to undermine his XO's self-confidence. LaMonte had taken seeing people shot to death in front of her better than he'd been afraid she would, but she was still shaken.

With all of her attention on flying the ship, however, that seemed forgotten for the moment.

An incoming call pinged and he redirected it from LaMonte's console with practiced ease. The whole point was that she didn't need distractions.

"This is *Red Falcon*, Captain Rice commanding," he answered briskly.

"*Red Falcon*, this is the Desdemona Security ship *Ravine*. We are approaching from your forty-five by sixty-two and matching velocities. Any problems with your prisoners?"

"My crew have a few sets of surplus RMMC exosuits," David told the man on the other end. "The prisoners seem thoroughly cowed."

Ravine's com officer chuckled as David checked their location.

There she was, exactly where they'd said. A hundred-meter-long flattened beetle shape, *Ravine* was a pretty standard system security corvette. *Red Falcon* could eat the ship's entire offensive armament without noticing and obliterate her in a single return salvo.

Though David *probably* shouldn't be considering how to engage the local police spaceship.

"That's about where I'd be in their place," the officer agreed. "There's a Lieutenant Soun waiting for you at dock six on Midsummer Station with a security team. We'll take them into custody and we'll find out what's going on."

"I think Cobalt will appreciate that," David replied, tapping a message over to LaMonte to give her their exact destination. "Are we clear all the way in?"

"You're clear to dock six," *Ravine* confirmed. "We'll fly escort all the way in. Our bosses are twitchy over corporate mercenaries here.

"Plus, well, armed megafreighters," he noted.

"I understand, *Ravine*. We'll play nice."

Once LaMonte had docked the ship, David joined Maria and Skavar in the main docking tube, leaving the ship in her capable hands. Despite his nerves, his XO had cut through Puck's danger zone with calm professionalism...and if her free hand had left potentially permanent indentations in her chair arm, it would be unfitting for him to notice.

The two mercenaries looked far less intimidating in the standard ill-fitting orange jumpsuits most ships kept on hand for unexpected brig inmates. Both were tall men with shaved heads, but much of their bulk had clearly been the coolant-laden stealth suits they'd worn.

With an exosuited escort apiece, they were being perfectly cooperative, too. Maria's arrival earned more askance looks as they noted the gold medallion at her throat that marked her as a trained Mage.

"Any problems with our guests?" David asked Skavar as he reached his security chief.

"None," the taller man said cheerfully. "It's amazing how cooperative people become when you're the ones with exosuits and stunguns...and they aren't."

David was sure he'd heard one of the mercs choke at that, but he smiled silently himself.

"We should be meeting a Lieutenant Soun to take them off our hands," he told his Chief. "So, you guys can go back to being glorified mall cops."

"I look forward to it," Skavar agreed, shifting to clear access to his holster as the indicator lights flicked to green to show atmosphere on the other side of the tube. "I'm told being a mall cop is nice."

The door slid open before he finished speaking, revealing a relatively open entryway for passengers to board the station. A clearly marked zone down the middle of the corridor had gravity runes, but most of the dock was zero gee.

Half a dozen cops in burgundy body armor were in the zero-gee section, locked to the metal floor with mag-boots and holding stunguns at the ready.

A seventh officer stood in the gravity zone in the same body armor. The man had removed his helmet and holstered his weapon, but his eyes were suspicious as he studied David and his companions.

"Captain Rice?"

"That would be me," he confirmed.

"You have prisoners for us to take into custody?" he snapped.

"Ivan." David gestured for his Security Chief to hand over the mercs. There didn't seem to be any fight left in the men, and they both followed directions out into the loading bay, where cops took hold of them and guided their manacled forms through the zero gravity.

Four of the cops remained behind Lieutenant Soun, their weapons still leveled.

"How else may I assist you, Lieutenant?" David said carefully.

"I also have a list of members of your security detail that will need to be detained until we've completed our investigation, and we will need to lock down the affected area," Soun barked. "No one can be allowed on or off your ship or the chunk of station the incident took place on until we've fully reviewed the situation."

...*that* was not what David had been expecting.

"I believe the right of my security team to use lethal force in defense of my ship is firmly established," he told the cop flatly. "I will *not* be surrendering any of my people to your custody.

"You will have to establish access to our cargo with Cobalt Interstellar," he continued. "You have no grounds to lock down my ship at all."

Soun smiled thinly.

"This is not *optional*, Captain," he said calmly. "You will either accede to my requirements or I will arrest you right here and now. By your own admission, six people *died* on your ship."

"In a firefight they started," David pointed out. "The right of a starship crew to defend themselves and their cargo is well established."

"Then I am certain that your crew and ship will be free to go quickly enough," Soun told them. "But my orders are clear—"

"And unconstitutional, Lieutenant," a new voice interjected. David looked up to see who had interrupted, but the speaker was a stranger to him.

The man was broad-shouldered with neatly trimmed gray hair, clad in a plain black robe of some kind and a dangerously calm smile as he strode along the gravity runes.

"I beg your pardon?" Soun demanded.

"I am Aubert Caron, Barrister at Law for the Desdemona System, expert in Protectorate and interstellar law," the newcomer reeled off brightly. "I must admit, an attempt by DesSec to *further* delay the arrival of Cobalt's parts is suspicious, given the fines to be collected by the system government in the case of late activation.

"Regardless, however, I was retained by Ms. Lauren to make certain there were no...complications with regards to Captain Rice's crew," he continued. "So, I repeat my original comment: the demands you have laid on Captain Rice are unconstitutional, a violation of his rights to self-defense, free movement, and security against illegal search.

"My client will be pleased to allow for DesSec investigators to sweep the smelter core—once it has been off-loaded from Captain Rice's ship and we have begun the assembly process."

"You can't just waltz in here and override my orders," Soun snapped.

Caron smiled and held out his hand.

"Then where, Lieutenant Soun, is your warrant for search and seizure?" he asked calmly. "For such extraordinary assertions of authority as you have made, you must surely then have a court order to back you up?"

The lawyer's hand didn't tremble. He held it out, palm up, in the magical gravity field for ten seconds. Fifteen. Thirty.

Then, without a word, Lieutenant Soun turned on his heel and barged past Caron.

The robed lawyer shook his head once the DesSec troopers were out of the docking bay.

"Captain Rice, I hope I arrived in time?" he asked.

"Well, none of my people are in irons and I haven't had to shoot my way out of the system yet, so I'd say yes," David agreed, looking after Lieutenant Soun. "What the hell was that?"

"Another piece of the puzzle," Caron said calmly. "I've made some quiet arrangements. Lieutenant Soun will *not* be keeping custody of those mercenaries."

"You think he's involved in the attack?"

Caron shook his head again.

"Captain, I am starting to fear that my *government* arranged the attack," he admitted. "The penalties Cobalt will have to pay if the refinery doesn't come online on schedule are...substantial.

"They would provide quite a slush fund for the Desdemonan government." Caron sighed. "One hates to think ill of the government of one's system, but that is quite the temptation. Your prisoners will end up in the hands of officers I trust to see their duty done, regardless of orders from on high.

"With that said, however, I suspect that Lieutenant Soun and his allies will have only limited difficulties acquiring a warrant to temporarily intern your ship. I have advised Ms. Lauren to arrange for the fastest possible unloading, but you are in danger of becoming a pawn in this game so long as you remain in the Desdemona System."

David considered his ship's status as a Martian covert ops vessel. An attempt by the Desdemona government to intern *Red Falcon* would draw far more attention to their little game than they probably wanted, but no one would work that out until after the fact.

And it would be too obvious.

"Megafreighters don't really...move without cargo," he pointed out. "I'll have to see what I can find."

"Look quickly, sir Captain," Caron told him. "We'll off-load as quickly as possible and I've already set into motion several legal measures to protect you, but we're talking about a potential conspiracy inside the system government.

"There is only so much protecting one law firm can do, even with Cobalt's resources behind us."

"I understand," David replied. "Thank you, Mr. Caron."

It seemed that he was going to have to be less subtle than hoped in making his connection here.

CHAPTER 10

"GREETINGS, CAPTAIN. Call me Ishmael."

David Rice stood in the entrance to the cheap trinket shop in Puck Station's bazaar and studied the man standing behind the counter. He was one of the many humans in this day and age that couldn't be traced back to a single ethnic group on Earth, with skin a mixed tan color and startling blue eyes.

"Greetings, Mr. Ishmael," David replied. "I'm told to look for Caleb Abel here."

"Ah, Abel," the stall proprietor agreed. "Come in, come in, Captain. Close the door."

"How do you know I'm a Captain?" David asked. He wore a plain business suit today, much the same as a good half of the people wandering the bazaar behind him. He listened to the strange little man, though, stepping inside the stall and closing the door behind him and Soprano.

"You can see it in a man's eyes if you know how to look," Ishmael told him. "His eyes and how he stands. Plus, well, I pay attention to who docks at this station, Captain Rice."

"I see," David allowed. He shared a meaningful glance with his Mage, who shrugged.

She clearly thought she could get them out of whatever trouble this man could create. Having seen Maria Soprano in action, David agreed with her assessment.

"And Mr. Abel?" he asked after a few moments' silence.

"Abel is dead," Ishmael said flatly. "Suicide, they say."

"'They', Mr. Ishmael?"

"DesSec coroner, in this case," the stall-keeper said quietly. "Don't blame them; the evidence all added up that way. Unless you had context."

"That's...unfortunate," David told him. "Though it leaves me wondering why I'm here."

"Caleb Abel had many names. Under all of them, was an idiot," Ishmael responded. "Smart man, brilliant man in many ways. But an idiot. He tried to play too many sides against the middle. For *your* purposes, Captain Rice, suffice it that it was not *Legatus* that killed him, and the cargo he was supposed to put you in touch with remains idle, waiting for a ship to haul it."

David studied Ishmael carefully.

"And how do you know all this, Mr. Ishmael?"

"I was Abel's handler for MISS," the little man replied. "Other things, too. Personal, professional, romantic." Ishmael shrugged casually, but his eyes turned to ice as he spoke. "I'm still culling down my list of who may have killed my lover, Captain Rice, but believe me: you should be happy you're not on it."

David shivered.

"I won't argue that," he said. "My cargo?"

"Seventeen point five million tons of raw ore, destined for the smelters at Legatus," Ishmael told him. "Transshipping to a vessel flagged under Integrity Galactic Transport at Junkertown—the primary orbital around Junkrat in Snap."

"Seems odd," David noted. "Why not ship directly to Legatus?"

"Two reasons. One, IGT is one of the companies licensed to transport directly to Legatus. They have a regular line between Snap and Legatus, but they never come to Desdemona. Minor MidWorld, not big enough for them.

"Two, the shipment is actually seventeen hundred and *sixty* ten-thousand-ton containers," he continued. "IGT knows what happens to the extra ten; you won't need to worry about it."

David held up a hand.

"I don't do no-questions-asked shipments anymore," he pointed out.

"So far as the *official* client is concerned, you do. Understand?" Ishmael asked. "But yeah, I know."

"So, what game are we playing?" Soprano asked. "If the client thinks we're not asking questions..."

"You don't ask the client, Mage Soprano. You ask me, and I tell you, and the client never knows you know."

"So, what are we hauling?" she asked before David could.

"Gems," Ishmael said flatly. "The authorities here were *accidentally* tipped off that someone was trying to smuggle an illegal gems shipment out; that's what kept the cargo held up until there was no one here to haul it. You're the first ship since with the capacity to carry Mr. Wu's cargo."

He shook his head.

"Mr. Wu thinks he's smuggling gems for monetary value," he continued. "Ninety percent of the gems you're hauling are just that: jewelry and industrial uses. Buried inside them, however, are ten thousand tons of crystals of sufficient grade for combat-rated laser optics.

"Mr. Wu is a smuggler of long standing here, and Legatus is using him as a proxy. We don't know where those optics are going, and from what little brief I got, tracking them isn't your problem."

Ishmael shrugged. "Presumably, someone *is* tracking them. I'll make sure that Mr. Wu is aware of your presence and cargo capacity before the end of the day."

"We're in a hurry ourselves," David admitted. "Reaching out directly here was a secondary option if the main plan failed, but we didn't have time."

"I didn't know the main plan," Ishmael told him. "So, it's a good thing you went straight for the backup. Wu will be in touch. If anything else comes up, let me know.

"In the meantime, however, people are going to wonder why you were in my shop. Buy a whelkie?"

Ishmael gestured at an array of hand-carved wooden statues beside David.

"Believe me," he added with a wicked grin, "they're expensive enough that people will believe we spent this long arguing over the price!"

"How long until we hear from Wu?" Soprano asked as they made their way back through the bazaar, the Mage's gaze flickering around, watching for threats.

"Hopefully not long," David replied. "From what Ishmael said, he'll be desperate to move this cargo before DesSec keeps poking at it—but we still need to finish off-loading Cobalt's gear."

He looked around. The bazaar was in the rotating portion of the station, kept at three-quarters of a gravity, and seemed to glow with an amazing mix of colors and smells. David had seen a thousand bazaars like it, though, and he had a feel for the patterns now.

And he didn't like the one he was seeing.

"Cops coming from the left," he murmured to Soprano. "They're probably not looking for us, but I think grabbing a bite at that restaurant over there is a good plan."

His Mage followed his lead as they slipped into an "open-air" patio. He tucked them against a wall as the server brought them menus, keeping an eye on the crowd.

They'd barely begun to peruse the tablets before he spotted the burgundy uniforms and clamshell armor, identical to the troopers who'd met them at the docking tube. A different officer led them, though, and he relaxed for a moment.

Only a moment. The cops were looking for somebody. It wasn't a regular patrol—people were moving away from them too deliberately, too quickly, for it to be a normal thing.

"They won't see us," Soprano murmured to him. "I'm blocking their view. Just in case."

Having a Mage along was useful far more often than he expected. They watched in silence as the armed cops swept by, relying on Soprano's magic to be safe.

Then the waitress reappeared to take their order.

"Is it normal to have entire squads of armored cops wandering through the bazaar?" David asked. "Seems...strange."

The woman shook her head.

"It is strange," she agreed. "Not the first time lately, though. Normally, there's only about thirty, forty DesSec guys on station, but they tripled their strength a month or so ago.

"Nobody's talking about why," she concluded. "Bad for business, though, when they're being that obvious. What can I get you?"

One decent, if not spectacular, meal later, they returned to the ship. Something in the tone of the station had clearly made it into Skavar as well. Normally, most of *Red Falcon*'s counter-boarding defenses were kept under wraps.

Today, four armed security troopers in the same style of clamshell body armor the DesSec cops were wearing stood around the entrance. Where the guards would normally be carrying stunguns, today they carried battle carbines with under-barrel stunguns.

Still nonlethal if they chose to be, but the carbines themselves were a pointed threat—and the tripod-mounted penetrator rifle they were alternating sitting next to was a reminder all on its own.

"Any trouble?" David asked.

"None so far," the team leader replied. "Some of the burgundy cops wandered by to take a look, but I think they got the message the Chief was after."

"It's not a subtle message," *Red Falcon*'s Captain noted.

"You'd be surprised. The fire team behind us is in exosuits."

David chuckled.

"I wish I could say Ivan was being paranoid," he said. "But...this is making me twitchy."

"You and us both, Skipper," the Marine replied. "Coming aboard?"

"Yeah."

The guards waved them through, keeping a careful eye past them.

"Hmm."

"Corporal?"

"Just noticed that there's a young lady over there who I've seen before," the Marine said quietly. "A few times. I think she's circling around to keep an eye on us. Where there's one spy..."

"There's more."

"Yep. We'll keep an eye out, but I think you need to assume everyone leaving and boarding this ship is being tracked."

LaMonte was waiting on the bridge when David and Soprano returned, rising from the captain's seat as they came in.

"Everything's under control, Skipper," she told them. "Cobalt's people started linking about twenty minutes ago." She gestured to the screen. "First of the big segments is coming off as we speak."

On the main screen, David could see the idling engines of at least a dozen dockyard tugs attached to the main smelter core, the component that had been their biggest headache all along.

LaMonte leaned back to the chair, tapping a control.

"Tug Lead, this is *Red Falcon*. We've released all clamps and connections. Segment One is yours."

"Confirming release; we have control of Segment One," the tug captain replied. "Initiating synchronized burn in fifteen seconds."

The engines on the dozen tugs lit up brighter and brighter, slowly pushing the massive station component away from the megafreighter. The farther they got, the brighter the engines grew, until the tugs were accelerating the smelter at one gravity.

"One down, six to go," David muttered. "Plus two hundred damn containers."

He shook his head.

"Was Skavar keeping you in the loop on our doorway situation?"

"Yes," LaMonte confirmed. "I reached out to the local MISS office with one of our covert drop codes. They may not know why, but they're poking into the kerfuffle around Soun trying to arrest us."

"That's risky," David observed. It was already done, so there was a limit to the degree he could undermine his XO, but...

"Calling them in to help watch *Falcon* was my first inclination, but that would definitely be risky," LaMonte told him. "And if I told them what was going on, that would be risky," she agreed. "I had them come at it the other way—I pointed them at the Cobalt fees and the risk that the government was trying to basically extort the company."

She smiled.

"I *may* have left our MISS friends with the impression that Mr. Caron had the drop code," she admitted. "Give them something to look at when they get curious. So far as I can tell, Caron is aboveboard, so that's safe enough."

David chuckled.

"Fair enough," he allowed.

Their covert drop codes were one-time command sequences that basically told the local Security Service station that the attached "suggestions" were to be regarded as orders at the highest level. In theory, they were dumped through the system network and untraceable.

In practice, MISS analysts were obsessively curious and were almost certain to find out who had used the code. They wouldn't *tell* anyone, they were almost as reliably discreet as they were reliably curious, but each person who knew what David's ship actually was was an increased security threat.

Directing them toward Caron and Cobalt Interstellar was harmless— or at least, if it *wasn't* harmless, it was because the megacorporation was up to things they shouldn't have been—and kept *Falcon* on the down-low.

While getting MISS resources on making sure the Desdemona government didn't start locking up David's crew.

"That'll do nicely," he continued after a moment's thought. "Anything else I need to watch for? Have we heard anything from a Mr. Wu?"

"Not much going on," LaMonte admitted. "Put in replenishment orders for food, life support and antimatter. No one even blinked at buying AM, which is always nice."

Few ships outside the military used antimatter engines, though *Red Falcon* wasn't unique in that aspect of her operations. She was rare enough, though, that buying antimatter was sometimes difficult and almost always attention-getting.

"We're fully stocked?"

"We'll be fully resupplied by twenty hundred OMT tonight," she confirmed. "Talking with Cobalt, we'll be off-loaded by about fourteen hundred OMT tomorrow. After that..."

"What we do and where we go is up to me," David finished for her.

"Thanks, XO."

CHAPTER 11

IN THEORY, Maria Soprano should have simply passed the executive officer the list of things the Ship's Mages needed. The tools and supplies were necessary aspects of the starship's operations, after all.

Long tradition, however, said that the Mages didn't have the mundanes purchase supplies for magic. It was a silly tradition, sometimes, but not always. Soldering irons and polymerized silver could be easily picked up by regular crew, after all.

The handful of premade runic artifacts the ship used, however, required a Mage to assess them. It wasn't like Maria could tell at a look whether the runes worked or not, but she could *read* Martian Runic.

Most people couldn't. With seventy-six characters and fourteen different ways of connecting them, the script was complex and difficult to read—and even a simple matrix on, say, an emergency personal shield, was tens of thousands of characters.

Even Mages had varying levels of competency with the script. The best were the Rune Scribes...a category which did not include one Maria Soprano.

Nonetheless, she was the most-qualified person aboard *Red Falcon* for that job, which left her in what looked like a knickknack shop off to one side of the bazaar. Only the most careful eye would have realized that the various trinkets were all marked with silver runes that described spells.

Very, *very* few of the artifacts in the store could actually be charged to function away from a Mage. Most of them acted as amplifiers, allowing a Mage to achieve more complex effects than most could muster on their own.

A few, like the shield bracelet Xi Wu was examining, could be. That artifact required near-daily charging but could protect the wearer from punches, knives or, well, *one* bullet. They were usually given as gifts to lovers by Mages.

"If you buy those, realize you have to charge it for them every morning," she murmured to the younger Mage, who promptly flushed. "And last I checked, Kelzin, at least, doesn't share quarters with you."

"Not *every* night," Wu admitted, still blushing. "Plus, I guess neither Mike nor Kelly is likely to get shot at, huh?"

"Neither the XO nor a flight leader is usually in the kind of trouble a shield bracelet can protect from," Maria agreed. "If a shuttle gets blown apart around Kelzin or, God forbid, *Red Falcon* gets blown apart around LaMonte, that bracelet won't make any difference."

"I guess." Wu touched the bracelets again, then nodded and stepped away. "Do we have what we need?"

"I think so," Maria told her. "Can you check over these for me?" She gestured at the range of runic items in front of her. "A double check never goes to waste."

Checking a runic artifact involved pulsing magic through it and seeing if it responded the way it should. Maria had occasionally heard rumors of Mages who could simply *see* how the runes worked, but she'd never met one.

"Mage?" the store's proprietor said quietly, seeming to appear out of nowhere and coughing delicately. "May I suggest that you hurry? A friend of mine at the local DesSec station said a call just went out for them to come here. No orders along with it...just the instruction that 'Lieutenant Soun would know what to do.'"

Maria sighed.

"Why are you telling me this?" she asked as she swept the artifacts off the counter.

"Because you're about to spend a large amount of money with my store," the woman said brightly, "and that buys you at *least* the same heads-up I got." She smiled. "I also have a back door?"

Sneaking out the back door, Maria and Wu made their way back around to the main corridor. The senior Mage stopped them before they stepped out into the thoroughfare, watching for the cops they'd been warned were coming.

It was always possible, she supposed, that the proprietor had lied to them to get them to buy the runic gear without checking it too closely, but...

There they were. Maria recognized Lieutenant Soun from the docking bay. The men around the officer may have been the same too—their helmets weren't closed up this time but had been before.

The squad was armed with stunguns, and several were carrying the heavy rune-covered manacles of Mage-cuffs. They'd almost certainly been coming for the two Mages from *Red Falcon*.

That...was not a good sign.

She tapped her wrist-comp, calling Cobalt's lawyer.

"Caron speaking," the man responded crisply.

"Mr. Caron, this is Mage Soprano from *Red Falcon*," she told him. "Did our friend get that piece of paper they were after?"

The channel was probably secure enough to be honest, but she was certain he'd know what she meant. The silence as he considered suggested she was right.

"Not that I'm aware of," Caron replied. "There *may* be some procedural games being played to keep them from doing so quickly. What's going on?"

"Lieutenant Soun just tried to arrest myself and one of my Mages," Maria said instantly. "The shopkeeper hustled us out of the way, but..."

Another silence.

"Unless they're playing some nasty games—which, sadly, I cannot rule out—Soun has no warrant for that," Caron finally said. "Can you get back to your ship?"

"We're in the main bazaar," Maria said. "Fifteen minutes to the ship. If they're hunting us..."

"They'll find you by then," he agreed. "My office isn't really closer. Are you safe where you are?"

Maria exchanged glances with Wu.

"Not really," she admitted. "We're in a side corridor near the store they know we were in. It won't take them long to find us if we don't move."

"Or even if you do," Caron completed the thought for her. "Damn. All right, Mage Soprano. Are you prepared to trust me?"

"My alternatives are looking unpleasant," Maria noted. They probably weren't what Caron thought they were: they started with using MISS overrides to order her own release and slid downhill from there, to a worst case of Skavar's Marines boarding the station in exosuits.

Red Falcon's crew could extricate themselves from this mess, but not without blowing their cover.

"There are two regional DesSec stations in the bazaar," Caron told her. "Spinward and counter-spinward. I don't know which one Soun is posted at, but I do know the Spinward Bazaar Station commander, a Captain Li Han.

"She was my second choice for taking on your prisoners if my first choice couldn't. I trust her explicitly. I need you to go to her station and ask for her.

"If Soun doesn't have an actual damned warrant for your arrest, Han won't give you up. Even if you are followed, she'll stall until I can get there.

"Understand, Mage Soprano?"

"Thank you," she told him. "I'd prefer not to have to transform anyone into newts to survive my day."

He coughed.

"Please don't," he noted. "So long as you keep your hands clean, I can protect you, but the moment you injure a DesSec officer, that all goes out the window."

"Understood," she confirmed a moment later, regretting the instant of levity. "I'll be speaking to Captain Han shortly."

"And I'll be there shortly after. Good luck."

On their way through the bazaar, Maria dialed the ship on her wrist-comp.

"*Red Falcon*, Second Officer LaMonte speaking," the XO answered brightly.

"Kelly, it's Soprano," Maria told the other woman. "We have a problem. Our friend Soun has shown up again, and he seems to be looking for me and Wu through this chaos."

"Damn. I'll raise Skavar; what do you need?" LaMonte asked instantly.

"I've contacted Caron and he's arranged sanctuary, he thinks," Maria told her. "We're heading for the Spinward Bazaar Station of DesSec, where I'm told we can trust the shift captain."

"And if Caron is wrong?" LaMonte asked.

"That's why I'm phoning home," the Mage said. "So you know where we are. Mobilizing Skavar's people is probably a good idea. Most likely, we won't need them, but this system is turning into more of a problem every second."

"I hear you," the younger woman agreed. "We'll have security on standby. Hopefully, we won't need them... I hear most space station administrators disapprove of firing boarding torpedoes into their stations."

Reaching the DesSec station, Maria realized they had another problem. Soun, it seemed, had either been eavesdropping or guessed what their next step would be. The Lieutenant himself wasn't waiting at the station...but four burgundy-armored DesSec troopers with helmets down, stunguns up, and Mage-cuffs at their belts were.

"Mage Maria Soprano, Mage Xi Wu," the tallest of them, the one with an extra gold stripe on her armored shoulder, barked. "You are summoned to surrender under the Covenants of Mars!"

Maria managed to conceal a wince. That was a weapon she couldn't argue with, not really. The Covenants regulated relations between Mage and mundane—and while they said that a Mage could only be tried by a court of Mages, they also called for Mages to surrender peacefully to mundane law enforcement.

Because either Maria or Wu could have killed all four Desdemona Security cops in a thought and a breath...but that would have made them Covenant-breakers, and the Protectorate *could not* tolerate Covenant-breakers.

She raised her hands placatingly.

"What am I being charged with?" she asked delicately.

"You will be advised of that in due time," the sergeant told the Mage as she and her men came forward, detaching the Mage-cuffs.

"If I am not being charged, why am I under arrest?" Maria said. "I am a Ship's Mage, registered in the Tau Ceti System. I have rights, Sergeant."

"And they will be respected. You will be advised of the charges by the appropriate individuals at the appropriate time."

Maria held out her hands...but used a tiny jet of force to fling the Mage-cuffs in the sergeant's hands against the window of the station.

"Oops," she murmured. "I'd hate to cause problems with your illegal detainment, Sergeant."

"You are bound by the Covenant," the cop barked. "Stand *down*, Mage Soprano."

"Sergeant Eleanor Travert," a new voice said from the door of the precinct station. "You're not assigned to this district. Hot pursuit is one thing, but it appears you were *lurking* outside my precinct station."

A tall woman with pitch-black skin and hair emerged through the door of the station, leaning sideways to scoop up the Mage-cuffs Maria had "knocked" with.

"Captain Han," Travert said stiffly. "This is a Special Security issue."

"Indeed?" Han asked. "You are aware, Sergeant, that the Special Security teams are supposed to provide notice when they'll be operating in my district? Indeed, in general, SS teams are not deployed unless regular security has failed."

The Captain smiled thinly.

"I was not even informed of any outstanding warrants against Mages staying on board the station." She tapped a sequence of commands on her wrist-comp. "In fact, the records available to me say there are no such Covenant warrants outstanding.

"Would you care to explain why, then, you are arresting two Mages outside my station?"

"You're not cleared for that information, ma'am," Travert replied.

"Right." The sarcasm in Han's voice was sharp enough to cut a knife with. "In that case, Sergeant, I will have to temporarily detain these two ladies in my station until such time as either Special Security can produce a warrant for their arrest or the constitutional limit on detainment without charge expires.

"Would you care to refresh my memory on that limit, Sergeant Travert? Or does Special Security no longer teach the constitution?"

"Twenty-four standard hours, ma'am," the Sergeant said reluctantly after several seconds silence. "Ma'am, you don't have the authority to interfere in this case."

The tall Captain walked over to Travert. One woman was in burgundy armor, the other in a plain dark gray working uniform, but Han towered over the armored noncom as she tapped the gold stripes on Travert's shoulder.

"Special Security has access to warrants that allow you to operate in my district and override my authority, Sergeant. *Do. You. Have. One?*"

The last four words could have been carved of asteroid ice.

"Not on me, ma'am."

"Then you will release these Mages to my custody," Han ordered.

"Ma'am..."

"My district, Sergeant. My authority. My custody. Now *go*."

The armored cops seemed to fold in on themselves, especially as several more gray-uniformed officers followed Captain Han out of the precinct station. Travert finally lowered the Mage-cuffs and left, gesturing for her men to follow her.

"Unfortunately, Mage, since Special Security *has* stated a warrant exists, I don't have a choice but to hold you for those twenty-four hours," Han told Maria politely. "May I ask your names?"

Maria blinked.

"Didn't Caron call you?" she asked. She'd assumed Han had raised that much trouble on their behalf because Cobalt's man had talked to her.

"The lawyer?" Han replied. "No. I haven't spoken to him to for a few days. What is going on, lady Mage?"

"I am Mage Maria Soprano, Ship's Mage off *Red Falcon*," Maria introduced herself with a shake of her head. "This is my junior Mage, Xi Wu.

"If I knew what was going on with any degree of certainty, I don't know if I would have left my ship this morning," she concluded. "A Lieutenant Soun seems to be trying to arbitrarily detain members of our crew, but so far as we can tell, he has no grounds."

"Soun," Han echoed, sounding like she'd found a piece of manure stuck to her boots. "I know Soun. Come on." She gestured for them to follow her.

"If Caron is involved, I probably won't have to hold you for twenty-four hours," she told Maria as she led the way into the station. "But barring legal intervention, I have to respect my fellow security officers' claim that there is a reason to detain you.

"I apologize, but that is where we're at."

"I understand," Maria allowed. She didn't really, but she *did* understand that Han had just stuck her neck out to protect them. "I wasn't aware of such a thing as 'Special Security.'"

"In theory, they're the system-wide upper tier of DesSec," Han told her. "In practice..." The police captain sighed as she tapped a keypad and opened a comfortable-looking detainment room.

"In practice, I can't officially say anything," she admitted after a moment. "The detainment room will block your wrist-comps from accessing the network. I'll advise Mr. Caron and your ship of the situation.

"That's the best I can do, ladies. I wish my system was showing you a better face."

Maria chuckled.

"Believe me, Captain Han, I've seen worse."

CHAPTER 12

CARON ARRIVED shortly afterward, the lawyer's credentials apparently sufficient to get Maria and Wu onto a conference call with Captain Rice with the lawyer in the room.

"What the *hell* is going on, Mr. Caron?" Rice demanded.

"You, Captain Rice, appear to have managed to get yourself stuck in the middle of an attempt by a group of government officials to use the contract with Cobalt to set themselves up as power brokers," Caron said flatly. "The department that will be responsible for administering the fines if Cobalt Interstellar fails to bring the smelter online appears to have decided to force that event.

"If they did so, that would give the bureaucrats involved a slush fund equal to a significant part of Desdemona's annual budget. With that slush fund, they'd be able to manipulate government priorities, elections...potentially even fund a coup, though I don't think we're that far gone."

"I hope that you saying this means you have handed proof over to the police and my Mages can make their way home," the Captain replied.

"I wish," Caron replied. "I have conjecture and hearsay at the moment. Several top DesSec investigators are working the file, however, and Cobalt has closed up security around their facilities."

"We'll have fully off-loaded Cobalt's cargo in under two hours," Rice told them. "I'll be making contact with our likely client for shipping out tonight. I'd *like* to leave as soon as my new cargo is aboard."

"That, frankly, will be best for everyone," the lawyer agreed. "While I can't guarantee that the people behind this mess will be prosecuted, we are now at the point that, barring them preventing you from off-loading, they have failed.

"The smelter will come online on schedule, there will be no fines to be paid, and there will be some *painful* questions asked about where funds and people have gone," Caron noted.

"Now, I *can* get Mage Soprano and Mage Wu out of here, but they might be safer inside a DesSec station until the cargo is entirely out of *Red Falcon*'s hands."

"I suppose having you teleport back is out of the question?" Rice asked wistfully.

Maria chuckled.

"We *could*," she pointed out. "But it would require detailed information on the station spin that I don't have and time for the calculation."

"And Captain Han might object to our abusing her hospitality so," Wu noted.

"Oh, I know," the Captain agreed. "I'm sending a team of Skavar's people to keep an eye on you, but I think Mr. Caron is right: stay put until morning."

"At least DesSec will feed us," Maria concluded with a sigh. "All right, boss, Mr. Caron. We'll be good."

"I apologize for all of this," Caron told them. "Money makes people stupid."

Maria nodded. It was almost nice, for her at least, to end up in trouble over something as simple as money as opposed to criminal syndicate actions or potential civil wars.

She was realizing, however, that David Rice was an absolute magnet for trouble.

Despite the thousand and one reasons they had to suspect something to go wrong, Maria and Wu spent the night in Captain Han's district office without any trouble. The detention room wasn't exactly comfortable, but they were used to living on starships.

It could have been *much* worse.

"I apologize for the inconvenience," Han told them. "As I expected, SS has failed to produce a warrant calling for your arrest, and Mr. Caron has produced a writ of *habeas corpus*. Since I have no grounds to charge you, you are being released."

She waved a long-fingered hand delicately at the waiting room.

"There is a collection of 'security officers' in my station who couldn't scream 'ex-Marine' any louder if they were actually shouting it," she continued. "I'm going to guess they're yours?"

Maria glanced past the police captain to the waiting room. The four troopers in plain fatigues were, in fact, *Red Falcon* Security.

"Yes, that lot is ours," she confirmed. A fifth individual was sitting with the troopers, she realized as she stepped out, but wasn't security.

Mike Kelzin wrapped Wu in a tight embrace and held the much smaller woman for several seconds.

"Kelly's keeping the ship together," he told the two Mages. "She asked me to make sure Xi was okay."

"I'm *fine*," Wu replied, but she interrupted herself to give Kelzin a fierce kiss. "It's good to see you."

"I also have a note from the Captain for you," Kelzin told Maria. He tapped his wrist-comp to hers, transferring the file. "I didn't read it, but he told me not to expect to be going right back to the ship."

He coughed.

"We have a shuttle standing by at a bay nearby," he noted. "It's not... one of the more dangerous ones, but we found ways to make up for that."

If Maria was reading between the lines correctly, that meant that Kelzin hadn't brought an assault shuttle but almost certainly *had* brought exosuited *Red Falcon* security troops for backup.

It could be worse, she supposed. *Red Falcon* had a full suite of boarding torpedoes, after all.

"Let's get out of the police station and see what the Captain has for me," she told them, glancing around.

She seemed to have acquired an entourage. The degree to which starship crews were protective of their Mages always amused her—even the least powerful Mage was more capable of protecting herself than the five armed crew escorting her and Wu.

It was a sign, she supposed, of respect.

Once they were away from the station, she opened the file Kelzin had bounced to her. It was a video file, David Rice's face appearing on the tiny screen of her wrist-comp.

"You can guess why this is being hand-delivered," he said dryly. "It appears our Mr. Wu is being spectacularly paranoid. He refuses to do business over the system network and demanded that I not transmit anything to do with this deal."

Given that Wu was apparently under watch for smuggling—and was trying to smuggle gems out of the system—Maria could understand his paranoia. Even if it was a headache for them.

"Of course, he can't meet with *me*," David continued, "as the Captain meeting him would be too obvious that there was something special going on."

The tiny image of Maria's Captain shook his head.

"But he'll meet with you or Kelly, no problem, and..." He shrugged. "Kelly is more than living up to expectations, but I'm not sending her into this kind of cloak-and-dagger bullshit negotiation. Which makes it your problem, Ship's Mage.

"Address is attached to the file. You're expected."

The message ended. There were some text details on what Rice was expecting her to negotiate—the fact that *Red Falcon* needed to take this cargo to Snap for their own reasons wasn't something they could allow others to realize.

That meant that despite the fact they had to take Wu's job, they also had to be *seen* to haggle.

Some days, Maria regretted ever agreeing to be a spy.

The address Maria had been given turned out to be a surprisingly respectable-looking office in an upscale portion of the station. The corridors there were double-width, with upgraded lighting and murals painted along the walls.

The occupants had probably been going for "welcoming" but most of what they were managing was "here is where money lives."

The scattering of neatly uniformed young men and women from a private security force didn't help with that impression, even if they were being perfectly discreet to anyone who wasn't feeling paranoid.

No one interrupted her cavalcade as they arrived at the office with the tasteful gold plaque declaring it to be Wu, Lee and Wong Import/Export. The door opened into a quiet reception area decorated with heavy viridian carpets and carefully selected art.

The young man behind the desk *probably* hadn't been picked because his green eyes matched the carpet, but the subtly green-hued fabric of his suit definitely had been.

"I am Carl Lee," the youth introduced himself, implying, most likely, a relation to one of the main partners. "You would be Mage Soprano and...party?"

"I am Maria Soprano, yes," Maria agreed. "We are here to meet Mr. Wu?"

"Of course. Zhao Wu is expecting you in his office," Lee confirmed. "May I ask that your escort remain in the waiting room?" he asked delicately.

"If you're concerned for your personal security, realize this entire neighborhood is guaranteed safe by Platinum Cerberus. No threats will be tolerated to anyone's safety."

Maria didn't exactly trust the local mercenaries to protect her from the system government, but she also wasn't expecting Wu to try and stab her in the back—literally or figuratively.

"All right, people, have a seat and get comfy," she instructed. "I don't know how long this will be, but I'm sure Mr. Lee will be glad to make sure everyone has drinks and perhaps some breakfast?"

The young man smiled, flashing brilliantly white teeth. "Of course. There is a deli around the corner; I'll have them bring sandwiches for everyone.

"If you'll follow me, Mage Soprano?"

Mr. Zhao Wu rose when Maria entered his office, bowing to her with an old-fashioned courtesy she'd rarely seen in her life. He didn't look as old as she'd expected—he was, in fact, not much older than Lee on the front desk, which led her to an interesting conclusion.

"I'm guessing that Mr. Lee is not the receptionist," she observed as the door closed behind her.

"Astutely observed, Mage Soprano," Wu confirmed. Like Lee, he wore a subtly green-hued suit that matched the expensive surroundings. "We take turns holding down the front desk when important guests are coming through. It allows us to make certain we don't do business with anyone at least two of us haven't met.

"And, well"—he made a fluttering gesture with his left hand—"it's always educational to see how people treat the receptionist."

"So, did I pass?" Maria asked.

"A middling B," Wu told her with a smile. "Good enough for our needs of the moment. Tea, Mage Soprano?"

Somehow, she got the impression that playing along with the exporter's games was going to be a requirement of this job. She nodded and took a seat as the man puttered about, finding a pot and pouring cups.

"You understand, Mage Soprano, that WLW normally deals with a very limited selection of shippers," he finally told her. "We have reasons for that, but we now find ourselves in an unfortunate position of not having any of our shippers available...and having, bluntly, run out of time."

"Whatever your cargo is, *Red Falcon* can carry it," Maria said confidently. She couldn't tell Wu, after all, that she knew exactly what his cargo was. "And with antimatter engines and four Mages aboard, we can get it wherever you need to go faster than anyone else."

"And that is why we are speaking," Wu confirmed. "But, as I told your Captain, this cargo has now been impounded for thirteen weeks. DesSec has failed to find any grounds to keep my cargo locked down and it has finally been released to me.

"I want to get our cargo underway before they change their minds, and, bluntly, your ship is the only one in the system capable of carrying it all."

"Conveniently, we are for hire," Maria said. "And DesSec has not... enamored us of them."

Wu chuckled.

"I have heard. I hear you need to leave the system quickly?"

"We could, of course, go to another nearby system and find a new cargo," she said lightly. "While no one likes to run empty, it's often true that no deal is better than a bad deal."

Wu chuckled again and leaned back in his chair.

"We have a seventeen-point-five-million-ton cargo of raw ore destined for transshipment at Junkrat Orbital in the Snap System," he said calmly. "There are an additional ten containers that will be loaded onto the transporting ship that will not be part of the official manifest."

"I see. Which means, I suspect, that DesSec was correct in impounding the shipment. Just what *are* you transporting, Mr. Wu?" she asked.

"Suffice to say, not anything worth impounding the cargo over," he said shortly. "This is a no-questions-asked arrangement, Mage Soprano. If you are not capable of meeting that criterion, then we can, if we must, wait for another ship."

She smiled, leaning back herself.

"No need to be hasty, Mr. Wu," she told him. She was glad that Ishmael had filled them in. Rice did *not* do no-questions-asked, but since they needed this cargo...

"So, you want a cargo delivered twenty-six light-years," she continued. A bit more than a three-day trip for *Red Falcon*. "You want it delivered discreetly, I presume, since you're sending us to Junkrat, and you want no questions asked."

"Speed is of the essence."

"There is no one faster," Maria told him. That wasn't technically true—most Navy ships, for example, carried five or six Mages—but there certainly wasn't anyone around to haul his cargo who was.

"But for speed, discretion, and no questions asked...each of these things comes with a premium, Mr. Wu. As does carrying cargo that doesn't hit the official manifest, since the cost for those containers is added on to the rest."

Wu winced, but made a "come on" gesture to her.

"I can't see us taking on this contract for less than five times normal carriage rates," she concluded. That, on seventeen and a half million tons of cargo over twenty-six light-years, was enough to make her brain refuse to calculate the total number.

The exporter exhaled, nodding as he studied her.

"You clearly have some flex in that number," he noted. "Especially since, as we discussed, you need to leave this system almost as urgently as my cargo does."

"Five light-years to the Carmichael System," Maria replied. "Six point five to Sherwood. Less than thirty-six hours to either. We can run empty that long to find a good deal."

He chuckled.

"You won't find five times carriage rate in Sherwood or Carmichael," he pointed out. "You won't find that for *anything*. I'll pay three point five."

She smiled.

"It's such a shame we've wasted each others' time," she told him. "My Captain doesn't *like* no-questions-asked, Mr. Wu. We might be able to do four and a half if we knew what we were carrying, but to keep secrets like this? Five."

Wu studied her for several long seconds, seeming to weigh her with his eyes.

"You're aware we're supposed to meet somewhere in the middle, right?" he observed with a chuckle. "You're asking a lot of money."

"And you're demanding a lot of secrecy," Maria told him. "You know our reputation. You pay the price, we'll deliver with discretion. If you don't..." She shrugged. "How many ships *does* Desdemona see that can haul eighteen million tons?"

"Fair," he allowed. "We do see enough six-million-ton ships that I can get the cargo where it needs to be soon enough. Fine. Four, Mage Soprano. Not a penny per ton higher."

She smiled sweetly.

"And you'll tell us what's in the ten extra containers?"

They held each other's gazes for a long time, and then Wu laughed. Years sloughed off his face, and she was suddenly certain he was at least ten years younger than her. The exporter had done well for himself in a relatively short time.

"Four and a quarter, Soprano. No questions. I'll personally guarantee there is nothing in those containers that will harm anyone. Sound fair?"

Rice had actually authorized her to go down to three and a half.

"Done," she allowed. "*If* you can have your cargo aboard inside twenty-four hours."

The exporter swallowed, hard, but nodded.

"We'll make it happen."

CHAPTER 13

NO ONE on *Red Falcon*'s bridge—most likely, no one aboard the entire freighter—was sorry to see Puck Orbital in their figurative rearview mirror.

Kelly LaMonte guided the big ship out of the chaos of the wrecked world with the same skill she'd guided them in. Bringing the ship in had been terrifying. Bringing the ship out...

Well, it was still terrifying. The fragment density was up about fifty percent, and even fewer of them seemed to be charted this time. *Falcon*'s sensors were as far above the norm as the rest of her, however, and that was enough for even a relatively rookie pilot to maneuver her way through the mess.

Almost.

The ship almost imperceptibly shivered as Jeeves pressed a button on his console, one of the RFLAM turrets spinning to fire three times.

"Thank you, Mr. Jeeves," Kelly said gratefully. She'd picked up the medium-sized, uncharted meteor too late to be able to avoid it without hitting something *else*. Fortunately, the gunner had been paying attention.

"Part of the job, ma'am," he replied brightly. Given a week aboard *Red Falcon* to slot himself into his new teams and remain freshly showered and shaved, Jeeves looked much less concerning to the XO than he had when he came aboard.

There appeared to be a solid officer under the grime after all.

"Can we flag the leftovers and pass them on to Puck STC?" she asked.

Jeeves had the grace to look almost embarrassed.

"Yes, ma'am; should have thought of that myself," he replied.

"Are *you* flying based on their debris charts?" Kelly said. "No. Why would you think of it?"

She tapped the controls, flaring *Falcon*'s antimatter engines to drift them past a properly charted meteor.

"But make sure STC gets the mass and vectors you left behind," she continued. "Might save some other poor pilot an actual collision."

"On it."

Kelly glanced back at where David Rice continued to hold down the command chair at the center of the bridge. If the Captain had any advice or comments, he was keeping them to himself.

Most of her attention was on the debris around them. It took over two hours for them to be clear enough of the debris field to point the ship at empty space and engage the engines at full power.

The gravity runes Mage Soprano's people maintained smoothly absorbed the acceleration as the big freighter leapt ahead at ten gravities.

"Clear of the debris field; now accelerating at full power," she announced. "Estimate seven hours to clear jump space."

"Thank you, XO," Rice replied. "You can stand down. I'll handle the rest of the flight."

"Sir?" Kelly asked slowly. That wasn't normal procedure, but Rice was smiling at her.

"Kelly, your girlfriend nearly got arrested and kidnapped, and I don't think you've had time for more than a quick hug since," he pointed out. "Our visit to Desdemona has been a complete shit-show.

"Go visit with Xi. She's last on the jump schedule this time. Go. Shoo."

The entire bridge was grinning at her as she shook her head at her boss and rose.

"With your permission, Captain."

"Get off my bridge," Rice told her with a laugh.

Kelly rapped on Xi's door when she reached it, then paused. After a moment, she knocked again.

"Who is it?" Xi finally replied.

"It's Kelly."

"Damn, sorry. Come in, come in! Door, unlock."

The verbal command unlocked the hatch, allowing Kelly to step into her lover's quarters.

She realized Xi wasn't alone immediately, mostly because the Mage was basically naked and pulled her inside instantly, closing the door behind her.

"Door, lock," Xi ordered. "Hi, Kelly," she added with a smile. The smell of candles and warmed oil filled the quarters, and Mike Kelzin was sprawled on the bed in a pair of shorts. "Mike was giving me a massage."

"I can come back later," Kelly offered, feeling somewhat awkward.

Xi's response was to drag her into a fierce kiss.

"We barely saw you in the Desdemona System," the Mage replied. "Not bloody happening. You, miss XO, are getting naked and on the bed, and then Mike and I are going to rub down every last muscle you didn't know was aching."

"You had a far worse few days," Kelly objected, but she found herself propelled toward the bed, where Mike also wrapped her in an embrace and kissed her.

"Yes, but I had time *off* after that," Xi told her. "You spent the whole time we were there running around organizing cargo and working. Time for you to rest."

Kelly's heart definitely wasn't in the argument, either, as her lovers began to carefully undress her.

"Besides," Xi concluded with a wicked grin, "if you think *I'm* not getting any relaxation out of this, you haven't guessed the full agenda."

David Rice watched the numbers trickle down toward the jump.

"So, Captain, would you happen to know where my most senior Mage is?" Soprano asked sweetly over the intercom.

"Why would it matter?" he asked. "I checked the schedule; she's not up for jumping for six more hours."

Soprano chuckled.

"That's fair, I suppose, though I expected her to answer her wrist-comp when I buzzed her."

"Well, given that I just made sure that Kelly, Xi and Michael were all off duty at the same time, I bloody well *hope* she wasn't answering your call," David pointed out dryly. "I may not be entirely enthused with my XO having her lovers aboard, but at least they're out of her chain of command."

"And allows you to arrange stress relief?" Soprano asked.

David chuckled.

"Oh, I'm trusting them to arrange that all on their own," he said. "None of the three of them are over twenty-six. I think they'll manage."

His Ship's Mage laughed.

"And this isn't a military ship, Captain Rice, for all of our oddities," she pointed out. "Chain of command isn't really a thing."

"Old habits die hard," he murmured. If anything, they should die harder for Soprano. He'd been out of the Navy for decades. She'd barely been out for a year and a half.

"They do. But on a civilian ship, there's no need for that one." Soprano shrugged. "Plus, they're sensible kids."

"They are," he agreed. "I make us far enough out to jump, Ship's Mage. You?"

"Everything looks clear on my end," she agreed. "Shall we be on our way to Snap?"

For a moment, David hesitated. Going to Snap was going to paint a giant target on his back...but it was also going to help put down the last of Mikhail Azure's leftovers.

"Yeah," he finally agreed. "You may jump when ready, Ship's Mage."

CHAPTER 14

JUNKRAT'S ORBITALS were both more impressive and *far* more ramshackle than David had been expecting from Stealey's description. The planet itself was a windswept dustball with a sad excuse for an atmosphere, barely bigger than Earth's moon.

Its only real value was as a gravitational anchor to the collection of stations forming a loose ring around Junkrat's equator. There was everything from structures assembled from welded-together collections of standard transport containers to a Legatan-designed ring station.

The latter had a squadron of six *Crucifix*-class gunships hovering protectively above it. The ships were currently sitting in combat mode, their weapons modules spread out in the extended X that gave the ships their name.

The ships had a pursuit mode that would have enabled them to police most of Junkrat local space relatively easily...but from their identifier codes, the gunships were actually Legatus Self-Defense Force ships.

They had no legal authority to police anybody in the Snap System and were announcing their lack of intention to do so as clearly as they could.

The Snap System government certainly wasn't doing any policing. A beacon positioned above Junkrat's pole was continuously transmitting that trading was permitted in Junkrat orbit, but any attempt by unauthorized vessels to approach Flytrap would be met with lethal force.

According to David's sensors, they'd reinforced that message with a set of about sixty buoys in orbit between the two planets that marked the "do not cross" line. A dozen container ships were locked into the long transfer orbit between Junkrat and Flytrap, cheaply carrying cargo that didn't need to arrive quickly.

A fleet of smaller ships, a mix of solar sails and fusion drives, also made the trip...but no jump-ships passed closer than Junkrat.

According to the MISS files, the Royal Martian Navy visited the planet two or three times a year for various reasons. The reports showed that Flytrap greeted its military visitors politely but unenthusiastically.

MISS files also noted that, despite the warning that crossing the line would be met with lethal force, Flytrap had never actually destroyed anyone. Their massive fusion missiles had a twenty-minute flight time from the orbital platforms—more than enough for anyone testing the locals' resolve to change their mind.

Apparently, the missiles had been designed to return home on orders, too, so the Snap Security Force could have their warning shot *and* get the weapons back.

It was an efficient design. Unlike, well, just about anything in Junkrat orbit.

"Please tell me we're heading to the Legatan station," Jeeves said plaintively. "Most of the rest of this place looks like we'll get tetanus just docking with them."

"Sadly, no," David told him. "I'm *told* Junkertown is relatively safe, through sheer size if nothing else, and it's the only place with the transshipment facilities we need. I'll contact Integrity's local office and make sure there's someone there to meet us."

"Junkertown," Jeeves repeated. "I don't know what sources *you* have, boss, but if they called Junkertown safe, what was their comparison point? *Darkport?*"

"Darkport is being converted into a RMMC zero-gee training facility," David pointed out. "It's pretty safe these days."

It had once been the center of the sex slave trade in the Protectorate. Then, of course, David Rice had visited.

He didn't feel particularly bad about that one.

"Junkertown isn't too bad," he continued. "It's not a place I want to go unarmed or unescorted, but the fact that everyone expects that actually keeps it relatively calm." He grinned.

"Most of the *rest* of the stations around here? I wouldn't trust the *air*, let alone the locals."

"Right. Why are we here, again?" the tactical officer asked.

"To drag our coats in front of the Azure Legacy and see if we can tempt them into a mistake."

"Right," Jeeves echoed. "Can I reconsider the whole prison thing?"

"Captain Rice, I am Administrator Nkechinyere Arendse," the dark-skinned woman in his screen greeted him. "I run Integrity Galactic's broker office here in Snap."

"Good to speak to you, Administrator Arendse," David told her. "I understand you were expecting our cargo?"

"Yeeees," Ardendse said slowly. "I believe there are...two components to it?"

"That is my understanding as well," he agreed. "I have seventeen point five million tons of raw rock from Puck's core for smelting, and an additional ten containers of 'no-questions-asked.'"

She smiled.

"Goood." She drew her vowels out again. "I don't, as it happens, have a ship on hand to take the cargo on at the moment."

David winced.

"The fees for keeping my ship sitting anywhere are not low, Administrator," he warned her. "To have us sit in an UnArcana system, let alone in a place with a reputation like Junkrat's..."

"Thaaat... won't be a problem," Arendse replied. "We have storage facilities here sufficient for those needs."

David nodded, managing not to visibly show surprise. Eighteen million tons of cargo storage seemed like a lot to have on hand, though he supposed if Integrity regularly ran ships that could carry that much, it made sense.

"We're on course for Junkertown," he told her. "Will that work for you, or should we be detouring somewhere else for drop-off?

"I'm presuming Junkertown is the best place for me to find a new cargo."

"Junkertown is fiiiine," Arendse told him. "We can arrange off-loading there." She paused. "I suggest you keep your security on duty and awake. Junkertown is safe so long as you appear ready for trouble."

"That was my understanding and my plan," he agreed. "If you have a referral for someone looking to carry cargo somewhere Integrity Galactic doesn't go..."

She smiled politely.

"Of course," she agreed, without meaning it at all. He wasn't really surprised. "I look forward to speaking with you further once you've docked, Captain. Fly safely."

"What in the gods' names is *that*?" LaMonte's voiced echoed in the bridge as Junkertown orbited past the horizon and *Red Falcon* finally got a solid look at her destination.

"Junkertown," David said redundantly, studying the ramshackle structure himself. "Which means, I suppose, what happens when a hundred different groups decided to build a space station in the same place for different reasons, and about the only thing they share is a center of gravity."

From the layout of the ugly assemblage of pods and work stations that made up Junkertown, it had *probably* started with the immense zero-gravity transshipment facilities that were still the single largest piece of the station.

Now, however, the ten tower-like docks and their connecting gantries and cranes rose like dead trees from a swamp. Someone had attached a fat O'Neill cylinder habitat to the transshipment center.

It had probably been at least two or three decades since the cylinder had rotated, and other habitat modules had been welded to it like tumors over those years. That nearly cancerous-looking growth formed as much of a core as Junkertown had. No less than seven different arms of the station spread out from there, each looking completely different from the others.

If David was counting correctly, there were easily twenty rotating habitat sections of various sizes, including what looked like it had once been a sister to the Legatan ring station at the near-opposite side of the planet.

Six—possibly more, but he could definitely pick out six—small asteroids had been towed in and attached to various sections of the station, both surface and interior consumed to provide more living and work space for a sprawling assemblage of humanity unlike anything even David had ever seen.

"Files say four hundred and fifty thousand permanent population, about twice that in transients and temporary workers," Jeeves read out. "Three-quarters of the spaceborne human population in this star system is in that mess."

"With no law enforcement and no central authority," LaMonte replied. "How? The whole thing should fall apart."

"There's also no central life support or power," David told her. "Each segment is run independently. Occasionally, they'll sell power or air to each other, but when I say Junkertown is a bunch of different space stations that happen to be in the same place, it's not a bad description."

"And somewhere in there, the Legacy is holding a conference to reunify the Blue Star," his XO noted, studying it. "Would the galaxy *really* miss this place if we vaporized it?"

"Over a million people, Kelly," he reminded her. "Even if they were all guilty of something worth death—and they're not—you wouldn't want that on your conscience.

"We go with the plan."

"Is that the one where you go and make a target of yourself?" she said sweetly.

He sighed.

"Yes. Exactly that one."

CHAPTER 15

CONNECTING *RED FALCON* with the cargo docks helped put the whole mass of Junkertown into perspective. The megafreighter was well over a kilometer long, and while the docking towers weren't long enough to cover her entire length, they covered most of it.

And if the towers were a kilometer tall, then Junkertown itself was roughly seven kilometers high, roughly the same wide, and twice that long.

Of course, most of that was empty space, given the sprawling and random nature of the spiderweb that made up the space station, but it was enough to make the clearly organic growth of the orbital impressive.

Once the ship was docked, a dozen tugs began a rapid approach to the freighter...rapid enough to make David uncomfortable.

"Jeeves, target those tugs with the RFLAMs," he ordered. "Be obvious about it."

A moment later, the indicators on his repeater screens showed the turrets pinging the incoming ships with active radar.

"Approaching vessels, this is *Red Falcon*," LaMonte said sharply into her mike. "Please state your intentions. We have made no arrangements for cargo pickup."

The ships continued on their course for a few more seconds, and then scattered like cockroaches when the light turned on. David sighed.

"Let me ping Administrator Arendse," he noted aloud, "and see if we can find our *actual* pickup. It seems we're going to need to watch for scavengers."

"We're being hailed by someone on the docking tower," LaMonte told him. "Do you want me to take it?"

"No, I'll talk to them," David replied. "I suspect this will be entertaining enough."

A command flipped the channel to his repeater screens, revealing a perfectly groomed bearded man with unusually black eyes.

"*Red Falcon*, I am dock control for Junkertown Tower Six," he introduced himself politely. "You are expected, but there are fees and costs associated with docking with the Tower." He coughed delicately.

"Integrity arranged your dock but has made it clear they are not covering any of your costs. We will need to make sure those are sorted before Tower Six can hook up umbilicals."

Docking costs normally were covered, but David had to admit that he was working for Wu, Lee and Wong, not Integrity. The Administrator had to sign off on receipt of the cargo before funds would be released to him, but she wasn't paying him.

Fortunately, he was being paid enough to cover this; he would just have preferred if Wu had mentioned that little complication in advance.

"And the cost for standard docking and air supply is?"

The groomed man quoted him a number.

David almost laughed aloud.

"And that includes antimatter resupply, I suppose?" he asked. The number was extortionate, far beyond anything that was reasonable, even for the ass end of nowhere.

"That is a standard docking fee including air," the other man said calmly. "Given the size of your vessel, we could easily see increasing it, given the amount of life support you clearly use. Any fuel, antimatter or otherwise, would be an additional charge.

"I have no negotiating discretion on the rate, Captain Rice. If you do not want to pay it, you are welcome to disconnect from our Tower and try and negotiate a better rate."

"And let me guess, you take no responsibility for our security while docked?" David said dryly.

"Of course not. We are a dock provider, nothing more."

"You sound more like a protection racket," the Captain muttered. "And what rate does *Integrity* pay when their ships dock?"

"Integrity Galactic is a customer of long standing with preexisting contracts," the man, who still hadn't actually given a *name*, replied. "They are a special case."

David smiled thinly.

"All right, I suggest you take a good, *long* look at my ship," he told the dockmaster. "This was an Armed Auxiliary Fast Heavy Freighter. While we're docked, your tower is inside our defensive perimeter. No natural debris, no meteors, no missiles, nothing will threaten you while we are here.

"We will happily guarantee *your* security...in exchange for paying the docking fees that Integrity Galactic pays for their own ships of our size."

Unspoken was that those same defensive systems could *gut* Tower Six. David wouldn't even need the main weapons; at this range, the anti-missile laser turrets would gouge twenty- or thirty-meter wide holes through the dock's framework at full power.

"I see, Captain Rice," the bearded man told him carefully. "I...think we can come to an arrangement."

He quoted a new rate. It was high enough that David suspected it wasn't actually what Integrity paid...but it was low enough to be merely highway robbery rather than grand theft.

"That's acceptable," he replied. "Transferring funds now. A pleasure doing business with Tower Six." He paused. "Will you be able to supply antimatter?"

The bearded man smiled, a shark-like expression that triggered a mental sigh in the back of David's head.

"That, Captain Rice, would be why Administrator Arendse sent you to us," he replied. "We are the *only* dock in Junkertown with access to antimatter supplies.

"Which means, of course, that supply is hardly cheap."

There was hiding from your enemies...and then there was what David Rice was doing on Junkertown. He'd drawn the line at having Skavar roll out exosuited security troopers, but the Security Chief had accompanied him himself—along with half a dozen men in the heaviest unpowered body armor they had.

Skavar and one of the other men actually went a step beyond that. They weren't in full exosuits, but they were both wearing powered harnesses over their armor that allowed them to carry the heavy penetrator rifles used by exosuits to kill each other.

Those guns were highly illegal in most space stations and planets...but Junkertown didn't have a central authority to enforce *any* law. Even sensible ones like "don't carry weapons that can punch through the station hull."

Xi Wu and Maria Soprano were easily missed amidst that collection of armor and weaponry, which was part of the point. If the seven security officers weren't enough to discourage someone from trying to take down Captain David Rice, the two Mages were almost certainly enough to *stop* them.

All told, it made for quite the crowd that made its way through the corridors of what had once been an O'Neill cylinder—a spinning habitat to provide massive quantities of habitable space—and was now a massive zero-gravity facility.

Parts of the cylinder had been converted into regular decks, but much of it remained as open, wasted space. Several smaller, more economical if less efficient, spinning habitats had been built *inside* the old cylinder, and it was one of these that their directions took them to.

There was a single point of entry at the center of the rotating ring, and unlike Rice, Integrity Galactic Transport had *not* refrained from using exosuited troopers for their defense. A small sign next to the zero-gravity entryway declared that the entire ring was extraterritorial, under the authority and protection of the Legatus government.

Hence the Legatan Self-Defense Force Space Assault troopers guarding the door. The difference between LSDFSA troops and Marines was...a matter of labels. Nothing more. The gear was comparable. The training was comparable

The dozen exosuited assault troops guarding the access to the ring would have been more than a match for the non-Mage component of David's bodyguard even if his people had been in exosuits. With one side in armor and one side not, David hoped his people were feeling meek.

The octagon of heavy remote-controlled turrets mounted around the hatch didn't help with the balance of force. He stopped himself just outside the line and leveled his gaze on the one unarmored woman waiting there.

She met his gaze with a cheerful smile...and a steady, square-pupiled look. There was a reason, he supposed, that the Augment hadn't bothered with armor. A Legatan combat cyborg was better protected inside an exosuit, but they weren't any stronger or faster.

"Captain Rice," she greeted him brightly. "I am Liza Sierra. I'm afraid I don't have you on my list."

He smiled back at Sierra.

"There must be some mistake," he told her. "I'm delivering a twenty-million-ton cargo; I need to meet with the receiving agent in person."

Nothing had actually been arranged, he knew, which meant Sierra was entirely correct. That said, it was odd that nothing *had* been arranged. He would have expected Arendse to have set up a meeting within a few hours of *Red Falcon* docking.

Of course, the point of this trip was to be seen, not to necessarily get business done.

"I will touch base with Administrator Arendse's office," Sierra promised. "I'm afraid I can't let you into the habitat ring without some kind of authorization."

"In this environment, I can understand the paranoia," David allowed. "Should we wait?"

Sierra nodded briskly, her eyes flickering in response to an image only she could see.

"Please do," she requested.

Clearly, the cyborg was communicating through her implants, a somewhat uncomfortable experience for everyone around her. There was no *reason* for her to be visibly responding to anything, except that under all the hardware, Augments were still human.

The square pupils weren't a necessary part of the technology, as David understood it. They'd been included intentionally to make combat cyborgs obvious to others, to provide some reassurance that no one was wandering around with weapons-grade implants without anyone knowing.

So, of course, David was quite sure Legatus had *also* built cyborgs without the obvious eyes. It's what he would have done.

"The Administrator isn't available at the moment, but you can meet with her chief of staff, if that works for you?" Sierra suddenly replied, concluding a conversation no one else could see. "Ms. Tran should be able to sort out whatever paperwork or assistance you need; she speaks with the Administrator's voice in most matters."

"That is more than acceptable," David agreed immediately. There was no harm in being accommodating, after all—and he'd expected to have to go back to the ship and return another time.

Meeting with Ms. Tran would at least skip that step.

CHAPTER 16

BY THE TIME they finished meeting with the chief of staff for Junkertown, David was beginning to realize that whatever they were *saying*, Integrity Galactic didn't own this particular chunk of rotating habitat.

From the number of troopers he could see, in uniform and out, there had to be at least a full space assault regiment stationed there. Possibly more. Over a thousand of Legatus's elite ground forces.

Plus at least a platoon from the Augment Corps. The Augments weren't being as obvious as the assault troopers, but they were definitely present. From the drills that both groups were going through, David could at least guess the purpose of their presence here.

In the case of a serious emergency or threat, Legatus would be able to seize control of Junkertown in minutes. The map on his wrist-comp confirmed his other suspicions: the rotating habitat linked to the outer edge of the original cylinder.

There was no official docking port there, but he suspected that there were probably more gunships stored here than anyone outside realized.

"Anyone else feeling paranoid?" Soprano muttered to him as they made their way out.

"Not really," he told her. "If I was, say, the Snap System Government... oh, yeah. Legatus has infiltrated a crack combat force under their noses. If I were the government here, I'd wonder why.

"As it is," he shrugged. "Somebody else's problem, Ship's Mage."

Soprano chuckled softly. Even from MISS's perspective, this was probably somebody else's problem, though they'd make sure to report it.

The meeting with Tran had been pretty straightforward, sorting out confirmation of receipt and payment release. The only oddity had been their need to insist on doing it in person—Integrity Galactic, it seemed, would have rather done that entirely electronically.

Now that David could see that Integrity Galactic's facility was concealing a Legatan strike force, he could understand why.

"Think we've made enough of a spectacle of ourselves, boss?" Skavar asked. "My shoulder blades are starting to itch."

"If I thought our blue friends were here, I'd say yes, but I doubt the Legatans would permit them to operate in their space."

David considered for a few seconds.

"This seems like a good place for us to pick up some gear for your people that won't be available most places," he pointed out. "Let's go see if we can find the arms bazaar."

The Security Chief chuckled.

"I know where *that* is," he admitted. "I was poking the station network to see if I could find some heavy anti-armor gear."

"Well, then, Chief," David replied, kicking off from the rotating habitat's exit hatch. "Let's go find you some anti-tank guns, shall we?"

Junkertown was a sufficiently disorganized mess of a space station that the net informed David that there were at least ten major markets he could call bazaars. Three—including, thankfully, the arms market—were in the old O'Neill cylinder.

It was the first time David had been in a bazaar of any significant size that didn't even have rotational gravity. It was an "open air" market, hanging in the middle of an area of open space in the cylinder, anchored on a set of storage containers but sprawling out in three dimensions with no sense of order beyond the ropes tying the stalls together.

Rows of weapons dangled in security cuffs at each station, and the smell of hot food drifted out from the solitary saloon—also, so far as David could tell, the only place in the bazaar with magical gravity.

That was odd enough on its own, given that Snap was an UnArcana System. Junkertown *really* didn't pay attention to its home system's laws.

"Over there," Skavar told him. "The big green exclamation mark is apparently Weinhauser's. They don't have the biggest selection, but their rep says they've got gear nobody else has.

"For the kind of esoteric systems we're looking for, they're our best hope."

"It's your shopping trip, Chief," David told him. "Lead the way."

Weinhauser's exclamation mark was made out of extremely old-fashioned neon tubes, glowing with a bright green unmatched by anything else in the mess. The three-meter-tall icon was attached to a suspended platform thirty meters on a side with a series of plain wooden trellis tables.

Given the lack of gravity, the throwback effect was entirely intentional—and like many other stalls in this market, the merchandise was chained to the tables with manacles normally used for high-security prisoners.

A figure came up to meet them, wrapped in a green suit almost as hideously neon as the exclamation mark.

"I am Weinhauser!" they announced brightly. "Purveyor of arms both extraordinary and mundane for the most discerning of customers. What can I set you up with?"

The androgynous glowing green figure looked over David's escort.

"You've quite the setup already, I see," they continued. "What do you need? Battle lasers? Explosives? Nukes?"

They paused.

"I don't actually have nukes," they noted. "Even in Junkertown, folk disapprove of keeping radioactives on a shop shelf."

"You have battle lasers?" Skavar asked. "I didn't think those were in practical use yet."

"Legatus Arms is up to mod five on their man-portable battle laser," Weinhauser told him. "Mod one and two were...less than useful, but mod three was a reasonably practical weapon, and mod four is a nasty little piece of gear. LSDF is using it as a squad support weapon, though they're holding off for mod five for mass rollout."

"And you have..." Skavar said.

"Six mod fours," Weinhauser said cheerfully. "They're great sniper rifles, though the mod *five* works nicely on armor. I don't have any mod fives," they concluded.

"No recoil? Good for EVA work, right?"

"Exactly," the arms salesperson agreed. "Want them?"

"We'll take them," Skavar replied. "But that wasn't what I was after. Looking for trooper- and exosuit-portable anti-armor gear—thinking multipurpose anti-tank and -aircraft systems."

Weinhauser nodded and gestured for them to follow. The salesperson was clearly *very* used to zero gravity, grabbing the ropes and guidelines around their free-floating stall with practiced ease as they led David's party deeper in.

"Real modern armor isn't something you see often," they noted. "Most folks settle for exosuits or, well, gear that wouldn't look out of place on twenty-second-century Earth. Only the LSDF and the Martians use real tanks."

"Let's just say my boss likes to make enemies," Skavar replied with a pointed glance at David. "I've learned not to underestimate their re-sources."

Weinhauser nodded, bracing themselves carefully to open a storage locker and slide out a coffin-sized box.

"We don't have exosuit designed gear for this," they admitted. "Exosuit teams tend to carry hyper-interceptors for that kind of gear, and people are even *less* enthused with antimatter on the shelf than they are with radioactives.

"This gear uses the same kind of powered supporting harness you're wearing," they continued, nodding toward Skavar's harness as they popped open the coffin. "I've never heard an official name for the things, nobody admits to mass-producing them and I've seen at least five differ-ent varieties, but everyone just calls them blasters."

Most of the coffin contained the support harness, an identical version to what Skavar himself was wearing. Nestled in the middle were three items that looked like nothing so much as beehives with chainsaw grips.

"Compressed-plasma gun," Weinhauser told them. "It's a fire-and-forget weapon—you fire it once, and then you forget you ever had it. Firing it vaporizes the interior of the gun.

"But it will put two point five kilograms of one-hundred-thousand-Kelvin hydrogen plasma on target with a two-centimeter divergence in beam for each hundred meters traveled," the salesman explained.

"I've got two sets like this," the salesperson concluded. "They don't move fast, but they're hard to replace, so they aren't cheap."

David smiled and held up a hand to his Chief of Security.

"So, how much is 'aren't cheap'?" he asked.

To David's surprise, they made it back to the ship with Skavar's prizes without being attacked. He summoned a staff meeting at that point, pulling LaMonte, Jeeves, Kellers, Soprano and Skavar into his office for a planning session.

"I'm pretty sure the bastards know we're here now," he told his officers. "But they didn't act while we were out, which leaves me wondering just what buttons to push."

"You've probably pushed the big ones already," Jeeves said quietly. "Right now, they're trying to decide if going after you is worth endangering their conference."

"Any thoughts on where the conference would be?" David asked.

"It's a big station," LaMonte pointed out. "I'd guess they're on Junkertown somewhere, I'd even guess in place with rotational pseudo-grav, but that still gives us a lot of potential targets."

"If we could narrow it down, we could see if we could dig up a potential cargo client in the area," Soprano suggested.

"That's exactly what I was thinking," David agreed. "I don't really want to just start randomly wandering through the rotating sections looking for trouble, though. Some basis for picking one would be good."

"Which ones are likely to *have* clients?" LaMonte asked. "I'd guess that the ones with docks, shipping offices, and conference centers are the most likely places to call that kind of meeting."

David nodded. As usual, his new XO had a point.

"How many places on this collection of junk actually have anything we'd call a conference center?" he asked.

"Five," Jeeves said instantly, gathering everyone's attention. He shrugged embarrassedly. "Guys, I got busted for arms running the second time I did it. There are only two places a rookie can find enough guns to make arms smuggling worth it.

"I don't know Junkertown well, but I've gone over the publicly available data a few times. The Old Ring"—he tapped the Legatan-style ring station rotating around one of the station's arms—"is probably the safest, cleanest, most up-to-date section of the station.

"Which, for those who aren't paying attention, means it's also the most corrupt and where most of the illegal transshipping is organized through," he concluded. "The group that owns it call themselves the Parchment Tigers, but they've spaced, shot and stabbed enough people that nobody thinks they're a paper tiger anymore."

David shook his head with a chuckle.

"You bought guns from them?" he asked.

"Yup," Jeeves agreed. "They aren't so much a Blue Star fragment as they were a Blue Star subsidiary, ran their own op but kicked up to Mikhail Azure at the end of the year."

"So, they've got a stake but are detached enough that people will accept them as neutral enough to host," David noted. "That sounds like a good place to start. I'll do some poking around the network to see if I can find someone looking for a cargo carrier."

"If you walk into the Old Ring, you are painting a giant target on your back, boss," Jeeves said quietly. "It's orderly because the Tigers keep it that way. If they decide you need to die—and they're clearly in bed with the Legacy—they have all of the power to make sure you die there."

"That's the risk we have to take," David replied. "We need to either make them be obvious or find them ourselves."

"What do we do if we find them before they attack?" Skavar asked.

Red Falcon's Captain chuckled again.

"Well, in that case, you do keep reminding me that we have boarding torpedoes."

CHAPTER 17

THE OLD RING felt almost sterile compared to the rest of Junkertown. Nowhere on the space station was actually *dirty*, exactly, as even the most casual of those who lived in space relied on the machinery around them to keep them alive.

But Junkertown was a level below most space stations David had visited. There was litter in corners and visible grime on some of the walls. It probably wasn't to the point where it was causing problems for life support...but there were spots where it was definitely closer than he was comfortable.

The Old Ring, however, was perfectly clean. The type of clean that spoke to hard labor by either humans or robots. The walls and ceilings had been painted a dull white to reduce glare, and the noise of machinery that was present throughout the station calmed to the normal soft hum here.

His escort, the same group he'd taken to meet Integrity, stayed close to him as they moved through the main corridors. The Old Ring was surprisingly empty of people, and what residents they passed quickly removed themselves from the way of the group of armed spacers.

"Shippers' Guild is on level seven," Soprano told him. "Stairs are that way."

David nodded his thanks. Any of them could look up the map, though they were trying to pass specific places as they made their way. That required them to at least look a little lost.

He gestured for his Ship's Mage to lead the way, keeping his own eyes peeled down each of the side corridors as they traveled.

It was *too* quiet.

"This is the largest section of Junkertown with gravity," he said softly. "Where is everyone?"

"Staying inside," Skavar replied. "And not because of us. We're too new. Something *else* has everyone gun-shy."

"A crime syndicate holding a reunion conference would do that, wouldn't it?" David agreed. "We're already watching our backs...but watch them harder, I think.

"I think we've found the enemy—which means it's time to walk into their trap with eyes wide open."

The Shippers' Guild—a fancy name for a cargo broker—was located on a large open promenade that linked through levels five, six, seven and eight of the Old Ring's ten decks. It was large enough that the curvature of the ring could be seen and tall enough that the "higher" levels had noticeably weaker gravity than the "lower" ones.

This promenade was apparently one of Old Ring's main commercial areas, with dozens of offices, restaurants and stores. It didn't have the stalls and chaos of a regular bazaar; this was more of a ground-style mall—more official and organized.

Unlike the rest of the Old Ring, the promenade was still busy with people. The populace might have realized there were more gangsters and thugs around than usual, but work still needed to get done.

The presence of the crowds meant that David began to relax. Nowhere on Junkertown was safe, not with the game he was playing, but his enemies seemed unlikely to start a firefight in what was basically a crowded mall—that they owned.

He was almost right.

They passed through the crowds without incident, the shoppers and office workers scrambling out of the way of the David's escorts with a calm assurance that suggested armed groups were far from uncommon there.

The promenade had broad ramps connecting the levels, home to carefully constructed fast food kiosks. The smell of cooking food swarmed anyone traveling between levels, a clever trick to sell burgers and pre-boxed fried rice dishes.

Soprano was leading the way still, crossing onto level seven and heading toward the subdued but still visible offices of the guild, when everything went to hell.

The sniper was good—but not good *enough* to fully account for the rotation of the promenade on their first shot. The tungsten armor-penetrating dart had been aimed at David but flashed by high and to the right.

The screams from behind him suggested that they'd hit *someone*, but they hadn't been aiming at innocent fast food workers.

"Shields!" Soprano barked at her subordinate, but the Mages weren't quick enough.

Skavar's Marines were. One of the armored escorts had David on the ground before the Captain could even begin to run for cover himself... and the sniper didn't miss twice.

David felt his bodyguard spasm as the heavy dart slammed home... and then again as the sniper kept firing.

The clamshell body armor his people wore was solid, capable of standing off most small arms. It wasn't up to withstanding the penetrator rounds designed to punch through exosuits. The third shot punched clean through David's protector and into his leg.

The fourth punched into his gut. The fifth into his lung.

If there were more bullets, he was unconscious before he registered them.

CHAPTER 18

"FUCK!"

Maria didn't even try to swallow the curse, instead focusing on getting the defensive shield up. Several more bullets slammed into it once she was covering the *Falcon's* crew, but she was already too late.

"Skavar," she snapped. "Medical."

"Already on it," the Marine replied, pulling a medkit from inside his powered harness as he knelt next to the two dying men. "Spiros, you handle Akkerman. Let's try not to lose *anybody*.

"Reyes, Tsao, *find that shooter.*"

Reyes was the trooper wearing the other powered harness, the tall man tracking around the promenade with the heavy penetrator rifle.

"The shooting stopped," he said grimly. "Why don't I think that's a good sign?"

"Because it's not," Maria replied, still focusing on holding the shield. The crowds around them were scattering, *fast*. On a station with as much gang involvement as Junkertown in general and the Old Ring in particular, the local populace knew when to take cover.

"Top level, jumpers," one of the guards snapped, bringing his own carbine up. "Ma'am, ROE?"

"If they're armed, put them down," Maria ordered grimly as the reason for the question sank in: with Rice down, *she* was in command.

Carbines barked around her as she refocused her shield to allow the gunfire. Half a dozen attackers in light body armor were coming down from the top level, taking advantage of the mixed gravity to parkour their way down the promenade in a way no other environment would allow.

If their approach, armor and weapons hadn't been enough of a clue, they started shooting in almost the same instant that *Falcon*'s crew did. They didn't have the benefit of two Mages providing defensive shields, however, and the gunfight rapidly proved uneven.

The attackers took cover behind the promenade walls, carefully firing around corners as they began to approach more conservatively. They had Maria's people pinned, though, and it wasn't like they could move Rice or Akkerman.

"Xi?" she asked.

"Ma'am?"

"Take over the shield," she ordered the younger Mage. "I need to deal with these assholes."

Xi Wu *could*, she was sure, take out the remaining attackers. But the young Mage had yet to have to use that level of combat magic in the real world. If someone had to have nightmares over this, well, Maria already had that type of nightmare.

She felt Wu take over the shield, covering them from the attackers' gunfire, and released her part of it as she took a moment to carefully study their advancing enemies.

They were still coming, which didn't seem right. It wasn't like Maria and Wu were being subtle about their presence—and four men with guns, however brave or skilled, weren't enough to take down one Mage, let alone two.

Which meant there was another string to their bow.

She threw up a new shield, wrapping the entire group in a sphere of impenetrable force that stopped their own bullets, just in time. Even as the shield flickered into existence, glittering white fire hammered into it from at least three locations.

"Mages," she hissed. "They brought Mages."

"It's nice to be respected, I suppose," Skavar said flatly. "Look, I've stopped the bleeding and covered the lovely *sucking chest wound*, but the Captain needs real medical attention—fast."

"Akkerman is gone," Spiros said, her voice cold and distant. "Too many wounds, too much blood. There's nothing we could have done."

More Mage-fire and gunfire hammered into Maria's shield, and she hesitated. Everyone was looking to her for an answer and she didn't have one...and then she met Xi Wu's terrified eyes and realized she did.

"Xi, your wrist-comp has the program for jump calculations, right?" she asked.

"Yeah..."

"We've got *Falcon*'s scans of the Old Ring for angular vector. Plug it all in, calculate the jump. Get the Captain and Akkerman back to the ship with you. These fuckers are here for the Skipper; if he's gone..."

"They're not going to want to fight a full-on Mage duel in a space station," Skavar concluded. "How fast can you run that calc?"

Wu didn't answer him, already focused down on her computer.

"Not that fast," Maria admitted. "This could still be a really bad day."

The Marine Intelligence officer grimaced, then picked up the penetrator rifle he'd dropped to check on Rice.

"Let's share that bad day with our new friends, shall we?"

A fully trained Combat Mage knew half a dozen tricks for hiding their location while they were bombarding a target. It was rapidly becoming clear to Maria that their attackers, while quite well trained and powerful, were *not* Combat Mages.

Most of her focus was kept on protecting everyone, weaving and reinforcing the shield of force that was deflecting bullets and Mage-fire. More shooters had begun to materialize out of the woodwork as well, including somebody with a penetrator rifle who was quite probably the original sniper.

"Ivan, do you have that sniper dialed in?" she asked.

"Mostly. I can drop him, but it's a long-range shot with a high-power weapon," Skavar replied. "Collateral mess is inevitable."

"I'll weep for the Parchment Tigers later," she said. "Right now, I don't care if you breach the damn hull. Take that fucker down."

"Oh, I was *hoping* you'd say that," Skavar purred. The powered harness helped him lift the heavy rifle as he tracked his target. "To quote my drill sergeant from long ago: 'Hey, y'all, *watch this!*'"

An RMMC heavy penetrator rifle was usually a single-shot weapon. It fired a discarding sabot that contained a single tungsten flechette dart designed to punch through any body armor, up to and including exosuit armor.

The Royal Martian Marine Corps being the paranoids they were, the gun was heavily overengineered and entirely capable of fully automatic fire. Even an exosuit or a power harness couldn't absorb the recoil of a 22mm cannon firing half a dozen rounds a second.

Ivan Skavar ended up on the ground on his ass—but he kept the gun on target for three entire seconds, covering the sniper's location in a hail of armor-penetrating death.

"I really *hope* that got the bastard," he said after a moment, sounding short of breath. "Because that hurt a *lot* more than I expected it to."

For a few precious moments, the gunfire stopped. Part of it, Maria was sure, was sheer shock at the raw firepower Skavar had unleashed— but a lot of it was also waiting to see whether the hail of high-velocity penetrators had managed to breach the station hull.

As the silence faded, Wu made a soft cheer.

"I've got it." She hesitated. "I don't know how many I can take with me."

"Take the Captain and Akkerman," Maria said instantly. "The rest of us can get out of this on our own. Go!"

The younger Mage crouched over the wounded and dead men, laying a hand on each as she studied the numbers on her wrist-comp screen. She exhaled, closed her eyes...and was gone.

"I really hope she got the numbers right," Maria muttered to herself.

"Can't you tell?" Skavar asked.

"No," the Mage admitted. "I can't track a jump. There apparently are people who can, but I'm not one of them!"

A renewed hail of gunfire battered her shield.

"I don't think they've noticed he's gone yet," the Marine said grimly. "What do we do?"

"We move. Without the wounded, we can *do* that," she replied. "Come on. I think our appointment with the Shippers' Guild is going to have to wait."

One of the enemy Mages had made the mistake of both getting too close and getting between Maria Soprano and the way out for the people under her protection. She'd been playing softball because, frankly, she didn't want to have to kill anyone she didn't need to.

Her priority was getting *her* people out.

Her shield bubble moved with her and her team, back toward the corridor they'd originally come in through, but there were a Mage and half a dozen gunmen blocking the way. Probably intentionally positioned to make sure that Rice's people couldn't retreat.

The Mage had enough time to meet Maria's eyes before he learned that while the Navy didn't train Combat Mages, the officers of an amplifier-armed starship learned a lot of ways to make people die.

They were throwing fireballs. Maria threw ball lightning. A bolt of plasma arced from her hand to land at the Mage's feet and then exploded into a fragmenting cluster of electricity and superheated air.

None of the syndicate thugs even had time to scream before they died, and Maria's shield flung their bodies aside as she led her people to safety.

Once in the corridor, the gunfire died down and she looked around.

"Is everyone okay?" she asked.

"A few scrapes, but you kept us all pretty well covered," Skavar told her. "Do we expect trouble between here and the ship?"

"Probably," she admitted. "We'll see how brave they want to be after that mess, though. Plus, well." She gestured at the recessed and semi-concealed cameras. "They know David's gone now. We *should* be safe."

Skavar shook his head.

"Fuckers. I hope the Captain is okay."

"Dr. Gupta is good at his job," Maria said as reassuringly as she could. "He'll be fine."

The Chief of Security had had an even better look at the Captain's wounds than she had. His expression...wasn't promising.

CHAPTER 19

KELLY LAMONTE wouldn't call her obsessive watching of the radio channels and *Red Falcon*'s sensors paranoid.

Paranoia would require there not to be a real and active threat. Since she had every reason to expect both enemies and attacks, watching for them was hardly paranoia.

Potentially, the fact that all of *Red Falcon*'s RFLAM turrets were currently fully online and operating in a semi-autonomous defense mode was paranoia. If so, she could live with that. She didn't trust the Blue Star Syndicate's survivors not to decide to try and destroy the docked freighter.

Especially not as Skavar's people began to report in about the attack.

"Gupta, it's LaMonte," she snapped into the ship's intercom. "We have incoming wounded. The Captain's been hit—I'm not sure how bad, from what I'm getting, but it does not sound good."

"Damn," the ship's doctor replied. "How quickly? They're at nearly the opposite end of the station!"

"Wu's bringing him in," Kelly told him as she listened to the com chatter. "Teleport. Not sure where she's going to come in, but I'm guessing one of the flight bays."

They were big open spaces, and while Kelly wasn't a Mage, if *she* was teleporting fifteen kilometers with a dying companion, she'd go for the biggest open space she had.

"Nicolas," she pinged the ship's first pilot. "Wu is going to teleport in with the Captain. He's been shot; I'm guessing she's going for the big open spaces, which would be your bays.

"Have your people watching—we need to get the wounded to Gupta ASAP."

"I hear you," Nicolas replied grimly. "I'll pass the word."

Kelly continued to run down her list.

"Lieutenant Armand," she said, reaching out to Skavar's second in command. "Do you have a response team ready to go?"

"Aye," the Marine replied instantly. "One in exosuits, one in regular body armor."

Exosuits were rare enough aboard civilian ships that sending them out would draw far too much attention to *Red Falcon*, and with the Captain hopefully extracted...

"Load the exosuit team onto a boarding torpedo and prep it for if everything goes to absolute hell," she ordered. "Take the rest in to meet our people. Bring them home, Armand."

"Will do," the other woman replied. "I'll get everyone moving while *I* get out of this armor. Nobody else is taking my people into that shithole."

"That's your call, Armand," Kelly told her.

"This is Kelzin," her boyfriend's voice interrupted. "We have Wu and the Captain on the deck in Bay Bravo. I've got a stretcher team moving in; we'll have him in the medbay in sixty seconds."

Kelzin paused.

"We've got Akkerman as well, but...he's not as urgent."

Kelly winced. That was what she'd expected from listening to the coms.

"Understood," she said grimly. "Mike...can you prep the assault shuttles for a strike flight? I *think* this mess is resolved for now, but I want everything ready if we have to go full-court."

"On it."

Kelly leaned back in the Captain's command chair, hoping she'd covered everything—and hoping she wasn't going to have to order her crew to blow their cover to extract the remaining people aboard Junkertown.

If she had to, she'd blow holes in the station big enough to fly *Red Falcon* herself into. Hopefully...hopefully...things were enough under control to avoid that.

"David is in surgery with Dr. Gupta now," Kelly told Soprano over the radio. "Gods only know how that's going to go, but he's in the best hands he can be.

"Where are you at?"

"Moving halfway back to the cylinder," the Mage replied grimly. "So far, people seem to be just getting the hell out of our way. No new incidents."

"Armand is on her way to you with another squad," Kelly told the older woman. "I've got backup standing by if anything else goes to hell, and I've brought the RFLAM turrets to full defensive mode."

She shook her head.

"Short of shooting holes in the station, we've gone as far as we can."

"I don't think that'll be required," Soprano said with a chuckle. "I think our *friends* have realized David is back aboard; they certainly seem to be leaving us alone. We'll be back aboard in fifteen minutes."

"Okay. Your orders?" Kelly asked quietly.

"Fuck."

Soprano was silent for several seconds.

"Do we have anyone off-ship *other* than us and the rescue squad?" she finally asked.

"No," Kelly confirmed. "We had a few people outside, but I've pulled everyone back except a small guard outside the personnel connection. I've locked down every other way aboard the ship."

"Good call. Keep that one open till we get aboard, please, but then button up the ship," Soprano ordered. "We'll still want to find a cargo if we can, but I think we want to cut free of Junkertown for now.

"Start the clearance process."

"And if they don't want to expedite for us?" Kelly asked. She could guess the answer, but she wanted the confirmation.

"Then cut the umbilicals. They can sue the damn Tigers for it."

Tower Six's controllers clearly understood *exactly* where Kelly and her ship were. All of the umbilicals and connections were retracted by the time Soprano and the security troops made it back aboard, and Kelly had no problems breaking the big ship free of Junkertown and moving her away from the station.

"So, XO, how obvious are we being about the fact we've dialed in the Old Ring for weapons fire?" Soprano asked as she walked onto the bridge.

"I would never *dream* of threatening innocents like that," Kelly replied virtuously. "I just have the defensive-turret radar going at full force."

"Which, of course, we can't *possibly* use to target the missiles or battle lasers," Soprano replied dryly.

Kelly chuckled and gestured to Jeeves.

"Guns? I think that one is yours."

"Junkertown itself is basically unarmed," the Third Officer pointed out. "I don't think any of us actually want to be pointing guns at it, pissed as we all are. With the defensive radar going, I could certainly drop missiles into it and vaporize large chunks of the station, but nothing is overtly prepped for that.

"*These* six ships, on the other hand, are docked with the Old Ring and have power signatures that suggest they could be armed," he continued. "And while I'm using the turret radar...yeah, I doubt any of them missed us rotating the ship to align the battle lasers on them."

Kelly smiled.

"For some reason, they haven't so much as twitched."

"Good," Soprano replied. "Any news on David?"

Kelly's smile faded as she shook her head.

"Gupta's been in with him for over half an hour," she said in a small voice. "That means he's still with us, but..."

"Gupta is a fantastic doctor," Soprano told her gently. "If anyone can save David, it's him."

"We walked into this, hard."

"We did," the Ship's Mage agreed grimly. "That was the plan, but we misestimated our enemy. They'd been paying attention to how many guns we'd been swanning around with and went for a solution that negated all of that.

"If the sniper had been more experienced with distance shots in a pseudogravity environment, David would be gone already. These fuckers are *good* and we need to not let ourselves forget that."

Kelly looked at the screen showing Junkertown.

"Do you think we dragged them out into the open enough?"

"We won't know anytime soon," Soprano admitted. "Could be weeks."

"What do we do now?"

"What we did before we were MISS, I guess," the Mage said. "We find a cargo, we keep moving.

"We make sure the Captain doesn't die."

CHAPTER 20

"HE'LL LIVE."

Dr. Jaidev Gupta looked exhausted as he stripped off his gloves and looked frankly at the three officers standing in his waiting room.

"That's about as good as the news gets," he continued. "Right now, Captain Rice is in a medically-induced coma and hooked up to a ventilator, replacing the function of his left lung. He's lost about a meter of his intestines, though that injury is otherwise repaired and the long-term consequences pale in comparison to the rest.

"His left leg is gone about halfway down the thigh, and his right shoulder is shattered."

Gupta shook his head.

"I've pieced together the fragments of his shoulder and have them in a recon matrix. That will heal. The leg and the lung..." He sighed.

"The lung will need to be replaced. Cybernetic or vat-grown, it doesn't really matter. The leg will need a cybernetic.

"Obviously, I don't keep cybernetic lungs and legs on hand," the doctor concluded. "I have the skillset and gear for implantation, but we would need to acquire the parts. I *can* grow the Captain a new lung, though it will take time, and he can survive with only one once the initial injury has healed.

"Junkertown would have the cybernetics we need," Gupta told them. "So would the Legatans if we decided to dock there instead. In the absence of those replacements..."

He shrugged.

"I'll be able to bring him out of the coma in about thirty-six hours, at which point he'll be off the ventilator but completely unable to use his right arm for about another week. It will take me two months to grow him a cloned lung, or a single overnight surgery to install a cybernetic replacement.

"Same surgery time for the leg, though we have to buy the part. Until we have the replacement limb, however, he'll be wheelchair- or zero-gee-bound."

Maria sighed.

"I don't want to make the decision on cybernetic or regrown for him," she said. "If he'll be conscious in a few days, we'll want to hold off until then."

Gupta nodded.

"That would be my preference as well, obviously," he told them. "Even in the case of the leg, where cybernetic is the only replacement option, I would prefer to go over the potential options with the Captain before acquiring the part. Even if the selection here is limited, I would prefer to wait to install a limb that met his requirements than install hardware that didn't."

Hardware.

Maria sighed. She hated that word when it came to replacement human parts. Most cybernetics were good enough that no one could tell the difference—and she'd met Legatan Augments who were something like ninety percent machinery by body mass and could pass for unmodified if you didn't know what to look for.

"Keep us informed, Doctor," she told him, then looked around at the other officers.

"For now, I'm acting captain unless one of you or Kellers has an issue?" she said.

Jeeves looked *terrified* at the thought of arguing, and LaMonte just laughed.

"I don't feel qualified to be XO, let alone Captain," the younger woman told her. "I'm behind you."

"Good. Because thirty-six hours is too long for us to just sit here, orbiting Junkertown and looking threatening. We need to find a cargo to get us *out* of this godforsaken system."

"Well, let's see if that broker at the Shippers' Guild is willing to talk to us still," LaMonte suggested. "I doubt *she* knew it was a trap, after all."

"And if she did?" Jeeves asked.

"Then I doubt she'll take Mage Soprano's calls!"

"Ma'am...ma'ams...officers." Skavar found them right outside the clinic, stumbling over his words. The security chief looked...afraid?

"You need to hear this," he told them.

"What is it?" Maria asked.

"The news."

Skavar hit a button on his wrist-comp and the audio starting playing again, an unfamiliar jingle ringing in *Red Falcon*'s plain corridors.

"...those just joining us, this is Junkertown Stationwide News, coming to you every hour of every day until this shithole falls apart.

"To repeat and bring everyone up to speed, we appear to have a follow-up to yesterday's gunfight in the Old Ring.

"Now, folks, this is Junkertown and we are not strangers to the odd murder or gang violence, but yesterday was something else entirely...and today is something completely new.

"What passes for authorities in the Old Ring tried to keep our reporters out, but they've hauled too many bodies out of the Vesuvius Hotel to hide it now, and they've let our Jorge Daniels onto the scene."

A new voice came on.

"This is Jorge Daniels, for JSN, from inside the Vesuvius Hotel in the Old Ring," the new speaker introduced himself, swallowing after speaking to try and gain some level of calm. "It is...a slaughterhouse in here. The Tigers aren't talking as to what they know or what the cameras saw, but I'm standing in the lobby and I can see...eight, nine bodies they haven't got to yet.

"Cut up, shot down, dead. Like discarded toys..." There was the distinctive sound of someone about to throw up, and the sound cut back to the first speaker.

"As Daniels said, we don't have a lot of information beyond that the Vesuvius Hotel appears to have been the scene of a massacre unparalleled in Junkertown history. What JSN *has* confirmed is that Parchment Tiger Blue Dragon Antonio Lawrence was in the hotel and has been removed...in pieces.

"No one is quite sure who was present in the building or why one of the Tigers' top leadership was there, but from the images Daniels has sent back, there was some kind of meeting or conference going on...and someone decided to end—"

Skavar turned off the channel.

"They started talking about it fifteen minutes ago," he told *Red Falcon's* senior officers. "I'd say the Vesuvius was hosting the conference we were looking for."

"*Was* being the operative word," Maria replied, shaking her head. "I doubt anyone is going to weep for a bunch of gang lords, but...damn. That's a lot of dead people with a lot of money and power behind them.

"*I* certainly wouldn't have picked that fight."

"Whoever did this either didn't expect to be traced or is backed by enough firepower that they have no fear of Blue Star's successors," Jeeves said quietly. "The only group that comes to mind for that is...well...MISS.

"Us."

The word hung in the room like a stone for several moments, but then Maria shook her head.

"That's not MISS's style," she said. "Use them as stalking horses? Sure, that *was* the plan—but we had agents in place to try and follow everyone home, use the conference as a center point to bring down all of the successor syndicates.

"If we were going to crush the conference, we'd do it with Marines and stunners and mass public arrests," she continued. "No, I don't think this was Mars—if only because I *know* what MISS's plan for this mess was."

"What about the other syndicates?" LaMonte asked. "I know we dealt the Mafia a blow helping take down Darkport, but last I heard, Julian Falcone had been broken out of prison. And they're not the only ones out there."

"No, they're not," Maria agreed. "The Blue Star Syndicate absorbed a dozen lesser crime organizations to get to its size and made a lot of enemies along the way. There are a lot of people out there who wouldn't want it rebuilt—and many of them are ruthless enough to massacre an entire hotel to make sure it didn't happen."

Most of them would probably have gone in for bombs, in her experience, but that didn't mean there weren't groups that would have sent in thugs with knives as a matter of *style*.

"We don't have enough data, and frankly, it's not our problem now," she told the rest of them. "We keep our ears to the ground and we find a cargo and we get *out* of this system before someone decides to start trying to chop us up."

She shook her head as the others shivered.

"We're a target as long as we're here," she concluded. "If we don't find a cargo in the next twenty-four hours, we get the hell out of Snap regardless.

"Unless we're loading cargo, the Captain does *not* wake up in this star system!"

Back in her office, Maria took several moments to simply rest her face in her hands and breathe. She couldn't think of anything she could have done differently—beyond not letting the Captain trawl himself out as bait—but she couldn't help feel responsible.

Maintaining the shield for the entire trip would have been impossible; at her best, she could only hold a defensive screen for about thirty minutes—and that time dropped dramatically if she was moving it.

Maybe if she'd got it up faster...but that was borrowing trouble. She could easily what-if her way into paralysis, and she had an entire starship to take care of.

Pouring herself a coffee, she focused and brought up the file Rice had put together on the broker they were talking to. She had contacts throughout Junkrat and even on Flytrap itself. If anyone could find them cargo, it would be her.

When she punched in the number, however, it connected instantly... and *not* to the broker she'd been calling.

Her screen now showed her what looked like a mid-tier hotel room, the camera looking down from a wallscreen across a row of empty bottles at a cross-legged man in a kimono with his eyes closed.

"I'm sorry, I think this is—"

"You entered the correct number, Mage Soprano," the stranger told her. Something in his build and stance warned her that this wasn't a man to take lightly. His scalp was shaved clean, with specks of dark stubble across it, and the kimono was tight across shoulder muscles that might have been distracting for Maria in other circumstances.

"You have the advantage of me," she told him. "Not least in hacking my communications."

A small smile flitted across the man's face.

"I didn't hack your communications, Mage Soprano," he noted. "I hacked the Shippers' Guild's communications. *Red Falcon*'s systems defeated my people. I am...impressed."

"All right, so you're showing off," she said sharply. "Who *are* you?"

"You don't need to know my actual name," he replied. "It's better for everyone if you don't. You can call me Blade."

"'Blade'," Maria echoed sardonically. "Is that supposed to be intimidating?"

"No," Blade said shortly. "I find I rarely need to attempt to be intimidating. You can call me Agent Blade, if you prefer. I work for the Legatus Military Intelligence Directorate, and I owe you a small thank-you."

Maria managed to hide a shiver. Sussing out more of LMID's operations was part of *Red Falcon*'s mandate, but she hadn't been expecting to have an LMID agent simply...open communications with them.

"A thank-you?" she asked carefully.

"We'd been using the Parchment Tigers as a window into the operations of the Blue Star Syndicate's leftovers for a while, but we missed the Azure Legacy using them as hosts for their little reunion conference.

"Legatus finds the fragmented syndicates *far* too useful to allow Blue Star to reform. Measures had to be taken, and we wouldn't have known if your presence hadn't brought the Legacy into the open.

"So, again, thank you."

That had not been an expected result of poking Legacy with a stick. Maria made the connection between the name he'd given her and the description of the bodies in the Vesuvius as "cut up."

"You could have sent flowers," she said drily.

"I could," he agreed. "Or money. Money always seems to go over well with private contractors. As it happens, however, I think we can both be of use to each other still."

Maria hesitated, then sighed.

"I'm listening, Agent Blade."

"Azure Legacy wants to destroy you," Blade said calmly. "For various reasons, LMID wants Azure Legacy destroyed. We share an enemy, and you possess a resource I do not: a jump-ship."

"You need transportation," she said slowly.

"I and ten others, mostly Augments, need to reach the Atlatl System," he confirmed. "We are quite capable of keeping to ourselves, Mage Soprano, and I assure you we will cause no trouble.

"My team are *not* counter-Mage enforcers like the Augments in Legatus," he continued. "Indeed, the non-Augment member of my team is a Mage, though not a Jump Mage."

"And other than striking at a common enemy, what do we get out of this?" Maria asked.

He smiled, opening his eyes for the first time. There was no question in Maria's mind that this man was an Augment, but he didn't have the square eyes typical of them. He was clearly one of the infiltration models MISS was quite certain existed but had no proof of.

No proof of until now, anyway.

Blade's eyes were actually quite pretty, she noted absently, a sparkling warm green that contrasted sharply with his flat expression—and the fact she was quite certain he'd personally cut up half a hotel in the last twenty-four hours.

"As I said, money always seems to go over well," he noted. "There is a cargo destined for Atlatl that is waiting for an Integrity Galactic freighter that is scheduled to arrive in a few days.

"I will arrange for that cargo to be carried on *Red Falcon*. You will be paid above-market rates for rapid delivery and to carry twelve extra persons alongside the cargo.

"Is this sufficient, Mage Soprano? More can be arranged, but this would be the cleanest method of compensation."

"I will need to consult with my Captain," Maria replied.

"Please, Mage Soprano, I don't know how long David Rice will be out of affairs, but I know you are acting Captain," Blade pointed out. "The call is yours. There is only so much time to work with."

"I will need to consult with my other officers, then," she told him. "I will not make the decision on the spur of the moment, *Agent* Blade."

He smiled.

"Fair, Mage Soprano. The number you have will continue to reach me for some time longer. We will speak again."

He didn't move or touch a control, but the screen cut to black, and Maria exhaled a long sigh.

This was not making life simpler.

CHAPTER 21

"SO, THAT'S LMID'S OFFER," Maria summarized to her small audience. In a normal ship, the Chief of Security didn't really have a role in this kind of decision. They were often an unofficial "Fifth Officer", but since they weren't Mate-certified or Mages, they didn't usually get a vote.

Since *Red Falcon* wasn't really a civilian freighter anymore, however, the man in charge of the Marines who pretended to be her security detail at least got to sit in the meetings.

Part of that, Maria reflected, was that with the Captain out of commission, they were running sorely short on experienced senior officers. Kellers was a solid, competent engineer, but he didn't *want* to be in charge.

Jeeves was an oddity, unused to his current role though doing well as a department head and experienced in general. LaMonte was still inexperienced, learning her job—though proving to be damn good at it.

But the five of them felt...lacking in something that David Rice had. Confidence forged by years of experience, knowledge...something like that, Maria reflected.

"We need a cargo," LaMonte finally concluded. "There aren't many to be had in this system that are worth us hauling. And they're right that we share an enemy."

"There's a certain value in delivering a hit squad from one of our enemies to the other," Skavar pointed out. "Amusement value, if nothing else. 'Hey, guys, let's you and him fight.'"

"I'd prefer more value than amusement if we're going to be hauling Augments on this ship," Maria said dryly. "They may not be specifically Mage-killers, but killing Mages is what Augments were built for.

"And these appear to be infiltration models—Blade is, if nothing else."

"Confirming the existence of those alone has value to the Protectorate," Skavar reminded her.

"I can set up a program in the ship's internal scanners to watch them at all hours," Kellers noted. "We'd be certain they didn't do anything we didn't allow—and we'd have a massive quantity of data on the infiltration Augments to provide the Protectorate."

"If we betray LMID's trust that badly, they may realize it," Jeeves warned quietly. "These aren't guys who play nice. They just *wiped out* a conference of gang lords to maintain a temporary advantage. Blue Star scares me...and these are the guys who scare Blue Star."

"So are we," LaMonte said flatly. "Both MISS and us, specifically. We've left pieces of Blue Star, Azure Legacy and other Blue Star successor syndicates scattered across half the fucking galaxy.

"If LMID wants to play? We'll play. They want to fuck with Azure Legacy? Let's throw our enemies at each other. We work for *Mars*, people. Are we really going to be intimidated by Legatus?"

Maria chuckled.

"For a moment there, XO, you sounded like a Navy officer," she told LaMonte. "And you're right. I see a lot of possible benefits for us and for MISS if we take this deal—and I won't deny I want to be out of this system *yesterday.*"

"A bird in the hand is worth two in the wind," Kellers said quietly. "This gets us out of Snap—and out of UnArcana space, too. Your call, Ship's Mage."

"But you think we should do it," Maria concluded for him. She looked around. "Anyone got a counterargument?"

"Not really," Jeeves admitted. "Just a general sense of foreboding doom. But...don't we need some cyber parts for the Skipper?"

"Eventually," Maria agreed.

"Legatus makes the best," the gunner reminded her. "See if they can throw them in as a bonus. If we're gonna do this, let's soak them for all we can!"

Whatever Maria wanted to say about LMID—and she had a *lot* to say about a covert organization that seemed to be busy with treason— they were certainly efficient. From her getting back in touch with "Agent Blade" to the cargo being confirmed to the cargo starting to load was under twelve hours.

The cargo in question was...less innocent than she'd prefer. Apparently, among its other magnificent qualities, Junkrat was the primary trans-shipment point for arms exports from Legatus. Atlatl, it appeared, was completely re-equipping its ground, sea, air and space forces with new equipment.

The containers being loaded onto *Red Falcon* contained two hundred assault shuttles, a thousand orbital cutters, five thousand tanks, three thousand aircraft, ten thousand armored personnel carriers, eight thousand exosuits and over a million carbines, battle lasers and penetrator rifles.

Plus, approximately three million tons of munitions for all of the above. It was almost a surprise that the rearmament program was actually mentioned in their most recent MISS updates. Atlatl was being quite up-front about replacing the gear their planetary forces were currently equipped with—since the average age of their existing gear was apparently around sixty years old.

It seemed there was also an order in with Tau Ceti for four destroyers to provide heavy support to that fleet of assault shuttles and cutters.

MISS suspected there was more going on than just a desire to re-place an aging fleet of armored vehicles and light spacecraft, but if they'd dug anything up that wasn't public, it wasn't in Maria's update.

Atlatl was far from poor, but the level of upgrading they were do-ing was staggering. They had to have invested enough money in the purchases from Legatus to have built a homegrown armament industry—though such an industry probably wouldn't have been able to provide as wide a breadth of equipment.

"Ship's Mage?" the voice of Corporal Spiros interrupted her review of the data on the cargo.

"Yes, Corporal?"

"Our guests are here."

Maria nodded grimly.

"I'll be right down."

The guards had been smart enough to pull the entire party aboard *Red Falcon* while waiting for the officers, and the four women and eight men were standing calmly next to their gear when Maria arrived.

Agent Blade was standing in front of his people and nodded cheerfully to her as she arrived.

"Mage Soprano," he greeted her, sweeping his hand back over his people. "This is my team. If you let us know where you want us to set up camp, we'll get out of your hair for the rest of the trip to Atlatl."

He smiled. For a murdering psychopathic cyborg, he had far too nice a smile.

"I imagine everyone will be happier if my people stay out of the way of your crew," he continued. "None of us know an ion engine from a power conduit, so we wouldn't be much help."

"That's fair," Maria agreed with a nod. "I'll have someone show you to the quarters we've set aside. Do you have any particular needs we should be aware of?"

Blade shrugged.

"The Augments need a far higher quotient of minerals and metals in their food than you'll have in your kitchen, but we brought supplements for that," he told her. "Feed us what you'd feed anybody else and we'll be fine.

"As for needs..." He picked up one of the two duffle bags at his feet and handed it to her. Despite the casual ease with which he lifted it, it was surprisingly heavy, and she opened it to find two shrink-wrapped plain white boxes. One was the full length of the bag, easily a meter long, where the other was maybe twenty centimeters by thirty.

"Military Augment-grade replacements," he noted. "One leg—adjustable to be either right or left if your surgeon is capable of the installation at all. One lung—hooks into the airway, provides full control of oxygen intake and a secondary oxygen reservoir."

Blade tapped his own chest.

"I've got two of the lungs, and they're the best upgrade we have," he told her. "I hope this all helps your Captain get back on his feet. My superiors are quite enthused with your Captain Rice."

"It should," Maria agreed, closing the bag. "We can only hope. He was quite badly injured."

"Believe me, Mage Soprano, the people who ordered that are *much* worse off," Blade told her with that same warm grin.

What had been attractive when he was being helpful was disturbing when he was bragging about mass murder.

CHAPTER 22

DAVID WOKE SLOWLY. Very slowly. It was like a fog was slowly lifting from his mind as he came back to wakefulness and then began to blink.

He blinked several times before his vision could focus, and then he remembered how he'd ended up unconscious and reached toward his chest. One of his arms refused to respond and he half-panicked, looking over to see his right shoulder coated in a heavy, immobilizing cast.

His chest was wrapped in bandages and several tubes still protruded from his immobilized right arm.

"Take it easy, Skipper," Dr. Gupta's reassuring baritone told him. "You had a rough few minutes and you're still coming back together. I kept you in an induced coma while the worst of the damage that could heal did."

"*Could heal*, huh?" David echoed, then coughed. His throat was dry and clogged—and the doctor was handing him a glass of water.

"Drink," Gupta ordered.

David obeyed, the doctor watching in silence.

"How bad?" he asked after finishing the water, his throat feeling less like a desert.

"You're short a lung and a leg," the doctor said flatly. "Your shoulder will be immobilized for at least another two weeks—and be thankful for modern medicine at that! We're not that many years away from when the degree of shattering your scapula underwent would have meant you needing an artificial replacement from the shoulder down."

Wincing, David patted at the blankets covering where he thought his legs had been. He might be conscious, but he was still tanked to the gills on painkillers, so he hadn't *noticed* he was missing one.

As the blankets settled over his limbs, that became obvious, though, and he sighed.

"How long was I out?" he asked.

"Just over three days," the doctor told him. "We're four jumps out from Snap now."

"Heading where?" David demanded. It was entirely within Soprano's authority to take on a cargo and move the ship if he was out, but he did need to know where they were going.

"Atlatl, carrying cargo for the military there," Gupta explained. "I don't know a lot of the details; you'll want to pin down Soprano or the rest of the senior officers for that."

David nodded, sighing as he studied his battered body.

"So, one lung, huh?" he asked. "I don't feel short of breath."

"You won't, unless you try and carry out strenuous exercise," the doctor told him. "You'll feel it pretty damned quickly then. Of course, exercise will be hard when you're missing a leg. I've got a wheelchair ready for you until you tell me you're ready for surgery."

"Cybernetics," he said quietly. Protectorate medical science wasn't up to regrowing limbs, though it could regrow most organs. "What about the lung?"

"I have the gear to clone you a new one," Gupta told him. "Or, well, the ridiculously insane cyber-leg we have as an available option came with a matching lung."

"What cyber-leg are we talking about?" David asked.

"Thanks to our Ship's Mage, there's a military Augment-grade cyber-limb—with hip reinforcements, thankfully—sitting in a sterile box on the other side of sick bay. There's a military Augment-grade cyber-lung to go with it."

David considered the full meaning of that.

"Augment-grade?" he asked.

"Legatan," Gupta explained. "They make the best cybernetics in the Protectorate, and they keep the military-grade stuff to themselves...and the Augment-grade stuff under even closer watch.

"LMID apparently *likes* you, Captain. This stuff is outside my training and experience, though thankfully, the installation is basically the same."

"LMID gave us Augment-grade cybernetics for me?" David asked. "When did we even start talking to LMID?!"

"After an LMID Augment infiltrator team fucking *massacred* every member of Azure Legacy's little conference," Soprano told him. He looked up to see his Ship's Mage closing the door behind her.

"We cut a deal: they got us a cargo and the best possible cybernetics for you, we carried that infiltrator team to Atlatl," she continued. "They're keeping to themselves and haven't turned into a problem yet.

"How is he doing, doc?" she asked, addressing the question to Gupta.

"I woke him up, didn't I?" the doctor said grumpily. "Look, I need time to examine him, and then *he* needs to decide if he wants to go down for implantation now or later.

"I know he's the Captain and he needs to be briefed, but..."

"But that's enough for now?" Soprano asked.

Gupta sighed.

"Not really," he admitted. "That's up to you guys. Look, I'll run the scanners while you jabber.

"Here."

He passed a tablet over to David. "That's the specs on the two parts the Legatans gave us. There isn't anything *better* out there, though there are other options if you'd prefer. I can get you a catalog later.

"For now, you read, she talks, I poke. Got it?"

The loss of breath from the missing lung became more apparent to David over the course of the conversation. It was hard for him, though some of that was almost certainly the painkillers, but Soprano's summary of the events of the last few days was breathtaking.

"I see we owe Ms. Wu a raise," he noted after she told him about the Mage teleporting him out. "That was clever and effective. Why didn't you bring everyone out that way?"

"Wu could bring two with her. I could bring three. Maybe four," Soprano told him. "Evacuating the wounded, sure, but I wasn't leaving half of the security detail behind. Not while we were still under fire and, well..." She shrugged. "I was relatively sure I could get everyone out. It was only really a question of how many people I had to kill."

Her last sentence was so matter-of-fact, it sent a shiver down David's spine. Just what had he dragged his officers—his *friends*—into when he'd signed up with MISS?

"And this Agent Blade?" he asked.

"He seems to be aboveboard, if fucking terrifying," she said. "But... he's an infiltration cyborg, an assassin." She shook her head. "I'm afraid of what we might be delivering him to do, even if it is being done to Azure Legacy."

"'Pay evil unto evil' and all that," David agreed, his working hand gently tracing the outline of the cast over his shoulder. "My sympathy for Mikhail Azure's leftovers is limited, but the concept of cyborg assassins makes me uncomfortable."

"And becoming a cyborg yourself?" Soprano asked, gesturing at the tablet in his hand.

He sighed.

"How long until we arrive in Atlatl?"

"About fifty-two hours," his Ship's Mage told him. "If you give Gupta the go-ahead, you should be walking and breathing by the time we get there."

"That's optimistic," the doctor interrupted. "The cyber-lung is autonomous. The leg is not so much, and even the lung has functions you will need to learn.

"*Implantation* will be done by the time we arrive in Atlatl, but it will be...days, at least, before you can walk normally.

"Weeks before you can fully use the extended functions of the implants. You will still be wheelchair-bound when we arrive in Atlatl, whatever we do."

"But that rehab and learning can't start until the limb is attached," David said.

"Exactly," Gupta agreed. "Whenever we do implantation, you'll be down for twenty-fours for each implant. Unconscious, general sedation. Nerves are *not* attached easily. The lung will be perfectly functional for normal uses as soon as implantation is complete, and some of the toxin filters and similar defenses will operate automatically.

"The oxygen reservoirs and some of the other options will require training to use. The leg will definitely require training, but...the sooner everything is *in* you, the sooner we can train you to use it."

David nodded.

"How's the ship, Maria?"

"Kelly has it surprisingly in hand," his Ship's Mage reported. "I play Captain so that she doesn't feel *too* overwhelmed, and she takes care of everything. She's turning into a damned fine XO, Skipper."

"Well, if you have everything in hand, it sounds like I can take a nice long nap," David replied. "Any concerns if I tell the good doctor to get started?"

Soprano snorted.

"About twelve and a half million of them, but nothing critical," she told him. "I won't say I'm not eager to give you the ship back, but I'd rather have a whole Captain in a few days than a stressed, exhausted, broken one right now."

"Thanks, I appreciate the vote of confidence," he replied, then looked over at Gupta. "Would you even let me get back to work if I said to hold off on the implants?"

"Not a chance in bloody hell," the doctor replied. "Regardless of whether we proceed with implantation, you need to spend the next week resting. Briefed and consulted, yes. In command from the bridge? No."

David chuckled.

"Then I see no reason to delay," he noted. "Let me get a meal into me, and then I think you may as well knock me out and start hooking up nerves."

CHAPTER 23

"JUMP COMPLETE," Xi Wu reported in a drained voice. "Welcome to the Atlatl System."

"Thanks, Xi," Kelly told her girlfriend, her attention torn between her exhausted-sounding lover and the sensor data on the star system.

Duty won out.

"Go rest," she ordered the Mage. "Next stop is Nahuatl, but we're still twelve hours out."

Wu nodded and the video link to the simulacrum chamber closed, leaving Kelly looking over the sensor data flowing in from *Red Falcon*'s various passive arrays.

Atlatl was an odd system in that the inhabitable worlds didn't orbit inside the normal liquid water zone for their F-type star's strength. Instead, a midsized gas giant named Teotihuacan orbited just outside the regular habitable zone, the additional heat from the gas giant's presence rendering three of its moons habitable.

Nahuatl, Macahuitl, and Tepoztopilli were each significantly larger than Earth's moon, dense enough with heavy metals that all three had gravities ranging from seventy to eighty percent of Earth standard.

The three moons would have seen massive mining efforts for those heavy metals—except that Teotihuacan had four other moons that had been too small or too fast to retain atmosphere or life. With three distinct ecosystems to protect and learn from, and four barren rocks to work from, Atlatl's populace had chosen to place all of the mining and most of the heavy industry either on the barren moons or in orbit between the seven worldlets that orbited Teotihuacan.

Nahuatl was the largest moon and the farthest out. Its thick atmosphere and wide oceans actually made it the warmest of the three moons, a temperate tropical paradise that had inevitably ended up as the seat of the system government.

"Well, at least flying through this mess is easier than traveling around Puck," Kelly observed aloud. "Jeeves, what have we got for company?"

"Half a dozen local militia corvettes, Mars-built but old," the Third Officer reported. "Looks like forty to fifty in-system ships making their rounds around Teotihuacan. Bunch of jump-ships docked at the orbitals—looks like five or six total.

"It's hard to say. Lots of small orbitals."

Kelly nodded. Each of Teotihuacan's seven major moons had its own orbital station. Nahuatl's was the biggest and the main stopping point for jump-ships, but any of the seven could handle ships up to *Red Falcon*'s size.

Nahuatl Orbital was the only place where you could dock more than one starship, but the seven stations provided the system with an impressive port capacity, all told.

The executive officer tapped a few commands, lighting the freighter's engines up.

"Twelve hours, twenty-six minutes to Nahuatl Orbital," she announced aloud. "The cargo is for the system government, and for some strange reason, they hang out on the planet with the beaches."

Jeeves chuckled.

"I can't blame them. Any idea what our chances of shore leave are?"

"Ask the Captain," Kelly replied with a grin. David was all but strapped to his bed in the infirmary to stop him injuring himself with his new leg, but he was conscious enough to be the one making calls like that.

And once they'd off-loaded their various deadly cargos, it would be up to him where *Red Falcon* went next.

"Unknown vessel, this is Teotihuacan Security Control," a calm female voice said on the transmission. "Please identify yourself and your purpose for approaching Nahuatl. You aren't on our list, and frankly, antimatter engines make everybody nervous."

"They're being a bit more than nervous, ma'am," Jeeves reported. "All six of those rustbuckets they call a militia are maneuvering to rendezvous at an intercept point along our course, and we just got pinged by long-range sensors from something *much* more modern in Tepoztopilli orbit."

"How are we defining 'much more modern'?" Kelly asked. "That covers a lot of bases."

"I'm defining it as 'has enough stealth and ECM that I can't make it out from this far away'," the gunner said bluntly. "I'm *guessing* remote radar platform feeding a set of orbital missile batteries, but it could be a destroyer."

Kelly shook her head.

"There is *definitely* more going on here than they've told anyone," she murmured. "Well, let's chat and see if we can calm them down."

She activated the microphone of the captain's chair and turned on her camera.

"Teotihuacan Security Control, this is Second Officer Kelly LaMonte of the independent charter freighter *Red Falcon*," she greeted them chirpily. She didn't have to fake bright cheeriness very often, but she was perfectly capable of doing so when she wasn't actually feeling cheerful.

"We're operating under contract to Integrity Galactic Transport to deliver your shipment from Diamond Arms Brokerage on Legatus." She smiled. "We would *very* much prefer not to get shot at, but as you can see from the engines, this is a former Navy Armed Auxiliary Fast Heavy Freighter. If you feel you have to shoot missiles at us, we can take it."

Most of a minute ticked away slowly...and then the female voice responded with a chuckle as her video feed kicked in. The voice's owner was an older woman with short-cropped silvering hair and a loose-fitting dark-purple uniform.

"I think we can refrain from that, Officer LaMonte," she replied. "This is Commodore Aleksandrina Al-Mufti. If you've got my assault shuttles and cutters aboard, you may be my new favorite merchant ship, regardless of our local heart attack at your arrival."

"From the bills of lading I received from Integrity and Diamond, we have the full order," Kelly told her. "From the shuttles to the exosuits."

"A lot of people are going to be very happy to see you, then, Officer LaMonte. You're clear to Nahuatl Orbital. Would you object if my corvettes escort you in?"

There was about a forty-second lag between each of their communications, but the Commodore kept her smile focused on the camera as she waited for Kelly's response.

"I'm always fond of having cops between me and potential bad guys," Kelly told her. "Your ships are more than welcome to bring us in, though I'll note that *Falcon* is quite capable of taking care of herself." She paused.

"Is there a reason for the paranoia, ma'am?" she asked. "This all seems...a bit much."

"I wish it was," Al-Mufti replied. "I can't say much, Officer LaMonte, but let's just say I have reasons to want to be *very* sure your cargo arrives unharmed!

"I look forward to speaking with you and your Captain when you arrive. Safe flight, Officer LaMonte."

The channel cut out and Kelly shook her head, her cheerfulness subduing.

"Who died?" she wondered aloud.

"I don't know," Jeeves replied. "But I think you're right. Somebody died...or perhaps more accurately, was killed."

CHAPTER 24

THE FIRST FEW HOURS of physiotherapy hadn't achieved much more than highlighting to David just how far he had to go. As *Red Falcon* made her way in toward Nahuatl, he and Dr. Gupta bundled him into a wheelchair, with the governors on his new leg turned up to maximum.

Without the governors limiting what the limb could do, he was at risk of accidentally destroying the wheelchair with an unexpected "muscle" spasm. With them limited, the leg wasn't much more than an expensive paperweight of metal, polymer and electronics, but it would improve.

With his right arm still immobilized, one of the crew had to wheel him into the transfer bay where the Legatan detachment was waiting. From what the crew told him, they'd kept to themselves the whole trip, which was about all anyone had wanted from them.

"Captain Rice," the tallest of them, presumably Agent Blade, greeted him with a smile. "A pleasure to meet you at last. Your crew has been most accommodating and helpful, but it is always a privilege to meet a man of your reputation."

David chuckled.

"There's only about half of me left," he noted. "How much of my reputation is attached to that?"

Blade echoed the chuckle, shaking his head.

"It will not be long until you feel you are all you again," he told David. "The initial dysphoria passes quite quickly. Your leg will feel like yours long before it's actually properly working."

"You would know, I suppose," David allowed. Right now, it didn't feel much like a limb, more like a weight attached to his hip. That had to pass. Blade, for example, probably didn't have an actual organic limb left, but he didn't seem bothered.

"I must thank you and your crew for your assistance," the LMID agent continued after a moment. "We have ways to enter the Protectorate, but most of them are known to the Legacy, as several of our former Blue Star partners have betrayed us.

"You have allowed us to enter Atlatl without our shared enemy knowing we're coming." Blade's smile narrowed, turning more predatory.

"They will regret making an enemy of us both," he concluded. A harsh vibration ran through the decking as *Red Falcon* connected with the dock, and Blade winced. "I see your pilot is still learning," he said drily. "That's...much more noticeable to me than you, perhaps."

"She was an engineer; she's learning," David replied. "She's doing fine."

Blade chuckled again.

"That she is. It's just the *learning* is very noticeable. Nonetheless, I think that is our cue." He gestured to his people to start collecting their bags.

"I wish you the best with your new parts, Captain Rice. We have our own way home from here once our mission is complete," he told David. "Thank you once again for your assistance."

"I hope your mission won't spill back on us," David told him. "You'll pardon me if I don't wish you luck."

"Legacy may make the connection," Blade admitted. "They'll have the data and they're not stupid; they just have incompatible objectives to you and me.

"There will be no...formal repercussions, let us say," he promised. "The authorities will not trace us to you; I can promise you that."

"I'll hold you to that," David told him. He didn't really have a way to hold LMID to that, but the promise stood anyway.

And in the worst case, well, it wasn't like David didn't have a get-out-of-jail-free card for local authorities. It was just that using it would leave his enemies and allies asking questions he didn't want them thinking about too hard.

David's caretaker slowly wheeled him onto the bridge, where Kelly LaMonte and Maria Soprano were both standing by his chair, watching the screen.

"Ladies, how are we doing?" he asked, stopping to cough in the middle as he suddenly found himself short of breath. His new lung was working, but it occasionally got confused and cut out, leaving his organic lung to try and carry the weight on its own unexpectedly.

"Aren't you barred from the bridge?" Soprano asked.

"Barred from *commanding* from the bridge," David corrected. "But since we're not in flight, I figure it's okay. Our good doctor will tell me later if I'm wrong," he finished with a smile.

"It's good to see you around and about," LaMonte told him. "The locals want to meet with the three of us once they start off-loading. They seem…"

"Twitchy," Soprano finished. "Or paranoid, however you want to phrase it. They almost started shooting at us when we showed up."

"And it was the antimatter engines that freaked them out," David's XO added. "Something odd is going on here."

"We'll keep our ears to the ground, see if we can fill in MISS on what's going on," he told them. "We probably don't want to get involved, not unless it turns out to be the Legacy. There's an entire local MISS branch to take care of Atlatl's problems."

"About that…" LaMonte shook her head. "We pinged the com address we had with the call-and-response code. Nothing. Not a wrong response. *No* response."

"That's not good," David agreed. "Do our files include any secondary contact methods for this system?"

"Just the standard call-and-response and a communication address," she replied. "We don't know the physical location of the office or anything. I was hoping to get an update on the situation, see if MISS knows what the issue here is."

"If the office is out of communication, the Protectorate needs to know that," David said quietly. "Where's the nearest RTA?"

Runic Transceiver Arrays were massive constructions of magic and runes that allowed a Mage to project their voice across the light-years to another RTA. They took years and vast quantities of money to build, but they were the only method of interstellar communication faster than a ship.

"Sandoval," Soprano told him. "Sixteen light-years."

"Start charting a course," David ordered. "We'll come up with an excuse to fly without a cargo if we need to. We can't trust this to a courier, not if an entire MISS office has gone silent."

"I think you're all underestimating just how twitchy these folks are," Jeeves interrupted, the tactical officer joining them around the captain's chair and tapping a command on the repeater screens.

The screen on the chair arm now mirrored the gunnery officer's own console, showing a circle of glowing orange icons in orbit above Tepoztopilli.

"We got pinged from Tepoztopilli orbit on our way in," he reminded them. "I couldn't pick up what was pinging us, and I thought it was because they were playing games; there's not a lot you can do to hide in space, but there's a few things.

"The problem was that I was looking for *one* emitter," he concluded. "Tepoztopilli orbit is currently home to twelve, plus forty-two receivers.

"A distributed Very Large Array, providing them with functionally perfect resolution on anything on this side of Teotihuacan. It's homebuilt but *very* capable."

"Data like that is only useful if you've got something to use it with," David said quietly.

"The corvettes could use it for extra-long-range missile fire," Jeeves told them, "but its main intended user is these guys."

Larger orange icons flickered into existence in Tepoztopilli orbit. And Nahuatl orbit. And Macahuitl orbit. Sixty icons distributed unevenly between the three moons. Another dozen icons in their own orbits of Teotihuacan between the moons. A handful more above the barren moons being mined.

"Like the sensors, the missile platforms are homebuilt," Jeeves told them. "I got a good look at one of the ones in Nahuatl orbit. Same theory as Snap's platforms—massive fusion-drive missiles, probably only three, four thousand gravities of acceleration but lots of endurance."

"None of that is in our files on Atlatl," LaMonte noted. "How recently can they have built that?"

"That depends on how much they bought, how much they built, and how much of their spaceborne industry they took over to build it," Jeeves replied. "They could have built all this in as little as six months if they prioritized it highly enough."

"All right...so, who is threatening a prosperous, successful MidWorld enough that they went to this kind of extent to defend themselves...and *never told the Protectorate?*" David asked.

"You know," Soprano said, almost conversationally, "I actually hope the answer is the Legacy, because the last thing I want to find out is that there's someone *else* with this scale of resources."

Two women in dark-purple uniforms under black armored vests were waiting when David and his officers exited *Red Falcon*. As he'd expected, the docking area was zero-gee, but LaMonte and the two security officers helped him out of his wheelchair and folded it up.

The chair was designed for that, after all, and the two officers took the whole thing with cheerful grace.

"Don't worry, Captain; we're *delighted* to see you," the senior woman told him. "We've been waiting on your cargo for six months."

"It's quite the cargo," he noted as they "swam" through the zero-gravity dock. "And we saw a bunch of missile platforms on the way in. Are those new?"

"Very," she agreed. "I'm not cleared to say much, Captain; Commodore Al-Mufti will fill you in on what she's prepared to tell you."

"All right, then lead the way," David told them with a smile. "It's not like I'm going much of anywhere without help!"

Nahuatl Orbital was the largest single space station in Teotihuacan local space, but that didn't mean much. It had a grand total of four docks and was basically a large X in space with a spinning hab section around the central point.

The section was smaller—and therefore spun faster—than most David had seen, and the transition from the docking structure to the pseudogravity hab ring was nauseating. Even the locals looked uncomfortable as the elevator pod accelerated up to speed.

For its small size, however, there was a warm feeling to the Orbital that a lot of space stations didn't have. All of the walls were painted, and many had murals of agricultural or pastoral scenes from the moonlets around them—and others had decoration that had very clearly been designed and applied by relatively young children.

That decoration made up in color and enthusiasm what it lacked in style or comprehensibility, bringing a smile to even David's currently disgruntled face.

Unfolding the wheelchair and getting him back into it took longer than he'd like, but eventually they reached the security doors into Teotihuacan Security Control. Even there, the warm nature of the decorations continued. The scene painted across the heavy hatch was a cutesy bright one of sunlit meadows and white rabbits.

If only half the rabbits were really identifiable and the sun had a face, well, that helped reduce the threat level of the two exosuited guards standing outside the armored hatch.

One of their uniformed escorts handed the guards a plastic card, and there was a silent exchange before the door slowly opened.

"The Commodore is waiting for you, Captain Rice."

Commodore Aleksandrina Al-Mufti's office was just off from a planetary command center space that would have done a much larger military force proud. A massive holographic tank displayed every object in the Teotihuacan planetary system, with green icons marking the corvettes as well as the missile launchers Jeeves had pointed out.

There were also two larger green icons attached to a structure that David's people hadn't picked up orbiting Teotihuacan well inside the orbit of the moonlets humanity had taken for their own. David Rice was perfectly capable of reading the standard tactical iconography used by the Martian Navy and the system militias, which meant he identified the two destroyers instantly.

It was a non-standard code, one even most Navy veterans wouldn't be able to read—but David had been a CIC technician.

The codes attached to their icons told him neither warship was active. That could be for any of a dozen reasons, but he suspected they were still undergoing fitting-out while their crews trained.

Even if there'd been more data in the tank, he wouldn't have been able to pick it out before he was wheeled into Al-Mufti's office. Unlike the rest of the station, Security Control's space was austere and plain, and Al-Mufti's room was no exception.

The walls were currently a plain industrial white but had the telltale glimmer of wallscreens. The Commodore worked from a single desk with a standard console display. As they entered, she was standing next to the one wallscreen *not* pretending to be a plain wall, studying a visual of what David guessed to be the VLA assembled around Tepoztopilli.

"Commodore Al-Mufti," he greeted her. "You asked to speak with myself, my Ship's Mage and my XO?"

"I did," she agreed. She tapped a command on her wrist-comp and the door slid shut behind them, locking out the rest of the Commodore's people with a neat finality. "This room is as secure as Teotihuacan Security can make it," she noted.

The wallscreen blanked behind her and David's wrist-comp bleeped a calm *no signal* warning.

"Including having the ability to be turned into a Faraday cage," she continued with a small smile. "Your ship attempted to ping the MISS office here in Atlatl. I'm hoping my interpretation of that was correct and that one of you three, at least, is an MISS operative."

David sighed. He was *authorized* to brief local authorities on *Red Falcon*'s true nature, but it had been made clear that everyone preferred he didn't.

"Our status is classified," he said bluntly. "But yes, you can presume that at least one of the people in the room works for MISS."

Al-Mufti chuckled.

"I wouldn't expect more, Captain," she admitted. "As I imagine you noticed the lack of response, I guess it's not a surprise that two months ago, an office in El Dorado was destroyed by a planted explosive.

"We didn't realize it was the MISS base office until we dug into *why* someone would have blown it up with everyone inside."

David winced.

"We have no ability to access MISS communications," Al-Mufti continued, "but we were at least able to recognize that someone was trying to communicate and locate them. I have been praying that someone would make contact."

"Ma'am...if you have a problem, why aren't you reaching out to the Navy?" David asked. "From what I can tell, you've vastly expanded your system military in the last year. Surely, any external threat would be better dealt with by the Navy."

"We did," she told him. "Two years ago. A Navy destroyer squadron sat in orbit of Tepoztopilli for nine months. Nothing happened for those nine months. The ships left, quite reasonably in my opinion, for other duties.

"Inside seventy-two hours, we had a bombing, a planetary minister kidnapped and assassinated, and a civilian jump-ship hijacked," she said. "The Navy has been running random patrols through the system as best they can, but whoever is *fucking* with us seems to know when they're coming as soon as we do.

"I'm forced to conclude that either our military or our government has been penetrated by whatever organization is trying to destroy our economy and bring down the government," she finished.

"You don't even know who's doing this?" Soprano asked.

"Not a clue. Anonymous demands, occasionally. Some threats, similarly anonymous. Four jump-ships hijacked or destroyed. Sixteen in-system ships hijacked or destroyed. *Nine* government officials murdered. Four kidnapped and successfully ransomed."

Al-Mufti shook her head as she reeled off the list. "That's the last fourteen months," she conceded. "We shot down one ship a month ago that tried to jump a starship. That was after we got the missile suites online...but I can't help but fear that our shadowy enemy is already plotting to undermine that capability."

"You want our help," David said grimly.

"I want MISS's help," she agreed. "I need someone with the skills and the knowledge to *find* these people and protect my world. A system military doesn't produce a great many spies and counterespionage agents, Captain."

"That's not really our expertise, either," he admitted. "We can reach out to MISS, pass on a report. We'll need an excuse to head to Sandoval once we've off-loaded, but I can report in and make sure you get help."

"That's as much as I could safely hope for," Al-Mufti replied. "I'll reach out through some of my personal contacts, see if I can arrange a cargo heading to Sandoval for you.

"I don't want to use public resources," she admitted. "I'm not sure I can trust my own people, let alone my government."

"I sympathize," David told her, remembering his own problems with spies aboard *Red Falcon*. "We'll see what we can do, Commodore."

"Thank you, Captain," she said quietly.

CHAPTER 25

EACH OF ATLATL'S new orbital cutters took up an entire standard cargo container, despite only being half the mass of the normal cargo. The new squadrons of the fleet little ships that Atlatl had ordered were the first things off-loaded, several of the containers barely making it to Nahuatl Orbital before crews swarmed over them to get them into space.

The cutters weren't heavily armed by starship standards, but their short-ranged missiles were more than powerful enough to take down just about any civilian starship in a few seconds. They also had the engine power to act as tugs if needed and the excess life support to act as rescue ships.

Most systems didn't go in for *quite* so many of them as Atlatl had ordered, but any system government worth their salt usually had at least a dozen or so. They were useful little ships, and David didn't feel at all bad about delivering them.

He was a bit twitchier over the containers containing multiple divisions' worth of tanks that were being carried to the surface of the moon below him via heavy-lift shuttle. He could understand why the Atlatl System's government wanted to upgrade their spaceborne forces, given the threat pattern he could see in the data they'd given him.

The massive upgrade to their ground forces seemed to be, basically, because they could sell a legislature panicked by terrorist attacks and hijackings on it.

Looking through their data, he suspected that the people of Atlatl were overestimating the scale of the threat. The sheer number of attacks was terrifying, yes, but they all occurred some time apart.

He figured the people screwing with Atlatl had maybe three ground-strike teams and, with one ship lost, maybe two starships left. Light ships, too, from the scan data they had. The usual kind of refitted jump-yachts used by pirates and bounty hunters.

Demonstrably capable of taking down Atlatl's obsolete corvettes, but no match for their home-built orbital missile network, let alone the destroyers building in low Teotihuacan orbit.

The Captain shook his head as his wrist-comp pinged an incoming call. He didn't recognize the ID, but...well, he was cargo-hunting right now.

He flipped it to his wall...and then was forced to swallow down nausea at the scene that appeared.

"Oh shit, sorry," Blade said immediately, using the cloth in his hand to clean the blood splatter off the camera. "Wasn't sure where our Legacy friends had put the camera."

Once the camera was clear, the Augment went back to cleaning the forty-centimeter-long blade protruding from his other hand. The reason he was cleaning the weapon was clearly visible behind him in the scattered wreckage of what had been at least half a dozen human beings.

"I wanted to let you know my mission here is complete," the Legatan continued, "and I wondered if I could ask a favor?"

"I'm...not headed back to UnArcana space," David said faintly, focusing on the cyborg's face and trying to ignore the gory mess behind him. Several other Augments were moving through the chaos, checking over bodies.

"I don't need a ride," Blade told him. "I had one lined up, but since I found out where Legacy buried their escape ship, I don't even need that. We're good all the way home.

"This place, however, is at least *theoretically* an import/export office, the kind of place that might be trying to hire you. I need you to swing by, like this call was for an appointment, and then call the cops."

David swallowed. His own conversations with Commodore Al-Mufti meant he'd probably have to tell her where the Legacy base was. Doing it as a favor to the Legatans was, he supposed, a bonus.

"I...I can do that," he agreed slowly, still trying not to look at either the slaughtered people behind Blade or the implant weapon he was cleaning.

"Good. Give us about an hour to get out of here, then swing by and call the locals," Blade told him. "Hopefully, they're smart enough to look at the databases quickly. From what they told me before they stopped twitching, they've got at least two more hack-job pirate ships floating around, and while *I* can't do anything about them, I'm pleased as punch to let the locals finish wrecking their shit for me."

The cyborg grinned.

"Thanks, Captain Rice. You've been very helpful."

The channel cut, and David sighed.

He was starting to hate his new job.

It didn't look any more pleasant in person. David rolled his wheelchair into the ruined office, accompanied by Skavar and several of *Red Falcon's* Security troops. Most of the people hadn't died cleanly or quickly—he wasn't sure if the Legatans hadn't been able to get guns down there for some reason or had simply chosen not to use them.

The Augment's built-in blades had been more than enough. There were enough guns scattered around to show that the Legacy's people had been hardly defenseless, but they hadn't been equipped to stop a kill-team of cyborgs.

Few people were.

He tapped his wrist-comp.

"Nahuatl Orbital Emergency Central, what is your emergency?" a voice said swiftly.

"I was supposed to be meeting someone for an appointment, but their office looks like a massacre," he told the woman. "Someone killed *everyone*."

He knew he sounded more tired than upset. He doubted it sounded remotely right to the woman on the other end of the call, but it was all he could muster at the moment.

"What's your location?" she demanded after a second. "Is there any sign of an active attacker?"

David reeled off the location of the office.

"No attacker that I can see," he told her. "Just...bodies."

"We have a team in the area," she replied. "Please remain in position until they arrive."

"Of course."

The channel cut, and he shook his head. He'd given Al-Mufti the heads-up, so there should be a proper forensic team with computer specialists only a few minutes away. He'd needed to come in and make the call directly, just in case the Legatans were watching, but he was willing to abuse his other hat to get people in play faster.

He wasn't expecting Al-Mufti herself to show up, the Commodore entering the office at a carefully slow pace in the trail of her people.

They might not have been briefed in full, but the team knew what the priority was—and it wasn't the tired middle-aged man in the wheelchair.

The Commodore gestured for him to join her in the corridor, where any bugs the Legatans had set up to watch what happened next couldn't trace.

"We've killed any bugs and we'll have the computers open in a few minutes," Al-Mufti said quietly as he wheeled up to join her. "That'll tell us a lot—and if there's more ships, we'll find them. And deal with them."

"This is a damned mess," David told her.

"It could be worse," she replied philosophically. "From the firepower scattered around this room alone, I think we may be suddenly short a local problem."

He nodded.

"We're still heading to Sandoval," he said. "Mars needs to know what's going on. They'll probably send help."

"We can hope," she agreed. "I'm not going to trust the kind of psycho-path who did *that*"—she gestured at the office behind David—"to have given me all the information."

Al-Mufti shook her head.

"I can see how they did it with a handful of agents and three ships," she admitted, "though damn, does that make us all look like incompe-tents. Officially, all I know is we have a bloody massacre in a shipping office that we're going to eventually connect back to our pirate problem.

"Even unofficially, it's not like I'm sending LMID a thank-you card," she finished drily.

"You shared an enemy, Commodore. Nothing more."

"I know. And I'd frankly rather they'd just told us where the bastards were. Arrests sit better with me than this mess," she told him.

"From what I was told, the reason they wiped this particular cell of Legacy out was that they had data on LMID's operations in Protectorate space," David pointed out. "They didn't *want* us to interrogate these people.

"They just wanted them dead."

She nodded.

"I've arranged that cargo to Sandoval for you," she told him. "If I were you, I'd take something of a roundabout route. If these guys hate you as much as it sounds like..."

"They can try anything they like," David replied. "If all they've got is a pair of hack-job jump corvettes? They won't even scratch my paint."

Al-Mufti chuckled.

"I envy you that," she told him. "I don't suppose I can interest you in mercenary work once we've located them?"

"I prefer to have fewer witnesses when I fight pirates," David told her. "*Red Falcon*'s full armament is still something of a mystery to many of my enemies. I'd like to keep it that way."

CHAPTER 26

"WE'RE LOADING WHAT?"

Jeeves's voice was flat and surprised as Kelly laughed at him.

"Dirt," she repeated. "Fourteen point six million metric tons of prime-grade farm dirt, sterilized of Nahuatl microorganisms and reseeded with a Terran microbiome.

"Key ingredient in localized terraforming projects. Sandoval Prime has a nitrogen-oxygen atmosphere, but the local plant and animal life are inedible to humans. Farming projects require the replacement of the local ecosystem down to a microbiological level, hence..."

"Dirt," the gunnery officer said, looking at the flow of hundreds of containers drifting through space toward *Red Falcon*. "And we're being paid for this?"

"Standard carriage rates," Kelly agreed. "We're not getting *extra* to haul dirt, but we'll have it to Sandoval faster than anyone else would. So, we can pick up *another* cargo and move on from there."

"I understand the logistics of a fast freighter," Jeeves said drily. "Just the economics of shipping dirt between planets hurts my head."

"Only makes sense when the planet that's getting it can't grow food in the native soil," she confirmed. "But since Sandoval Prime can't, here we are."

"Twelve more hours to load our dirt," Jeeves pointed out. "And then what?"

"We head straight out, according to the Captain," she told him. "Sandoval has an RTA and we need to touch base with MISS on Mars."

"Yeah, 'cause the fact that I took a job on a covert ops ship is making me feel *so* much better," he replied.

"Did you prefer jail?" Kelly asked. She was actually curious. "This isn't exactly a harsh prison, as I understand."

"Ehhh. Medium-security facilities aren't too bad," Jeeves said. "I'll take *Falcon* over it except when we're being shot at, but still... might take it over the Navy. The Navy was *fine*, but I wouldn't put the uniform back on."

He sighed.

"Of course, they wouldn't take me either. Criminal convictions do that."

"What *did* they catch you for?"

"Arms smuggling." Jeeves shrugged. "Made what looked like a good deal with one of the Blue Star leftover groups. Seemed like a great way to turn my seed cash into a bigger investment, but there was a reason it was such a good deal.

"The syndicate got their guns and I got left holding the bag when the police arrived," he concluded. "I should have known better, but I wanted to be independent."

"And now you're with us."

"And Captain Rice is technically my jailer," Jeeves agreed with a shrug. "I owe him from way back, but this job isn't a favor to him. It's a favor to *me*. Learn from my lessons, XO. Don't deal in guns and don't work with crime syndicates."

She coughed.

"We just delivered eighteen million tons of weapons to Atlatl," Kelly pointed out. "Don't deal in guns, huh?"

Jeeves chuckled.

"I said *you* should learn from my lessons, Second Officer LaMonte," he replied. "The Captain has learned his own lessons. I can't speak for him."

-}-

Teotihuacan Security was on the move at the same time as *Red Falcon* was. As Kelly maneuvered the big freighter, now loaded with a stupendous quantity of high-quality soil, away from Nahuatl Orbital, the six corvettes were moving as well.

"I hope that the Legacy ships are even more crap than they are," she said aloud, watching their icons. "I wouldn't want anyone I liked aboard those ships."

"I would say that the locals agree with you," Jeeves told her, tapping a command to mirror his focus to the command chair. "Take a look."

One of the larger icons marking the Tau Ceti-built destroyers was moving. Kelly focused on it, running through its data and shaking her head.

"I'm a damned engineer," she said softly. "That ship is barely combat-capable, if she is at all. She's *leaking atmo*. Probably closer to finishing her fit-out than the other one, but that means her crew has barely touched her systems."

"She's still a destroyer, XO," Jeeves replied. "She out-masses all six of those corvettes combined *and* is about fifty years more modern.

"I see everything you do...and I'd still rather ride that destroyer than one of those corvettes."

She sighed and nodded.

"Not our call, if not necessarily not our problem," she concluded. *Red Falcon* shifted under her hands as she aligned the big ship. She checked a screen and nodded.

"We're clear for full engines. Bringing us to ten gravities."

The freighter vibrated under her and her navigation display updated. Eleven hours to jump. Then they would be safe. For now, at least.

They were still three hours away from jump when the first explosion lit up *Falcon*'s scanners. It was rapidly followed by dozens more as the Teotihuacan Security flotilla's missile salvo struck home.

Even from almost two light-minutes away, their scanners were good enough to show Kelly at least some detail on the battle that was going on.

Like most gas giants, Teotihuacan had a set of trailing trojan asteroids that followed along in its orbital wake.

Unlike many gas giants, it was close enough to its star that the trailing trojans were relatively close to Teotihuacan. They'd been close enough that the pirates had apparently been using them as a base, using their knowledge of the Atlatl System's defenders' systems to stay hidden.

The Legacy pirates had seen the flotilla coming in time to try and run—but Al-Mufti had expected that and brought her seven ships in on a vector where the Legacy couldn't reach space they could jump from in time.

Teotihuacan Security's missiles were only fusion birds—but that was also all the Legacy ships had. The missile duel was horrendously uneven. The two pirate ships outgunned any of the corvettes alone, but against six corvettes and a destroyer, however unready, they never stood a chance.

From the first explosion to the last, the whole battle lasted less than three minutes. One of the Teotihuacan corvettes was badly damaged, but both pirate ships were vaporized.

"Well, that couldn't have happened to nicer folk," Jeeves said grimly. "Though. Hmm."

"Guns?" Kelly asked cheerfully. "You see something interesting?"

"Yeah. Looks like there were a few more jump-ships than I originally thought docked at the orbitals." He shrugged. "I was counting freighters, but now I'm seeing four courier- or yacht-sized ships suddenly moving out.

"I'd guess one of them is Blade, but the others...friends or associates of the Legacy."

"Record everything you can; we'll leave it with MISS in Sandoval," Kelly ordered. "A few more bits of data on our enemies."

"Agreed. Wait..."

Kelly saw Jeeves suddenly focus more on one of those ships.

"Guns?" she asked again.

"One of them appears to be following us," he told her.

Kelly chuckled.

"Let him," she replied. "We aren't following the jump plan they'll expect. They'll never find us."

"True enough," Jeeves agreed. "I'm still going to keep a *very* close eye on him."

CHAPTER 27

"JUMP COMPLETE," Soprano told David. Their trip into Atlatl had been brief but exciting. This trip was turning into a demonstration of just why setting out to poke the enemy in the eye and see how they reacted was a dangerous plan.

"We are four light-years away from Atlatl now," she told the video link to David's office. The Captain was upright, leaning against his desk as he tried to get used to his new leg. "It will be eight hours before I'll want any of us to jump again, but we should be beyond anything anyone can track."

Not least because none of those four jumps had been along any of the standard routes. They were light-years away from anywhere anyone would expect them to be. It would take them an extra set of jumps to reach Sandoval, but eight hours wasn't going to change the timeline for their soil that much.

"Jeeves and LaMonte will keep an eye on things," David told her. "Go rest!"

"You don't have to tell me twice," she agreed. "See you in eight hours, boss."

The channel cut off, leaving David's wallscreen showing the space around *Red Falcon*. The empty void between the stars was both draining and relaxing for him. On the one hand, it was darker than it could ever be in a star system, with no source of light for untold trillions of kilometers in any direction.

On the other hand, it meant the stars were brighter and more visible here than they could ever be anywhere else—and it meant they were safe.

And if he still felt a bit paranoid, well, even paranoids have real enemies.

"Should you be up here?" LaMonte asked brightly as David limped onto the bridge. "Light duty, right?"

"We're four light-years from *anything*," he grumped, one hand on a cane to keep his balance as his new leg spasmed. He was out of a wheel-chair, at least, and the cane would be a thing for only a few more days.

"And if I can walk under my own power, cane or not, I can sit in my damn chair," he concluded.

Given the extent of his injuries, he knew Gupta was right to try and keep him away from work or stress of any kind, but the reality of his ship meant that wasn't possible. Being off the bridge was probably *more* stressful for him.

"You're the Captain, Captain," LaMonte allowed, rising from the command chair and gesturing him to it.

He smiled his thanks and took his seat, failing to conceal a heavy sigh of relief as he took his weight off his leg and activated the governors.

"I have to walk to teach it," he told his XO. "But walking with it sucks still. It'll pass."

"You sure you should be up and about?" she asked.

"Nope. Just that I'm sick of sitting in my office reading," he replied with a grin. "Jeeves! What's the deep dark void looking like?"

"Deep, dark, empty. Very void-like," his old friend replied. "What Captain Santiago used to call the quiet of the darkest sea."

"And our cargo?" David asked LaMonte.

"According to the container sensors, everything is just the right amount of not-quite-wriggly," she told him. "We're keeping all the containers at a set eleven degrees Centigrade. The microbiome is warming most of them a couple of degrees, just as they said it would."

She paused.

"I didn't think that shipping dirt would be quite so complicated and detailed a procedure," she noted.

"That, XO, is because you think of dirt as inanimate," David replied. "And the whole point of shipping *soil* is that we're shipping that microbiome. We'll keep it warm and alive, get it where it needs to go.

"It may not seem like much, but this dirt will allow Sandoval Prime to build thousands of hectares of new farmland and get that bit closer to food independence." He shook his head. "Not many MidWorlds aren't food-independent; that's got to be nerve-wracking for them."

"How'd they end up dependent?" LaMonte asked.

"More immigrants and babies than planned for," he told her. "They've had several economic booms based on resources and industrial projects, all of which needed workers. When every piece of farmland is bought with sweat and toil, balancing the food supply against the population is hard enough without massive waves of new mouths."

He shrugged.

"They were supposed to be temporary workers, in the main, but over three times as many chose to stay as they projected. For all of its food issues, Sandoval is a comfortable world, and a well-run one.

"I think we'll end up staying there for a few weeks for shore leave," he noted. "I think I want this damn leg working properly before I go sticking our nose in further trouble."

"I can appreciate that," his XO agreed.

"Wait," Jeeves suddenly interjected into the conversation. "That doesn't look right..."

"Guns?" LaMonte said sharply, and the lanky Third Officer looked up at them with nervous eyes.

"Jump flares," he reported grimly. "I have multiple jump flares!"

"Tracker," David said instantly, staring at the plot of space around *Red Falcon* as Jeeves dropped in the icons of the newcomers. "The sons of bitches have to have a *Tracker*."

"What in ever-loving *FUCK* is a Tracker?" Jeeves snapped.

"Weird people who can somehow make sense of the energy signature of a jump," LaMonte told him. Her hands were flying over the XO's station, turning the ship away from their new companions.

The ships were too close.

"Like the name says, they can track a jump. Mikhail Azure had two we know of; there's a third that works for Mars now." She shook her head. "Apparently, the Azure Legacy found one."

"What have we got, Jeeves?" David asked quietly.

"Four ships. Weird ships," his gunnery officer said drily. "Not jump-yachts, too big. Not destroyers, too small."

"Oh. Oh, *fuck* me."

"Jeeves?" David snapped.

"I know those ships," the gunner said quietly. "There's only six of them in existence and they were all built for one guy: Jason Aristos. The Admiral Commanding of the Golden Bears."

"They're...mercenaries, right?" David asked.

"In polite company, at least," Jeeves replied. "I guess the Protectorate could never *prove* anything, but their rep in the underworld is that if you need somebody dead with no records, no proof, just disappeared between the stars...the Admiral Commanding could make it happen."

"A Tracker and half a dozen baby destroyers," LaMonte said aloud. "Yeah, I can see how that would work." She shook her head. "Antimatter engines, boss. They're inbound at twelve gees. I can buy us time, but..."

"Not enough for the Mages to jump us," David concluded on his own. "They'll be in missile range in a few minutes if they have antimatter birds like we do. Jeeves—what do we have on these guys?"

"Seven hundred thousand tons apiece," the gunner reeled off, clearly half from memory and half from his scans. "Aristos calls them 'monitors,' though from what I know of the historical version, that's a crappy name for them.

"They're fast and well crewed. Not as heavily armed, ton-for-ton, as a true Navy ship—they're designed to board and capture as much as kill."

"Any idea what the armament *is*?"

"No amplifiers," Jeeves told him. "Amber-built, some upgrades slotted in at Tau Ceti and Legatus and...well, anywhere else they'd take money to put top-of-the-line gear in a starship.

"I'd guess antimatter birds, heavy battle lasers, RFLAM turrets.... We probably outgun each of his damn monitors on their own, but with four of them..."

"The odds go the other way," David accepted grimly. "Jeeves?"

"Skipper?"

"Take the ship to battle stations and make sure the antimatter birds are loaded. If they want to tangle with us in deep space where there's no witnesses, I see no reason not to take advantage of the situation.

"We'll see what this Aristos has to say...but the moment they enter missile range, you will open fire and *keep* firing until we run out of antimatter missiles, clear?"

"As crystal, sir."

"I don't suppose our friends are saying anything?" David asked several minutes later as the monitors continued to close with *Red Falcon*. They were still over fourteen million kilometers away, closing at a speed that expanded the already-impressive range of the modern Phoenix VII missiles in his magazines.

They'd carried a significant velocity relative to *Falcon* through their jump and were closing at two percent of light. Accelerating away was buying David's people time...but not much, not at those velocities.

Not the four hours he needed for his Mages to jump him away.

"Not a squeak," LaMonte replied. "Three minutes to missile range. Ninety-second communication turnaround."

"All right, let's see what they have to say," David said grimly.

He activated the recorder and leaned into his camera.

"Admiral Jason Aristos...or whoever is commanding the Golden Bear detachment. I know you're following me. I know you've used a Tracker to find me here in the middle of nowhere.

"I can only assume that you're in the employ of Azure Legacy. I'll warn you that this isn't going to go the way you think. You've apparently spent quite some time and energy preserving your license to operate in the Protectorate...but if you attack me, that's over. I have friends in high places, and they will hear of your actions, your crimes.

"Begin deceleration now, and we can both go our separate ways. No one needs to die today...but in the absence of communication and a reversal of your course, I have no choice but to regard you as pirates and defend my ship at the maximum range I am capable of.

"Withdraw or be destroyed."

He ended the recording and transmitted.

"If they start reversing course, give them extra time to communicate," he told Jeeves. "Otherwise...open fire as soon as you can."

"If they've got the same missiles we have, they could play enough games to get into range," his gunner replied.

"If they've got Phoenix Sevens, we'll deal with that, but there will be hell to pay later," David pointed out. "If they've got Sixes, though, we've got about a hundred seconds of range over them. Let's use it."

The Phoenix VII had a shorter flight time than the older missile but accelerated two thousand gravities faster.

Both missiles had a seven-minute-plus flight time at maximum range, though. If Aristos had Phoenix VIs, *Falcon*'s missiles would hit over two minutes before the mercenary missiles—but almost five minutes after the Golden Bears launched.

"Incoming transmission," LaMonte told him. "Relaying to your screens."

As soon as Jason Aristos appeared on David's screen, he recognized the man. The most successful mercenary in the Protectorate was famous enough that he'd seen Aristos's image before.

Aristos was a tall, thickly built man with tanned skin and pitch-black hair that hung to his shoulders. He lounged in a command chair very similar to David's, and he had an irritating smirk on his face.

"Captain Rice, I see you recognize my ships," he said calmly. "You are quite brave, but let's be honest: each of my monitors outguns your half-disarmed Navy auxiliary. Unless you're hiding a handful of destroyers in your cargo of mud, this is only going to end one way.

"But I have no desire to fight a battle I can avoid. You don't become a successful mercenary that way." His smirk expanded.

"I'll make you a deal, Captain. Surrender yourself to me and I will let your people leave. The Legacy is paying me to destroy *Falcon*, but we both know they only want you.

"Seems a fair deal, doesn't it?"

The recording stopped and David sighed.

"Does the entire *galaxy* think I'm enough of a sucker to surrender to torture and death to *maybe* protect my crew?" he asked aloud.

It wasn't the first time he'd received that exact offer since the Azure Legacy had started chasing him. The last person who'd given it was dead.

He sighed and leaned back in his chair.

"XO, Guns. Are we clear for action?"

"We're clear, sir."

"We're clear...but I'll remind you that this ship was designed by *Martians*, sir," Jeeves told him.

David chuckled. The Royal Martian Navy didn't design its ships to run away.

"That's right, isn't it?" he replied. "Kelly?"

"Skipper?"

"All of our guns point forward. Bring us about—it's time to show this 'Admiral Commanding' just how disarmed we actually are."

Red Falcon flipped in space, the mushroom shape of the megafreighter spinning in place to turn the "cap" of the ship, the part with the water tanks, the armor, and the missile tubes to face the pursuing enemy.

If the Golden Bears were surprised, they didn't show it—but when *Falcon* opened fire, they didn't respond.

Ten missiles flashed into space. Twenty seconds later, another ten followed. Then ten more in twenty more seconds.

Fifty missiles were in space before the Bears did anything. Once the range dropped far enough, they returned fire.

"Phoenix Sixes," Jeeves confirmed. "Closing at ten thousand gravities...eight per monitor."

Thirty-two missiles in each salvo. David shivered. That was more missiles than he had defensive turrets, and he really wasn't sure how well the RFLAM turrets would handle fire incoming at over fifty thousand kilometers a second.

In theory, they could handle it, but maximum-range fire was always the fastest and most dangerous.

"Dialing in their missiles," LaMonte announced. "Poor buggers."

"XO?" David asked.

"Unless they're being really, *really* clever, they haven't replaced the standard electronic penetrator suite on the Sixes."

"It's a damn capable suite; why would they replace it?" he asked.

His XO turned back to face him with an absolutely wicked grin on her face.

"Because we're *MISS*, boss, which means I have every line of the penetrator suite's code. Instead of making it harder for us to shoot down their missiles, they're actually making it easier."

"Given the number of weapons heading our way, I'm not complaining," he said calmly as a second salvo of thirty-two missiles launched into space.

The Golden Bears now had more antimatter missiles in space than he did.

"Want to take bets on how many of those missiles they have?" Jeeves said cheerfully. "Or how many they're willing to spend?"

"I know what Legacy is prepared to pay to see me dead," David replied. "I don't know how many missiles Aristos might have been able to acquire, but I guarantee you he's willing to spend them all."

"What did you *do* to these people?" Jeeves replied. "I mean, really, is killing someone's boss worth all this?"

"It is when said boss's will puts up a multi-*trillion*-dollar reward for the death of his killer," David pointed out.

Jeeves swallowed.

"Is it too late to change my mind about prison?"

"Yes. What are our odds of hurting these bastards?"

"Decent. They're not used to going up against the Navy's top-grade missiles," Jeeves admitted. "I doubt we'll get them all, but they're going to get more hurt than they expected."

"I don't suppose we can make sure we blow Aristos to hell?" David asked.

"Not enough data," his gunner replied. "And not enough control. Boss, we're still thirty light-seconds away from them. Whatever instructions I give our missiles are basically a minute out of date by the time they reach them."

"Terminal is always up to their computers."

"Which is why their missiles are screwed," LaMonte pointed out. "So... if I keep shooting down all of their missiles, what does Aristos do *next*?"

"If the rumors I've heard are right...each of those monitors is built around a single old cruiser laser. A ten-gigawatt beam."

"Ah," David said softly. "So, we do *not* want to court a laser engagement."

"It could be worse; they've only got one beam each so they're easier to dodge," Jeeves replied. "But yeah. We've got ten lasers to their four, but theirs are twice as powerful."

"Assuming they live that long," the Captain replied, watching the missiles head toward each other.

"Assuming, yeah," Jeeves told him, then sighed. "That was it, boss. We're out of Phoenixes. Fifteen minutes before we're in range for the Rapiers."

"Well, let's see what the good Admiral does."

Red Falcon's missiles closed on their targets at almost twenty percent of lightspeed, having crossed the intervening millions of kilometers in just under seven minutes. Ten missiles weren't a lot, not against four ships that had been based on the design of Martian Navy destroyers.

Against a flotilla of RMN destroyers, David probably wouldn't even have launched the missiles. On the other hand, against a Navy flotilla, he'd have already surrendered if he couldn't run. *Red Falcon*'s armament was designed around different parameters than a destroyer but was roughly comparable.

Four of them could eat his ship for breakfast. Their only hope today was that the Golden Bears' monitors were *enough* inferior to a Navy destroyer to make up the difference.

"First salvo neutralized," Jeeves reported. "We've got some ugly radiation hash, though." He shook his head. "I can't assist the further salvos at all now. It's up to the computers."

"Fortunately, we're *not* running the default code for Phoenix Sevens," LaMonte replied. "Kellers and I added some tricks while we were laid up in Tau Ceti. They're scarier independent than I bet these guys are counting on."

"I'll let you know in about, oh, twelve seconds," Jeeves told her dryly.

"Focus, LaMonte," David told his XO. "Our incoming?"

"Crossing the range of the RFLAMs now," she said. "Electronic warfare...let it run, let it run."

David swallowed as *Falcon*'s lasers remained silent.

"Kelly, there are thirty-two one-gigaton warheads heading for this ship," he pointed out.

She held up a finger.

"Trust me." She watched, typed in several more commands, watched again...and then hit an initiation key.

Ten seconds later, *Red Falcon's* skies were clear. The radiation hash inevitable to taking out antimatter weapons was still over three light-seconds away from them.

David checked his systems. The turrets had fired three times, a total of seventy-five laser pulses, to wipe out thirty-two missiles.

"Okay, that wasn't bad," he admitted. "What now?"

"We got one!" Jeeves snapped. "One hit...no, two! Monitor Charlie just ceased fire and is spinning out of control.

"She'll probably live, but she's mission-killed," the gunnery officer announced. "She isn't accelerating and is falling behind fast."

"Can we retarget the remaining salvos?" David asked.

"Already on it. They should do so independently, but I'm making sure," Jeeves promised.

"Second incoming salvo neutralized," LaMonte told them. "Rad hash at nine hundred and forty thousand klicks."

And there was the problem of even successfully stopping antimatter salvos. Each time LaMonte wiped out a group of missiles, the chaos created by dozens of antimatter warheads detonating created a zone where *Falcon* couldn't target the missiles.

And with each salvo, that zone crept closer.

"Nailing down their defenses," Jeeves reported as their third salvo died ineffectually short of the Golden Bears. "Looks like fifteen half-gigawatt RFLAMs apiece, same turrets we're carrying."

David nodded. That meant *Red Falcon* had better missile defenses than any individual ship she was facing, but the combination of the three remaining ships had enough to deal with *Falcon's* anemic salvos.

LaMonte's modifications to their missiles were helping—Monitor Charlie had managed to get part of her engines back online but was now actively withdrawing from the battlespace, for example—but they were simply outclassed by the flotilla they were facing.

What had to be driving Aristos crazy, though, was that LaMonte was consistently shooting down every missile he threw at them. It wasn't going to matter if the Bears had three times as many launchers as *Red Falcon* and twice the missile defenses if he couldn't land a single hit.

"Ten minutes to Rapier range," Jeeves announced. "About another eight after that for laser range."

"At this point, he's got to be planning to finish us there," David said. The Bears had finally run out of antimatter missiles, it seemed, but having fired fifteen salvos of thirty-odd missiles each, they'd spent a lot of resources trying to get at him.

"Do we think he's done with missiles?" LaMonte asked. "I've got one more trick in my quiver, but it's easily disabled if they have hard access to the birds."

"He's probably got fusion missiles, same as us," David told her. His Rapier IVs were one of thirteen different brand names, all with several tiers of roughly comparable weapon systems. He'd be shocked if the Bears weren't carrying something functionally identical to the Rapier IV, with its four thousand gravities of acceleration and seven minutes of flight time.

It was the most expensive tier of "civilian" available weapon out there, but he doubted Aristos had made it to the top of his field without being prepared to buy the best.

"But no more Phoenixes," his XO concluded. "Okay. Um. Boss...how all-out are we planning on going?"

"Kelly, he's going to vaporize us if we don't stop him, so I'm not too concerned about showing our cards. Why?"

"Included in my files on the Phoenix VI is a command override code," she told him. "Won't work if he's running the Navy security encryptions or if he's disabled the receivers, but if he's running them in the standard mode for *militia* use..."

"They put an override code in the missiles they sold the militias?" David asked. "Damn."

"I suspect every militia in the Protectorate knows about it and knows how to disable it if, for some reason, they thought they were going up against the RMN," LaMonte pointed out. "But even if Aristos *knows* about it, he definitely doesn't have the security encryptions to block it, and disabling the receivers reduces their effectiveness."

"Do it," David ordered.

His XO grinned at him again, the same brightly happy, terrifyingly wicked grin she'd shown when she'd realized the mercenaries were using the standard software suite on their missiles.

She pushed a button on her console.

"Done."

"So...what does that *mean?*" Jeeves asked.

"We're no longer a valid target in the missiles' systems," LaMonte explained. "Basically, I just overrode their identify-friend-or-foe sequences and set them to fully autonomous mode.

"The only thing they'll identify as friendly is us...and they're going to go after the closest ships they identify as hostile."

David swallowed, his gaze turning to the tactical plot as his XO's transmission swept out. The nearest missiles didn't have enough fuel to turn around and go after their motherships. Their suicidal little brains ran the calculation, assessed that they were a greater risk to friendlies than the enemy...and self-destructed.

The lightspeed lag meant he could watch their transmission spread in almost real time. Salvo after salvo self-destructed...until the signal reached missiles whose computers judged that they *could* reach the Golden Bears.

Those missiles flipped in space. Suddenly, instead of accelerating toward *Red Falcon* at ten thousand gravities, they were charging toward the Golden Bears at the same acceleration.

"Bring us up and over the radiation hash," David ordered. "Stand by the battle lasers and Rapiers; take us right at them and see how badly they panic."

Whatever the Golden Bears had been expecting from this battle, it hadn't been for their missiles to turn on them. *Red Falcon* picked up the fringes of increasingly complex and desperate attempts to re-override the missiles controls or even just self-destruct them.

None of them worked, and the Bears' missile defenses now came to life against their own missiles. The salvos came in far slower than the ones *Falcon* had launched, but they were also larger and unexpected.

Between the co-opted missiles and *Red Falcon*'s salvos, over three hundred missiles hammered in on Aristos's fleet. Space around them lit up with radiation and explosions, making it almost impossible for David and his people to track what was going on.

When the chaos finally ended, the space between *Falcon* and her enemies was clear...and two of the Bears' monitors were just...gone.

The last ship was now accelerating away from them, trying to rejoin the ship damaged earlier.

"From her acceleration, Monitor Alpha is still basically intact," Jeeves warned. "Even with Charlie's damage, I suspect they both have their lasers online... Chasing them would be a bad idea, boss."

David nodded silently, studying the icons. A single hit from one of the ten-gigawatt lasers the monitors carried would wreck his ship, but he had a decent chance of taking out both monitors before they could hit him.

Of course, since both of them had fusion-drive missiles, they had a not-insignificant chance of taking *Falcon* out, too. LaMonte's trick had evened the odds nicely, but even odds weren't what you want when you needed to get a cargo home.

"They now know exactly how much firepower *Falcon* has," he pointed out. "And from Kelly's trick, they can probably guess just what our affiliations actually are.

"That'll be a headache. A big one."

"Skipper...there are at least two hundred people on each of those ships," LaMonte reminded him. "Are we really willing to kill another five hundred people just to keep a secret, not to protect ourselves?"

In a moment of somewhat painful self-reflection, David realized that he *was*. Not so much to keep the secret, but to protect his people. He'd kill every last one of the Golden Bears to keep LaMonte and Jeeves and Soprano and everyone else aboard *Red Falcon* safe.

But...he couldn't quite bring himself to order LaMonte and Jeeves to take that blood on their own hands.

He sighed.

"Let's see if they're willing to talk," he said finally. "How far out of Rapier range are we?"

"About three minutes. Time for at least two exchanges, maybe three, depending on how fast you guys talk," Jeeves told him.

David took a deep breath, then exhaled in a fresh sigh as he came to a decision. They'd demonstrated that *Red Falcon* had one hell of a stick. Now it was time to see how Jason Aristos felt about carrots.

"All right, Aristos," David said into the camera. "We've flexed our muscles, flung missiles at each other and you've managed to get several hundred people killed so far.

"By now, you realize you can't destroy *Red Falcon*. We can evade you now—and by now, you can guess that we have enough friends in high places to *destroy* you. As things stand right now, the Golden Bears' mercenary license won't last ten seconds after we make it to Sandoval Prime's RTA.

"But you, Admiral, are *not* my enemy."

David leaned back in his chair, steepling his hands as he looked evenly at the camera.

"My enemy is Azure Legacy. They contracted you. Pointed you at me. And you came after me with everything you had.

"You have failed them. They don't accept failure lightly. They're going to want their money back, Admiral Aristos, and they may well take it in flesh and blood.

"I have an...alternative to us killing each other," David told Aristos. "I will refrain from exposing your extracurricular activities to the Protectorate and pay you one hundred million Martian dollars—not, perhaps, enough to replace your losses, but enough for repairs for your damaged ships.

"In exchange, you will tell me where to find Azure Legacy's leadership." David smiled. "It's a win-lose situation for you, Admiral. Refuse my offer, and either *I* kill you or the Protectorate destroys your little empire.

"Accept it, and you get to continue operating and I destroy your former clients before they can come after you.

"The decision is yours."

He hit TRANSMIT and shook his head.

"Think he'll buy it?" LaMonte asked.

"I don't know," David admitted. "Hold the pursuit course after them regardless. Jeeves?"

"Sir?"

"Get the Rapiers prepped. If Aristos doesn't want to play, I want him hammered to pieces."

Jeeves swallowed. He didn't look as assured about *Red Falcon*'s chances in a straight-up fight as David did, but he nodded his agreement and turned back to his console.

Radio waves traveled at the speed of light, crossing the void between the starships at what felt like a crawl sometimes. David couldn't help counting the seconds until the earliest moment he could receive Aristos's response.

Silence. They crept toward missile and laser range. There was no way to avoid weapons range at this point, even if they both vectored away. They would either come to an agreement or they would kill each other.

"Incoming transmission." LaMonte studied it for a moment. "From Monitor Charlie."

Aristos's image appeared on the main screen. The bridge around him looked the worse for wear, showing the signs of the antimatter missiles that had knocked Charlie out of formation early on in the fight.

The Admiral Commanding didn't look much better. He'd clearly been hit by a piece of debris at some point and made only the minimum effort to stop the bleeding. A bandage was wrapped around his head, but half-dried blood marked the entire side of his face and neck.

"You're a bastard, Rice," he said bluntly. "If I sell out my clients, I'm done. But if I let you tell the Protectorate what we've done, I'm done too. You call it win-lose? I call it lose-lose."

The dried blood cracked as he grinned, the expression truly horrifying on the mercenary's wounded face.

"So, the best choice *I* see is to sell out my clients and hope you finish them off before anyone knows what I've done," he concluded brightly. Hundreds of dead subordinates didn't seem to be bothering the Admiral much.

"I'm standing down my offensive weapons and sensors," Aristos told them. "I'm still running my antimissile turrets and defensive radar, but I will not engage you. Once you've sent the money, I will give you the information you desire. I know who the Legacy truly is, Captain Rice, because I insisted before I took this deal.

"I considered it an insurance policy. It appears it is time to make a claim."

CHAPTER 28

"SO, NOW WE KNOW," David told his senior officers.

The Golden Bears had limped off with their hundred million dollars and their lives, opening the distance between them and *Red Falcon* until Soprano's people were ready to jump them away.

Now David and his top officers and his security chief sat in his office, considering their next step. Dr. Gupta wasn't normally part of these meetings, but today he hovered at David's shoulder, continually consulting his wrist-comp's reports on the half-dozen sensors the Captain was wearing.

"We knew all along that the Legacy was mostly being organized by lawyers," David continued. "Now, we know that, at its core, Azure Legacy *is* lawyers. Every layer out from there is mercenaries, recruits, and fragments of the Blue Star.

"The core is the law firm of Armstrong, Lee and Howard in Corinthian," David told his people. "We have some files from MISS and our previous visit, but ALH doesn't show up much. They're a small, high-value firm that works with extremely high-net-worth individuals on interstellar affairs.

"From what Aristos has told me, they're actually larger than they like to appear, with a lot of underground resources and links into illegal markets. Their existence, it seems, is why the Blue Star Syndicate was never strong in Corinthian: you don't piss in the water being used to launder your money."

"Corinthian, huh?" LaMonte replied. "Are...you and I even allowed back in Corinthian, boss?"

The last time David Rice had visited Corinthian, he'd filled an entire precinct office with knockout gas to rescue Damien Montgomery. LaMonte, for her part, had *shot* at least three security officers with SmartDarts over the course of the rescue.

"All records were expunged and all charges dropped, according to the Hand," David replied. He'd gone back and checked before the meeting, too. His own memories of Corinthian weren't exactly pleasant.

"I can't imagine we'll be popular with anyone who remembers our faces," he continued, "but there are no legal problems waiting for us at the Spindle. That probably won't last once the Legacy realizes we're there, but at least we don't have to worry about the police shooting at us."

"If we know who they are and where they are...perhaps we should simply pass that information on?" Soprano suggested. "I won't pretend I don't like the thought of extorting some payback for the last few months of insanity, but this seems like a problem now better passed on to Marines and police."

"In the long run, yes," David agreed. "But if they sweep the offices, they'll have time to bury the records. We need them off-balance, looking in the wrong direction—if possible, to even pull their resources out of place entirely and leave their base nearly defenseless when the Marines sweep in."

"You sound like you have a plan," Skavar said, and David smiled.

He hadn't sat down and drawn it up, but he *did* have a plan.

"I think I do," he admitted. "A lot will depend on what the situation is in Corinthian, what assets MISS or others can put at our disposal. First, we need to get to Sandoval and report in. That just became even more important."

"And then?" Skavar asked.

"Then we go play agents-provocateur at the Legacy again," David told them with a grin. "See if we can poke one of our bears into a final mistake."

Kelly was sitting in her quarters, staring at the wall as her mind insisted on replaying the cascade of explosions that had resulted from the press of one button, when the admittance chime buzzed.

She ignored it at first. She didn't like to think of herself as a killer, but the count of people her clever ideas had left floating in the void was starting to get high enough to make that classification hard to avoid.

The chime buzzed again. Shaking her head, Kelly turned away from the door, sinking deeper into her funk.

That was when Mike Kelzin and Xi Wu discovered that she'd been too sunk into her imminent depression to remember to lock her door when she'd come in. The door slid open without hesitation, and her lovers entered in perfect step with each other.

"I see the wall remains utterly fascinating," Mike told her, sitting down next to her. He was close enough to invite physical contact and far enough not to force it...and she was moving into his arms before she even thought about it.

"Not really," she murmured into his shoulder. A moment later, a second set of arms wrapped around her and she found herself pinned between the two of them.

"The wall isn't what you're looking at," Xi said, kissing Kelly's hair as she spoke. "Memories and what-ifs are what you're looking at."

"Something like that," Kelly agreed.

"I'd like to note that, once again, you, Ms. XO, are the reason we're all still breathing," Mike told her. He squeezed her.

"And that I still have nightmares about Chrysanthemum," he murmured in her ear. "You?"

"Oh god, Chrysanthemum," she half-gasped. "All I did was lead the cleanup on the ship. That was bad enough."

"Chrysanthemum was the first place I killed someone," her boyfriend told her. "Not the last, not with the way this crew attracts trouble, but the first."

"That's where we got the fuel tanker," Kelly said. "*That* was the first thing I killed anyone with."

Blue Jay had fled the Chrysanthemum System after the local government had tried to kill Damien Montgomery and betray them all to the Blue Star Syndicate. Kelzin had flown the shuttle that had pulled the officers off the planet, covering their boarding himself with a battle carbine.

Kelly, in turn, had turned the fuel tanker they'd accidentally stolen into a weapon that had taken down the bounty hunter ship that had chased them from Chrysanthemum. *That* explosion was one of the memories she was reliving.

"You've both been to counseling," Xi pointed out, the Mage wrapping her arms around her lovers. "You know you were protecting others, doing what you had to do."

"Yeah," Kelly admitted. "I don't regret protecting us...just leaving quite a trail of death behind us."

"We didn't start this fight with the Legacy," Xi reminded her. "And if we're taking it to them now, well, they're turning into a bigger threat to others than we can stand by and watch.

"We agreed to a job with MISS. We may be making ourselves a target, but by doing so, we make others safer."

"That's the theory, anyway," Mike agreed. "And the Golden Bears... those *fuckers* do not deserve your sympathy. High and mighty they might pretend to be, but they were outright murderers for hire."

Kelly nodded, leaning into his shoulder. Off-shift and with the door closed, she didn't need to be *Red Falcon*'s executive officer. Here, she could just be a young woman, leaning on the ones she loved for support.

Sometimes, that was all you had. Often, it was enough.

The battle against the Golden Bears had been the first time *Red Falcon* had gone into combat where Maria and her Mages had literally done nothing. Usually, they were at least playing missile defense, but LaMonte had rendered that unnecessary.

It wasn't as though Maria could really feel useless aboard the twenty-million-ton spaceship that only her magic allowed to travel through the

208

stars, but it was an interesting comparison to when she'd served aboard Navy warships with true amplifiers.

For all that even an amplified Mage had a relatively limited range, a lot of the Royal Martian Navy's tactics were built around bringing enemies into that range. Missiles and lasers might have longer range, but there was no ship-killer so reliable as a Mage's ability to warp reality to their whim.

But neither *Falcon* nor her enemies possessed amplifiers, which left them restricted to relatively mundane methods of trying to kill each other.

By any reasonable logic, however, Rice shouldn't have been in command through the battle. From the way Gupta had hovered over the Captain after the incident, he'd probably run closer to doing himself real harm than Rice suspected.

But...Maria would never have thought of *bribing* the mercenaries to tell them where to find their true enemy. If she'd been in command, she'd have pressed the attack after LaMonte had evened the odds, using the fusion-drive missiles and even the lasers to make sure that the Golden Bears didn't live to tell anyone about *Falcon*'s capabilities.

David Rice might be in command by virtue of owning *Red Falcon* and *Peregrine* and having access to an amount of money that was still mind-boggling to someone with just their personal finances, but he was also still more a merchant than a spy.

Which meant sometimes he had solutions that wouldn't occur to the naval officer turned spy who teleported his ship between the stars.

Maria smiled as she studied the map. Two more jumps to Sandoval. Six days from Sandoval to Corinthian. They'd probably be delayed finding a cargo that justified them going to Corinthian from Sandoval, though she had faith in her Captain now.

That was an odd thought. She'd always trusted Rice and believed in his skills...but when had that turned into the near-unquestioning belief that, at least as it came to cargo and contracts, the Captain would simply get it done, no matter what?

Certainly, he was better at it than she was! She'd found a cargo only because LMID had wanted to use them to strike at the Legacy.

Maria Soprano was relatively comfortable that she could command a warship...but *Red Falcon* was no warship, and she still had a lot to learn.

At least she appeared to have one of the best teachers available.

CHAPTER 29

SANDOVAL PRIME was a strange and fascinating world to Maria. Even from orbit, the colors were utterly wrong, and the differences only became more obvious as Nicolas maneuvered the shuttle down toward the surface.

Her wrist-comp had the data to explain everything. The local chlorophyll-equivalent used iron in converting oxygen to energy, resulting in a deep rusty orange color instead of the green she was used to on other worlds. The seawater contained concentrations of copper that were instantly-toxic to Terran life, turning the oceans a stunning shade of pale green like no other world she'd ever seen.

But despite the oddities of its life and water, Prime had nearly the same gravity and atmospheric mix as Earth. It was the kind of world where the differences were enough to put a spring in your step and not enough to throw off your equilibrium.

And that same odd life naturally produced some of the most complicated ferro-organic molecules in the universe. The equivalent of Earth's oil deposits here was a viscous red sludge that was easily refined into high-strength alloys and plastics.

The settlements were a clear sign of the eternal conflict between Prime's reason for being and what humans needed to survive. The ash-black cleared zones around the farms of familiar green weren't there to protect the farms from Prime's life—they were there to protect Prime's priceless ecosystem from the food humanity needed to survive.

Easily half of Sandoval's food production was in orbit, but some things were simply most efficiently grown in real soil with proper gravity. So, Prime's cities were surrounded by fields of green crops, which were surrounded in turn by cleared zones where nothing from either ecosystem lived.

"Coming up on the RTA now," Nicolas reported. The pilot was listening to his headset. "We are clear to land, though they sound somewhat grumpy at our lack of appointment."

Maria grinned as she looked out the window, easily picking out Sandoval's Runic Transceiver Array from the orange forest surrounding it. The RTA was a massive structure of black concrete, the runes that covered it invisible from here except in the glittering sheen they gave the black sphere.

"They'll get over it," she told Nicolas. "What kind of spies would we be if we told people we were coming?"

Exiting the shuttle, Maria found herself met by two of the perfectly standard-robed Mages of the Transceiver Guild. They seemed to be stamped from a mold somewhere, combining a librarian's faint sense of disapproval at loud conversation with powerful magic of their own and a commitment to confidentiality matched by few in the galaxy.

"This is a Protectorate-secured facility," the taller Mage told her grumpily. She couldn't really see his face under the hood of his robe, but she could tell he was looking down his nose at her. "Access to the transceiver array is by appointment and arrangement only; that is no different here than on any other..."

He finally noticed the plain white card Maria was holding out to him. It was blank. The card itself was the message—well, that and the data chip concealed within it that held a Transceiver Guild encryption Maria was quite certain *Red Falcon*'s computers couldn't break.

The Mage sighed and took the card, pressing it to his wrist-comp and reading the text that flashed up on his screen.

"I see," he finally said, looking back at her. The faint air of disapproval was still there, but at least he wasn't looking down his nose at her.

"I am Zhao Fernandez," he introduced himself. "We have regularly scheduled communications going on right now. How confidential does your communication need to be?"

"The highest," Maria told him. "I need to contact Mars, Mage Fernandez."

"Ah." He nodded slowly. "If you give us about fifteen minutes, Lady Mage, we can clear the facility without drawing too much attention. I can clear it faster, but..."

"But that would draw attention," Maria agreed. "Fifteen minutes is fine, Mage Fernandez. My report is based on events from days ago; another half-hour won't make a difference."

He smiled for the first time.

"I agree with your logic, Lady Mage, but you'd be astonished how many couriers don't seem to understand that."

It took the Transceiver Mages just over twenty-five minutes to clear the various side chambers and recording facilities that allowed a single RTA to provide the sole source of instantaneous communication for an entire planet.

Finally, Fernandez escorted Maria into the central transmission chamber and bowed.

"We're running standard confidentiality procedures, ma'am," he told her. "We are still recording incoming communications in the other receiving chambers, but there are no recorders active in here, and we will purge any side chatter that makes it into the other recorders."

He shrugged.

"We can't do more without cutting Sandoval off from the universe, and, apologies ma'am, but your authority doesn't stretch that far."

Maria chuckled.

"It has stretched more than far enough for my purposes, Mage Fernandez. Thank you."

He bowed and withdrew, leaving her alone in the central chamber. She crossed the spherical room to the very center and focused her energies.

For most people, they would pay a Transceiver like Fernandez to send their message. He would enter this chamber, channel its energies, and speak the message he was given. Only a Mage's voice could be sent across the galaxy, which inherently limited the use of the RTA beyond even the sheer scale and cost of one's construction.

Any Mage, however, could fulfill the same role. Not all of them knew how, but it was part of both Jump Mage and Naval Mage training.

When she spoke, her words flashed across space to the RTA at Olympus Mons on Mars.

"This is a Bravo One Priority communication," she announced into thin air. "Authentication Kappa Kappa Bravo Six Three Lima Romeo Eight Niner One Charlie. I repeat, this is a Bravo One Priority communication.

"I need to make contact with MISS Command immediately. Please connect."

The room was silent for a few seconds, and then a voice responded out of the air.

"This is Mars RTA Control; we are receiving you," it told her. "We are clearing a confidential chamber and preparing a radio relay to MISS Command, please stand by."

"Belay that," a new voice cut over. It was an unfamiliar, a husky baritone that spoke with calm authority. "I'll take that confidential chamber, though."

"Understood. Please stand by; we are connecting you to Hand Lomond."

Hand Lomond? Hand Hans Lomond was the longest serving of the Mage-King's Hands, his roving troubleshooters. He was the one who tended to be sent along with the Mage-King's fleets...

He was the man they called the Sword of Mars.

"Mage Soprano," Lomond's baritone emerged from the air a few moments later. "Hand Stealey has briefed me on your operation, but she is not currently on Mars. Since I'm *here*, it seems wiser to pull myself into this than to wait for MISS to find someone senior enough to talk to you."

"My Lord Lomond, I did not expect to be speaking to a Hand," Maria admitted.

Lomond chuckled.

"You've met Stealey, haven't you?" he replied. "We're just ordinary men and women. Well...no less ordinary than any other Mage, at least. His Majesty has asked more of us; that is all.

"What is your situation? You wouldn't be reaching out at Bravo One if it wasn't important."

Maria breathed heavily and then launched into her spiel, explaining the events of their voyage so far, focusing on the conflict with the Golden Bears and the problems in Atlatl.

Lomond waited silently, poking with the occasional question as she continued.

"I see," he finally concluded. "Fortunately, I happen to have a trio of cruisers and, oh, a Hand spoiling for a fight. I think I shall need to visit Atlatl and make certain the situation is contained.

"We will keep your Captain's promise to the Bears for now," he noted. Maria might not have told MISS everything, including what they'd promised, but she wasn't going to lie to a Hand. Not even by omission.

"If they behave, they can keep their license. If we discover they are continuing to be knives for hire, they will learn the limits of the Protectorate's patience," Lomond said calmly. In some ways, his calm was scarier than another man's rage.

"What about Corinthian?" she asked.

"That depends on what Rice is planning," Lomond admitted. "I don't want to joggle the man's elbow, and we frankly don't have much in the area we can quickly commit. RTAs get sparse on the ground in that region.

"I can arrange for a cleanup team to arrive about a week after you do," he continued. "If you can pull them off balance, the team I'm thinking of will make sure to get all of their files...but Rice is correct.

"If we show up with destroyers and Marines and storm their office, they'll have a destruct built into their files. We'll gain nothing. We need to finish the Legacy off, *forever*.

"You and Rice know what you're doing," he concluded. "Whatever resources you need to commandeer, you have the authority to."

"We do?" Maria asked, surprised.

Lomond coughed.

"All right, then, get a recorder going and I'll *give* you that authority," he told her with a chuckle. "You know where the jugular of one of our most pernicious enemies is located. They wouldn't call me the Sword of Mars if I wasn't the type to tell you to go for it!"

CHAPTER 30

KELLY WAS RUBBING her head to try and ease away her headache when the Captain wandered into her office. He didn't look in much better shape than she did.

"How's the off-loading going?" he asked, his voice tired.

"I'm wishing we'd paid more attention to that 'multiple delivery location' clause in the contract," she told him. "I was expecting, I don't know, two, maybe three locales?"

"So was I," Rice grunted. "I know Nicolas's people have been run ragged. How bad?"

"A quarter of the cargo went to the orbital for later distribution," she told him. "The rest...forty different orbital food platforms and fifteen different surface locations. We're being reimbursed for fuel and time, but..."

She shook her head.

Fifty-six different delivery locations, varying from five containers of soil to over four hundred heading to the orbital. Sandoval Prime Orbital had transshipment facilities to handle most of their four hundred-plus themselves, thankfully, but the other deliveries had all fallen on *Red Falcon*'s shuttle pilots.

The heaviest shuttles *Falcon* had could carry two ten-thousand-ton containers. The big freighter had a lot of shuttles...but she also carried *eighteen hundred* containers.

It had been a busy few days, and Kelly suspected it might take Kelzin a day or two to have enough energy to even *look* at his lovers again. The surface flights were especially rough on the pilots—and so inevitably ended up on the most experienced and senior flight crews.

"Total up the fuel and time spent and bounce it to my comp," Rice told her. "We may as well get fully paid for this cargo."

The grouchiness in his tone warned her of the problem.

"We don't have a cargo to Corinthian?" she asked.

"We don't have a cargo. Period," the Captain told her. "Sandoval imports a lot of crap, including millions of tons of soil, but most of their exports are locked down by a group of Core World interstellars, and they use the big shipping firms.

"There's nothing shipping out of Sandoval worth loading up the *Falcon* with," he concluded. "You and I have an appointment with a shipping broker this afternoon, but that..."

The Captain shrugged.

"That's actually just cover for a meeting with the local MISS branch, seeing if they can help out. We need an excuse to go to Corinthian, and right now it looks like we'll be leaving Sandoval with a quarter-load at best."

"And we can't justify taking a quarter-load more than half a dozen light-years," Kelly agreed. "Not six days to Corinthian."

"Exactly." Her boss sighed, leaning against her desk. "I've run the data we have, and I *think* we can swing a quarter-load into Amber. From there, I'm pretty sure I can arrange a cargo to Corinthian, even if I have to beg a favor from Keiko."

Keiko Alabaster was the Captain's girlfriend—the fabulously wealthy mistress of an Amber-based shipping syndicate with a bad habit of getting involved in revolutions.

"Keiko doesn't know we work for MISS, does she?" Kelly asked.

"I think she *suspects*," David replied, "but she doesn't know." He sighed. "The major reason I think she suspects is that she hasn't asked. She doesn't want to make me lie to her, and she knows I couldn't tell her one way or another.

"I'd rather *not* use her connections here," he continued, "but we need to get to Corinthian without drawing too much attention to ourselves."

Kelly considered.

"Corinthian's one of the richer MidWorlds," she said aloud. "What about a spec cargo?"

"We'd need to find someone willing to *sell* us at least ten million tons of Sandoval's exports," David pointed out. "And the money to pay for it. Even just raw Prime sludge goes for twenty, thirty thousand a ton."

"Well, didn't you just say we were going to talk to MISS?" she pointed out.

The receptionist at Orange Autumn Exporters didn't seem to know there was anything unusual going on. The adorably nervous young man's nerves were pretty clearly entirely related to being brand-new at his job.

Kelly wanted to pat the puppy-in-human-form on the head and tell him he was doing fine, but she was reasonably sure that qualified as unprofessional. Instead, she let him get her a glass of water and waited for their meeting room to open up.

Eventually, the young man walked them to the neatly professional meeting room, where a woman in a dark pink suit, not much older than the kid escorting them, was waiting.

"Captain Rice, Officer LaMonte, greetings," she told them. "That will be all, Jason."

The receptionist bowed his way out of the room, closing the door behind him.

"Please forgive Jason; he's been on the job for all of, oh, three days," the dark-haired broker told them. "He's a trained MISS bodyguard and lethal with any object that weighs more than about two hundred grams, but he isn't quite sure how to be a receptionist yet."

She rose and offered them her hand.

"Elena Petrovich," she introduced herself. "Depending on the day, junior partner in Orange Autumn Exporters, or Deputy Station Chief, Sandoval for the MISS.

"You come to me with the authentication codes and protocols to command my complete attention, Captain Rice, though I'll confess that

I did not expect to discover that you were an MISS agent when your ship arrived. *Red Falcon* is in my files, yes, but not as one of ours."

"That's generally to everyone's advantage," Rice pointed out. "The fewer people who know your covert ops ship is such, the more useful that ship is going to be."

"This is very true," Petrovich allowed. "How may I be of assistance, Captain Rice?"

"We need to be in Corinthian," he said bluntly. "And we need to be in Corinthian for reasons that make sense to others, at least at first blush. If I were to simply pick up and head there, too many questions would be asked about just why I did so.

"So, I need a cargo."

"And no one in Sandoval is shipping to Corinthian. Yes, I see," Petrovich said. She considered for a moment, tapping on her wrist-comp and turning the long wall of the conference table into an active wallscreen.

"Honestly, your ship's capacity is simply too large for most exports from this system," she admitted. "If it isn't heading to the Core Worlds, most of Sandoval's needs are met by smaller ships in the three-to-six-megaton range. Not twenty.

"I'm not sure I can twist Orange Autumn's operations into anything remotely near enough of a pretzel to justify a shipment to Corinthian worth hiring your ship for," she admitted, flipping through screens and reports faster than Kelly could follow.

"We came to the same conclusions before we got here," Kelly told her, with a quick glance at Rice to make sure she could lay out what they'd concluded. "So, we found ourselves with one logical option that we think can work.

"Captain Rice's resources are known to be impressive at this point, as are his connections," she noted. "We now own a second ship, *Peregrine*, which is not something most independent shippers can claim.

"It wouldn't appear out of reason for us to pick up a speculative cargo that would fit *Peregrine*'s capacity here and transport it to Corinthian for sale. Assuming we could *find* a ten-megaton or larger cargo of Sandoval's unique organics to purchase."

"That…could work," Petrovich agreed. The wallscreen suddenly changed to a completely different set of reports as she continued to tap away at her wrist-comp.

"Of course, you wouldn't be able to find a single cargo like that," she noted. "You'd need to track down multiple batches from the independent producers, few of which will be over five hundred thousand tons…"

"We'd need a local broker," Kelly said with a smile.

"You would," Petrovich agreed. "And, I'm assuming, some level of financing? I don't know if your personal resources will actually stretch to this, Captain Rice, but I have discretionary funds available that should allow for us to pull this together."

"I was hoping you'd say that," Rice told her. "I could afford ten megatons of sludge at the current list price, barely, but buying it in smaller batches is always more expensive."

"Let's see what we can make happen, shall we?"

With all of the problems they'd been having with security on space stations across the Protectorate, Kelly and Rice moved through Sandoval Prime Orbital in a blur. Their trip to and from the MISS office masquerading as a brokerage was via the fastest in-station transport available, with an entire squad of Skavar's people riding shotgun.

They took a different route back to the ship than they took away from the ship, and so far, at least, the new precautions seemed to be working.

This time, they weren't *trying* to provoke an attack. Kelly's Captain was still having trouble moving with his new leg, even if he'd foregone both the wheelchair and the cane by now.

The young executive officer heaved an open sigh of relief when they reached the docking tube for the ship to find Soprano waiting for them. The Ship's Mage looked like someone had hit her between the eyes with a length of pipe, but she was still managing to keep a wary eye out as the Captain came aboard.

"My office, both of you," Rice ordered as they passed Soprano. "Kelly, can you ping Jeeves and Kellers as well?" He glanced over at their escort. "If one of you scary gentlemen and ladies wants to spare the XO the hassle of telling Skavar to get to my office, I'd appreciate it."

Corporal Spiros grinned.

"On it, Skipper."

"Come on," he told Kelly. "It's time to start lining all of the pieces up."

Once again, Kelly and the rest of the officers gathered in David's office. The Captain stumped over to his desk and dropped into his chair with an audible—and concerning—sigh of relief.

In Kelly's unqualified but informed opinion, he was pushing himself too hard. But how did an XO with experience measured in weeks tell that to her Captain whose experience was measured in decades?

"My attempt to contact MISS command got short-circuited," Soprano told them. "By Hand Lomond."

"Another bleeding Hand?" Rice growled. "Who do we work for again?"

"The Mage-King," Soprano replied gently. "My report is being passed on, but Lomond is going to deal with the Atlatl situation personally.

"I now have his explicit authorization to commandeer any Protectorate resources necessary for our mission, on an authenticated recording," she continued. "Terrifying as that feels, it should let us pull together whatever we need."

"I think the resources we need are already in place," the Captain said. "But that may come in handy regardless. The Navy has set up a general trap for anyone hunting down remnants of the Blue Star Syndicate that I intend to try and lure the Legacy into.

"Thanks to a brainstorm of Kelly's, we now have a reason to head to Corinthian. We're going to receive a number of separate deliveries over the next forty-eight hours that add up to about a twelve-million-ton cargo of Sandoval sludge and various refined ferro-organics.

"Technically, we're paying for it all ourselves. In practice, MISS is underwriting most of the bill. It's a spec cargo, but Corinthian is one of, oh, four MidWorlds that might actually be able to justify a regular run from Sandoval," he concluded. "So, it's a decent excuse."

"I also reached out to Campbell," Soprano told the others. "*Peregrine* will be meeting us in Corinthian. Neither of our ships are true combatants, but *Peregrine* has enough firepower to make having her around reassuring."

"So, what is our actual plan in Corinthian?" Skavar asked. "No offense, Skipper, but I think we need to be *very* done with the 'wander around and see who shoots at us' plan."

Rice chuckled and smacked his leg. The polymer was wrapped in faked skin relatively well—and was designed so that it would over time function as a matrix for his skin to grow over—but right now, hitting the limb created a very mechanical sound.

"I, my leg, and my lung agree with you completely," he replied. "I have some names to poke at in Corinthian for contacts, if they're still in business and willing to talk to me. I'd like to approach these lawyers through an intermediary, but if none of the people we know in the Spindle are willing to talk to us, well...showing up in their front office will probably make an impression."

"Not necessarily the impression we want, since we'd rather take their files intact," Kelly pointed out. "They won't have anything incriminating hooked up to the system net. We need to get Marine or MISS techs physically in that office before they can start wrecking shit."

"Hence why I want to talk to them," Rice confirmed. "They've chased us across half the damn Protectorate at this point. Let's see if they're at least willing to talk peace."

CHAPTER 31

IT WAS PERFECTLY FINE, David reflected, for an Augment who was only about thirty percent human by mass to say that the leg would feel like his before it worked properly. Blade's legs probably hadn't even been the first thing the cyborg's employers had replaced.

For David, the dysmorphia wasn't fading at all. He barely registered the odd weight in his chest where his new lung sat; that one had been easy enough to get used to.

His leg, though...

He could walk again, after a fashion. Zero gravity was fine. *Red Falcon's* magical artificial gravity was a different story, but he could clunk around like a man with a robot leg that didn't quite want to obey him.

It wasn't really a metaphor.

He thumped back into his office alone after the jump away from Sandoval and collapsed into his chair. He didn't even have the emotional satisfaction of breathing hard anymore. Anaerobic exercise was apparently a thing of the past once you had a lung that was perfectly willing to top up your oxygen supply from its own reserves.

The manual said it could take up to six months for the dysmorphia to fade. He wasn't looking forward to spending half a year with a hunk of metal on his hip that mostly followed his instructions without quite feeling like it belonged to him.

Red Falcon was back in deep space again, where she belonged. Sandoval Prime was behind them and they were once more out of communication with everybody. Six days and over seventy light-years from now, they would reach Corinthian, and David Rice would challenge the lawyers who were trying to kill him.

There was something...extra evil about that concept. They weren't sending killers and mercenaries after him out of malice or even truly personal benefit. It was simply that was what the will said they had to do...so that was what they were going to do.

Hundreds—possibly thousands—of people were dead because of that. An entire regional syndicate, a successor organization to the Blue Star, had been ground to pieces by the Navy after their attack on David had exposed them.

Both David and MISS would rather he could focus on Legatus. The UnArcana Worlds were moving in the shadows, and the whole mess with Azure Legacy was a distraction from what MISS suspected were the opening moves of a civil war.

All because a group of lawyers apparently respected their client's will more than they respected laws or even human lives.

When this was over, David was going to make them pay for that.

And for his leg. There were a lot of things he was angry about at this point, but his leg was pretty high up the list.

"Mage Soprano, can I have a moment?"

Maria looked up to see Kelly LaMonte standing in the door of her office, and gestured the young XO in. Unlike her junior Mages, Maria at least had her own separate office. The juniors shared their space with the soldering workbenches and three-dimensional holograms used for jump plotting.

The office wasn't big, but there was enough room for Maria to have meetings, and it had a fridge and a coffee pot.

"Sure. Want something to drink? Coffee? Water?"

"Coffee, please," LaMonte replied.

Maria slid a cup across the table.

"What's up, XO?"

"The Captain," the younger woman said quietly. "He's...not in a great headspace right now, and we're about to go toe-to-toe with the folks causing us all kinds of grief. I'm worried about him."

Maria sighed.

"I don't know him as well," she pointed out. "You've served with him longer; you saw him through the whole mess on *Blue Jay*. This is a smaller-level clusterfuck than that, from what I can tell."

"Yeah, but..." LaMonte shook her head. "The thing is, while he took losing people hard, I don't think the Captain has ever actually been seriously injured himself before. He *wants* to be the kind of person where his people matter more than he does...but he lost a goddamn leg, Maria."

"Nobody bounces back from that as quickly as he's trying to."

Maria sighed.

"I know," she admitted. "And I suspect he thinks he's failing us by not being at his best."

"We're supposed to be at his back, holding him up," LaMonte said. "How do we do that when I'm not one hundred percent sure he's thinking clearly?"

"By using our judgment, XO," Maria told her. "Preferably better than I have historically."

LaMonte winced at that. She knew at least the high level of why Maria had barely avoided being dishonorably discharged from the Royal Martian Navy.

"We'll meet Campbell in Corinthian, too," Maria continued. "She knows Rice better than anyone alive—far better than even Alabaster, I suspect. Alabaster's just sleeping with the man. Campbell was his XO for over a decade."

"And what do we do if we think he's about to go off the deep end?" LaMonte asked quietly.

"We find bungee cords, XO, and we pull him back up," Maria replied. "That's the damn job, isn't it?"

Maria didn't bother to knock as she walked into Ivan Skavar's spectacularly chaotic office. She knew the Marine intelligence officer far too well to believe the room was as disorganized as it looked, but paper and datapads were strewn over every surface like a hurricane had swept through.

"Welcome, welcome, have a seat," Skavar said dryly as she shifted a pile of papers off a chair with a gesture and a flick of magic.

There were clear chairs, but the one with paper on it looked far more comfortable, and she dropped into it with an exaggerated sigh.

"Four metal folding chairs, one stuffed armchair, and which one do you fill with papers?" she asked rhetorically. The papers spun in the air distractedly.

"I presume you want these somewhere specific?" she continued.

Skavar snorted.

"That chair?" he replied. "Otherwise, drop them on the end of my desk here." He pointed. "That's the 'to be sorted' pile."

"As opposed to the rest of the room?"

"Those piles each have a purpose," he objected, then grinned. "Of course, the chair was an expansion of the 'to be sorted' pile."

Maria shook her head at the Marine, adding the papers and datapad from the chair to the designated pile. She straightened it up with her magic as she did so; the datapad would probably have fallen off if she didn't.

"So, our Captain is about to shove his head into the dragon's mouth," she noted. "He's smarter about it than some I've met, but I'm wondering if you have any particular ideas for making sure we get him *back* from that."

Skavar sighed.

"I don't think I can justify rules of engagement that call for exosuits on the Spindle," he pointed out, referring to Corinthian's primary space station. "Not least, given the Captain's history there, I suspect the local authorities would take a poor view of us traipsing around in heavy battle armor."

"There comes a point where we stop caring what the locals think," Maria replied. "We have the authority to do whatever we need to."

"Yes, but if we fire boarding torpedoes loaded with exosuits into the damn station, no one is ever going to believe *Red Falcon* is an innocent merchant ship ever again," Skavar told her. "*An* assault shuttle? Sure, people might believe we bought that with the ship."

"Boarding torpedoes? Exosuits? Attack flights of armed shuttles? We could very easily blow any chance of us ever having a cover again!"

"If it's a choice between that or losing the Captain, what do we do?" Maria asked.

Skavar winced like she'd hit him.

"I could argue that we should accept losing the Captain," he said levelly. "I won't, but I could. If it comes down to it, I and my people will go all-out and we will *fuck up* the Legacy with everything we've got.

"Is that what you want to hear, Mage Soprano? I'll have a boarding torp loaded with exosuits ready to go, but..." He shook his head again. "There's a limit to what we can do in an inhabited system under eyes of a few million people.

"Drag the Legacy out here into the void and the shadows?" He gestured at the screen showing the empty space around *Red Falcon*.

"Out here, I'll go all-out. But in-system, we need to be subtler."

"So, what do we do?" Maria asked.

"We get the Skipper to wear a tracker, just in case," the Marine told her. "I'm going to quietly make sure I have a *lot* more armed people on the Spindle than anybody knows, and I'm going to make sure I've got the links and the codes to call in the local Marine garrison if needed.

"After the Skipper's last visit to Corinthian, my understanding is that there's a trio of destroyers and an entire RMMC regiment standing guard, plus the locals," he continued. "I can think of all kinds of uses for those folks."

"And I can think of a few other people we can poke," Maria admitted. "If we get a target...well, one of the dead drops we have to contact LMID is only a few jumps from Corinthian."

Skavar blinked.

"We have dead drops to contact LMID?" he asked.

"Well, the Captain does," she told him. "He briefed LaMonte and me—and now I've briefed you. Legatus has him marked as an asset. That's something they're going to regret in the long run, but I'll be damned if I'll let it go to waste today!"

CHAPTER 32

"A TRACKER?" David asked, looking cautiously at the large-seeming hypodermic in Dr. Gupta's hand.

"A modification of the standard Marine-issue challenge-response beacon," Skavar told him, standing behind the doctor and very clearly trying not to seem like he was forcing any part of this issue. "If it gets hit with the correct signal, it responds at random intervals for the ensuing ninety seconds."

"As I recall, that beacon is built into the dog tags," David replied. "And you want to *inject* me with that?"

"It opens up a lot of options and possibilities," his security chief told him. "Plus, bluntly, you have a habit of getting in trouble, Skipper. This would make sure we could track you down, no matter what."

"Within limits," the Captain pointed out. "It's not like it's some magic interstellar beacon. Radio waves, right?"

"Not many other options I'm aware of," the Marine agreed. "And while I'd love to borrow a Tracker, the only people I know with one, well, we blew half their fleet to pieces and bribed them to sell out their clients."

David sighed.

"And if I were to promise to be a good boy and do everything by electronic coms?" he asked.

"We both know that's not an option. Even if we weren't coming to Corinthian to try and sort out a meet with the Legacy, the kind of spec cargo we're bringing in requires you to meet with people," Skavar concluded. "Much as I'd *love* to lock you on the ship, behind a wall of armored troops and maybe a battle tank or two, the job requires you to leave the ship.

"So, this lets us keep an extra eye on you and know where to come barrelling in with all the troops and guns if something *does* go wrong."

"Does it have to be *quite* so intimidating a needle?" the Captain grumbled.

"We could, in theory, install it in your leg," Gupta told him. "That would require me to have more faith that Legatan hardware will play nice with Martian hardware than I do. The injected chip is honestly the best option."

David looked at the needle again and shivered.

"I've had worse," he admitted. "Fine."

"Pull up your sleeve, boss."

There was a sharp stab, and then a swab of cooling coagulant.

"That's all."

"Thanks, boss," Skavar told him. "After the last few months, even one extra arrow in our quiver makes me a feel bit better. Surprises...well, I like having surprises to spring a lot better than I like running into them."

"Me too," David agreed. "Plus, well, more likely than not, the person this is going to save is me!"

The PA system crackled to life as he was speaking and Kelly LaMonte's voice sounded across the ship.

"All hands, all hands. Stand by for final jump into Corinthian System."

There was a nearly imperceptible flicker of reality changing, and then the XO spoke again.

"All right, folks, welcome to Corinthian. Those of us who made an impression last time...well, let's not remind people about that.

"I promised the Captain we wouldn't stun any cops this time!"

David waited until they were close enough to the Spindle for a reasonable conversation before reaching out to his contacts. A few seconds'

delay as messages flew back and forth was easily handled by experienced spacers.

Longer called for recordings, and this wasn't a conversation he wanted to have via recording. He wasn't even sure that the contact code he had would work.

When the screen lit up with the image of a reception desk and a perfectly coiffed young woman in a purple dress, he was certain he had the wrong number. He had a few other ways to try and get ahold of the man he was looking for, but they were all complicated.

"Spindle Spider Information Consulting," the young lady happily chirped at him. "How may I assist you?"

Well…information consulting was more promising that he'd initially thought.

"Good afternoon," he greeted her. "I had this contact number for Travis Carmichael. Would you be able to put me in contact with him?"

From the woman's complete non-reaction, Carmichael clearly had some connection to the consulting company David had reached.

"I am aware of Mr. Carmichael," she said carefully. "SSIC does some business with him, but I'm afraid I have no way of getting in touch with him immediately.

"Certainly, SSIC is not in the habit of passing on contact information without explicit permission."

"Of course," David allowed. Carmichael, it seemed, had kept the old contact code he'd given David before *Blue Jay*'s visit to Corinthian had gone sideways, but attached it to a filter.

"If you could pass on a message to Mr. Carmichael," he continued, "please let him know that Captain David Rice is looking to get in touch with him with regards to a potential business arrangement."

He smiled.

"Mr. Carmichael knows who I am."

The woman nodded.

"Of course, Captain Rice. I'll talk to the partner who works with Mr. Carmichael and see if we can pass on your information. How would he be able to get ahold of you?"

"I'm aboard the freighter *Red Falcon*," David told her. "We'll be docking in an hour or two."

"Thank you; I'll make sure that Mr. Carmichael hears."

He nodded his thanks and closed the connection. She'd messed up at the end. She was supposed to be pretending that she didn't work for Carmichael, but her final phrasing had been that of an employee promising their boss would be in touch.

David made a checkmark in his mental book of bets with himself as his wrist-comp chimed. He'd barely had enough time to hit the head and refill his coffee.

"Rice here," he said into the little computer.

"Skipper, we've got an inbound call for you from a Travis Carmichael," the current com technician told him. "Should I put him through?"

"I've been waiting for him," David told her. "Connect him to my office system."

The last couple of years didn't seem to have changed Carmichael much. The tall information broker was still just as slim and fit as he had been, and he'd lost none of the sheen to his red hair or the piercing glare to his eyes.

"Captain Rice," Carmichael greeted him. "The last time we spoke, I believe I told you never to come back to Corinthian."

"You certainly advised against it," David agreed. "Though it was more in the order of warning what the government and local thuggery would do if I came back. Things have been sorted with the government.

"Should I be concerned about the criminals?"

Carmichael chuckled.

"Between one thing and another, I don't think anyone you pissed off is still in play," he admitted. "Carney would probably want you dead, still, but he drank a vial of poison in lieu of being arrested about a year back."

The younger man on David's screen shrugged.

"His organization was all but gone at that point anyway. Half got arrested; half abandoned him for a new flag. Hell, the guy they abandoned Carney for is dead now too, but he didn't go quietly on his front porch."

Last time he'd been in Corinthian, David Rice had made a deal with the crime boss Carney to break out his Ship's Mage. He'd also left Carney swinging when Hand Stealey arrived to clean up the mess.

"So, you're probably safe to be here," Carmichael admitted. "Can't say I'd have come back in your place, but I'm presuming you've got a reason. What do you want, Rice?"

"I want to engage your services," David told him. "I've brought in a spec cargo, which means I'm going to need to track down buyers. I can't imagine you haven't rebuilt from whatever losses the Hand inflicted on your network."

The broker chuckled.

"I took the arrival of a Hand as unto a sign from God, Captain Rice," he replied. "I keep my finger on the pulse of the underworld here in self-defense, yes, but I keep my nose clean. Your spec cargo is exactly the kind of work I do most of these days.

"What kind of cargo are we talking?"

David smiled.

The channel was sufficiently secure that they could talk about past potential criminalities, but not secure enough that either of them would risk admitting to current crimes or problems.

"At the high level, it's ferro-organics from Sandoval Prime," he told the broker. "Buying a spec cargo there, however, means I've got a bunch of hundred- to five-hundred-thousand-ton lots of slightly different things.

"I'd like to go over the details in person."

Carmichael nodded slowly. Just as David had picked up that he had more underworld contacts than he'd admitted, he'd picked up that David needed more than someone to put him in touch with buyers.

"All right, Captain Rice," he agreed. "My office is still in the same building, even if it has a different owner these days. I'll have my staff send yours the address. Say, tomorrow at eleven AM Olympus Mons Time?"

"That sounds acceptable," David said. "May I bring my Ship's Mage?"

"Feeling paranoid, Captain?"

"You remember my last visit to the Spindle," David pointed out.

"Fair enough. Is it still the young Montgomery?" Carmichael asked.

"No. Montgomery moved on to different pastures. Mage Maria Soprano leads my Mages now."

"That's right; you have a much bigger ship these days, don't you?" The broker nodded, his gaze flickering as he clearly ran a data search on a screen David couldn't see. "Very well, Captain, feel free to bring Commander Soprano with you.

"Her record sounds *fascinating*."

CHAPTER 33

THE CORINTHIAN SPINDLE wasn't necessarily unique in human space, but it was spectacular. Like the core piece of Junkertown in Snap, it was an O'Neill cylinder. Unlike Junkertown, however, the Spindle's builders had managed to put the resources in place to keep the Spindle operating.

The primary cylinder continued to spin fast enough to provide a semblance of one gravity on the outer edge, and massive quantities of soil had been lifted from the surface to allow for planting forests and farms. With the surface area available on the inside of a fully functioning O'Neill cylinder, the Spindle had towns, cities, farms, even carefully manicured parks.

Making the transition from the zero-gravity "caps" on the end of the cylinder, kept motionless so ships could dock, to the verdant glory of the primary Spindle was impressive even to David, and this was his third visit to the Spindle.

Soprano had never been here before, and the Mage stopped dead as she stepped out of the elevator terminal and into the neatly arranged rows of trees that shaded the exit from the carefully controlled brightness radiating from the core pillar at the center of the cylinder.

"Damn," she murmured.

"There are other places like the Spindle," David agreed, "But none that managed the concept quite so well. It's like a chunk of Old Earth in space, except you can look up and see Germany."

His Ship's Mage chuckled.

"I didn't think there were any fully ecosystemed O'Neill cylinders outside Sol, let alone the Core Worlds. I knew Corinthian had a cylinder, but..."

"You figured it was something like Junkertown, where someone had started and never finished?" David asked. "There's a few of those. But... Corinthian takes a lot of pride in this place, though they don't mention the real reason for it."

"What's that?" Soprano asked carefully.

David pointed "Yard-wards" as they exited the park around the elevators. Halfway along the length of the artificial ecosystem the Corinthians maintained, a massive black iron fortress rose out of the surface. Its harsh exterior was softened by trees planted on its terraced exterior, but even from here you could tell that it was a fortress against the world.

"The Citadel. It's the center of the Mage Guilds in Corinthian—and the Mage Guilds underwrote most of the cost of building the Spindle. The system had some major problems with anti-Mage sentiment, including some ugly riots and bombings just as the Spindle was being started."

Soprano shivered.

"Right." She shook her head. "How do we get to this Carmichael?"

"We walk over to the Length-way over there," David gestured, "and grab a taxi. The station's pretty well set up."

The discreet three-story office building tucked into the outskirts of one of the Spindle's small towns was much busier this time than the last time David had visited. A bakery-style café had moved in on the main floor, and the beginning of the lunchtime rush was already filling its tables.

Their directions took them to the second floor, where a young lady in a dark green dress greeted them in front of a stylized logo of a jeweled spider. It was a different woman from the one who'd answered the call the previous day, but she was cut from much the same distractingly attractive, probably dangerously smart cloth.

"Captain Rice, Mage Soprano," she greeted them cheerfully. "A pleasure to meet you both. May I show you to your meeting room?"

"Of course," David told her.

The moment the woman stood up and moved, he realized he'd still *dramatically* underestimated her. The only people he'd seen move with that kind of liquid grace had been the genetically augmented assassins employed by Turquoise of the Silent Ocean syndicate.

He had a Mage beside him, so the odds were *probably* in his favor if Carmichael's new bodyguard decided he was a threat, but it wasn't a chance he wanted to take!

She led the way up to the top floor and a familiar office looking out over the Spindle's artificial world. The room was still paneled in imported Sherwood oak, and any filing cabinets or storage space was concealed behind the panels. A single desk of the expensive hardwood filled the center of the room, and several overstuffed chairs, also framed in oak, were scattered comfortably around the room.

In person, it was easier to see the silver that had begun to sneak its way into Carmichael's hair. The information broker was closing the blinds as they came in, hidden panels in the roof adjusting their glow to keep the light constant.

"Thank you, Lisa," he told the bodyguard. "You shouldn't need to remain. Captain Rice is no threat."

"Of course, Travis," the woman replied. "Your next appointment is lunch at twelve thirty. We'll need to get moving at about twelve fifteen to be there on time."

"Thank you, Lisa," Carmichael repeated with a smile. The young woman bowed herself out, closing the door behind her.

David was watching for it and felt the Faraday cage built into the room activate as the door closed.

"Still sweeping the building for bugs every day?" he asked.

"Of course," the broker confirmed. "Even if *I* was willing to let that up, Lisa and her sister wouldn't." He smiled. "They were apparently intended to be sold at a slave auction when I came across the information on their shipment.

"Programmed for obedience to their designated client." He shook his head. "There are lines in this galaxy, Captain Rice, that even those of us who often work in the shadows should not cross."

"You rescued them?" David asked carefully.

Carmichael chuckled.

"In a manner of speaking. I arranged for the transport carrying them and two hundred other slaves to be raided by security, handed the man who organized the shipment over to the Marine garrison, and watched his successor flail his way into an open firefight with a Navy landing team.

"Lisa and Maria tracked down the source of the information that freed them and volunteered their services. They are extraordinarily capable employees who do not let me pay them *nearly* enough."

He tapped a hidden control on his desk, and a two-way screen rose out of the wooden surface.

"Now, you didn't come here to talk about my new hires. You had details on the cargo that you wanted me to help find buyers for?"

"I do," David confirmed, pulling a datachip from inside his blazer and sliding it over. "There are about thirty-seven different lots with about ninety different variations of source material, target refined product and state of refinement. With this kind of spec cargo, a broad variety is useful to find who in Corinthian will be interested in buying it."

"That's correct," Carmichael agreed, sliding open a concealed panel to reveal a reader he dropped the chip onto. "From what I know of Sandoval's products, I'm quite certain we can find buyers for everything, but I don't know in what quantities or at what prices yet. It may well prove that only certain products are profitable enough to be worthwhile—and those may not be desired in sufficient quantity to be worth shipping."

"I know," David conceded the warning. "But it's worth testing. We have a second ship now, so using *Red Falcon* to test routes we then have *Peregrine* take is useful. Plus, well…*Falcon* and I are a bit of a target these days."

Carmichael chuckled.

"And has that worked out any better for the current collection than it did for the last bunch?" he asked.

"Not really," David said. "But I'm getting sick of losing people and having to kill people. I'm a merchant captain, damn it, not a soldier."

The broker's chuckle turned to a sigh.

"And so, you come to me," he murmured. "I figured there was more going on than just needing a sales broker."

"Don't get me wrong," David told him. "I need a sales broker and you're the only one I know here—and I owe you for the mess I got you stuck in last time."

Carmichael ran his finger down the numbers on his side of the screen, then flipped them over to their side.

"I'll need a six-percent cut of the final price," he said. "This includes your purchase price, so I'll be targeting at least a five-percent profit on everything after my cut for you. That will probably be average," he warned, "with some products taking a loss and some getting higher.

"Sound reasonable?"

"That does," David confirmed. He could probably argue the broker down...but he did owe Carmichael. Plus, MISS had paid for three-quarters of the cargo, and they weren't charging him interest.

"As for other business...what do you need?" Carmichael asked, rising from his desk to study the closed blinds.

"What do you know about Azure Legacy?" David asked.

"Mikhail Azure's revenge," the broker replied instantly. "The organization created by his will to try and kill whoever killed him and put his syndicate back together. They've been quiet in this region—Blue Star was never strong here—but I'm hearing some ugly rumors of what they've been up to."

"I killed Mikhail Azure," David told him flatly. "They're the ones coming after me these days, and they've killed a lot of good people along the way."

Carmichael remained facing the closed windows.

"You have my sympathy, Captain, but I'm not sure how I can assist you. Like the Blue Star Syndicate before them, the Legacy isn't active in Corinthian, and my reach only goes so far outside this star system."

"What do you know about the law firm of Armstrong, Lee and Howard?" David asked.

The broker froze.

"Fuck me," he said quietly. "Armstrong, Lee and Howard are a collection of lawyers who work for boutique clients and don't blink at breaking laws, tax codes, or anything *else* they think will make the clients happy.

"They are *exactly* the type of pricks who'd take on Mikhail Azure as a client—and demand he left *their* star system alone as part of the payment."

"That's roughly my understanding of what happened, yes," David confirmed. "Armstrong, Lee and Howard *are* Azure Legacy. The beating heart at the core of it, if nothing else.

"You know them. You guessed."

Carmichael sighed.

"Not until you started asking questions about the Legacy and I wondered why you were here," he admitted. "The pieces added up pretty quickly at that point."

"You have channels?" David asked.

"Of course I have channels," Carmichael snapped. He finally turned back to face them, glancing over at the impassively quiet Soprano sitting next to David.

He clearly understood the implicit threat of even having a Mage in the room.

"I'm not going to help you fight a vendetta in my home system, Captain Rice," he finally said. "I don't *like* ALH, but you don't have the sanction or the firepower to deal with them, understand me?"

"I don't want you to help me *fight* them," David told the other man.

"I need you to set up a meeting with them," he continued. "I want to sit down with the lawyers behind this mess and talk peace.

"Sooner or later, even they have to admit the killing has to stop."

Carmichael sighed and nodded.

"Okay," he admitted slowly. "A meet, huh? I can organize that. But if you *fuck* me again..." He held up a warning finger.

"I guarantee you, Mr. Carmichael, *we* will not start a fight at the meet," David told him.

He had his plans for the Legacy's final fate, but attacking anyone at this meeting wasn't among them. He wasn't so sure about the Legacy themselves...but that was the risk he had to take.

CHAPTER 34

"RED FALCON, this is *Peregrine*; how's your feathers?"

Kelly chuckled as Jenna Campbell's voice echoed over the bridge radio.

"Good to see you, *Peregrine*. Our feathers are a bit ruffled and grumpy, but we're still here," she told Campbell. "Yourselves?"

"Sailing with the Skipper, I'd forgot what smooth flying was like," the older woman replied. "I'm presuming, from the note I got, that things haven't been as clear for you."

"That's the understatement of the century or so," Kelly told her. "I think Captain Rice wants to brief you in person. What's your ETA?"

They were close enough that only a few seconds were passing between responses, so they couldn't be too far away.

"*Peregrine* will make dock in about two hours," Campbell told her. "Entertainingly, we're carrying cargo for Bistro Manufacturing again. I'm guessing the old man is experimenting with different materials—this time, it's three million tons of Erewhon pine.

"Which, I'll have you note, is *blue* and does not have anything resembling needles or even leaves," the new-fledged Captain concluded.

"I saw what Sandoval Prime calls trees," Kelly replied. "They're orange. And their sap is a contact poison for humans."

"Oh, the worlds we find," Campbell agreed. "I'll set up docking clearances to bring us in beside *Red Falcon*. Looking forward to see you all."

"Likewise, Captain Campbell," the younger woman replied. "I have an entire *list* of 'dear gods, how do I executive-officer this man?' questions for you!"

"I'm not surprised in the slightest. We'll talk when I get there. You and Maria and I can go for drinks—if your voyage was anything like what I suspect it was, you both need them!"

The eggbeater-esque shape of *Peregrine* nudged into her dock slowly and carefully, her ribs still spinning to provide gravity in her crew decks. Kelly watched the big twelve-million-ton ship dock, then turned her attention to her original task of keeping an eye on the traffic around the Spindle.

Even with *Red Falcon* and *Peregrine*, the station was quieter than it had been when they'd visited with *Blue Jay*. There were one other jump freighter and a selection of smaller ships, some of which might have jump matrices.

Most of what shipping she could see was in-system ships, however. They drifted around orbit or moved cargo from the sky to the ground. The system only had the one inhabited planet, and humanity hadn't moved out much from Corinthian itself.

A lot of people and cargo moved from the Spindle to the planet, though, and that was enough to require tight traffic control. Kelly was sure the people running that just *adored* the trio of Martian destroyers in high orbit and their fifty-thousand-kilometer safety bubbles.

The system was still trying to lure a Navy base out there, as she understood, so they'd put up with it. A permanent picket like the one Hand Stealey had ordered installed was an advantage for their argument.

Right now, Kelly was just glad to see the white pyramids of the destroyers. The Legacy seemed to operate on the theory of not pissing where they lived, which would help protect *Falcon*'s crew while they were in Corinthian, but a battalion of Marines and a trio of warships were reassuring regardless.

"Ma'am, the Captain and Ship's Mage have returned aboard," the security guard at the docking tube told her.

"Thanks, Corporal," she replied. "Secure the tube for now; that's everyone aboard. Captain Campbell will be on her way shortly, so keep an eye out for her."

"Understood, ma'am."

David drifted into the bridge several minutes later. He was limping slightly, the governors on his leg clearly activated after a long day of pretending he wasn't injured.

"*Peregrine* made it in?" he asked.

"Docked right next door," Kelly confirmed. "Campbell sent over the cargo list. Biggest chunk is a load for Bistro Manufacturing—pine from Erewhon to go with the oak we delivered from Sherwood last time."

David chuckled, shaking his head.

"Given the scale Bistro works on, I'd be stunned if they have any of that left," he pointed out. "They make something like thirty percent of *all* furniture sold on Corinthian. Even a few million tons of wood disappear in the face of that kind of demand."

"You found our contact?" Kelly asked.

"I did," he confirmed. He looked around, but the bridge was empty except for the two of them.

"Carmichael's going to work on selling our cargo for us, and he knows ALH," he continued. "He didn't know they were the Legacy, but he wasn't surprised in the slightest. He's going to try and set up a meeting."

Kelly shook her head.

"That seems risky, boss. These guys are specifically after you."

"I'm relatively confident the *lawyers* aren't going to pull a gun in the meeting and blow my head off," David told her. "Have someone shoot me before or after? Sure. Shoot me themselves?

"I doubt they're the type. We'll move with an escort, and we'll wire ourselves into the Navy and Marines. I'll be careful, I promise."

Command, it seemed, agreed with Jenna Campbell. It was hard for Kelly to put her finger on why, but there was a new air of confidence and self-assuredness around *Red Falcon*'s old XO. Campbell was still the stocky, heavily built woman she'd always been, but now she carried herself like a *Captain*.

She joined the meeting of *Falcon*'s senior officers without hesitation, taking a seat directly opposite Captain Rice.

"I'm the only one here because nobody else on *Peregrine* knows who you lot actually work for," she said without preamble. "I'm not sure how much help we can be while keeping that screen in place, but whatever I can manage, I will.

"It's not like we're even heavily armed," she half-complained.

"Hell, I know I'm missing our antimatter missiles about now," Jeeves noted. "Any way for us to resupply those, Skipper?"

"Outside of a major naval base, no," Rice replied. "There'd be too many questions as to why a random civilian ship was buying antimatter weapons."

"We're allowed one hundred, but it's not like the Navy is going to give us more," Kelly added. "We'd need to be at a Navy base that's also got enough of an MISS presence to pull weight and get the missiles.

"That limits us to...well, Tau Ceti or Sol," she concluded.

"Not quite that bad...but close," her Captain allowed. "Jenna, we've managed to identify who the core lawyers behind Azure Legacy are. They're here in Corinthian, out of the way of all of Blue Star's operations."

"So, what's the plan?" Campbell asked.

"We see if they're willing to talk peace. They've lost a lot of resources coming after us. Sooner or later, it has to stop being cost-effective to keep coming.

"I've retained Carmichael to make the first contact," he continued. "He'll set up a meet in neutral space; we'll go to talk to them with all of the guards and toys we can think of.

"Our major playing chip here is the location of *Azure Gauntlet*," the Captain noted. "That's a trap, but they don't know that and it makes pretty tempting bait."

"So, you're going to try and negotiate peace using a trap as your peace offering?" Campbell replied. "I'm sure that's going to go over well."

"In the short run, they don't know it's a trap," Rice reminded her. "In the long run..."

He shook his head.

"In the long run, it is their task to preserve Mikhail Azure's legacy, and I have every intention of seeing that legacy burnt to the ground. We work for Mars, and Mars will *not* permit the Blue Star Syndicate to be rebuilt.

"But even if we didn't, they started this damn war, people. I intend to finish it—and if that means I'm lying to the people who are trying to kill us all, I am *entirely* okay with that."

"You realize that the meeting is probably going to be a trap of *theirs?*" Skavar pointed out after a few seconds of silence.

"Quite possibly," Rice agreed. "Kelly?"

"The plan is go in with an escort and leave with an escort," she laid out. "Captain Rice's wrist-comp is linked to *Red Falcon* by an encrypted frequency-hopping channel. We will be relaying that continuous to the Navy picket.

"If anything goes wrong, Ivan, we'll want your people to move in immediately—but you'll have Marines and heavy fire support within a few minutes."

"And you stuck a tracker in me, which gives us a further backup plan," Rice pointed out. "Plus, Maria and Kelly both know where the fake *Gauntlet* location is. We've got a few layers of fallbacks here, people.

"But the risk exists, yes. And we're going to take it. Because—understand me, people—we *are going to bring these bastards down.*"

CHAPTER 35

DAVID LEFT *Red Falcon* accompanied, once again, by what felt like a small army. Ivan Skavar led the way, and a full dozen of his security people ran a perimeter around them.

Corinthian had quite strict weapon laws, so they weren't carrying battle carbines and penetrator rifles today. Stunguns were the order of the day, though David was certain that Skavar's people were at the least carrying arguably illegal sidearms.

David was carrying one himself, after all.

Carmichael met them at the elevator terminal with a trio of low-slung dark-blue SUVs. The ubiquitous Fords wouldn't have looked out of place on any planet in the Protectorate, even though these particular vehicles lived on a space station.

"I booked a conference room at the Hollister Grand Hotel," he told David as the Captain and his guards got into the second vehicle. "You're meeting the middle partner of Armstrong, Lee and Howard, Ms. Sarah Vandella-Howard. She might *look* pretty, but don't be fooled. The list of disbarred lawyers on this planet is littered with people who got on her wrong side—and there's at least a few who ended up in graveyards."

Carmichael shook his head.

"Not least Mr. Richard Howard, the original Howard of Armstrong, Lee and Howard, and her second husband," he noted. "Vandella-Howard is sharper than you think, and if you underestimate her, you *will* get cut.

Step carefully, Captain Rice. I'm not sure you realize how dark the waters you've stepped into are."

"They dragged me into these waters; I didn't choose to be here," David pointed out. "They started a war."

"Mikhail Azure started this fucking war," Carmichael told him. "This is just a bunch of lawyers who don't let *anything* get in the way of their contracts. That's...almost worse in a lot of ways."

"They've got enough mercenaries and troublemakers on retainer that I wouldn't trust them as far as I could throw them," David replied. "Unless they've insisted on it, you don't need to be in the meeting, Carmichael.

"You're probably better off as far away as possible."

"You can say that again," Carmichael muttered. "Don't worry, Captain Rice; I'm going to be very visibly on the opposite side of the station, negotiating with a potential buyer for your cargo.

"Driver! Stop here," he ordered.

The SUV came to a halt and Carmichael smiled.

"The drivers are my people," he noted. "They'll take care of you. Good luck!"

The Hollister Grand Hotel definitely lived up to the name. Despite having visited the Spindle several times, David had never actually been to Spire City, the largest urban area in the space station and its effective capital.

It said a lot about the scale of the Spindle that Spire City was home to roughly three hundred thousand people and took up roughly a tenth of the available surface area inside the Spindle. It was a small city by surface standards but absolutely immense by the standard of "we built a city inside a space station."

The Hollister was one of several hotels on a carefully arranged street on the edge of the downtown area, all of them structures that seemed to tower in the Spindle. Tall buildings in a centripetal gravity environment were a risk. Tidal forces stressed the building, and pseudogravity reduced as you grew closer to the center of spin.

But, if you were determined enough, you could build yourself a set of thirty-story hotels. Four broad, tall, hotels that looked like they belonged in a surface resort district marked the Dock-ward frontier of downtown, and the broadest and grandest was the Hollister.

Uniformed valets waited for the vehicles, stepping forward as David's convoy arrived. The drivers waved them off.

"We're on call," the man driving David's SUV told him. "Ping us via your comp when you're done."

He smiled grimly.

"Ping us three times in succession if you're having trouble, and we'll ignore traffic laws on the way. Be careful, Captain Rice."

David nodded his thanks and stepped out of the vehicle, his people emerging and closing in around him.

"Let's go," he told Skavar.

Quite intentionally, Skavar was the next-most senior officer from *Red Falcon* with him. If worse came to worst, his ship would have LaMonte, Soprano, Jeeves and Kellers left to run it as they came after him.

He pitied the idiot who thought those four would be easier prey than he was.

The Marines pretending to be security guards folded around him with practiced ease as he moved forward into the hotel. He didn't expect to make it far, and he was entirely correct. A uniformed manager intercepted them halfway across the lobby.

"Excuse me, sir, may I ask where you're going?" he said politely. The man managed to make it sound like he was being helpful instead of demanding what they thought they were doing...but both messages made it through loud and clear.

"I am Captain David Rice," David told him. "I have a meeting scheduled here."

"Yes," the manager said slowly, consulting his wrist-comp. "In the Brisbane. May I show you to the meeting room, Captain Rice?" He coughed delicately. "I can have some of my people escort your...security to the bar. I'm sure we can find some way to keep them entertained."

David exchanged a look with Skavar that the manager actually caught.

"The Hollister prides ourselves on our security and privacy measures, Captain Rice," he told David. "I promise you, you do not need to worry about your safety here."

"Ivan, you're with me," David finally ordered. "The rest of you, find the bar. Snacks only, no booze." He smiled at the manager. "I only trust the *hotel*."

David was surprised by the sheer scale and emptiness of the meeting room when he stepped into it. The room was large enough to hold a mid-sized wedding or a large corporate presentation, but all it currently held was a single round table.

A tall blonde woman in a conservatively cut black business suit sat at the table, with one chair across from her. An unusually large man leaned against the wall behind her, wearing a similarly expensive suit.

There was no question what the man was. He might be wearing a designer suit, but his stance and awkwardness made it clear he was a hired killer stuffed into a designer suit.

Vandella-Howard, however, wore her suit like a second skin. She was a stunningly attractive woman, with a heart-shaped face and bright blue eyes. From what Carmichael had said, it was a sign of respect that she'd dropped many of the games today.

"Captain David Rice," she greeted him. "I must admit I was surprised to hear you reach out to us."

"Did you expect that the true nature of the Azure Legacy would remain secret?" he asked, stepping up to the table and taking the empty chair. Behind him, Skavar took up his own portion of the wall, matching glares with Vandella-Howard's bodyguard.

She smiled.

"You seem very certain of that identification, Captain," she pointed out. "I'm afraid I have no idea what you're talking about."

"I'm impressed," David told her. "You managed to say that with a completely straight face. I won't betray my source, Ms. Vandella-Howard, but I have no reason to doubt them.

"Armstrong, Lee and Howard held Mikhail Azure's will. Since his death, you have been executing on that will—a process that has left a trail of blood and fire across the Protectorate, much of it spent chasing me.

"I figure I should, at the very least, look in the eyes of the people determined to see me dead."

The lawyer sighed.

"I see that I shall have to have some harsh words with the Admiral Commanding," she noted. "The only way I can see you acquiring that information is if Aristos traded it for his life. One expects better from one's mercenaries."

"I'm sure the galaxy weeps for the failings of your hired killers, Ms. Vandella-Howard."

"I will note, Captain Rice, that a large quantity of the blood you speak of was spilled by you," she said quietly. "It is easy for you to speak of 'hired killers,' I suppose, but you have left entire mercenary fleets shattered in your wake.

"Few of Admiral Aristos's colleagues could share your kill count, Captain Rice. If you did not hold a hand of corpses and shattered ships, we would not be speaking. You know this."

"You sent them after me," he told her flatly. "You started this damn fight."

"Mikhail Azure's will is very clear," Vandella-Howard replied. "One half of all his assets goes to the organization that kills you. We are simply coordinators of the bounty, accessing funds to cover operations against you."

"And half goes to put the Blue Star Syndicate back together, as I understand?" David asked.

"Exactly." She shrugged. "This is business, Captain Rice. Nothing more. We signed a contract that says how Mr. Azure's money was to be split. However much money you think is on your head, Captain, I guarantee you that you underestimate it."

"And I promise you that however much you think it will cost you to collect it, you underestimate that," he replied. "I want to bring this to an end, Ms. Vandella-Howard. There has to be a way to make peace here."

"Several of our...contractors, shall we say, have made the offer very clear," she reminded him. "Surrender yourself to us, and your crew and employees will go unharmed. We are prepared to restrict the responsibility for Mr. Azure's death to you.

"That is as much flexibility as the will gives us."

"I have no intention of blithely committing suicide to make your lives easier," David told her. "If you want my head, you're going to pay the price for it in lost lives, lost money and lost ships."

"You know, the wonderful thing about offering a bounty is that we don't pay anything unless they bring you in," Vandella-Howard noted. "You've cut quite a swathe through the galaxy's undesirables, but you honestly haven't cost us that much money yet.

"We can keep this up for longer than you can, Captain Rice. If you hoped to buy us off, you don't have the money. If you wanted to threaten us, you don't have the firepower. If you planned to turn us in to the Protectorate, you don't have the evidence.

"You have nothing to hold over Armstrong, Lee and Howard, Captain. I'm not sure what you expected to get out of this meeting other than to meet me in person. This is business," she repeated. "Nothing more. And my firm's reputation requires that we fulfill our clients' wills, or we have no business."

"How much would it take?" David asked, bluntly. "If there's a price Azure offered, perhaps I can match it."

She laughed.

"You speak of *Mikhail Azure*," she pointed out. "Your *ship* would count for only a fraction of the wealth he left for us to manage. How many trillions do you have hidden down the back of your couch, Captain Rice?

"I think we're done here," she concluded, rising. "As I'm sure you've guessed, we don't like to cause trouble here in Corinthian. You are safe to return to your ship. Remaining in Corinthian, of course, will simply allow us to calibrate our attacks so as to...limit the trouble."

"There are things money cannot buy, Ms. Vandella-Howard," David said. "Things that could turn the tide of the rest of your plans. Half of Azure's money is tied up in killing me...but what if I could offer you something that would guarantee your success in reunifying his syndicate?"

The blonde stopped, standing with her back turned to him, then sighed.

"There are only a handful of things I can think of that would meet that description," she noted. "I do not believe you have access to any of them."

"I know where *Azure Gauntlet* is," he told her. "She's damaged, yes, and her crew is long dead. But my understanding is that she may be reparable."

"*Azure Gauntlet* was destroyed," Vandella-Howard replied. She wasn't continuing to leave, though.

"And who told you that?" David asked. "She fought us and *lost*, her crew were killed and she certainly isn't combat-capable without work... but she's intact. How much money, Ms. Vandella-Howard, would it cost you to acquire a new cruiser?"

"We both know that mere money would not suffice," she said sharply. "Azure spent years and tens of millions assembling the connections and the blackmail necessary to steal *Gauntlet*. Money could arrange for the acquisition of an *export* cruiser...but those lack amplifiers."

"Exactly," he said quietly. "*Gauntlet* may not be capable of flight or combat without repair...but her amplifier is intact. What price, then, for that?"

She was silent for several seconds, letting the quiet drag on before she turned to face him.

"Is that your offer, then, Captain Rice?" she said slowly. "You lead us to the godforsaken patch of void where Azure died, and in exchange, we let you live?"

"Basically," he agreed. "Though I was thinking more on order of 'give you the coordinates and we go our separate ways.'"

"That would not suffice," Vandella-Howard said flatly. "If I am to even *consider* this, you will come with me, as hostage to your good intentions."

"That's a rather...different situation," he replied carefully. That would be a problem, especially since he doubted the Navy was going to be particularly interested in taking prisoners when the Legacy showed up.

"Regardless. That is *my* offer, Captain Rice," she snapped. "You leave here with me. We board a ship, we meet the fleet the Legacy has assembled for our tasks, and we go recover *Gauntlet*.

"If all is as you say, you will be released, and we will lift all bounties on you. If you have lied...then we will fulfill Mikhail Azure's will."

David glanced back at Skavar.

"Choose *now*," she snapped. "Your bodyguard can return to your ship to tell them what has come to pass."

"No one else knows where *Gauntlet* is," David protested as he met Skavar's gaze. He was telling the truth in one sense—no one knew where *Gauntlet* was. Vaporized debris was hard to track.

Both Soprano and LaMonte knew where the location for the fake ship was, however, and *Skavar* knew that.

"Then that is a better guarantee for me," Vandella-Howard told him. "You have my word and the bond of Armstrong, Lee and Howard, Captain Rice, that if you fulfill our bargain, the bounty will be lifted and you will be released safely to a world where your ship can pick you up.

"That is the same word and bond that binds us to hunt you to the ends of the galaxy to honor Azure's will. You will find no greater surety."

She'd phrased her promise carefully, too. There were no loopholes or gaps they could betray him through without breaking their word.

He could lead them into his trap, but only if he stuck his head in with them and trusted his crew and his allies to get him out safely.

Fortunately for him, he *knew* his crew.

"Very well, Ms. Vandella-Howard," he said levelly, intentionally letting fear color his voice. "You have a deal."

CHAPTER 36

"THE CAPTAIN DID *WHAT*?" Maria demanded, staring blankly at the wall of her office.

"He agreed to go with the Legacy to 'recover *Azure Gauntlet*,'" Skavar repeated. "He left with them. I'm on my way back to the ship; I think most of this is a conversation we should have in person."

"Fair," she allowed. She didn't trust the walls of the Spindle to keep their secrets at this point. "I'll pull the rest of the senior officers together."

"Start brainstorming," the security chief told her. "This is about sixty percent disaster, forty percent opportunity."

"Agreed," she replied. "Get back here on the double, Chief."

The channel cut and the Mage leaned back in her chair, breathing carefully to try and control any incipient panic.

If Rice was now in the custody of the Legacy, they had to have promised him his safety in a manner he trusted. The problem was that Rice *wasn't* going to uphold his end of whatever bargain he'd made. He was leading his enemies into a trap that would almost certainly kill him, too.

Maria Soprano wasn't going to allow that. With her Captain in custody, she now commanded *Red Falcon*, and if she couldn't change David Rice's fate with just this ship, well...she had a lot of other resources at her command.

"Kelly," she pinged the XO. "We have a problem."

"I know. Skavar sent me the rundown in text while he called you," she replied. "What do we do?"

"Right now, I'm calling a meeting," Maria said with a chuckle. "But near the top of our priority list is to make *damn* sure we know which ship he leaves on.

"We know where they're going; we can probably beat them there," she concluded. "But I need to know when they leave so we can make sure of that."

"What will we do if we beat them there?" LaMonte asked.

"That's what I'm hoping to think up at the meeting," Maria admitted.

"Should we grab Jenna?" the XO asked.

Maria paused. That was a good question. One of the reasons that Campbell had got *Peregrine* was because she'd wanted out of the new employment that Maria had talked Rice into. But...she had their second ship, and that wasn't a resource they could pass up.

"Yes, ping her," she ordered. "Let's get everyone in one place where we're sure nobody is eavesdropping.

"I only know two things for certain: if the Legacy goes after that cruiser, they are *not* going to like what they find—and I have no intention of leaving the Skipper to burn with those bastards!"

"Well, don't *you* look promising?" Jeeves murmured as Maria stepped onto the bridge.

"Guns?" she asked immediately, the old Navy slang falling off her tongue unintentionally.

"Well, my math says that the earliest anybody could have made it from the Hollister to any of the docks was about five minutes ago," he noted, then tapped his screen. "And, about twenty seconds ago, what looks like a neat, fast little yacht just popped clear of one of the private ports built into the Spindle itself.

"Some *nice* piloting, too, taking the best advantage of the spin to get themselves going," he continued.

"Let me guess: the right kind of yacht for an Amber-converted jump-corvette?" LaMonte asked from the command chair. The XO started to rise but Maria waved her back to her seat.

They would be collecting the senior officers for their planning session in a few minutes. There was no point in shuffling seats at this point.

"A bit too small, actually," Jeeves concluded. "You could fit a nasty punch into a girl like that, but no sustained fight. If she's armed, it's 'kick 'em in the nuts and run' gear, not pirate gear."

"Interesting," Maria said. "Jeeves, you've got the trigger pulse for the beacon on the Captain, right?"

"I do, but if we ping it now, they might pick it up," he warned. "The more often we ping it, the more obvious it is..."

"Let's take the risk," Maria told him. "We need to know for certain if that's where the Captain is."

"Understood." Jeeves tapped a command and waited. A few seconds later, a tiny green dot flashed into existence on the ship before disappearing a moment later.

"That's him," the gunner confirmed. "They moved fast, though having a ship attached to the Spindle made it easier for them to get going."

"I'm not surprised. I'd love for the Legacy to be slow off the bat, but that's not the evidence we've seen so far," Maria replied. "Now we know, which means we have our timeline. How long till she jumps?"

"She's running standard fusion engines, but she's a small ship and they're big drives," Jeeves told her. "Burning hot and hard; looks like eight gravities. She'll be clear in about sixteen hours."

"And after that, it depends on how many Mages they have aboard," LaMonte concluded. "Can we catch them, Maria?"

Maria smiled thinly.

"We have four Mages aboard, all of them capable of sustaining six-hour jumps for several days," she reminded them all. "Our target is thirty-three light-years away. Just over two days for us if we push it.

"Even if they've got four Mages aboard, they won't have all Navy-quality Mages. It'll take them most of three days to get there.

"We're not going to just catch them, Kelly. We're going to beat them there."

Maria waited for Campbell to take her seat, *Peregrine*'s Captain the last to arrive of the collection of officers.

"All right, everyone, you all know what the Captain has gone and done," she said without preamble. "I'm sure we're all shocked that David has done something daring and stupid after attracting trouble to himself.

"We now need to get him *out* of that trouble, and I don't see a lot of easy options."

"That yacht didn't look like it was very well armed," Jeeves noted. "We could easily chase it down and capture it."

"They'd kill Rice the instant they worked out what we were doing," LaMonte objected. "Remember, killing the boss is basically a win condition for them. He's offered them something worth giving that up for, but if they think for even a *second* that things are hinky—"

"David dies," Maria concluded. "A degree of risk to the Skipper is inevitable, people, but an open attack with *Red Falcon* will all but guarantee his death. If we're going to pull this off, we need to come at them sideways."

"Just what *did* the Captain offer to get them to play nice?" Campbell asked. "I mean, he's hardly poor, but he doesn't have *that* much money."

"He offered them *Azure Gauntlet*," Maria explained.

"...That's impossible. *Gauntlet* was vaporized," Campbell replied. "Damien blew the containment on her antimatter capacitors. There wasn't even time for the safeties to engage."

"I know that," Maria agreed. "You know that. Who else knows that, really? With certainty? The people who were on *Blue Jay*'s bridge, most of whom are on *Red Falcon* or *Peregrine,* and all of whom were sworn to secrecy—and a bunch of naval officers who take their oaths seriously.

"So, the Navy set up a trap. A ship of the same class, lurking where *Gauntlet* died, rigged up to look like a wreck. When the Legacy shows up, they'll find their *Gauntlet*...and then the Navy will blow them to hell."

Campbell winced.

"With David aboard their ship now."

"And therein lies the flaw in our Captain's brilliant plan," Maria agreed. "The only option *I* see is to remove him from their ship before the Navy vaporizes them."

"That's...doable," Skavar said grimly. "In theory. But...boarding torpedoes may have the range to get at them without giving away *Falcon's* position, but they are *not* stealthy on their own."

"Damien once hid an entire ship from *Azure Gauntlet* itself," LaMonte suggested. "Could we hide the boarding torpedoes?"

Maria hesitated. She'd, in theory, been trained in hiding something in space. But she'd never actually *done* it. She could read up on the spells again, though, and make it happen.

"We can do it," she confirmed. "Or at least *I* can. I hesitate to say any of our other Mages can.

"In any case, though, it'll work better with a distraction."

"Especially because there's a wrinkle I don't think we've all processed yet," Skavar noted. "She said they were going to meet with a *fleet*. That, to me, suggests they're going to have a lot more than just a lightly armed jump-yacht for us to deal with."

"We can get the Navy involved," LaMonte said, then paused. "Except that has the same damn problem as us showing up. The Navy shows up, they'll blame us and kill the Skipper."

"...But the idea works," Maria said slowly, then looked over at Campbell.

"I don't want to drag *Peregrine* into this," she told the other woman. "This isn't going to be the kind of mess where an extra half-dozen missiles is going to make a difference. But..."

"You want me to play courier," Campbell guessed. "We can do that."

"You say that," Maria replied with a smile, "but you haven't heard who I want you to play courier to.

"We have a dead drop in the Erewhon System with the Legatans," she told Campbell. "I'm presuming they have access to the RTA, hence the drop being there. I want you to give them everything we have—where the ship supposedly is, that the Legacy is going after it, and that the Legacy has David as a hostage."

"The Legatans," Campbell repeated. "LMID, I'm presuming? What do you expect them to do?"

"I have no fucking idea," Maria admitted. "But there are systems closer to this whole mess than we are right now, and if they happen to have spaceborne assets in position to intervene, I'm not going to object to a whole new player in the mess David is courting."

"What about the Navy?" Jeeves asked.

"I'm going to use the authorization we've got to steal a couple of destroyers from here, just in case," Maria told them. "But I also want you to report everything to the Navy commander in Erewhon. I'll give you the authentication codes for a confidential RTA connection."

"I think the nearest real fleet presence is Commodore Cor at Ardennes, but if she can spare a cruiser or three on top of our 'bait,' that'll be an ugly wake-up for our Legacy friends."

"And what about ALH here?" Skavar asked. "We can't let them continue on as they are."

"And we won't," Maria agreed. "But that's no longer our problem. I'm guessing that when *Peregrine* and *Red Falcon* ship out, they may get suspicious...but they'll also probably relax a bit with us gone.

"And then Hand Lomond has a follow-up team coming in. Top-level MISS operatives, the kind that Armstrong, Lee and Howard won't see coming.

"The kind with a warrant signed and sealed by a Hand of the Mage-King of Mars. Vandella-Howard thinks we don't have the evidence to nail them to a wall? Those operatives will find it. They'll be in their systems before they know there's a problem."

"And everybody who's followed David to the ass end of nowhere is going to end up running into the maw of a fully armed and operational battlecruiser," Jeeves said with satisfaction.

"The only real kink is whether or not we can get the Skipper out before everything goes to hell," Skavar concluded. "If we can sneak some boarding torpedoes up to them under a magical cloak...I think we can do it."

"That sounds like a plan," Maria confirmed. "Let's get to it, people."

CHAPTER 37

DAVID'S TRIP with Vandella-Howard was going surprisingly pleasantly so far. One rushed taxi ride, crammed into the back seat with the unnamed mountain of genetically modified muscle that had escorted her to the meeting, and then hustled aboard a well-appointed fast jump-yacht.

The room they'd put him in was gorgeous, easily the same size as his Captain's cabin aboard *Red Falcon*, and kitted out with insanely comfortable furnishings. The door had sealed behind him, and his one attempt to knock on it had attracted the attention of what he was *reasonably* sure was a different muscle mountain.

It was hard to be certain. He was starting to suspect that the Blue Star Syndicate had been running a larger genetic modification program than anyone had guessed.

Mountain or not, the guard had been quite polite and had shown him how to work the small auto-chef attached to one wall. It wasn't designed to provide all of a person's meals, but it would do to keep a man alive with hors d'oeuvres and tiny sandwiches.

A quick check showed that his wrist-comp was blocked out of most of the yacht's computer network, but he was at least linked into the entertainment library. He was definitely a prisoner, but at least they were being *polite* about their hostage-holding.

He was nonetheless surprised in the middle of the evening when there was a knock on the door, shortly followed by the entry of his guardian mountain carrying a suit bag.

"The ship's tailor says this should fit you, based on his scans when you came aboard," the man rumbled. "Ms. Vandella-Howard invites you to join her for dinner on the observation deck."

David grinned.

"How much trouble am I in if I refuse?"

The mountain shrugged.

"I would guess you could get away with it once," he said. "The next time, she'd probably 'ask' me to bring you up forcefully."

They were polite and honest mountains of muscle. Odd fit for the bodyguards of a criminal, though perhaps not a lawyer.

"The observation deck sounds fascinating," David allowed as he checked the contents of the bag. He wasn't surprised to find it contained a gorgeously cut dark gray suit. The color was exactly his own preference, though the cut was more stylish than he usually preferred.

"I will dress and join Ms. Vandella-Howard," he promised. "I presume you will be escorting me."

"Of course," the mountain rumbled. "It's a big ship. You might get lost."

It was not a big ship.

It took David longer to get dressed in the suit—which, as promised, fit him perfectly—than it took him and his escort to cross the length of the yacht and travel up three decks. Following along behind the mountain, he noted the intriguing nature of the suit's cut.

The clothes fit perfectly. They were amazingly comfortable. But he also found his movements restricted, contained. He might be comfortable so long as he moved at a normal pace, but the moment he tried to run or fight, the suit would turn into a trap.

And he doubted the fabric would tear as easily as his usual suits. It was a gorgeous piece of prisoner wear, but it remained very definitely prisoner wear.

Sarah Vandella-Howard had also changed. Gone was the conservatively cut black suit. In its place she wore a long, skintight dress in midnight black decorated with stars.

The stars, he realized after a moment, were gemstones. Each glittering little dot was a ruby, sapphire, diamond or emerald. Her "casual" dress was probably worth a million or more...and done in such a way that it managed to be tasteful and not gaudy.

The dress was slit all the way up to her hip, showing flashes of athletically trim tanned skin. He suspected the purpose was more to free up her legs for movement rather than distraction, and the cut of the shoulders of the dress and tightness of the bodice matched that idea.

He doubted the distraction factor of the outfit was an accidental bonus, but the unnamed tailor had designed the dress to allow her to run and fight without impediment. It also showed off her curves and muscles in a way that David suspected had left more than one man making one of several possible fatal mistakes.

He bowed delicately as he entered the observation deck, and saw her turn to face him at the far end of the room. This was a woman who was perfectly prepared to use any weapon at her disposal, and his own experience with crime lords and ladies had confirmed an old adage for him:

The female of the species was deadlier than the male.

"Ms. Vandella-Howard," he greeted her. "You look lovely."

"I find this dress goes nicely with the void," she replied. "I don't have many opportunities to leave Corinthian; it's all arm's length and couriered recordings. Please, have a seat."

He took the indicated seat, realizing that the bodyguards had stayed outside. He was alone in the room with the lawyer, looking up at a transparent dome that showed the stars outside.

From the depth of shadow and interplay of light, an experienced spacer like David could judge they were no longer in a star system. They'd clearly made at least one jump since he'd come aboard.

"This is a fast ship," he noted. "I wouldn't have expected us to have left Corinthian yet."

"She's no navy ship like yours, but *Luck* can keep up quite a pace when she needs to," Vandella-Howard agreed. "We're on our way to the rendezvous."

"Of course." She had said something about a fleet. That was a nerve-wracking thought on its own—just how many ships and mercenaries did the Legacy command? What kind of monster had Mikhail Azure birthed to try to keep his empire together?

There were already silver serving dishes on the table. She gestured for him to open his as she removed the cover over her own dinner, allowing steam to waft up from the steak and lobster on the plate.

His own dish was much the same, expensive food spectacularly prepared. It was unlikely she was trying to poison him at this point, so David dug in.

To his surprise, the lawyer ate in silence, allowing him to enjoy the food and the view out the roof. He carefully did *not* enjoy the "view" that Vandella-Howard's dress presented. That, in his opinion, was as deadly a trap as the one he was leading her into.

"You have a good cook," he said carefully.

"The staff aboard *Luck* is the best I can find," she replied. "As I said, I do not travel often, but I see no reason not to travel in comfort. My partners occasionally use the ship as well, but I inherited her from my late husband."

David nodded silently. That opening was also, he judged, a trap. From his dinner companion's smile, she was enjoying teasing him.

"There is no reason not to be polite at this point, Captain Rice," she told him. "Events may yet require that I will have to have you killed, but for now, let us presume we are all playing fair with each other. It's far more pleasant."

She winked at him and David chuckled.

"If you're half as informed as I suspect you are, you know better than to think I would do anything to offend Keiko Alabaster's sensibilities," he pointed out. "Her reach is long and her claws are sharp."

And if he didn't think Keiko would object to his seducing his way out of a death sentence, Vandella-Howard didn't need to know that.

She giggled, a bright and cheerfully infectious sound.

"That is true," she allowed. "Though I suspect you'd find my reach is equally long and my claws equally sharp."

She glanced at her wrist-comp.

"And perhaps now is the time to demonstrate that better than any other," she purred. "Look up, Captain Rice, as *Luck* jumps."

He looked up, studying the stars. He was watching as they *shifted*, the world changing as the yacht leapt an entire light-year in the blink of an eye.

There were new stars. More of them than you usually saw in deep space...bigger, too.

Bigger because they weren't stars. They were *starships*. A lot of starships. He was counting them up when *Luck* rotated, allowing them to see the yacht's immediate destination.

At this distance, they were tiny triangles, but Vandella-Howard tapped her wrist-comp and part of the dome above them zoomed in, optics and computers magnifying to allow David to see the three Tau Ceti–style export destroyers that formed the core of the Legacy fleet.

There were at least two dozen other ships around them. His experienced eye marked most of them as jump-corvettes, the mix of refitted freighters and secret-shipyard-built light warships used by freighters and bounty hunters.

A handful, though were of a similar ilk to the Golden Bears' monitors. Not as large, barely half the size of the million-ton destroyers at the core of the fleet, but he could pick out at least six half-megaton ships, probably built as sublight defense ships.

But someone had installed jump matrices in those SDSes and provided the Legacy with a second tier of warships to rival any system government.

He stared up at the Legacy's naval might in shock.

"Like I said, Captain Rice, money can acquire the ships they build for export," Vandella-Howard said softly. "But it cannot acquire an amplifier. Deliver that to me and I will finish the task laid before my firm.

"But betray me...betray me, and as you said...my reach is long and my claws are *very* sharp."

They didn't return David to the quarters they'd put him in. Instead, the mobile mountains that guarded Vandella-Howard led both of them directly to a shuttle bay. This, it seemed, was as far as *Luck* came.

The lawyer watched him with obvious amusement as he studied the destroyer they were approaching through the shuttle's windows.

"She's Tau Ceti-built," Vandella-Howard told him. "Sold to a system government—forgive me if I don't tell you which one—that found themselves in serious financial distress. If they'd actually come clean about how bad the finances had become, the government would have fallen.

"So, they sold the destroyers under the table." She shrugged. "They got the money they needed to hold their infrastructure together and save the next election. I got the destroyers I needed to complete my task.

"Everybody wins."

"I'm sure their constituents might disagree," David said dryly.

Vandella-Howard laughed.

"Since when have politicians cared about what the common mob thinks, beyond what it takes to get elected?" she asked cynically. "Most of our clients are politicians of one stripe or another, Captain Rice. Believe me, however low your opinion of them is, the truth is worse."

It occurred to David, at least, that the nature of what Armstrong, Lee and Howard did would inevitably filter things so their partners only saw the worst of the worst.

He wasn't going to argue with her, though. Four of her bodyguards had joined them aboard the shuttle, and they'd traded in their expensive tailored suits for equally expensive body armor with low-profile power assists.

Or, at least, he *hoped* the armor had low-profile power assists. Otherwise, the genetically augmented giants watching Sarah Vandella-Howard's back expected to be able to use the full-size penetrator rifles they carried without assistance.

He wouldn't disbelieve that. It just said terrifying things about just what Blue Star had been up to while no one was looking.

"*Bleeding Sapphire* is the flagship for now," the lawyer told him as their shuttle dropped towards the destroyer's shuttle bay. "If you have lied, it will be your grave."

There was no malice or threat in her tone. She was simply stating a fact.

"If you have told the truth, however, *Azure Gauntlet* will replace her as the flagship. Even damaged, *Gauntlet* is a symbol of power that will force the syndicates into line."

David kept his peace. He was the one who wanted her to believe he could deliver the cruiser...but at the same time, he could have told her a cruiser wouldn't be enough to bring the Protectorate's crime syndicates in line.

Mikhail Azure had kept his *Gauntlet* as a trophy, not a tool.

After all, if all it took to bring syndicates in line was a cruiser, well... the Royal Martian Navy had over sixty of them and they'd never managed to stop the Syndicates.

CHAPTER 38

KELLY LAMONTE WATCHED their escorts move back into place after the latest jump. The two destroyers weren't much in the grand scheme of things, but compared to the regular run of jump-corvettes and such that they expected the pirates to field, one probably would have been enough.

Or none, given that they were supposed to be luring the Legacy into range of the guns of a Martian cruiser.

A polite young officer appeared on her screen. Technically, Soprano was in command of *Red Falcon*, but the Ship's Mage was down in the simulacrum chamber. That left Kelly in the captain's chair on the bridge, commanding the freighter's weapons and handling her communications.

Fortunately, despite the age difference, Jeeves had yet to so much as blink at following her orders.

The Martian officer on the screen had skin as dark as his black uniform matched to shockingly white hair. The hair was probably the result of either dye or genetic tampering, given that the man was younger than Kelly herself.

"Mage-Captain Michel sends her compliments, Officer LaMonte, and the task group is in position to follow you into the next jump," he told her. "After the last one, she's asked that our Mages directly confer with Ship's Mage Soprano to make sure we avoid miscommunication."

That was a polite way of saying "Mage-Captain Irune Michel is *furious* at her Jump Mages for making her look bad in front of the civilians and dishonorably discharged ex-Navy Mage, so she's going to make them take orders from Soprano so they don't fuck it up again."

Or at least that's how Kelly read it. *Red Falcon's* Mages had come out of the last jump exactly on target, after all.

"I'll inform Acting Captain Soprano," Kelly replied cheerfully. "She can coordinate the calculations for the next jump." She checked her screen. "I make it in just over two hours."

It had taken the three ships four hours to rendezvous and match velocities after the mis-jump—and that was with everyone accelerating at ten gravities. If *Red Falcon* had been a more conventional freighter, it would have taken a lot longer.

"I show the same, Officer LaMonte," the Lieutenant confirmed. "Mage-Captain Michel suggests that she and Mage-Commander Irving set up a videoconference with yourself and Acting Captain Soprano after the next jump.

"As we understand, we're going to be jumping into quite the mess on the other end, and Mage-Captain Michel wants to be sure the task group does their part."

"Of course," Kelly agreed. "I'll confer with Acting Captain Soprano, but I don't see a problem."

"Our thanks, Officer LaMonte." The Lieutenant bowed slightly. "The Mage-Captain will make herself available for the conference."

It was hard for Kelly not to feel out of place in the videoconference several hours later. Soprano might be a civilian now, but she'd once been an officer of the Royal Martian Navy. As the video links opened up to bring the two starship captains online, she couldn't help thinking there was an entire layer of communication to the body language between the three officers that she wasn't picking up.

"As I understand it," Michel noted after the initial pleasantries were over, "there is already a Navy cruiser at our final destination. They'll have spent time preparing their cover and positioning, which allows for a degree of stealth impossible under normal circumstances."

"More, anyone arriving is going to be *expecting* them to be there," Soprano pointed out. "They'll have disguised themselves as a derelict."

"The Legacy expects to find *Azure Gauntlet,* a wrecked *Minotaur*-class armored cruiser," Kelly said. "Instead, they're going to find *a Minotaur*-class cruiser, with her emissions stepped down or concealed and surface work done to appear as if she's been severely damaged."

"That won't hold for very long," Mage-Commander Deepali Irving pointed out. The Earth-native Indian man looked fascinated with the entire concept, but that didn't seem to be stopping him from poking holes in it. "There's only so much heat they can conceal, and a radar sweep will give up the game instantly."

"They're not going to get a detailed-enough radar sweep outside of *maybe* ten light-seconds," Kelly replied. "Remember, these are pirates. At best, they're running export- or militia-grade sensor suites.

"And if they approach inside five million kilometers of the cruiser, it's game over."

"That depends on how paranoid they are," Michel pointed out. "Yes, her ten-gigawatt lasers have a five-million-kilometer effective range, but you have to *hit* the target with a sixteen-second delay for both targeting data and beam propagation.

"Even the most cursory of evasive maneuvers will reduce the kill chance. The cruiser is a trump card, yes, but don't overestimate her capabilities."

"And the problem with letting the cruiser resolve the situation is that it doesn't get your Captain back," Irving noted. "I'll confess I'm not certain how exactly you are planning on doing that."

"I have four Navy-grade Mages aboard," Soprano told them. "We've been practicing concealment spells. While I can't conceal *Red Falcon* underway, we can conceal her heat signature relatively easily if she's on full standby.

"After that, it's a matter of letting them close enough. We have a full suite of boarding torpedoes aboard, and I'm quite comfortable in our ability to conceal *those*."

"You are aware that is basically suicide, correct?" Michel said crisply. "It sounds like a Marine's plan."

"We will have assault shuttles standing by for extraction," Soprano told her. "We have the ability to identify which ship Captain Rice is on, and the ability to board it.

"Once we have boarded the vessel and retrieved Captain Rice, Security Chief Skavar will make the assessment of whether we can take control of the vessel or withdraw. If we have to withdraw, that will be the main portion of this mission we need you for."

"You want us to cover the assault shuttles," Irving said quietly. "We may be smaller than *Red Falcon*, Mage Soprano, but our power density is even higher. We are not easily hidden. There is a reason even Navy Mages are inexperienced in cloaking spells—they're mostly bloody useless."

"The only other option is for you to wait one jump out," Soprano replied. "We have no way of contacting you in that case short of jumping *Falcon* herself, which I doubt the pirates will miss."

"Unlikely," Michel agreed. "I would love to consider all pirates incompetent, but if the Legacy didn't have access to some competent people, this whole mess would have been over long ago.

"But the same assumption of competence is in play if we try and hide in the system with you," she pointed out. "One ship, with her reactors stepped down and concealed by magic, may pass unnoticed with the prize of the cruiser on their screens—but every additional vessel we add increases the odds of this entire plan coming apart.

"And this plan, Mage Soprano, is fragile enough already."

"Without covering fire, I'm not certain we can get assault shuttles in to extract our Marines," Soprano admitted. "And given that I intend to go in with the Marines, and that the whole purpose is to bring Captain Rice out, failing to extract the Marines isn't an option."

"Fragile," Michel repeated, then smiled. "But daring and necessary. We may be looking at the problem the wrong way."

"Oh?" Soprano said noncommittally.

"Once the boarders are trying to withdraw, the pirates will be looking for someone coming to extract them," the Mage-Captain said. "If we were to, say, use cloaking spells to cover the two or three shuttles you need to extract your people, they'll know something's up and they will spam space with heavy radar."

"Cloaks are only so effective," she noted. "If they have multiple ships and they know somebody is out there, they will find the shuttles. And they will destroy them."

"So, what do we do?" Kelly asked as levelly as she could. Her boyfriend was almost certainly going to be flying one of those assault shuttles—and if they were concealing them with magic, her girlfriend was almost certainly going to be aboard as well.

"We let them see what they want to see," Michel replied. "*Red Falcon* only carries a handful of assault shuttles, as I understand. *Unrelenting Pursuit of Justice* and *Sword of Untrammeled Liberty* both carry full sets."

"And the RMN's assault shuttles are fully rigged for remote control," she concluded. "They're expensive...but so are Marine Forward Combat Information units. I don't think anyone will object if we expend a dozen or so of them to cover the extraction."

"And since they saw and blew up the assault shuttles they *thought* were the rescue effort..." Kelly nodded. "They won't be looking for the cloaked ones."

"As for keeping us in a position where we can intervene..." The Mage-Captain sighed. "I'm not sure we can. There's nowhere for us to hide."

Kelly looked at the data they had on the location everyone was converging on, with the estimation of the location of the Navy cruiser playing bait, then smiled.

"That's not *entirely* true."

CHAPTER 39

DAVID'S QUARTERS aboard *Bleeding Sapphire* were no less comfortable than his quarters aboard *Luck*. He suspected the Azure Legacy's lawyer leaders had insisted that a portion of the destroyer be refitted to the standard of comfort and luxury they were accustomed to.

Of course, he had no more access to the ship's systems there than he'd had aboard *Luck*. Less, in many ways, since the destroyer was properly set up to contain prisoners. He did, to his surprise, have access to a feed of space outside the starship.

It didn't give him sensors or anything as silly as that, just a link to the ship's basic opticals and some computer zoom functions, but it was enough for him to assess the fleet that the Azure Legacy had assembled.

He presumed that the lawyers had other weapons in their arsenal. A star fleet was not a subtle tool and an odd choice for a criminal syndicate to have mustered. Piracy and slave raids were possible, he was sure, but he couldn't see a lot of use for the Legacy's fleet.

Not unless they were planning on robbing entire Fringe Worlds...or there were more hidden secret pirate stations out there than David knew about.

Either of those would justify the fleet, and he knew that the kind of massive-scale pillage that this fleet could unleash on a Fringe World would help earn the Legacy the respect they *actually* needed to bring the syndicates into line.

At best, he was seeing only one aspect of their plan gathered around him. Money and blackmail and negotiated agreements were more likely tools for the task the Legacy had been set—and those were all tools Vandella-Howard and her partners were intimately familiar with.

The admittance buzzer to his quarters chimed. He didn't even bother to respond—correctly so, as Vandella-Howard simply walked through a moment later. She didn't even give him enough time to get dressed.

She'd changed into another suit, though this one was worn over a low-cut top and managed to draw even more attention to her figure than the skin-tight dress had. While David doubted Vandella-Howard had ever killed anyone herself, he suspected that more than one man had died while being distracted by the woman's physique.

"Ms. Vandella-Howard," he greeted her politely, keeping his eye on the "window" showing the outside of the ship. "How may I assist you?"

"We'll be coming up on the moment of truth in a few hours," she told him. "Feeling nervous?"

David shrugged.

"If the ship isn't there, there is nothing I can do about it," he pointed out. "I know where it *was*, but if someone has moved it since, then I am aware of the remaining value of my bargaining chip."

"A fatalist, I see," she replied. "You amuse me, Captain Rice. I might almost be sad if we have to kill you, though I'll admit mostly I'll be disappointed in the lack of a cruiser."

He shivered. Vandella-Howard's ability to deliver a threat of death in the same tones she'd discuss a mortgage or a contract was...terrifying.

"What do you want?" he asked flatly.

"Checking in on the potentially condemned man," she replied. "Want anything? A last meal? Cigarette?" She ran her hands distractingly down her body. "You're either about to die or do me a huge favor; either way, I'm not averse to a pity fuck."

David rolled his eyes.

"And how many people have ended up dead taking *that* seriously?" he asked.

She laughed and kissed him gently on the lips.

"Enough that I am always impressed to be turned down," Vandella-Howard noted. "Six hours until we jump to *Gauntlet*'s supposed location, David Rice. Spend them wisely."

David Rice had a great deal of faith in the promises of the Royal Martian Navy. He had even more faith in the promises of the Hands of the Mage-King of Mars.

The moments after they arrived at the godforsaken piece of nowhere where Mikhail Azure died, however, were still a strain. The optics he had access to couldn't pick out a cruiser from the background light, not at any practical deep-space distance.

With the coordinates he'd given Vandella-Howard, they could have arrived at exactly the spot *Azure Gauntlet* had died. The wreckage would have drifted from there. Even seemingly empty space had its gravity and its orbits.

Calculating from the location *Gauntlet* had died to where its wreck would be was child's play for any navigational computer. He suspected that the slight haze of slightly denser-than-normal deep-space molecules was the *actual* remnants of the battle cruiser, regardless of what he'd told the Legacy.

The cruiser *should* be out there. He couldn't see it, but he knew that the sensors mounted on the flotilla would be able to pick out the "derelict" at upward of a light-minute.

Nonetheless, as seconds turned to minutes, he began to pace uncomfortably in his quarters. He wouldn't put it past Vandella-Howard to lie to him about which jump would bring them to their destination, just to see what he did, but...

"Captain Rice," the lawyer's voice suddenly cut through the intercom. "Congratulations. It appears you get to live."

"Ms. Vandella-Howard?"

"Please, David, call me Sarah," she told him, her voice warmer than it had been at any point so far. "We have finished scanning the area and confirmed the presence of a derelict, quite badly damaged cruiser.

"We jumped in quite a way out and it will take us time to get close enough to make an assessment of how damaged she is, but we now have the proof we needed that you played fair with us.

"I have some preparations to do up here, but I suggest you find that nice suit we made up for you aboard *Luck*," she continued. "You *will* be joining me for supper, David, as we celebrate our agreement—and the now-inevitable success of the Azure Legacy!"

To David's surprise, his wrist-comp beeped at him a few moments after Vandella-Howard ended the call. The device had been authenticated onto a new network—still not even basic crew-level access, but now the access for passengers instead of prisoners.

He linked the device into the wallscreen and pulled up the sensor feed. He focused the view on the big cruiser. That was what everyone would expect—and while they could tell where he'd focused the screen, they couldn't tell where he was actually looking.

There was no sign of any other ships. Any jump flare had dissipated, which meant if there was anyone here, they'd arrived at least two hours before, but it wasn't like ships were easily hidden.

He was...reasonably sure the *Minotaur*-class cruiser the Navy had left here could handle Legacy's little fleet. Especially if they got too close before realizing there was a problem.

The problem, however, was that if it came down to the cruiser, he was going to get vaporized along with everyone else.

A quick check confirmed that he was still locked in. They were trusting him more now they had proof he was playing fair, but Vandella-Howard was still regarding him as a risk.

Which was fair. He was doing everything in his power to bring the Legacy down.

Time. All he had was time—the pirates had emerged a full light-minute from the cruiser. It was going to take them a full day to close the distance. He had options and tools his enemies didn't know about, but if he tried to break himself free right now...

Well, he had nowhere to go and the Legacy had all of the time in the world to try and bring him back in.

He trusted the Navy and he trusted MISS...but most of all, he trusted his people.

It was time to wait and see what they were planning.

CHAPTER 40

DAVID WAS reasonably sure that *Bleeding Sapphire* had come with an observation deck. Most starships did. He was also reasonably sure that the observation deck hadn't been rigged out as an atrium and luxury dining room before the destroyer had come into Sarah Vandella-Howard's hands.

The woman clearly had her preferences for where she liked to eat: surrounded by greenery and looking out over the stars. She certainly had the money and power to make sure any ship she served on had the ability to meet that preference, even if it was an odd one.

He was escorted to join her by what he was *reasonably* sure was the same mountain who'd been his guard before, but it was hard to tell. There were at least four different men and they were by no means clones or twins, but they all had the same haircut, build and coloring.

Plus, it was hard to look past "two hundred and twenty centimeters tall, hundred and fifty kilograms, no fat" to try to pick out distinguishing features. The bodyguards had a presence beyond any attempt to identify or individualize them.

Dinner this time was cold fish. Sushi, in fact, though David wasn't sure *he'd* have trusted a starship to have fish that was high-enough quality and fresh enough for sushi.

He also wouldn't want to be the cook who gave Vandella-Howard even a minor stomachache. The food was almost certainly safe.

She was still dressed in her suit from earlier, but there was a loose relaxedness to how she sat that he hadn't seen before. He hadn't realized how much tension there had been in the woman every time they'd spoken until he saw her without it.

"David, please, sit down," she told him. "I brought my cook over from *Luck* after we boarded. He does fantastic sushi; try it!"

David carefully took a piece of raw fish and rice without saying anything. It was as good as he expected.

"Thank you...Sarah," he replied. She had instructed him to use her name, after all. It was roughly on par with shaking paws with a trained tiger. It was *probably* safe, but the claws were still there.

"We're going to be here for a while," she warned him. "I suspect that *Gauntlet* won't be movable in her current state, so we'll need to move more resources out to make sure we can either tow her or repair her in place.

"The courier I send back to my partners will have the stop order for the bounty on you," she promised. "Your ship will have been unmolested in Corinthian, and so long as they are there until the stop order starts propagating, they hopefully won't get anywhere before it does.

"You've done us a service," she concluded. "We pay our debts, David."

"And Mikhail Azure is still dead," David observed.

"That he is," Vandella-Howard agreed, taking a sip of wine. "And my partners may even still think we're giving the rebuilt syndicate over to one of his sub-bosses, but if they were leadership-quality, well, we wouldn't be doing all the work for them."

David managed not to wince. He'd suspected that was where she was going with this.

"And your partners?"

She made a throwaway gesture.

"Now that we have assembled this fleet, have access to *Gauntlet*, and have our fingers already moving through the rest of the galaxy, my partners have become expendable," she said. "They will fall into line or...be removed from my way."

Like her husband had been. Not that David was going to say that aloud.

The female was deadlier than the male, indeed.

"Why are you telling *me* this?" he finally asked.

"Two reasons," she replied, holding up a pair of fingers. "Firstly, there really isn't anything you can do at this point to change what's coming. The Blue Star Syndicate will be reborn, and *I* will control it.

"Secondly, you've proven yourself spectacularly capable and to have connections in the oddest of places," she told him. "I'd be willing to offer you a position at the top of the organization. *Consigliere*, I believe the Cosa Nostra call it. Advisor and right-hand man."

"Tempting," David lied. "I don't suppose you'd be willing to give up the slave trade and illegal genetic augmentation?"

Vandella-Howard laughed ruefully.

"I didn't expect you to accept," she admitted. "We'll go our separate ways, Captain Rice. And believe me, my people will be warned never to try and hire you. The new syndicate will keep its distance from you.

"I've seen too many die who failed to learn *that* lesson."

Dinner continued calmly for several more minutes, until one of the ship's crew knocked at the door. One of the bodyguards went over and had a quiet conversation that David pretended not to be trying to overhear as he tested the several varieties of soy sauce Vandella-Howard's chef had served.

The bodyguard then came back, leaning down next to the lawyer-turned-crime-boss to whisper in her ear.

David's hearing wasn't good enough to hear what the guard was saying...but he didn't miss the reaction of the woman across from him. Every gram of tension that had disappeared for this dinner suddenly returned tenfold as the man spoke.

He never saw her draw the guard's gun from his holster. The first David was aware of it was when he found himself staring down the spectacularly large barrel of the hand cannon.

He doubted Vandella-Howard had the wrists to absorb the recoil of even a single shot from the ugly weapon, but she was holding it in a perfect two-handed grip, and there wasn't even a tremor as it trained directly on his head.

"What?" he demanded.

"You betrayed us," she said flatly. "I don't know what game you're playing, Rice, but this is *not* going to end the way you think."

He very slowly raised his hands. Whatever his crew had got up to, his best chance of getting out right now was to play innocent.

"Would you care to tell me *how* I apparently betrayed you?" he asked. "I mean, if I'd somehow predicted your exact route and timing to get here well enough to allow for someone to show up three hours after you did, I'd be seeing how large a chunk of the Royal Navy I could send.

"Assuming I'd somehow predicted that we'd end up out here, anyway," he continued. "I wasn't exactly planning on getting dragged out to the ass end of nowhere, no matter how gorgeous the Legacy's boss turned out to be."

"Four ten-megaton-plus jump flares, Captain Rice," Vandella-Howard said flatly. "Ten million kilometers from us, emerging from jump on a direct course for *Gauntlet*."

That was cruiser-mass. There was no way his crew had managed to find four cruisers and get them there this quickly. He seriously had *no* idea what was going on now.

"I'll note," he said quietly, "that my ship is over twenty million tons fully loaded. And while *Peregrine* is in the mass range you quote, she's only one ship."

"It's about right for two-thirds of a Martian cruiser squadron, though, isn't it?" she snapped. "Just like you were saying."

He sighed.

"What's their acceleration?" he asked.

"What?" she snapped.

"Their *acceleration*," he barked back. "This *isn't* anything I arranged, but if they're coming at us at ten or more gravities, it *is* the Navy. If they're coming slower..."

The gun didn't move, but Vandella-Howard cocked her head at her bodyguard, nodding the mountain toward the crewman at the door.

The crewman looked terrified as the bodyguard approached, but followed him to the table at a silent gesture.

"What was the question, ma'am?" he asked cautiously, taking in the
entire scene of David, Vandella-Howard, and the gun.

"Acceleration," she demanded. "The bogies. What's their acceleration?"

The man swallowed and checked his wrist-comp.

"They've adjusted course to come for us," he said very, very quietly.
"Acceleration is...two point eight gravities."

"That's not Navy," Vandella-Howard said, mostly to herself. "Thank
you, Mikael. Get back to the bridge and inform Captain Jandaček that I
will be joining him shortly."

She lowered the gun.

"That's a freighter acceleration," she told David. "Who the hell would
have forty million tons of freighters out in the back ass of nowhere?"

"Someone *else* who tracked down rumors and fragments and worked
out where Azure died," David finally admitted. Stealey had warned him
that they were using the location as bait. They'd apparently managed to
get someone else here and walking into the same trap.

The timing had nearly got him killed. Even if the other ships were
completely unarmed and "innocent" salvagers, this was going to be an
ugly headache.

"They're burning for us," Vandella-Howard said. "That means they're
looking for a fight."

She smiled coldly.

"Captain Jandaček and the rest of my people will have to oblige them.
Karls!"

Her barked word brought one of the massive bodyguards forward.

"Take Captain Rice back to his quarters and lock him in," she
snapped. "Sorry, David, but while this may not be your problem, it
sure looks questionable when you assured me no one else knew where
Gauntlet was."

He sighed and rose to follow Karls.

"Of course, the rest of my bridge crew knew," he pointed out.
"Montgomery knew, if no one else, though he never struck me as the

type to sell out. Most of my crew came with me to *Falcon*, though, or never saw the data.

"Doesn't mean someone didn't pull it from the system and sell it later."

"You keep telling yourself that," she replied. "Just hope that you didn't like whoever it was, David, because if they're on those ships, they're going to die."

CHAPTER 41

"THAT...IS A LOT MORE ships than we were expecting."

Jeeves's comment echoed in Maria's ear as she studied the boarding torpedo in front of her, trying to work out where she was going to squeeze herself in.

"Okay," she replied. "What *are* we looking at?"

"I make it twenty-nine, possibly thirty ships," the gunnery officer said softly. "Three are real warships, megaton-range ships with antimatter engines. The rest are smaller, two hundred to five hundred k-tons. Mix of fusion and antimatter thrusters.

"It's a fleet, Soprano. What do we do?"

She looked over her shoulder at Skavar and gestured for the Marine to start loading his people into the three torpedoes they'd prepped for the mission.

"How close are we?" she asked.

"We're about eight million klicks away from them," Jeeves replied. "We're off the direct-line course between them and the false *Gauntlet*. Closest approach looks like...fifteen light-seconds. Four and a half million kilometers."

The boarding torpedoes had several hours of endurance but didn't have much better acceleration that an assault shuttle. They were designed to be fired at close range, using the ship's launchers to give them a boost the shuttle wouldn't have, not used for stealth ambushes.

"You're the expert, Jeeves," she told him. "Can we catch them with the boarding torpedoes?"

She heard him swallow. He was silent for several seconds, running numbers.

"Yes," he finally concluded. "Launch in the next ten minutes. You'll have a two-hour flight time, and you'll intercept them as they reach their closest approach to us." He paused. "Your relative vee at intercept is going to be well over a thousand KPS. That's pushing the limits of what the crush compensator can handle."

"I've used them before," Maria told him. "The scribes who put them together underrate the damn things for safety. The crush compensator should be able to eat almost twice that before the passengers are in danger."

Jeeves swallowed again.

"You're the one riding fire, ma'am," he conceded. "Once you're in space, there's only so much we can do to keep you in the loop. We'll send updates via directional laser for as long as we can, but we won't be able to see you, either."

"I know," she said. "Ping the Captain's beacon, Jeeves. Let's know what ship we're shooting ourselves at."

"Shouldn't we wait?" Jeeves asked. "That's probably the thing they're most likely to detect."

"We need to know what we're aiming for. We'll take the risk."

Leaving Jeeves to his work, she turned back to the Marines. Exosuited troopers were packing themselves into the torpedoes like sardines in a can.

"You folks going to be comfortable?" she asked Skavar.

He chuckled.

"Exosuits aren't too bad. *You're* the one getting packed in with us in a vac-suit."

Maria made a *touché* gesture. That part was going to well and truly suck.

"We'll have a target in a few minutes," she told him. "We'll launch as soon as we do."

Skavar shook his head.

"I heard," he confirmed. "You sure you can hide us all the way in?"

"Keep the torpedoes within fifteen hundred meters of each other," she ordered. "Inside that bubble, yeah. Realize, though, that it's going to take a lot of my reserves just to get us there."

"I know," Skavar said. "Thirty exosuited Marines and one exhausted Mage against an entire starship. They won't know what hit them."

Maria laughed softly. Even thirty ordinary Marines could probably take a pirate corvette with surprise and exosuits—and Skavar's people were Marine Forward Combat Intelligence. They were infiltrators and spies, covert ops troops who'd gone through the same training as Marine Force Recon.

There were probably better troops in the galaxy, but she knew these ones. She'd walk into hell with them.

"Ma'am, we've got him," Jeeves announced. "Destroyer in the center of the formation. No sign that anybody detected the pulse."

"All right," Maria said, looking into the torpedo and the almost-exactly-Maria-sized space left in it. "Here goes...everything."

Red Falcon had four boarding-torpedo launchers mounted in the engine pod at the base of the "mushroom" of her superstructure. The big freighter, currently being concealed in space by Xi Wu and the other two junior Mages, had been rotating slowly since the pirate fleet had been detected.

The moment of launch was hell. Maria had a momentary sensation of crushing weight before she blacked out. She woke up quickly enough, feeling utterly wrung out but still well enough to cast the spell that would shield them all from the Legacy's scanners.

"You okay?" Skavar asked.

"I'm not used to being sat on by giants," she said sourly. "It's been a long time since I was in anything without gravity runes. You forget what ten-plus gravities actually feels like."

The Marine chuckled.

"This *has* gravity runes," he pointed out. "Xi Wu charged them yesterday. That's why we *only* felt twenty gees."

She grunted.

"If it makes you feel better, half the damn Marines passed out too, and *they're* in exosuits," Skavar told her. "Are we cloaked?"

"We're cloaked," she confirmed. "Get comfortable, Chief. It's not going to be a short flight."

She could *feel* his grin.

"If it was going to be *easy*, they wouldn't have sent us, Maria," he said gently. "Are you going to be okay?"

"Yeah, this is a bit easier than I was afraid of," she admitted, continuing to spin light around the three metal capsules to shield them from prying eyes. "Anything new on the scanners?"

"Nah. We've got the destroyer the Captain is on dialed in." He paused. "I probably can't take a destroyer with thirty Marines, ma'am, even FCI Marines. Not if they've got any kind of real security force."

"I know. We're back to the extraction plan."

"Even with the decoys, that plan sucks."

"Do you have a better one?" Maria asked sweetly.

"Nope. Just warning you that the odds that we all die on this stunt are easily sixty-forty," he replied.

"I see, Chief Skavar. You're an *optimist*."

CHAPTER 42

IT WAS STRANGE, to put it mildly, to watch an entire fleet blast its way through space and know you were completely invisible to their sensors.

Kelly had full faith both in Soprano's ability to hide the torpedoes and in Xi Wu's ability to hide *Red Falcon* herself. She trusted the Ship's Mage—and she trusted her girlfriend without question.

"You want to know just how deep the shit is, XO?" Jeeves asked.

"Spill it, Guns," she ordered.

"Okay. *These*"—three icons on the display adjusted, flashing into the standard icon for Protectorate destroyers—"are Tau Ceti-built export destroyers. Not sure of the class, but there's a dozen identifying characteristics you can't hide without doing a lot of work.

"Work these guys haven't done." Jeeves shrugged. "They might have done enough that we won't be able to tell which ships they are and trace them back, but we'd need to be much closer for that. If we even had the databases for it."

"Record everything you can," Kelly ordered. "MISS *does* have those databanks."

"True enough," he agreed. Six more icons flashed on the display, changing into smaller, square icons. "These are system-defense ships. Might have been built by any of six systems—my money is on Alpha Centauri, though."

"Why Centauri?" she asked.

"They're the only ones who actually build SDSes for export," he told her. "The others who build them use them for local defense. Alpha Centauri's are designed to be carried by big-enough freighters, though this set clearly had jump matrices added.

"They're half a million tons apiece. If they're Centauri-built, the builder doesn't have access to antimatter missiles, so they build their ships with no missiles at all. Heavy laser armament, though. Six-, seven-gigawatt beams."

Kelly nodded. So, *Red Falcon* had heavier beams than anything she was facing. They'd restocked their own antimatter missiles from the destroyers' magazines on the way—*Falcon* was actually in range to use those missiles on the Legacy fleet.

They wouldn't do much beyond exposing the freighter's presence, though. Salvos of ten missiles could threaten one or two of the SDSes. That was it.

"And what's the rest?"

"The other twenty ships are what we were expecting to see," Jeeves told her. "Jump-modified corvettes and jump-yachts with weapons added. Your general collection of pirate and bounty hunter junk. One fifty to two fifty apiece."

"Can the Navy handle them?" she asked.

He laughed.

"Yeah," he told her. "They can handle the entire collection. But..."

"But?"

"We were expecting half a dozen pirates. Not thirty. Our bait can take them...but she's going to get hurt a lot more than anyone expects. Which means..."

"They can't be careful once everyone's in range," Kelly said grimly.

"Exactly. Maria and Ivan need to get the Captain off that ship before the Navy opens fire."

"They know that," the XO said firmly. "As well as we do—they're both better trained at this than I am."

The ex-NCO laughed.

"Better trained than either of us. They'll get it done, XO. They'll bring him home."

There was a translucent green oval on the screen, marking the likely location of the boarding torpedoes. It had broadened enough that they could no longer rely on tightbeam transmissions to hit the torpedoes and nothing else.

Soprano and the Marines were now blind. They would bring up the torpedoes' own sensors for the final approach, but until then, the price of invisibility was complete blindness. The boarding torpedoes weren't big enough for passive scanners.

"Wait, that's strange," Jeeves murmured. The Third Officer was focused on something on his console.

Kelly resisted her curiosity for all of about a second, then mirrored his display to the repeaters on the Captain's chair.

There was a new icon on the screen. A pulsing orange shape that the computers hadn't resolved into anything useful. Jeeves was already running several different programs to try and identify it, and as she watched, it slowly resolved into four icons.

Then he looked up at her.

"XO, we have a new player," he told her. "Four new jump flares. Engines are coming online; I'm reading them as fusion drives, pushing ten-megaton ships at just under three gravities."

"That's strange," she echoed. "Not military?"

"They're cruiser-sized, but cruisers have antimatter engines," Jeeves concluded. "They're freighters of some kind, at a guess. I'll know more as they get closer, but they're fifteen million klicks from us. Ten million from the Legacy."

About the same distance from the false *Gauntlet* as from the Legacy, Kelly noted absently.

"What are they *doing*?" she asked.

"If I knew who they were, I might be able to answer that," Jeeves replied. "But...I have no idea."

Kelly studied the display with its now four sets of icons.

"MISS was using this location as bait for a few groups," she noted.

"But the odds of any of them showing up this conveniently aren't high.... It's got to be Legatus."

"Legatus? Even if they'd sent an RTA message as soon as they got Campbell's note, the ships would need to have been perfectly positioned!"

"Then we got lucky," Kelly concluded. "What are they doing?"

"Accelerating towards the pirates," he answered. "Ma'am...they're freighters. What can they be planning on doing?"

"I don't know. But they do," she told him. "And they seem willing to pick that fight. For now, we watch. Whoever they are, they've volunteered themselves as the distraction Mage Soprano needs."

She switched open an intercom channel.

"Mike, what's the status on the shuttles?"

"We're ready to go," he replied. "We've got a stack of spares flying drone-mode with us, too, but remember they'll see you and the decoys as soon as we launch."

"I know," Kelly confirmed. Wu was currently hiding the entire ship, but she was on the flight deck of Kelzin's assault shuttle. To hide the three shuttles was going to take all three of *Red Falcon*'s remaining Mages, and Kelly LaMonte was going to send both of her lovers into harm's way.

"I'll give you the signal when the time is right," she continued. "Two more hours, give or take."

"We'll bring them all home, Kelly. I promise."

"You'll bring yourselves home, too," she ordered.

"I included us in 'them all,'" he told her with a chuckle.

"Okay, now, that is *really* weird."

"Jeeves?" Kelly asked in cheerful exasperation. Whatever he was seeing was almost certainly valuable, but she would give quite a bit for prompt information.

"Our potentially-Legatan-friends just started having babies," the gunner finally replied. "They just spat out a dozen new drive signatures...and there they go again."

Kelly looked at the data.

"And again," she murmured. "That's...a gravity-rib rotation cycle for a big freighter like that. Every twenty-five seconds. What are they *doing*?"

"And again," Jeeves agreed. "Forty-eight new drive signatures. Fusion torches, same as the freighters, but much smaller. Pulling five gees apiece...and there's another twelve."

Sixty smaller engine signatures. That was...really weird.

"Do you have a mass estimate?" Kelly asked.

"Bang on a hundred thousand tons apiece. And there's another twelve. Seventy-two of them."

Something was ringing a bell. A hundred-thousand-ton spacecraft, hidden under the ribs of a freighter...

"Son of a *bitch*," Kelly swore. "Gunships. Jeeves, do they match the profile for Legatan gunships?"

Red Falcon's bridge was silent for several seconds.

"Yes," he concluded. "Older units, most likely, but yes. What the hell?"

"*Blue Jay* was hired to transport gunships once," she told him. "We had eight of them tucked away under the gravity ribs. We were just moving them, though; these guys are rigged out to deploy them, probably using the ribs themselves as an orbital hook for their initial velocity."

"Hence one batch of them each rotation cycle," Jeeves agreed. "Damn. *Jay* was a *Venice* class, right?"

"Yeah."

"These guys are *Troubadour* class, or of much the same size. Six ribs, ten megatons. They could be carrying a lot of these things."

"There's another squadron," Kelly noted. Eighty-four gunships were now in space, adjusting accelerations to match velocities with each other as they closed with the pirates. "Any idea when they'll be in range?"

Jeeves shook his head.

"Depends on what they're carrying. LSDS uses either the Phoenix VII or their home-built Excalibur missile. Both would be in range already.

"If they're using general-market missiles, though, a Rapier equivalent...they'll range around eight minutes before Skavar and Soprano make contact. Just enough time to land a salvo before we board."

Kelly shook her head.

"That's the perfect distraction for our people," she noted.

"Assuming they don't accidentally blow the Captain to hell."

"Assuming that," she agreed.

CHAPTER 43

LOCKED BACK IN his room, David was surprised to realize he still had access to *Bleeding Sapphire*'s sensors. He couldn't change anything about them, but he could at least access the feed—and his wrist-comp had a collection of programs he'd acquired over the years.

With both of those, it took him just under five minutes to identify the four strange ships as *Troubadour*-class heavy freighters. Twelve megatons fully loaded, so the mass that *Sapphire* was picking up suggested that they only carried partial loads.

But also, he noted, meant they were carrying far more cargo than would make sense if they'd shown up to loot *Azure Gauntlet*. If he'd been coming to scavenge something of value from what he believed to be a derelict ship, he'd either have brought an actual refit ship to try and make it flyable again, or he'd have brought a small amount of cutting gear and left as much cargo space as possible to fill with pieces of starship.

Plus, well, a *Troubadour* had no business intentionally flying in the direction of a flotilla of armed ships, no matter how many friends she'd brought. The four ships had maybe thirty or so anti-missile turrets between them. That was it.

And then the gunships started launching. David worked out what they had to be almost instantly, watching their numbers continue to grow as he realized what was going on.

LMID was there, it appeared. That was...potentially awkward. They were about as likely to vaporize him as the Navy was, and they probably didn't even know he was aboard. The Navy, hopefully, did.

Eighty-four gunships were now heading toward him, and he could do the math easily enough. That was roughly a thousand missile launchers, enough to give the Legacy's fleet an ugly hangover.

The Legacy's fleet probably had a slight edge, mostly in that they were flying actual starships with armor and defenses. The Legatans, though, were almost certainly veteran military crews.

Either way, it was starting to look more and more like David Rice needed to be somewhere else. Anywhere else. Anywhere that *wasn't* locked in the guest quarters aboard a destroyer that was about to run into more enemies than its crew realized.

Now if only there were an easy way for him to escape...

While David was no hacker or software expert—he'd left that to James Kellers and Kelly LaMonte in recent years—his collection of programs acquired over the years included several that were designed for brute-force cracking.

He'd opened locked doors with them in the past to get out of tight spots or into places he wasn't supposed to be, so he was reasonably confident they'd get him through the door.

He was, in fact, confident enough that he'd been trying for over half an hour when he finally accepted that no, it wasn't going to work. He was probably lucky that he hadn't triggered an alarm.

Looking back at *Bleeding Sapphire*'s sensor feed, he saw the pirate fleet had opened fire several minutes before. Just two salvos, a probe to see how significant the gunships' missile defenses were.

If he had full access to the destroyer's sensors, he could probably have identified the gunship class. With only the "guest feed," he couldn't tell...but he suspected that the pirates were going to be surprised by the lack of effectiveness of their missiles.

If Vandella-Howard's people took full advantage of their possession of antimatter missiles, they could take out the entire incoming gunship force without losses. But every second they waited to see how their first salvoes did was a second closer to the gunships' range.

David needed to get out of this room.

If software and smarts weren't going to do it, then at least he had brute force on his side.

He pulled a chair over to the door to balance on and positioned himself carefully. His hip had been reinforced, but not enough to take the full force of his leg at maximum strength.

His new *knee*, however, was part of the cybernetic. Holding himself carefully in place, he kicked from the knee, a snap forward of his booted foot that blurred even to his eyes.

He winced. He'd left a visible dent in the metal door next to the lock, but it was still intact. The force had pushed him off-balance, but he'd managed to stay upright, and he was uninjured.

No one came running to see what the noise was, either.

That was enough. He kicked the door again. And again.

It took five tries and his boot was half-wrecked by the time he was done, but the insanely overpowered cyber-limb the Legatans had given him smashed the door open. The corridor beyond was empty and he inhaled deeply as he considered his options.

His guest access happily disgorged a basic map of the ship and a "you are here." The ships Tau Ceti built for export were much the same as the ships they'd built for the Navy in his long-ago days of military service.

He could find the shuttle bay. He could *fly* a shuttle.

And with the missile duel that was about to start, he might well get off the ship he'd led into a trap before it killed him.

Bleeding Sapphire might be crewed by pirates, mercenaries and criminals, but they at least understood battle stations. The corridors were empty as David made his way down to the shuttle bay.

That area, however, was much less empty. *Sapphire's* shuttles were civilian models, not assault craft, but they'd all been retrofitted with various types of weaponry. Deck crews were fueling and arming them, presumably preparing them for potential boarding operations against either the incoming impromptu carriers or the *Gauntlet*.

The deck crews were the first people he'd seen since escaping his quarters, and their appearance really drove home what kind of vessel he was on. *Bleeding Sapphire's* corridors were clean and her systems well maintained; she didn't live down to his mental image of a pirate ship at all.

Her *crew*, however, were dressed in a motley collection of clothing that seemed intentionally picked to be as ununiform as possible. Vacsuits on the flight crews were painted with strange symbols and murals; the deck crews wore bright colors and only barely seemed to refrain from frills and tassels that would be actively dangerous in this work.

And every last person in the shuttle bay was armed. Everything from simple pistols worn at the belt to assault carbines strapped to backs. If David was spotted, he was probably going to die very, very quickly.

It wasn't like there were any stunners out there, after all.

"We got one," somebody announced loudly, to cheers in the open space. "Don't know who these idiots are, but the missiles blew one of them to hell."

The cheers petered off after a moment.

"Didn't we just fire the entire fleet's launchers at a bunch of basically corvettes?" somebody asked. "Shouldn't we have got, well, more than one?"

The shuttle bay was very silent.

"Bridge says we're opening fire again," the first speaker replied after a few moments. "So, shut your beaks and get back to work. If the lady says we're going to board and retrieve *Azure Gauntlet*, that's all *we* need to worry about. Got it?"

As the crews returned to work, David slowly worked his way around the outside of the bay. One of the shuttles was facing away from the others, its boarding ramp close enough to a pile of crates that he was pretty sure he could board without being seen—and if he was seen, he could probably get to the pilot's console before anyone managed to catch him.

Reaching the final set of crates, he realized there was a new commotion back at the entrance he'd come through. Three of Vandella-Howard's massive bodyguards had emerged into the shuttle bay, the leader studying his wrist-comp and ignoring the questions being asked by the shuttle bay crew.

He looked up from his wrist-comp and pointed directly at David.

"He's over there!"

David swore. What was... He looked at his wrist-comp, still showing him the sensor feed from the destroyer's guest network.

Of course they could track his comp while he was tied into that network. He cursed himself for an idiot and ran for the shuttle.

It turned out, thankfully, that Vandella-Howard's bodyguards *did* have stunguns.

David was still twitching when the human mountains dragged him back into the observation deck, his hands cuffed in front of him, and tossed him on the floor.

"You know," the blonde lawyer told him coldly, "it really doesn't help convince me that you *didn't* betray me when you try to steal a shuttle and run."

"I have surprisingly little faith in the ability of your pirates to fight off the Legatus Military Intelligence Directorate," David gasped out, struggling to his knees.

Vandella-Howard apparently hadn't given her bodyguard the hand cannon back. She was seated now, with the massive black pistol sitting on her lap.

"So, you *do* know who has decided to interfere," she noted. "Keep digging, Captain Rice."

"I don't know why they're here now or where they got the data," he pointed out. "I just know that LMID had been experimenting with using freighters to transport gunships and that those are definitely Legatan gunships."

"Are they, now?" she asked sweetly. "Doesn't the LSDF use antimatter missiles? These idiots appeared to have launched a lovely salvo of fusion missiles at my fleet."

She gestured and a middle-aged man in a plain shipsuit activated a project display, showing the main sensor feed. The gunship formation had taken losses, but there were still over seventy gunships in play, now accelerating back toward their carriers.

There were also hundreds of missiles in space. Probably close to a thousand, enough to cause serious damage to the Legacy fleet. Even with fusion-drive weapons.

He sighed.

"If *you* were running a covert operation in Protectorate space, would *you* arm your ships with antimatter missiles?" he asked. "They want it to look like people like you killed their targets. Anything they destroy, they want Mars to write off as pirates."

"An interesting chain of logic," she observed. "They're going to make quite a mess of my lighter ships, I suspect, and have done a surprisingly good job of shooting down our missiles."

David shrugged.

"How many of your missile people are vets?" he asked bluntly. "How many of them know how to use the electronic warfare systems on their Phoenix VIIs to their full potential?

"You might have the second-best missiles in the galaxy, but they're badly degraded if your people don't know how to use them. Where these guys are using a Rapier-equivalent—but they know what they're doing."

Vandella-Howard grunted. She hadn't picked up the gun yet, so he figured he wasn't currently marked for death, but he wasn't being un-cuffed or helped to stand, either.

"Why are they accelerating away from us?" she asked the crewman standing nearby. "Wouldn't they want to close?"

"They only have a few missiles per launcher," David told her before the crewman could speak. "Once they've emptied those magazines, they want to fall back on the freighters. They'll do what damage they can and then jump out. Given your people's demonstrated competence, they may not leave much of your fleet when they do."

The lawyer snarled.

"And what would *you* have done?" she snapped.

"Opened fire with antimatter missiles as soon as I realized they were dropping gunships," he replied. "Possibly even lasers. Your SDSes have big beams; you might have been able to cause them headaches even at this range.

"You probably wouldn't have stopped them deploying most of the gunships, but without motherships, they have no way home—and I doubt they're feeling particularly suicidal."

"And now we just eat their best shot and they fly away?" Vandella-Howard asked, her voice surprisingly clinical. She shifted moods from angered to calm far too quickly for David's peace of mind.

"Most of your ships have gravity runes," he pointed out. "You could almost certainly close with them, bleed them. You'd lose more of your own ships in the process, though."

"You'd love that, wouldn't you?" she asked. "You've been setting us up from the beginning."

"God, I do not fucking care what you do at this point," David snapped. "You're going to get yourselves killed because you're so impressed with the firepower you've assembled, you didn't bother to make sure your people could actually *use* it.

"Those gunships? They're no match for your fleet. But your people have screwed this up so badly that you're going to get *hammered* and they're going to extract three-quarters or more of their ships after the strike is over.

"There is no way in hell that I am planning to die with you, Sarah Vandella-Howard," he told her. "You're trying to rebuild Mikhail Azure's empire on the backs of the same murderers and slavers he built it on. You want to reclaim and rebuild his legacy—and I want to see that same legacy *burnt to the ground.*"

He struggled to his feet, glaring at her.

"If you live, you will bring misery and death to a hundred worlds for your own profit," he continued. "If the Legatans kill you, I will *laugh*, even if I have to die with you. All you ever had to do was decide that the will of a megalomaniacal crime lord wasn't legally binding on your firm. Instead, you did this."

He gestured around them.

Vandella-Howard giggled. The sound made her appear even younger than she regularly looked, and she *grinned* at him.

"Such fire," she remarked. "Such passion. I'm hardly surprised at your opinion of my plans, Captain Rice. I'm not even surprised that you've betrayed me, one way or another. I do have to wonder how you managed to get the Legatans to do your dirty work."

"I didn't!" he snapped. "If I'd thought I could have, I would! But these idiots showed up all on their own."

She was on her feet again now, the gun finally in her hands and trained on him as he glared at her.

"Sorry, David, I don't believe that," she admitted. "Plus, well, you've given me what I wanted. I was going to let you go, but now...now I don't think I can trust you.

"And that, my dear Captain, only leaves me one real option, doesn't it?"

She wasn't paying attention to the sensors anymore. Her focus was on David—who *was* watching the sensors and knew that the Legacy fleet wasn't going to stop nearly all of the missiles.

Gravity runes were wonderful things, but they were designed to create a gravity field and counteract acceleration along specific planes.

They couldn't do much about the impact of a dozen kinetic missiles hitting at five percent of the speed of light. The ship lurched. Vandella-Howard stumbled, the heavy gun falling from her hands as she cursed.

David dove forward, dodging under a swinging arm from one of the mountainous bodyguards and scooping up the pistol. Tucking it into his chest, he rolled away from the lawyer, managing to keep the gun in his cuffed hands as he came up to a kneeling position.

310

It didn't matter how big the bodyguards were. How strong they were. The human body could only take so much hydrostatic shock, and the gun was firing *big* bullets.

Both of the guards in the room went down in a spray of blood, and David pointed the gun at Vandella-Howard and the crewman.

"Seal that door," he ordered the crewman.

"Okay, okay!" The man raised his hands, crossing over to the door and hitting the command to close it. The moment David started to relax, however, he went for his own gun.

Everyone on this damn ship was armed. Relaxed or not, though, David had a gun in his hands and the crewman didn't. The hand cannon boomed again, and David and Vandella-Howard were the only living people left in the room.

She had backed into the table, her eyes wide and her breath coming short and sharp. Her cheeks were flushed as she met his gaze, and David realized she was in no sense afraid.

"You are one sick woman," he pointed out, training the gun on her. "I'm guessing, though, that you'll make a decent hostage to get me off this boat before the Legatans wreck it."

"I can arrange that, I suppose," she allowed. "I can get you to a shuttle, off the ship without being challenged.... I don't know where you're going to go, though."

Behind her, new red icons flashed into existence on the scanners as *something* pulsed the entire fleet with active radar at point-blank range, and he smiled as three new symbols appeared on the screen—moments before a new sequence of impacts shook the ship.

"I *do* know," he admitted. "Because you're right. I did betray you— and *that*, Ms. Vandella-Howard, was my ride arriving."

CHAPTER 44

RAMMING A BOARDING TORPEDO into a target starship at thousands of kilometers a second was...not inherently a survivable process. Maria could probably protect the people aboard her own torpedo, at the price of not being able to do much else in the boarding action.

Since the Royal Martian Marine Corps liked their Combat Mages to actually be able to engage in combat, they'd come up with a solution: the crush compensator.

The crush compensator was an expensive one-shot runic artifact that happily absorbed hundreds of thousands of newtons of force, reducing an impact that could easily have qualified as a kinetic weapon and liquefied the boarding torpedoes passengers to merely uncomfortable.

Skavar and his Marines were trained for the process. They snapped the sensors to life as Maria dropped the stealth spell, sweeping the pirate flotilla at point-blank range with active radar and pinging Captain Rice's beacon.

There was only so much adjusting they could do to their course at this point—enough to make sure they hit a specific ship but not necessarily enough to hit an exact location.

"We seem to be missing some pirates," Skavar noted.

That was all anyone had time to say before the torpedo hammered home and Maria lost consciousness again.

She blinked back awake a moment or so later, spitting a sick taste out of her mouth and looking up at the armored Marine next to her. The torpedo had half-emptied while she was blacked out, and she shook herself ruefully.

"You're fine," Skavar told her. "Our pirate friends aren't. They've lost a destroyer, a couple of SDSes and half the damn light ships."

"What the hell *happened*?" Maria asked.

"I suspect it has something to do with the gunships falling back onto freighters and trying to get out of here," the Marine replied. "It looks like the Legatans got our message in time and decided to get involved. They have *hammered* Legacy's fleet—hell, this ship's been hit at least a half-dozen times."

"My heart bleeds for them," she said. "Is the Captain okay?"

"Beacon is still responding to interrogation pulses; it doesn't have a biomonitor, but he's still moving, so..."

"Ha! Fair enough. Where is he?" Maria demanded.

"This way," Skavar replied. "We haven't run into anybody so far, but we are avoiding battle-station positions. Damage control teams are our biggest threat until someone works out what happened and starts sending security after us."

"Let's see if we can delay that as long as we can. What's the ETA on our pickup?"

"Assuming they followed the plan and launched the shuttles as soon as we went visible, fifty minutes. About twenty-five minutes before this whole assemblage reaches the Navy's range."

"Cutting it closer than I'd like," Maria admitted. "Let's go find the Captain."

"I don't suppose we have any access to the ship's systems?" Maria asked as they caught up with the first Marine teams. One of the exosuited troopers was pulling cables out of a linkup to the computers, after all.

"No," Corporal Spiros replied. "I tried the MISS codes LaMonte gave me. No dice. They've loaded a custom operating system. I've loaded some standard worms in that are going to screw up their internal sensors, but that's all I can do. They can't see us...but we can't even pull a damn map without more time."

Time they didn't have.

"All right," Skavar cut in. "The Captain is moving. He's that way," the Marine pointed, "but heading towards the base of the pyramid. If this ship is designed anything like a Navy destroyer, I'd say he's heading for the shuttle bay."

"On his own?" Maria asked. "If we came all this way and the Captain freed *himself*..."

"He'd still be screwed," the Marine replied. "A rogue shuttle launch in the middle of the flotilla? The Legatans may have kicked their asses, but they've still got over a dozen ships out here. Stealing a shuttle is just going to get him vaporized."

"If we know where he's going, can we head him off?" she asked.

Skavar was studying something on the inside of his helmet.

"No," he admitted. "But we can get to the shuttle bay just after him—and while I don't know what the Skipper has for resources, we have thirty exosuited Marines and a Navy Mage.

"I think we'll make a bit of a difference."

David was surprised to reach the shuttle bay again without even running into interference. Vandella-Howard wasn't exactly being cooperative, but she also wasn't running away, screaming for help.

With her now wearing the handcuffs her bodyguards had slapped on him, he pushed her against a wall and studied the hangar again. It hadn't changed much from before. More of the small spacecraft had been closed up since, but the deck crews continued to swarm over the space.

His previous visit had resulted in one change, though. A squad of security troopers, clad in matching body armor if not matching uniforms, stood watch over each of the two main entrances. Looking around, he also picked out the sniper team hanging out on top of the main flight control room.

He had one heavy pistol and a hostage. Somewhere on the ship, hopefully, was a rescue team. There was a decent chance he could get onto a shuttle on his own using Vandella-Howard as a bargaining chip, but he didn't know what that was going to do to his people's plan.

Of course, while he was considering that, the crime boss promptly made all of his plans irrelevant. She kicked him in his still-original leg, dropping him to the ground as she ran out into the hangar bay.

"Rice is back there!" she shouted. "A million in cash to the man who kills him!"

For a single moment of cold rage, David seriously considered shooting an unarmed woman in the back. It would end most of this mess, end Mikhail Azure's legacy. It would even, by just about any standard, be justified.

But he couldn't bring himself to do it. Instead, he fired in the general direction of the closest armed security squad, sending the armored men and women ducking for cover with a pair of bullets before dodging back into the corridor.

With the magazines he'd taken from Vandella-Howard's bodyguard, he had a total of about twenty bullets. Even if he was a good-enough shot for one bullet, one target, there were more than twenty security troopers in the hangar.

And that was before counting the fact that *everybody* in the hangar except the lawyer-turned-crime-boss was armed.

He'd underestimated Vandella-Howard.

Damn it.

"Scanners are showing gunfire ahead," Skavar reported. "A *lot* of gunfire. I'd say the boss just poked the hornet's nest."

"Then let's go save him," Maria replied. It had been a long time since she'd tried to use an exosuit to carry herself forward, but Skavar clearly picked up her intent and deployed the stirrups built into the back of his legs for just that purpose.

As soon as the Mage was secure on the chief's back, he took off at full speed after his people. If the shooting had started, now was not the time for subtlety anymore.

The *Red Falcon* boarding team smashed into the hangar bay like the fist of god. Whatever the pirates had been expecting, a fully armed and armored Royal Martian Marine platoon was *not* on their list. Only a handful of the pirates had heavy-enough gear to threaten the exosuits, and all of them were focused on the opposite end of the hangar.

For a moment, everything went the boarders' way. They cut through the armored and unarmored opposition alike—but then the enemy woke up. A heavy penetrator smashed into Skavar's armor, sending the security chief crashing to the floor with Maria.

Magic flared around her, pulling her out before he could crush her, and then shielding the entire force from the sniper who'd shot Skavar. A team of men was setting up a bipod-mounted penetrator cannon near her—and a blast of fire ended their involvement in the battle.

The sniper had spotted her, though, and was falling back on the training of every soldier in the modern galaxy: Threat Priority Mage!

The single-shot sniper rifle they were using couldn't punch through her shield in one shot, but the heavy penetrator rounds it was firing could do a number if they put *enough* on target and if she was distracted enough.

"Skavar?" she snapped. "I can shield us, but I can't track for counter-fire!"

"Right," the wounded Marine gasped. "I can't stand, servos shot. Spiros!"

The Marine Corporal was there before Maria could even ask what he needed the woman to do—and she didn't need an explanation as the next penetrator hammered Maria's shield.

"Right," she said briskly, her own rifle twisting around in her armored gauntlets. The sniper got one more shot—and then Spiros emptied half of a thirty-round clip into the suspended control bay they were using as a perch.

Maria was reasonably sure Spiros got the sniper. She *definitely* destroyed the flight control center and sent pieces of it scattering across the hangar bay.

"Remind me not to piss you off," she muttered, half-hiding behind the exosuited Marine as she scanned the bridge. "The Captain is at the other entrance," she barked. "Cover me?"

"Well, I'm not moving yet," Skavar replied, levering himself into a sitting position with Spiros's aid. "Cover is all I can provide.

"Go!"

Maria charged across the space, the two Marines opening fire on everything that moved near her. Magic flared around her, deflecting the gunfire the only unarmored person in the attack naturally attracted.

None of the shooters kept up their fire for long. Any of them that didn't drop when they realized they were shooting at a Mage were put down by the Marines.

She was a distraction as the exosuited troops advanced behind her, clearing the hangar bay as they came, but she was also the best hope of protecting the Captain that they had.

She reached the other side of the hangar as a group of armored troops made a rush at the corner. The loud report of a heavy handgun echoed several times, but at least four of the Legacy troops made it around the corner.

Unfortunately for them, she was right behind them, fire flashing from her hands as they charged at Rice. They'd run him out of ammunition, but she took them down before they managed to shoot him themselves.

For a few seconds, she stood over the bodies, looking at where her Captain was leaning against a wall, looking absolutely exhausted.

"Hey, boss," she finally said. "Want a ride?"

"Oh god, yes," he replied. "Do we have one?"

"Not yet," Maria admitted. "We came in by torpedo. Kelzin is on his way with a set of shuttles being stealthed by the rest of our Mages and a pile of decoys we borrowed from the Navy. It'll make their lives a lot easier if we hold the shuttle bay, though."

"That it will," he confirmed. "Skavar?"

"Back in the bay," she told him. "Shall we?"

Rice nodded, levering himself carefully off the wall. Now Maria could see that she hadn't been as in time as she thought—he'd been shot several times. His rebuilt shoulder was going to need new work, though it looked like the other rounds had hit his cyber-leg.

"The leg is armored," he murmured. "The shoulder isn't. I...wouldn't turn down painkillers, Ship's Mage."

"I don't have anything," she replied, stepping over to support him. "But I bet the Marines have *nice* drugs."

A trio of exosuited troopers joined them around the corner as she was speaking.

"Skavar is setting up a command post where he fell," the senior trooper told them. "Good to see you, Skipper. We'll take over this doorway."

Maria half-carried David back to where Skavar was still sitting. From the way he was refraining from moving, she suspected the Marine had taken some serious damage.

"Are you all right, Ivan?" she demanded.

"No," he admitted. "Suit has hit me up with nerve-blockers; I'm lucid but my left leg may as well be gone below the hip." There was a tired, fatalistic note to his voice. "If I'm reading my medical displays right, that's about where I'm going to end up, too."

"We can get matching 'I flew on *Red Falcon* and all I got was a shitty cyber-leg' t-shirts," Rice told him. "Anybody got some painki—oh."

The audible sigh of relief was from Spiros slamming a trauma patch over the hole in his shoulder.

"Okay, that'll do," he continued, his voice somewhat dreamy as the painkillers took effect. "What's the plan, Chief?"

"Kelzin is on his way with the assault shuttles, like I said," Maria told the Captain. Skavar wasn't in any better condition than Rice was. "They've got a mix of decoys to attract hostile fire and get them all the way in.

"Then, well, we load everybody up and run, using the Mages to hide us."

"At close range, that won't work as well," Rice pointed out.

"It'll work better than stealing a shuttle and just flying outside to see what they do," Maria replied.

Rice chuckled.

"Fair, I was running out of options." He looked around. "Did anybody see the blonde lunatic running this asylum? I had her prisoner, but she broke free and was somewhere in here..."

"We traded fire with a lot of people," Corporal Spiros noted. "Nobody who looked like they were anything other than security or flight crew." She shook her head. "We're digging in; we'll see what they do.

"Our ride is still twenty minutes out."

"Let's get some of these shuttles turned around," David suggested. "Their guns will make a nice mess of the approach corridors if the pirates want to push it."

Spiros laughed.

"We left our pilot-trained people with Kelzin and Nicolas," she told him. "None of us could even manage that—and we are *not* letting you at the controls of anything with a hole in you!"

"I can fly the shuttles," Maria replied. "I figure you have someone who can run the guns if I turn a couple of them around?"

Skavar barked a laugh, following by a whimper of pain.

"Now, *that* adds up," he concluded. "Spiros, work with the Mage. Let's get some defenses set up."

Before they could move, however, the announcement system crackled to life.

"You may think you've won, David Rice," a female voice snapped—one Rice definitely recognized. "But you're still on *my* ship. We're evacuating the air from the hangar bay now. I hope you enjoy vacuum."

Skavar swore.

"Spiros, get the Mage and the Skipper aboard one of those damn shuttles and seal it up *now*," he ordered. "The rest of us have exosuits, but they're both *squishy*."

Maria didn't even have a chance to argue before gauntleted hands had her and the Captain off the ground as Spiros's fire team *ran* for the closest shuttle.

She was guessing the woman on the PA was Vandella-Howard. She hadn't met the woman—but she was already acquiring a list of reasons to hate her!

CHAPTER 45

KELLY WATCHED as the last gunship dropped inside the rotating ribs of the freighters that had delivered them, almost dismissively ignoring the hail of missile fire still incoming from the pirate fleet.

The freighters weren't carrying anything more than the usual defensive armament of the class, but with dozens of active gunships locked to their hulls, they had a *lot* of defensive lasers.

And as soon as the last set of gunships locked on, the four freighters vanished in the Cherenkov-blue flash of jump flares. LMID had clearly achieved whatever they had decided to do—most likely, utterly hammer the Legacy's fleet in a way that could only undermine the morale of the fragile edifice the lawyers had put together.

The Legacy had destroyed nine gunships. They'd lost, in exchange, a destroyer, four system-defense ships, and fifteen jump-corvettes. Over half of their fleet obliterated by a force they should have been able to crush.

It wouldn't be good for their morale. What would probably be worse in the long run, in Kelly's opinion, would be when they dissected the fight afterward...and concluded that there were half a dozen ways they *could* have won.

"Legatans are clear," she announced. "Jeeves, what are our positions?"

"Kelzin is twenty minutes out and they're starting to take potshots at the decoys," the gunner replied. "We can throw some missiles into the mix to help cover them."

"How much attention is that going to draw to us?" Kelly asked.

Jeeves shrugged.

"They know we're here now, but with our drives down, they have no idea what we are," he said. "If we open fire, I'll want to bring the engines up and keep us in motion. Just to make sure they don't throw long-range laser fire our way. We're outside range, but...not by much."

"Can we try and not be obvious who we are?" Kelly said. "I doubt we're going to get a clean sweep, and if they associate antimatter missiles and real assault shuttles with *Red Falcon*, it could cause a lot of questions we don't want asked."

Jeeves pursed his lips.

"I can make it less *obvious*," he agreed. "I can't make it impossible for them to tell, though. We just have to hope they're more distracted by the fact that *Maze of Glorious Victory* is going to stop pretending to be dead in about thirty minutes."

And the missiles would, conveniently, make sure that Kelly's lovers and friends were more likely to make it through alive.

"Carry on, Guns," she ordered. "Bringing up the drives for evasive maneuvers now. Let's see if we can make these bastards blink."

The missiles blazed past the assault shuttles at roughly a thousand times their acceleration, leaving trails of fire and radiation as they spiraled around the decoy craft to try and protect them.

Red Falcon maneuvered as she opened fire, Jeeves emptying her launcher magazines to cover the assault shuttles. Even with refilled magazines, they only had a hundred missiles—but that was a hundred targets that the Legacy ships had to regard as far more important targets.

It wasn't enough to save all of the shuttles, and Kelly watched with a mix of amusement and horror as the decoys came apart. Each of those shuttles would normally have carried between thirty and sixty men and women.

And even if they were empty right now, they also represented millions of dollars of hardware apiece. Hardware that *Falcon*'s crew was expending like cheap tacos to cover their *actual* approach.

"Are we keeping Kelzin updated?" she asked.

"Punching a tightbeam through to several of the decoy shuttles; they're relaying," Jeeves confirmed. "All three ships of Shadow Flight are unharmed. They are decelerating to contact now."

Kelly looked over her data. That was odd.

"Our target is venting atmosphere," she told Jeeves. "She was leaking a bit before from the hits she took, but...she just dumped the entire contents of her shuttle bay."

Jeeves chuckled.

"Want to bet that's where our friends are?" he asked.

"No bet," she replied. Hopefully, everyone had *survived* that. "Make sure Mike knows—if everyone is in one place, that makes extraction a *lot* easier."

"I'll send it on," Jeeves confirmed. "That narrows down everything a bit. Time to contact ninety seconds and dropping."

"How long until they realize *Maze of Glorious Victory* isn't a hulk?" Kelly asked.

"That depends on how much attention they pay," he replied. "She'll be in laser range in twenty-five minutes."

"It's all down to how fast they can get aboard the shuttles now."

The shuttle Maria had boarded vibrated underneath her again as she pressed the firing key once more. Whoever had retrofitted this particular spacecraft for the Azure Legacy had been thinking in terms of planetside raiding: the pair of chain guns mounted in the chin were useless as space-to-space weapons but would have made for a nasty strafing run on the surface.

Trapped inside an airless open space aboard a spaceship, they made an ugly mess of the latest attempt to rush the bay. Explosive shells walked their way across the entrance. The vacuum robbed the explosions of much of their force, but they still ripped apart vac-suited pirates with ease.

The handful of exosuited attackers went down to Marines with penetrator rifles. The security hatch over the shuttle bay had been history for at least ten minutes. By now, most of the wall around it was wreckage too, and a massive portion of the ship had been opened to space.

So far, the gravity runes in the bay decking had gone undamaged. The boarding party still had gravity, even if they no longer had atmosphere and the bay doors were wide open.

Maria, unfortunately, had discovered that there were remote locks built into the shuttles. She'd managed to bring the weapons in the craft online, but the engines remained in cold shutdown. The two Marines who'd squeezed aboard with her and Rice were working on that with the Captain as she provided cover for the men and women outside.

"There you go," Rice's voice suddenly sounded over the intercom. He sounded exhausted. "Software locks overridden. Hardware locks removed."

He paused.

"Any other shuttle will take at least ten minutes as well," he noted. "We're not stealing Legacy's ships to get out of here."

"That's fine; our ride is on its way," Skavar interrupted. "You can fly?"

"I can fly anything, just not well," Maria replied.

"You two get the hell out of here, then," the Marine ordered. "You can hide the shuttle from the sensors and visuals, right?"

"I can, but what about the rest of you?" she asked.

"Our ride is due any minute now," he repeated. "But we came for Rice and you've got him and can get him home. *Go.*"

"And you're wounded yourself," Maria reminded him.

"They're going to have to haul my carcass onto the shuttles; we'll worry about that then," he replied. "We'll hold. Go."

Red Falcon's security chief was clearly not going to listen. She sighed, sent another spray of explosive shells into the entrance to discourage the pirates, and then brought up the shuttle's engines. Even with everyone in the bay in exosuits, getting out safely was going to require careful maneuvering.

She angled the jets to lift the ship off the deck carefully, then brought up the main engines—pointing the nozzles at the entrances from the rest of the ship as she activated them. The heat would expand the holes they'd already made, and somehow, Maria Soprano didn't care much if she tore massive holes in the guts of Vandella-Howard's ship.

She summoned magic around the shuttlecraft as they blasted out into space, concealing it from scanners even as she threw it into a painful series of loops. Behind her, the destroyer's anti-missile turrets flared to life, laser beams stabbing through where she would have been.

"Rice just passed out," one of the Marines reported from the back. "We're checking in on him. You do what you got to do, Mage Soprano, but I'm not sure he can take another sequence like that."

"We're clear," she replied, also transmitting to Skavar. "Heading for *Red Falcon* nice and slow."

"And Kelzin is here," the Marine replied. "You can't see him, but his people are hovering just outside the bay. We're moving out by fire teams."

Maria was sufficiently skilled and powerful that she could open a tiny gap in the stealth shield, allowing her to watch as the Marines leapt from the pirate destroyer, tiny fireflies flickering in the night as they flashed across—and then disappeared into the stealth fields.

"Make sure you move yourself, you big lug," she told Skavar.

"Two people are hauling me," he replied. "We're moving."

A slightly larger firefly flashed out into space...but the Legacy seemed to have finally worked out what was going on. The closest RFLAMs came to life, flickering invisibly deadly beams across the target zone.

"Everyone else is aboard; it's just you and your escorts," Kelzin's voice said in a worried tone. "Sending Shadow Two and Three back. We're holding for you, Chief."

"Spiros, Conners, go," Skavar barked. "Even a cripple can pilot the damn thrusters; I don't need an esc—"

There was no screaming. No drama. Just an invisible beam that suddenly became visible as half a gigawatt of coherent light washed over three armored figures.

Then both the beam and the figures vanished.

"Skavar, come in," Kelzin barked. "Ivan!"

Maria didn't even try. She knew *exactly* how likely it was that the Chief had survived that.

"He's gone, Michael," she said quietly. "Pull back to *Falcon*. Our part in this is done."

Kelly LaMonte only barely had enough resolution at this range to guess what had happened. At least some of the Marines hadn't made it—and she'd lost track of all of the shuttles they'd sent over. They were wrapped inside the stealth spells now.

Most of the decoys were destroyed as well, but she found one still intact to serve as a relay, opening a channel.

"Guys, you need to get out of there *now*," she told them. "*Maze of Glorious Victory* is in range. This is all about to be over, but you need to not get caught in the crossfire!"

Seconds ticked away, the pirate flotilla continuing to close with the "derelict" cruiser. With over fifteen light-seconds still separating the Legacy from *Maze*—and more separating either force from *Red Falcon*, many of the pirates never even realized they'd been trapped.

Maze's heavy battle lasers spoke without warning. Every destroyer and system-defense ship vanished in a single cataclysmic instant, each of the five remaining heavier ships now the target of ten ten-gigawatt lasers.

The jump-corvettes panicked. Even from millions of kilometers away, Kelly could see that in their suddenly panicked maneuvers, their desperate attempts to clear enough space to cast their jump spells.

But there were already missiles on the way, and the two destroyers *Red Falcon* had brought with her emerged from hiding behind the cruiser, their engines fully warmed up and active in a way *Maze of Glorious Victory* could never have concealed on herself.

The cruiser's mass had hidden the destroyers, however, and they now lunged forward at fifteen gravities. Even with the gravity runes, that would be punishing for the crews aboard them—but it was three times the best acceleration the pirate raiders could muster.

Lasers flashed in the night, the raiders finding the nerve to fire on the Martian Navy in a desperate attempt to survive.

A hopeless attempt.

Watching from the sidelines, Kelly picked out three ships managing to escape. That was it. Three ships with Mages who were ready to jump and paranoid enough to already be in the simulacrum chamber.

That was it.

Azure Legacy was *done.*

CHAPTER 46

TAU CETI *E* WASN'T exactly a pleasant world. Neither of Tau Ceti's habitable planets was known for tropics or beaches, after all.

That said, most settled planets had enough variety in their climates to have at least one place where people could install a beach resort. Tau Ceti *e*'s Bree Isles were tucked into a microclimate zone on the planet's equator, shielded from the worst of the planet's weather by a range of "islands" that were actually sharp-peaked mountains, rising from the bottom of the ocean to tower a full kilometer above sea level.

Those islands were all but useless, but they turned the Bree Isles into a semitropical paradise containing the best resorts in the system. Several of those resorts belonged entirely to the Martian military. Some of the *islands* belonged entirely to the Martian military, and MISS had taken over an isolated corner of one of those to set up a rest, recreation and rehab facility for their often overstressed agents.

Kelly LaMonte was not currently overstressed. She was currently wearing a bikini, sitting in inch-deep warm water as gentle waves washed over her, eyeing her lovers farther up the beach.

Xi Wu was taking advantage of the privacy to sunbathe topless on the beach, not that her Asian-descended skin needed to tan. Mike Kelzin was slightly more dressed in a pair of long shorts, but he was completely passed out on a hammock near Xi.

He might have been asleep, but Mike still wore the stunned smile of a young man who wasn't quite sure what he'd done to deserve his luck. It was an improvement, at least, over the survivor's guilt he'd been dealing with over most of the trip back to Tau Ceti.

Mike had been in charge of the shuttle extraction. He felt...he *was* responsible for the operation that had failed to extract Skavar, Spiros, and Conners.

But command and responsibility did not constitute control. The therapists there seemed to have finally drilled that into his head.

With a smile, Kelly rose out of the water and crossed to her partners, giving each of them a soft kiss as she joined them.

"He's not going to wake up soon," Xi purred. "This is nice. Reward for a job well done, huh?"

Kelly chuckled as she sat on the edge of her girlfriend's sunbed. "Mike hasn't worked out what he did to deserve us."

"I know," the Mage agreed. "That's a good bit of *why* he's so adorable."

Before Kelly could respond further, there was a chime from the pile of clothes she'd left further up the beach. She sighed.

"We're on vacation," Xi told her. "You could totally tell whoever it was that we were having sex. For that matter..." Kelly's lover waggled her eyebrows suggestively, and *Red Falcon*'s XO laughed.

"The true reward for a job well done is another job, my heart," she told Xi. "I'll go see what it is. We've had a couple of weeks to help put ourselves back together. We can only hide here on Tau Ceti and pretend to be a normal freighter crew for so long."

"Fair. Tell Soprano I said hi," Xi conceded.

Kelly wasn't at all surprised to see that her lover was correct—the call was from Soprano.

"LaMonte here."

"Kelly, can you get back to the main hotel?" Soprano asked immediately. "We have a guest asking to meet the three of us."

There was no question as to which three that was.

"I can get back in five minutes, but I'm guessing clothes might be an idea?" Kelly replied.

David Rice and his crew weren't the only guests at the Silent Horizons Resort...but since the Silent Horizons Resort was *actually* a Martian Interstellar Security Service RRR facility, the other guests were also maximum-security-clearance covert operatives.

Or, well, the medical professionals tasked with making sure none of those covert operatives were going insane. They'd finally managed to get him over the last vestiges of his dysphoria over the cyber-leg, for example.

And helped Mike Kelzin and others past survivor's guilt. Losing Ivan Skavar had been a shock to the system.

The lack of uncleared personnel, however, made it convenient enough for him to commandeer a meeting room for himself, Soprano and LaMonte when the word of their visitor came down.

Black-suited Protectorate Secret Service agents swept the room after the three of them took their seats, the women calmly professional and polite as they made sure that the Captain of one of the Protectorate covert ops ships hadn't decided to assassinate a Hand.

Then Hand Alaura Stealey came into the room. Like every other time David had seen the middle-aged Hand, she looked tired, but she dropped herself into the chair at the head of the table with a smile.

"David, Kelly, Maria," she greeted them. "It's good to see you all."

"We made it. Others didn't," David replied softly. "What's the word, ma'am?"

"Lomond's team rolled up Armstrong, Lee and Howard without much difficulty once you'd drawn away their attention and much of their firepower. We took the files intact, which means that regular MIS cops are sweeping up Legacy cells across the Protectorate."

The similarity between the acronyms for the Martian Investigation Service, the Protectorate-wide police service, and the Martian Interstellar Security Service, the Protectorate's internal security and covert ops organization, was *not* unintentional.

"They're done?" LaMonte asked.

"They're done," Stealey confirmed. "And their records should allow us to sweep up a bunch of the fragments of the Blue Star Syndicate. Mikhail Azure's empire is finished."

David felt a fierce sense of satisfaction at that.

"So, what now?" he asked.

"If the Legacy is gone, then Legatus becomes our priority," Stealey told them. "Infiltration Augment kill teams? Secret carriers?" She shook her head.

"The reward for a job well done, Captain Rice, is another job," she told him. "LMID appears to be willing to use you as a resource and regards themselves as being in your debt, to some extent at least.

"We need you to *use* that," she said grimly. "Use everything—from your links to this Agent Blade and to Major Niska to your connections with Keiko Alabaster.

"We don't know what they're planning. We clearly underestimated their resources. You three already provoked one enemy of the Protectorate into a fatal misstep.

"Let's see what we can do with Legatus, Agents."

ABOUT THE AUTHOR

GLYNN STEWART is the author of Starship's Mage, a bestselling science fiction and fantasy series where faster-than-light travel is possible–but only because of magic. His other works include science fiction series Duchy of Terra, Castle Federation and Vigilante, as well as the urban fantasy series ONSET and Changeling Blood.

Writing managed to liberate Glynn from a bleak future as an accountant. With his personality and hope for a high-tech future intact, he lives in Kitchener, Ontario with his partner, their cats, and an unstoppable writing habit.